WINTER'S CORRUPTION

First in the Messengersmith Series

BRENNAN D.K. CORRIGAN

ISBN: 1517777569
ISBN 13: 9781517777562

DEDICATION

For Mom and Dad

Prologue

Never before had the Alliance council watched an entire species nearly destroy itself. The four representatives sat in the Assembly Chamber, baked by an oppressive desert sun that only frayed their tempers more. Recently appointed ambassador Kon-Ren An-Tun, of the planet Daalronna, listened nervously as his counterparts from other planets sparred on the issue at hand.

"I cannot fathom how anyone in this assembly could even consider establishing first contact with the humans at a time like this!" declared Legate Thelano Neralja, the frail, pale-skinned representative of the planet Wenifri. "Not even a day ago, they came within a thread's width of total self-annihilation. Their entire planet is polarized for war. If we make contact with one nation, its enemies will immediately be hostile to the Alliance."

"I never heard that complaint when Wenifri and Daalronna made contact with my homeworld for the first time," said Ambassador Delaro, the scaly-skinned representative of planet Andaros. "A naval war and a radical religious uprising didn't seem to deter you from landing a Messenger envoy in the Kastal Mountains."

"The extremists' prophet did not have the capacity to order a *nuclear missile strike!*" Neralja screamed. "You cannot compare the two!"

The representative of Naris, appearing to the assembly by video feed from a water-filled tank, spoke up via translator. "Neralja's point is sound. With respect to Delaro, Andaros' Takathist Awakening and Earth's nuclear crisis are two very different situations."

Neralja smiled, looking eager to drive the final nail into Delaro's rhetorical coffin. "What say you, An-Tun? Surely the evidence is as clear to you as it is to me. "

An-Tun swallowed hard. Apparently, Neralja thought it would be easy to pressure a new ambassador into agreement.

Not so fast, An-Tun thought. "Actually, my government supports making first contact with the humans. We have already taken some rather irrevocable actions to that effect."

Neralja frowned. "And those would be?"

"Two years ago, Prime Minister Na-Kember of Daalronna authorized a team of linguists and diplomats to make contact with young citizens of Earth's nations, selecting representatives from current and upcoming superpowers.

We have begun a cultural exchange and political research program, operating from a base on one of Earth's remote plains regions. I—"

"Daalronnans contacted a volatile species without so much as a notification to the Alliance Council?" Neralja asked, standing up abruptly and pointing an accusatory finger at An-Tun. "Do you have any idea how severe of an affront this is to my government? I will be lodging a formal complaint with the Regulatory Committee—"

"The Committee will not find us at fault. Nowhere in the original Alliance Treaty, the Andarite or Narissan Amendments, or the Regulatory Statutes is it stated that the any planet requires Council approval to act on non-military matters. Reread them yourself, if you wish. The military alert was only imposed upon Earth a few days ago. We acted years ago."

Neralja grimaced and sank back into the chair. "The Earth governments know about this?"

"No. We limited the program to carefully screened civilians, each of whom I have come to trust and respect. Today, I am accompanied by a friend and colleague from Earth. Without further ado, I would like to introduce you to the American Cultural Liaison, Dennison Smith."

An-Tun signaled to the aide sitting behind him, who strode to the chamber annex and brought back a human. Dennison had pale skin without scales, spines, or other protrusions, except for a tuft of golden fur atop his head. He had only two arms, and was short by Daalronnan standards.

He addressed the diplomats in their own language, thickly accented by his American English.

"Good afternoon, ambassadors of the Alliance. My name is Dennison Smith. I represent the planet Earth and the nation known as the United States of America." Dennison clicked a button on a remote control that An-Tun had given him, and a map of Earth appeared on the projection screen that took up one wall of the council chamber. Each nation's name was written in Wenifrin Script, the common alphabet of the Council. "As you know, Earth has recently resolved a nuclear conflict between the United States and the Union of Soviet Socialist Republics, or Soviet Union. I know this is disturbing to many in the galactic community, but An-Tun and I believe that Earth is nevertheless ready for contact with the Alliance."

"What makes you think that your world has truly resolved this conflict?" the Narissan representative asked.

"To tell you the truth, Ambassador, I think we needed that little scare. For a few days during the movement of Soviet nuclear missiles, the prospect of nuclear war was very real to us. We proved that day that humans recognize the very real, worldwide threat of nuclear annihilation. With that still fresh in our minds, I hope the Alliance will decide to make contact with world leaders of my planet in the near future, before we forget that lesson."

Ambassador Delaro smiled and nodded. "You make a good point, Liaison Dennison. Tell me more about this cultural exchange between Earth and Daalronna."

"Yes, tell us," Neralja interjected. "How are the Daalronnans so confident that this project is secret from your leaders?"

Dennison clicked through the presentation projected on the board, to an architectural diagram of a subterranean construction built like a stepped pyramid. From the small opening hall at ground level, each underground floor was built larger than the one above. There were four large pillars aboveground, equidistant from the door at the center.

"This is our base, located in Mongolia, one of the remotest places on Earth. The structure has twenty bedrooms currently in use by humans and Daalronnans, as well as five extra suites for guests. Also, self-contained water and waste systems, radio and laser communications, 100-capacity Messenger aviary and maintenance workshop, dining, nursing and aeroponics facilities, library, and Level 2 wormhole transport anchoring station." Dennison indicated the pillars with a laser pointer. "Daalronnan magicians installed a cloaking system designed to make the base invisible to all human methods of detection."

"You mentioned Messenger workshop facilities. Is there a Messengersmith on your Daalronnan staff?" Delaro asked.

"Yes. An-Tun himself staffs our Messenger facilities when he isn't on council business. Several of the humans, including me, have taken up his offer to receive training as Messengersmiths."

"An-Tun! Is this true? You offered to do this?" Neralja snapped.

"Dennison and the other humans are making great progress on the basic enchantments," An-Tun replied. "I am very proud of them."

"You thoughtless renegade! If I had the authority, I'd—"

"Eject me from the council? Remember, Neralja, the Daalronnan government that I represent was not in violation of its rights, per the Treaty or any other laws."

Neralja snarled. "But now that a military alert has been declared on Earth, the Council is within its rights to dismantle this project. I make a motion to order the Daalronnan government to stop its involvement with Earth."

All eyes turned to the Council Moderator, who until this point had remained in silent observance of the proceedings. "Will someone second the motion?" he asked. No one spoke. Neralja glared around the room. "Will someone second the motion?" the Moderator asked again. Still silence. "Very well. Motion defeated."

"What would you have them do with the base they built on the plains, Neralja?" the Narissan asked. "Abandon it and wait for a human to find the cloaking pillars once they fall into disrepair? Destroy it, and watch the human nations accuse each other of test-firing their weapons into the wilderness? I make a motion to place the Earth base under military jurisdiction until such time as the humans are fully ready to be contacted."

"Is that allowed within the Treaty?" Dennison asked.

An-Tun grimaced. "Yes, it is."

Dennison shouted, "People of the Council, please! The Daalronnans are acting responsibly in this interaction between our species! Give us another chance, and I'll prove—"

"An-Tun, quiet your guest or I will hold *you* in contempt of this council," the Moderator hissed. Dennison fell silent. "All in favor?"

Neralja and the Narissan raised their hands.

"All opposed?"

An-Tun and Delaro raised their hands. Procedure held that in this case, the Moderator was the tiebreaker. An-Tun held his breath scrutinized the Moderator's stoic face as he weighed the arguments.

"Motion approved."

An-Tun cursed, and Dennison stormed out of the Council chamber.

After the Council had adjourned for the day, An-Tun found Dennison standing on one of the garden tiers of the great Ziggurat inside which the Council chambers were contained. He stared down at the bustling civilians of Daron City. Beyond that lay the dunes and rocky outcroppings of a great desert, baked under the light of a red star low in the late afternoon sky.

"What happens now?" Dennison asked.

"Not much, I don't think. Neralja is determined to keep the Alliance from having diplomatic contact with Earth's governments. For now, I think we'll just have to wait out the storms and teach each other what we can under the circumstances."

"Have Daalronna and Wenifri always been at each other's throats like this?" Dennison asked.

"Before the Alliance Treaty, the two planets were at war. Things are peaceful now, but politics is far more complicated."

"Earth would probably complicate things further."

"Or so Neralja thinks. I, for one, think we can still manage a good cultural exchange, even in secret from your governments. After you left the Council, Ambassador Delaro and I spent most of the day trying to negotiate leniency on some of the military policies. You're still my apprentice Messengersmith."

"That's great," Dennison muttered. He didn't smile.

"I know this is difficult," An-Tun said, "but at least Neralja couldn't cancel the program entirely. You and the other humans still have four planets full of new things to discover."

"Four? What happened to the fifth?"

"Iyerayñan is withdrawing its application to join the Alliance. A new political faction there is persuading their executive council to remain independent of any other planets. They seem to be taking quite a hard stance on migration."

"What? No! What about Katya and Marion, and their families? Will we still be able to visit them?"

"I warned them when they decided to move off Earth that this might happen. I promise you I will send you everything I hear about the new Iyerani government, especially migration policies. But, regardless of how bad it may seem to us, Katya and Marion will make their own decisions about whether to leave or stay on Iyerayñan."

"I'm tired of politics," Dennison said.

"You've had a long day. Remember, this planet rotates in thirty hours, not twenty-four! Get some rest, and we'll head back to Earth tomorrow."

"I will." Dennison started to leave, then paused at the door. "An-Tun? One more thing."

"Anything."

"You said I could tell my sister about the project, and I did. I trust her. She always wanted to settle down and start a family, though."

"You're worried about the children," An-Tun surmised. "True, it may be hard for them, growing up keeping the secret of the galaxy from their peers."

"They'll be legally bound to never fully be honest with their friends," Dennison said.

"But, they will grow up with opportunities unavailable to any other human," An-Tun replied. "We can only hope that will be consolation enough."

"I hope so."

Chapter 1

Hot July sun dominated the forest, without the slightest breeze to temper it. Inside a tree house on a tall, proud oak, a boy of sixteen called out into the air, "Celer, Hurry up! We'll be late if you don't come back."

"Coming!" called a high-pitched voice from above. Celer, a magical being called a Messenger, flew down out of the canopy in a flurry of leaves. Celer was made of fine, sky-blue cloth, tied back with a length of orange yarn, completed with glass-bead eyes. The final product was no bigger than a sparrow, and gave the semblance of a bulbous head and fluttering, ghostly body. The shape of the eyeholes gave Celer wide, curious-looking eyes. He flew down to the boy's eye level.

"Aw, Ben!" he said. "Can't we stay out a little longer? It's so nice out." When Celer spoke, it was magic that made the sounds, accompanied by waves of light that showed his emotions. He glowed a soft, mildly annoyed orange.

"Nice? Not for us humans. Besides, we should get going."

"Yeah, okay. Wouldn't want you to miss the big surprise."

"There's no chance of me getting you to spill the secret?" Ben prodded.

Celer laughed. "Dennison swore me not to tell! I can't ruin it for you. It wouldn't be fun that way, now would it?"

"Fine. I hope you don't mind killing me with the suspense."

Ben and Celer left the woods and came out into the backyard of their home. It was a modest, cream-colored, one-story house seated in the woods of rural New Hampshire. The home had a small front porch furnished with two rocking chairs that had mismatched cushions. Ben went inside, Celer floating beside him. Inside, Ben's mother was finishing a phone call.

"Alright, forty-five minutes. See you soon, Dennis. Love you." She hung up the phone. "Ben!" she said. "Good, you're back. Dennison called; he'll be here soon. Go clean up and finish packing."

Ben ran to his small bedroom, where three walls were covered in bookshelves. Fiction, nonfiction, reference, and history books were all piled in formidable stacks. Two whole walls composed Celer's library, which was devoted to language and history. On the sections of wall unoccupied by books were pictures of Ben, Celer, and Ben's mom and dad on their many camping trips: the White Mountains, the Grand Canyon, Yosemite, the Everglades, the Mongolian plains.

Ben changed clothes and then turned to packing. He had already packed cool-weather clothes for a three-day trip into his carryon bag, and now was gathering other essentials. Even though it was the middle of July, Dennison had said to be ready for three days of autumn chill. He had only given a mischievous wink when Ben asked where they were going.

"Travel chess board, language book, toothbrush, tooth-paste…" Ben muttered as he stuffed things into his bag. Some items took longer than others to find in Ben's cluttered space. He picked up a forgotten summer camp pamphlet, then tossed it aside with other rubbish. He continued his packing list with, "flashlight, pocketknife…" He paused just before he slid the red Swiss Army knife into his bag, then set it on his chest of drawers. "Can't bring that on the plane." Satisfied that everything he might need for the surprise trip – minus the pocketknife – had been packed, Ben went out to the front porch to wait for Dennison to take him to the airport.

Soon after, a blue SUV pulled up onto the long driveway. Ben got up, hefted the carryon bag, and made his way towards the vehicle.

"Celer," he said, "go tell Mom that Uncle Dennison's here!" Celer whizzed back into the house through the open window and called Ben's mother outside. She and Celer came back out just as the passenger door of the SUV opened and Dennison came out to say hello.

Ben's great-uncle, Dennison Smith, was in excellent health for someone nearing his seventy-fifth birthday, with brilliant blue eyes and a brisk, purposeful step. His once-blond hair was now a whitish gold, and had receded substantially. Dennison wore jeans and an untucked blue button-down shirt. The shirt had flecks of black and green ink on the cuffs. Ben dropped his bag and ran forward to give his granduncle a hug. Celer was close behind, twittering and chirping with excitement.

"We missed you!" Ben said.

"We've missed you as well. Aquila has been yearning to speak with Celer again for months."

A Messenger poked his head out of Dennison's shirt pocket. Aquila had ovular eyes and an analytical, yet mischievous gaze. His yarn neckband was colored in alternating dashes of red and white. As was customary for their kind, Celer and Aquila took to flying above their keepers' heads in a small circle, like two planets around an invisible star. They conversed rapidly about what had happened in the months they were apart.

"Dennis!" Ben's mother called to Uncle Dennison. "Thanks so much for coming. Ben and Celer have been counting down the days for a month now." Ben's mother beamed. "Don't worry, I didn't give anything away about your trip."

"He'll find out soon enough. I'd love to stay and talk for a while," Dennison said, checking his watch, "but we have a flight to catch and an appointment to keep. I'll send Aquila with a message in the morning so you know we've arrived safely. Now Ben, say good-bye to your mom and let's hit the road."

Ben, Dennison, Aquila and Celer drove to the airport and boarded the first flight on the trip to Mongolia. This was usual; Dennison lived there, and took Ben and Celer for the school year. However, Ben still itched to know what special occasion warranted a trip in the middle of summer. Celer was hidden from the view of other passengers, concealed safely in Ben's sweatshirt hood, which Ben had put on for that purpose.

"Can you get the Voleric grammar out of the bag for me? I'm bored."

"Sure," Ben said, pulling a book about the size of his palm out from his bag. The title read *Essentials of the Voleric Language: By Kon-Ren An-Tun and Tira Kliaro. Translated by Dennison Smith.*

Ben opened the book to the page Celer requested, and turned them as needed. A few minutes later Dennison called out,

"Ben, look! See the sunset?"

Ben and Celer looked out the window at what Dennison had pointed out. At flight altitude, the sun appeared like a band of gold, set on fire and stretched thin across the surface of the ocean. Even as the brilliant sunlight faded, it painted the clouds purple and the sky a dark orange. Slowly, Ben's eyelids drooped as the sun sunk slowly below the horizon. As the ocean snuffed out the last ray of sunlight, Ben and Celer drifted off to sleep.

Ben, Celer and Dennison slept as much as they could on the connecting flights to Chicago, Beijing, and finally Ulan Bator, Mongolia. Once they landed at the international airport, they exited the plane with the throng of other travelers, and made their way out into a back lot. Here, they boarded yet another plane, this time a small, four-seater Cessna, piloted by Dennison himself. Aquila ushered the group into the plane, the propellers whirred, and then they were off into the clear blue skies over Mongolia.

Ben watched as the cities below him gave way to grassland that seemed to stretch on forever. Other than the occasional group of nomadic herders, Ben could not make out anything in particular as the plane flew farther over the rolling green hills.

Soon, Ben spotted a familiar disturbance ahead. The air in front of the plane was blurred and wavering, like a mirage. This phenomenon, though, was a giant, dome-shaped barrier, and was getting closer as the plane flew onward. When the plane hit the barrier, the air cleared and revealed four huge, golden pillars. These were positioned at a half-mile radius around what could have been any ordinary patch of grass on the Mongolian grassland, except for a landing strip and a small shed. The barrier's strange fluctuations, though, were invisible once the party was within their influence. Ben had always spent his school years here. He, Dennison, and a few other select families from around the world lived here, in one of the least inhabited places on Earth, waiting patiently for long awaited orders from the Alliance Council.

Ben had heard the history of the Daalronnan Alliance and more, as he had spent many nights around the hearth during his apprenticeship to Dennison, learning to build and enchant the flying Messengers that maintained contact between the distant worlds. As the group of humans and Messengers entered the Ziggurat, Ben recalled the thousand memories that he had made in every room. Here, Ben had spent every September to June, learning how to become a full-fledged member of an order called the Messengersmiths. He learned math, science, language, ethics and history. Down the hall, Ben had always eaten breakfast in the kitchen, a room that carried the sharp scent of Daalronnan *onqari* root and *ko-imensi* tea. Here, Ben had also learned to appreciate omelets turned purple by the alien spices that Dennison used. Ben spent holidays with the tight-knit family of the base; Dennison, the Messengers, and the multilingual, multinational community that An-Tun had chosen all those years ago.

The original chosen representatives and their adult children were going about their daily business when Ben arrived, but he had no time to say hello. The airline had suffered a delay in Beijing, and Dennison was exhorting Ben to run as they deboarded the Cessna.

"Come on, we can't miss our appointment," he said. Dennison jammed the *down* button on the elevator. At the cheery *ding* that signaled their arrival on the deepest subterranean floor, he pushed the doors open, racing by other national representatives as he led Ben down a long hallway. Ben barely had time to wave and shout "Ni hao" or "Salaam" as he ran past his extended family.

"Isn't this the hallway to the Portal room?" Ben panted as he ran beside Dennison. "Is this trip even on Earth?" If not, it would be his first trip off his birth planet.

Dennison smiled. "I knew you'd figure it out."

"So where are we going, then?" Ben asked.

"Andaros' annual Literature Festival," Celer said. "The biggest gathering of authors, playwrights, and other entertainers in the known galaxy. I've been learning the native Voleric language for months. So, what do you think?"

"This is awesome!" Ben exclaimed. "Thank you, thank you, thank you! Let's go!"

Dennison punched a key code into a pad on the heavy steel door of the Portal room.

"This door," Dennison explained, "is an airlock. Before we open the portal to another planet, we seal it, because different planets have different atmospheric pressures and compositions. If we didn't seal the doors, then pressure and content would equalize on a planetary scale. Luckily, we're not late for acclimation, which can take a while."

Dennison pushed the door open and led Ben and Celer into the room, then sealed the door with a pneumatic hiss. Taking up the entire back of the room was a huge device made of tanks and tubes and uncountable wires. In the center of this device stood a round, empty door that led nowhere except for the steel paneling of the front of the machine. The piece of technology reduced the usable space in that gymnasium-sized room down to an area about as large as a bedroom. Dennison started entering data into a computer panel, which stood on a podium in the center of the usable space.

The computer hummed. In its computerized voice, it said, "*Interface open. Please select your destination.*"

"Andaros, Alarzi Municipal."

"*Your appointment is confirmed in computer logs. Your transit to Alarzi Municipal Station, Republic of Dawta Volaero, planet Andaros will commence in one hour, thirty minutes. Please stand by for atmospheric equalization.*"

For the hour and a half in which the atmospheres of Andaros and Earth gradually mixed to prevent shock, the group had to wait without much to do. Celer entertained Ben with the story of a religious war of the extremist Takathists versus the mainstream priesthood, which had inflamed at the same time as when the Alliance wanted to make first contact with Andaros. Just as Celer had finished describing the unlikely triumph of a single embattled Messengersmith versus an army of a thousand, an alarm bell sounded. Ben felt the floor rumble, sending vibrations up through his bones. He eyed the empty door, and momentarily, the steel seemed to ripple as if it had become water. Like a cloud of mud clearing from a pond, the steel seemed to dissolve into a different sight: that of a huge room like an airport terminal, with signs written in the vertical script Ben recognized from the Voleric phrasebook. Once the image had snapped into complete focus, Dennison announced it was safe to cross onto planet Andaros.

Ben was surprised at how normal crossing between worlds felt. In fact, it seemed no stranger than walking through a door that connected two rooms of his house. Ben had to remind himself that he had just crossed between planets, an unfathomable distance of interstellar space.

The terminal that he and the rest of the group had entered seemed all the more empty because of its size. Like any airport on Earth, this building was meant to accommodate hundreds of people at a time, who came in droves from mass transit "wormhole anchors" all over the Alliance. Dennison waved at the native Andarite attendant, who closed the wormhole from his computer panel. The Andarite was about five and a half feet tall and covered in deep green scales. Two horns protruded from above his eyes, and the back of his head was wreathed in a thick frill of bone.

"Good job, Ben," Dennison said as he, Ben and the Messengers exited the main terminal.

"With what?" Ben asked. The process had seemed easy enough.

"Not staring at Mr. Ralazaro," Dennison said, referring to the attendant. "Most people are taken off guard by the native species on their first off-world adventure."

"Oh, okay," Ben said, laughing a little. He checked his watch, which read 3:30 p.m. "I hope we're not going to be late! I can't wait to get to the Festival."

"Not to worry, Ben," Dennison said, pulling out a silver pocket watch. He tapped the face three times and said, "Alarzi, Dawta Volaero." Suddenly the watch rearranged itself. The twelve disappeared, and the numbers rearranged so they were evenly spaced, and the eleven was on top. The hands spun until they read 10:05 am. "This," Dennison said, "is an interplanetary watch. It's designed to reset to whatever interplanetary timezone you need. It also resets to the length of the specific planet's day. For example, Andaros only has twenty-one hours in its day. Also, it's still morning here. So, we'll catch plenty of the festivities, but we should be in bed early so it's easier to deal with the galactic jet lag tomorrow. Now, let's drop off our bags at the hotel and we can get to sightseeing!"

After they had dropped off their bags and changed into cool weather clothes in a small hotel near the anchor station, the group proceeded towards the bustling downtown of the city of Alarzi. Ben shivered in the cool autumn air, and zipped his jacket.

"Is there anything you're hoping to see at the Literature Festival, Ben, Celer?" Dennison asked.

Celer was the first to respond. "I'd love to look through some more Alliance history," he replied. "Especially Narissan history and the feudal schisms."

"Ben? How about you?" Dennison asked.

"You caught me off guard with the surprise, so I don't really know. Any suggestions?"

"Celer has good ideas," Dennison said. "And I think you'll also like a set of novels dictated by a colonial Wenifrin Messenger named Avanti. They're the type of wilderness adventure story I think you'd like."

"Alright, thanks!" Ben said. "I'll look for it." Just then, Ben, Dennison, Celer and Aquila rounded the street corner onto downtown Alarzi. Ben stood agape at the sight before him. He and Dennison were standing on the rim of a huge bowl. Downtown Alarzi was a huge valley filled with gleaming buildings of metal and glass. Throughout the area, monorails shot around on elevated tracks, traveling fast enough to cross the huge valley in seconds. Ben imagined himself reaching out and picking one up, for the city looked like an idyllic little model train display, full of life and excitement, but on a tiny scale. At the bottom of the bowl, there was a huge park that surrounded a blue, sparkling lake. Colorful festival tents took up the entire area. The downtown's five main roads shot out from the fairgrounds, each filled to capacity with a flowing mass of pedestrian traffic. The fairground, full of flashing lights and the bustle of activity, was a huge heart, pumping life and energy out into the city along those five giant arteries. Celer vibrated with excitement.

"Let's go already!" he said.

Dennison checked his watch, and then pointed towards an open-air pavilion next to a set of monorail tracks. "These trains have the most precise arrival and departure times on this planet." Dennison and Ben boarded the monorail along with a few other Andarites. At the door, Celer, Aquila and the Andarites' Messengers flew up above the train car, joining an already large swarm hovering there. Ben didn't begrudge the separation; Messengers preferred the open air to confinement in any artificial transportation. Besides, Celer had little contact with other Messengers when he wasn't at the Mongolia base.

Once inside the monorail, Ben was surprised by how ornate the inside of the train was. The seats were made of a cream-colored native hardwood with an intricate, swirling grain. The cushions were made of blue leather that felt scaly to the touch. All along the train, Andarites sat in silence, most of them reading books or pamphlets.

"Nice train," Ben commented.

"The Andarites like the simple pleasures of life," Dennison said. "Stories, fine arts, home cooked meals. They have little interest in mathematics or the sciences. This train was most likely sold and installed by a company from Wenifri. The interior was probably installed by a small team of master Andarite craftsmen. The Wenifrins are always ready to sell their technology to others, for the right price."

Ben nodded. "This is really cool," he said. "Everything seems so balanced. Seems like Andaros has a really nice system going on here."

Dennison shook his head and frowned. "You would think that, having only seen Alarzi. The rest of Dawta Volaero is deep in debt to Wenifrin corporations. Cities amassed huge deficits from buying expensive technology, and the Voleric economy is suffering for it. Many cities have under-funded public services, and many of those have been forced to cut back on things like law enforcement and fire control. Joraw and Diwo Rovisiro are hotbeds for organized crime."

"How does Alarzi look so good, then?" Ben asked.

"Tourism," Dennison replied. "This city relies on the income from the Literature Festival. That, and Alarzi is lucky enough to be seated in the middle of the Barali Mountains." Dennison motioned out the monorail window to the towering, snow-capped peaks, glistening with ice and dominating the rim of the valley. "Without those draws for tourists, Alarzi would be as underfunded as the rest of Dawta Volaero."

Ben nodded and looked down at his shoes, but Dennison gave him a reassuring smile. "You and Celer don't need to worry about that, though. I just want you to focus on enjoying yourselves during this trip."

The monorail ride into Alarzi took under five minutes, which seemed far too short, considering how vast the valley looked from its rim. Excitement welled up in Ben's chest as the monorail doors slid open with a soft hiss. He and Dennison left the monorail, joining the long queue of other passengers. All those exiting raised their fists in a nonverbal call. The cloud of Messengers slowly dispersed, each called back into orbit around each keeper's head. Ben and Dennison raised their fists, returning Celer and Aquila to the group. Ben flashed Celer a big, excited grin, and Celer released joyful waves of yellow light in reply. They took off at a sprint down the street.

"Wait up!" Dennison called. "No use turning down the wrong street when you leave me behind."

Ben, though, couldn't help running once he started hearing the alien, but beautiful, Andarite music in the streets around the park. The smells of new foods to try followed soon afterwards, and finally Ben saw the towering gates, hung with embroidered banners, behind which lay everything Ben was so excited to see.

"Alarzi's two hundred eightieth Literature Festival," Celer said, translating the text on the banners. "That would mean the Festival was established in about 1730 in Earth measurement."

"That's right," Dennison said. "This event happens every year, and I'd say it is more prestigious here than the Olympics are on Earth. Any book being sold here is at the top of its genre."

Dennison stepped up to the ticket counter and began speaking to the park attendant in fluent Voleric. At the end of the exchange, Dennison handed the Andarite five silver rings and three bronze ones. Dennison, Ben, Celer and Aquila passed through the gates and into the vast press of people who were doing business, reading, or otherwise enjoying the festival. Billboards marketed a plethora of other services, from *Ul-Ncu's Herbal Tea Supplements* to *Dhilnara Enterprises' Economical Storage & Transport Solutions*. Booksellers shouted their wares in every Alliance language, and enchanted banners whirled and danced through the crowds.

The number of people of all different species was staggering. While the majority of the crowd was made up of Andarites, other Alliance species milled about as well. There were imposing Daalronnans, reptiles with four arms and seven-foot stature, and spindly Wenifrins, whose slick skin was a pale lavender-gray. Every so often, the crowd parted for a wealthy Narissan, suspended on a fifteen foot-long metal rig and kept breathing by a continuous flow of water through a buzzing aerator. The fairgoers seemed all the more diverse because of their clothing, which seemed to come from a thousand different galactic cultures. The fairgrounds were shaded, as from a passing cloud blocking the sun. When Ben looked up, though, all he saw were Messengers. Messengers of every color and shape, from every Alliance world, were spiraling and weaving through overhead throngs of their own kind. What light could reach the ground did so as a thousand tiny pinpricks, each poking though the press of flying bodies for a moment and then disappearing. All of the fairgoers were walking on pavement that had become a river of shadowy fish, each of which followed a Messenger along its course through the crowd.

Dennison handed him a bag of gold, silver and bronze rings like the ones he used to pay for admission to the festival. Dennison said, "If you see a book or some snacks that you want to buy, use these. The gold ones are worth about two dollars, the silver ones are worth one dollar, and the bronze ones are about fifty cents. Just stay in sight of Aquila and me."

"Thanks," Ben said. He didn't waste any time making his way to the nearest vendor, an Andarite whose storefront was decorated with exquisite watercolor maps of the Alliance worlds.

"Zeyeujaga rijaudi veroi?" the shopkeeper called.

"Translation, Celer?" Ben asked.

"Would these products interest you?" Celer replied. Ben took a moment to look at the shopkeeper's stacks of books. Hoping to catch his attention, the shopkeeper pointed at a three-book boxed set. Each one was the size of an encyclopedia. Celer's translation in English overlapped the Voleric sales pitch:

"*Yil ridi...* These are the three volumes of the *Complete History of the Daalronnan Alliance.* The first volume covers the formation years all the way to the Alliance's expansion onto Andaros. The second covers the Narissan feudal schisms and the Kalofri colonization years. The third covers everything from the third Iyerani Roianx Revolution to the Earth Nuclear Crisis."

Ben reached for the first volume on display. With Celer translating, he asked,

"May I?"

"Go ahead," the shopkeeper replied. Ben opened the book and flipped through its pages. Guiding Celer by dragging his finger along the columns of Voleric script, he listened to the translation:

"The Daalronnan race was the first to have created Messengers, which they called *ha-daal-wes-mik-ha-ter,* or, 'those who fly with the stars.' The sent them forth from their native world, and, flying across the stars, they made contact with the Wenifrins." Ben had heard the early history of the Alliance before. He remembered how the Wenifri had sent spaceships in response to the Messengers' contact. Transit at near light speed, one way, had taken forty years between the planets. Once the Wenifrin ships landed, the explorers created a colony. At first, there was bitter cultural and military strife that pitted magic against advanced technology, but peace won out when neither side could keep fighting. The treaty that created the Alliance was signed at Daalronna's capital, Daron City. Ben closed the book, and gave Celer time to inquire to the shopkeeper about the Narissan schisms. Ben obligingly turned the pages as Celer read some of the Narrisans' history from Volume II. Suddenly the shopkeeper became irate. Ben couldn't understand the rapid exchange, but he could tell it was escalating. Ben plucked Celer out of the air by his tail and pulled him away.

"What was that all about?" Ben asked.

"He said I had to buy the book before I read the whole thing. Said I was in the way of his paying customers."

"Well, you kind of were," Ben said. "Come on. There are other books around here. *Lots* of other books."

"Alright, fine. How about the fiction section?"

"Sure." Ben checked over his shoulder to make sure Dennison was still within sight, then picked up a book of short stories from the fiction writers' section. Celer translated the title as *Tales of The Messengers*. Ben opened it to a page near the end, half of which was taken up by a strange picture.

It was a sketch of a man wrapped entirely in the high-quality cloth used only to make Messengers. He appeared to have baseball-sized, black glass marbles for eyes, similar to those of a Messenger. He wore gauntlets and greaves that looked like Messengers' fluttering cloth tails. The subtitle said, *the legendary half-Messenger.* Celer skimmed the story and gave Ben a summary. The tale seemed based on how a man, who had become a hybrid of Messenger and man, saved the world from many different calamities. He had both the capacity to fly at near light speed like a Messenger, and the appendages of a human. Ben was fascinated.

"Do you think this could be possible?" Ben asked of the old Andarite woman behind the counter. Again, Celer's translation kicked in:

"Zau... No, impossible. Besides, Messengers and surface-dwellers must rely on each other's powers. It keeps balance. The impulsive thoughts of all beings can produce great evil when combined with great power. Walkers and flyers must always be able to second-guess each other."

Ben nodded. "So what happens to the half-Messenger at the end?"

"He dies."

"What?" Ben exclaimed, indignant.

"Maybe," the woman replied, smiling mischievously. "I thought I'd keep you guessing. Three gold and one silver if you want to read the ending."

"Alright," Ben said, reaching into the pouch. "Here you go." Ben handed the woman the payment she had asked for.

She pulled out a cash register composed of three rods designed for the rings to slide onto.

"Have a nice stay at the festival," she said, "And enjoy the book."

"Thanks," Ben said. Then he heard a Messenger's high-pitched voice from behind him.

"Ben! Celer! Uncle Dennison would like you to follow him. We're moving on to another section of the Festival," Aquila said, flying down to Ben's eye level. Ben and Celer followed Aquila back to where Dennison was buying snacks for Ben and himself. He handed Ben a strange delicacy that looked like a blue French fry.

"I'm sorry I had to pull you away from whatever you were reading, but we have a lot of festival to cover! We have to get through the science section and the Hall of Memoirs by the end of today so we can finish everything by tomorrow evening! Trust me, there's a lot to see!"

Ben nodded as he put the blue, crispy strip into his mouth. "Wow!" he said. "These are great! What are they?"

"Andarite tortoise liver jerky," Dennison replied, handing Ben a sealed bag of his own. "Save those for later. You can eat out of my bag for now."

"Don't mind if I do," Ben said, helping himself to another strip from Dennison's bag. Along with its basic meaty flavor, the liver jerky also had hints of something like almond. Ben had never tasted anything like it, but he loved it. Dennison ushered him and Celer on through the festival, while Ben tried to absorb as much as he could from every book he passed. After flipping though the picture panels of *Edible Plants of the Andarite Mountain Ranges,* he paused for a good laugh with a book called *Spaceships! Understanding Messenger Humor.* Ben's interest faded as his group passed into the science section, where the familiar embrace of a good story faded into the hard, emotionless lines formed of mathematical equations that Ben couldn't decipher. The vocabulary Celer had studied for the trip didn't include the scientific terms piled so thickly into the text. Finally, the science section faded out into the 'Hall of Memoirs.' Ben picked up the autobiography of a nationalist fighter who had been exiled from his home planet. He was about to ask Celer for the translation of the first page when he noticed something out of the corner of his eye. Ben did a double take.

Could it be? he thought. He knew that no one else from the base, besides Dennison and the Messengers, had come with him to Andaros. Still, Ben was sure that there was a human girl of his age, sitting on a bench, barely twenty feet from where he stood.

Chapter 2

Ben stared as possible explanations ran through his mind. None made sense.

"Aquila?" Ben asked. "Are we meeting someone else from Earth?"

"No. Why do you ask?"

"I found another human," Ben replied, pointing. By now, Ben and Aquila had attracted Dennison's attention. He, too, looked wide-eyed at the girl.

"Did I ever tell you about Katerina and Marion?" Dennison asked Ben.

"Yeah, the ones who moved off Earth?"

"With their families, yes. This must be their grandchild. Go say hello! She might like to meet someone of her age from Earth."

Ben nodded and went to sit on the bench next to the girl. She was ascetically thin, had red hair cut close to her scalp, and wore a shirt, winter jacket, and pants all of the same drab gray material. She didn't seem to notice as Ben sat down, but instead kept working with the silver tablet that sat in her lap. On its screen were scrolling columns of symbols. They weren't the flowing, cursive Andarite script, and didn't look like any of Earth's languages either. The girl tapped the symbols in complex patterns, causing the screen to flash blue.

"Hi," Ben said. Distracted, the girl tapped a symbol incorrectly, and the screen flashed red. She looked up from the tablet.

"Hello," she said. She looked over at Ben, raking her eyes up and down his body, like a detective appraising a cold corpse at a murder scene.

"How did you arrive at the Festival?" Her accent was foreign yet untraceable, each syllable spoken with flat, equal stress, each sound articulated with mechanical precision.

"My uncle brought me because he comes every year. Do you know Dennison Smith? Or the cultural base in Mongolia?"

"I know of it. Are you also a Messengersmith, like him?"

"Technically, yes," Ben said. "Well, an apprentice, really, but—"

"So you practice magic."

"Yeah."

The girl was silent for a moment. She looked at Ben, but blankly.

"I'm Ben, and this is Celer," Ben said to break the silence.

"Seren," she said.

"Do you want to check out some of the books around here?" Ben asked.

"Yes." She left without a word, heading over to a particularly large tent of "*Vio Yidaro's Collected Personal Essays: Limited Time Special Edition 6-Volume Set.*" Ben and Celer followed her into the tent, and perused books that, upon Celer's translation, seemed to be the densest, driest selection of literature in this section of the fair. The bookseller himself was asleep, feet propped up on a desk in the back corner. Nevertheless, Seren picked up one of the ponderous tomes. Ben walked over to her.

"Is there something in particular you need from me?" Seren asked. She stared Ben down, hawklike in her intensity.

"Ah, no... Just trying to make conversation." Ben floundered mentally for something more.

"Do you need a translation of any of these books?" Celer asked.

Seren took out what looked like a hearing aid.

"This is a translation device," she said. Ben noticed that the white of Seren's left eye was actually sky blue. The iris was riddled with golden circuitry. She indicated the eyepiece and said, "This handles translations of text. Also, when I need to speak in the Andarite language, it displays a phonetic transcription of what I want to say."

"Wow," Ben said.

"And you receive your translation from the... magical robot?" Seren asked. She pointed a finger at Celer.

"Excuse me?" Celer asked, glowing a disgusted shade of green. "I am a fully sentient magical *being*, miss! Just because

I'm not technically a metabolizing life form doesn't mean I can't—"

"Celer!" Ben said. "Calm down." Ben turned to Seren and explained, "The Messengers are intelligent. They have emotions and opinions like we do. And, yes, Celer is my translator. Just don't call him a robot, alright?"

"Understood," Seren said. "I apologize, Celer."

"That's okay," Celer said, still sounding hurt. "This morning I thought everyone off Earth knew about magic. Everyone here is paired with a Messenger, you know."

"There is little communication between the Alliance and Iyerayñan," Seren said.

Ben nodded solemnly. Dennison spoke little about the time Iyerayñan had withdrawn its application for Alliance membership, but whenever he did, it was bitter. He sat in silence for a while, unsure what to do as Seren read.

Ben awoke from the solemn memory when a choked gurgling sound and a thud sounded in the tent. Ben peered out from around the corner of the bookshelf. Two people had entered the tent while Seren had been reading. One was at the shopkeeper's table: a short, rust colored alien on tall robotic legs. He towered over the shopkeeper, who was now awake and stuttering something in Voleric. His voice quaked with fear. Beside the desk, another Andarite lay on the ground, bleeding out from the throat. A deep blue blood-stain spread from the wound. The red-skinned murderer's tone was threatening as he began to speak to the shopkeeper in a language Ben could neither understand nor recognize.

The Andarite shopkeeper reluctantly pulled a blue rectangular device out of his coat pocket and handed it to the murderer. As the murderer examined the device, the shopkeeper reached for what appeared to be a telephone receiver with one shaking hand, while holding a handgun in the other.

The murderer reached out and disarmed the shopkeeper in a lightning-fast motion of his hand, then shot him a weapon that gave no sound except a soft *puff*. Blood gushed from the shopkeeper's chest, and he slumped over. The murderer then removed a different device from his pocket and pressed a button.

Seren yelped in pain as her earpiece gave off a loud, high-pitched tone. The murderer turned and looked at the bookshelf behind which Ben, Celer and Seren hid. Ben didn't have time to think as the murderer drew a gun. He stood up and extended his hand, and torrent of magic threw the bookshelf like a house of cards in a gale, slamming it into the murderer.

Ben immediately felt like someone had poured boiling water on his back and down his arm. Dizziness and nausea came over him in waves, and he fell to the ground. As he caught himself, another rod of pain shot up through his right arm. Through the pain, Ben struggled to keep his mind in the moment.

The murderer struggled under the heavy piles of books, extricated himself from the crushed remains of his robotic legs, and ran away, as fast as his short natural legs would carry him. He pushed out of the tent, leaving Ben, Seren and Celer inside. Seren knelt over Ben.

"What happened?" she asked.

"Magic burns," Ben said through grinding teeth, "Happen whenever the nerves can't handle the magic you put through them."

"Will it heal?" Seren asked.

"It will, but I can't use any more magic for a couple weeks, maybe months."

"Understood," Seren said. "If you are able, we should report the murder." Ben nodded and pushed himself to his feet with his left hand, the hand without the magic-burned nerves. Seren went over to the desk and picked up the blue device.

"He must have dropped this while disarming the shop-keeper," she said. "We should give it to the authorities."

The uneasy crowd of fairgoers gave the group a wide berth as they exited the tent. The police had not yet arrived. Everyone in the crowd eyed Ben, Seren and Celer, but then turned towards the sound of screaming coming from down the row of tents. Messengers scattered from where they orbited their keepers' heads, fleeing from the disturbance making its way through the throng. Celer flew above the crowds for a better vantage point. He returned to Ben's eye level and exclaimed, "Run! The attacker's back – and he brought friends!" Ben ran, pulling Seren along as she looked back over her shoulder, surveying the crowd and the red-skinned, robotic-legged assailants coming through.

"Come on!" Ben yelled. Finally Seren started running in earnest, and they managed to put some distance between themselves and the attackers. The crowd parted wide before them. Ben risked a look back and saw the aliens gaining on him and Seren, their robotic legs pumping like professional athletes'. These attackers wielded Andarite rifles and did not hesitate to aim them at terrified bystanders. The alien in the lead started firing, the weapon giving quiet bangs like a silenced gun.

"Over here!" Seren shouted, pointing down an alleyway. Ben followed her through and came out of the alley beside a stopped monorail. She slid past the ticketing line, ducked under a security officer, and pushed deep into the crowd of people already on the train. Ben followed.

The three attackers rounded the corner. The leader spoke to his two subordinates, and the three split up, searching the platform for Ben and Seren. The monorail's doors closed with a *thump*, and it started to move. They arrived at their destination near the edge of the city in a few seconds. Seren scanned the area, then grabbed Ben's arm and led him through the crowd. He bit back a sharp remark as pain shot up his burned limb.

"One of the people chasing us boarded the train and followed us here," Seren said. "Follow me and stay quiet."

Ben obliged as Seren kept her head low and followed the crowd. The assailant was speaking with an attendant farther down the train. When they had almost passed him, he turned and Ben's breath caught in his throat. The assailant, though, did not have time to chase him before the attendant he was speaking with kicked his robotic legs, at just the right angle to reduce them to sparking, twitching paperweights. The assailant fell and the Andarite stomped on his hand as he reached for a gun. The Andarite yelled, "*Wevaw! Rijoraghe wevaw! Averiae!*" which Celer translated as "Go! Get away from here! Quickly!"

Ben and Seren ran out of the terminal, being jostled by the other panicked passengers who heard the shout.

"Celer, fly up over us," Ben said. "I want to make sure we don't walk right into an ambush."

Celer flew up and quickly returned from his survey. "More of them coming down every street leading here. Five of them at least, all converging on the terminal."

"Options?" Seren asked.

"We leave the city," Celer said. He flicked his tail at a high fence to the group's left, behind which was a forest of tall, broad-leafed trees. Footsteps and the clank of metallic legs echoed from down the streets.

"Out of the city it is, then," Ben said. He ran to the wall of metal mesh and scrambled over, heart pumping. Seren got over and dropped into the leaf litter before he did, as every time he grabbed the fence, his right arm jolted again. The footsteps grew louder as Ben reached the top of the fence. He jumped and rolled into leaf litter to cushion his fall. Seren pulled him into the concealment of the leaves. They held their breath as they watched the group of red-skinned aliens converge on the monorail station. The aliens conversed for a moment, and then entered the station, one by one. Celer flew out of hiding to check that the coast was clear.

"We're clear!" he said on his return. "We should get deeper into the woods before they realize we're not in the station."

Ben, Seren and Celer pushed through the thick undergrowth and ducked tree branches until they could no longer see the buildings of Alarzi. When they stopped, Ben could feel the adrenaline leaving his system. His legs wobbled under him, and the pain surged back into his arm. He leaned against the trunk of a tall tree and gasped for air. All three took a moment to let the events of the last few minutes sink in.

Ben was the first to speak up, saying, "We have to get back into the city."

"We should not act until we have assessed the situation," Seren replied. "By what we saw, the force we are against is highly organized, and will not hesitate to kill. I agree we should return to the city, but not before we know that we are dealing with."

"I can find that out for you," Celer said. "You two stay put here and I'll come back with some usable intel."

"You could be noticed," Seren said.

"To them, I'm just another Messenger among a million others," Celer replied. "They won't notice me." Celer shot directly up through the canopy to begin reconnaissance, leaving Ben and Seren beneath the trees.

"Crazy day," Ben said. "It's my first time off Earth and I'm being chased by aliens already. Yep, crazy day…"

"Whoever they were," Seren said, "they were from Iyerayñan."

"Is that species who chased us native to your planet?" Ben asked.

"Yes. I also recognize their technology."

"You speak their language since you're from their planet, right? What was he saying to the sales clerk at the festival?"

"The Iyerani seemed to be scolding the Andarite about an overdue delivery. I think it was this item."

Seren handed the blue device to Ben. He found that one face of the item was covered in gold dots. He handed the device to Seren. "What is it?" he asked.

"This is a data storage device from Iyerayñan, but not a standard model. This appears to be made to fit in a custom access port. It must have been shielded somehow from the electromagnetic pulse."

"The what?" Ben asked.

"Our assailant used a device to release an electromagnetic pulse to disable the vendor's communicator. It overloaded my translator as well. I am sorry that it revealed us."

"It wasn't your fault."

"How is your arm?"

"Still hurts," Ben said as he ventured at massaging the muscles. The pain had faded slightly into a throbbing ache, and no longer flared up when he touched it. "If I had some Annalalh with me, it would heal faster."

"Annalalh?"

"It's a plant salve that helps train the nerves to carry more magic without being hurt. It heals magic burns, too."

"Interesting," Seren said. "I do not know enough about the science behind magic to know how the burns could be treated with what we have."

"They'll heal on their own," Ben said. "How about you? Are you alright?"

"I am not injured."

"That's good," Ben replied. He examined the Andarite forest. The trees were broad-leafed and tall, and the thick canopy choked out much of the daylight. There was a sound like the cawing of birds, paired with a hum like dragonfly wings, high in the canopy. Ben looked for the source for a moment, then gave up. The foliage was too dense above to see anything except the occasional darting shadow. He picked a stick up from off the ground and brushed leaf litter away from a patch of dirt. As he waited for Celer to return, he occupied himself with doodling random shapes in the dirt.

He was drawing a Wenifrin spaceship that he had seen in a book illustration, when he looked over at Seren. She had resumed the appraising, analytical countenance that had so unsettled Ben earlier, while they talked at the festival. Ben had heard the expression 'staring daggers' before, but Seren seemed to be staring scalpels at him; dissecting his expressions, movements, breathing rate, anything. Ben returned to his drawings in the dirt and tried to clear the unsettling expression from his mind. He surprised himself when the stick snapped in his hand; he had been pressing furiously into the dirt, leaving inch-deep scars in the ground. Thankfully, a moment later, Celer dropped through the canopy and leveled out so as to look Ben and Seren in the eye.

"What did you see?" Ben asked.

"The entire city's full of them!" Celer exclaimed. "Everywhere I looked, there's at least one or two. Every once in a while they talk into earpieces."

"You are sure that all of these agents are working for the group that pursued us?" Seren asked.

"Definitely. None of them are doing anything except pacing. Each one of them is patrolling a well-defined course, each of which is long enough that it always looks like they're going somewhere, not just pacing in place."

"What are their weapons like?" Ben asked.

"Concealed handguns, mostly under coats or tucked into hiding spots. They're being extra careful not to arouse suspicion. Ben, I'm sure the entire city's full of them. This mob has control of Alarzi, and the people have no idea."

Ben nodded pensively. "Highly organized Iyerani mafia with the manpower to control an entire city. That's what we're up against. Ideas?"

"Leave the city entirely," Celer said. "We hike to the next nearest city."

"How far is that?" Ben asked.

"I checked from the lower boundary of the stratosphere, and there's a city north of here. I'd estimate it's about a week's hike from here to there."

"That would depend upon the terrain," Seren said.

"I took that into account, don't worry. Alarzi is on the south end of a mountain pass that extends north. The other city is up there, and it's bordered by huge, flat meadows for about ten miles. The pass is basically all flat terrain, intersected by one river. I already found a safe place to cross it. But Ben, shouldn't we go try to find Dennison?"

"The mob will start patrolling the forest to find us, I'm sure of it. We can't linger around here while we look for him. Besides, there are only three humans in the city. He'll attract attention and they could ambush us."

"Good point," Celer replied.

"Alright," Ben said. "Seren, think you're up for hiking to the next city?"

"It is a risk," she replied, "but I think our odds of surviving the wilderness are greater than our odds of surviving a confrontation with the mafia in Alarzi. We should begin."

They hiked towards the mountain pass without stopping for hours. Eventually, Ben looked up and estimated the sun's position in Andaros' skies.

"Hold on," Ben said. "There's only an hour or so of daylight left. We should construct a shelter and catch up on sleep. Tomorrow, we'll keep going."

Seren nodded her assent and surveyed the area for shelter-building materials. She located a long branch and started breaking off the smaller twigs until she was left with a stave about five feet long. She wedged it horizontally between two trees, beginning the frame for a lean-to. Ben went about gathering more long, leafy branches to complete the back wall. Soon, they had made a suitable lean-to. Ben completed the shelter using leaf litter to cover the multitude of holes in the slanting roof. He decided he was satisfied as the sun touched down against the horizon in an orange blaze. He sat down in the shelter. His stomach growled, and then he remembered the bag of snacks that Dennison had given him earlier that day. He pulled the bag out of his pocket, substantially more battered than when he had put it in. Nonetheless, he opened it and took out one of the bluish liver strips inside.

"Have some of these," Ben said, waving the bag at Seren. She sat down in the shelter with Ben and took a few of the strips.

"Does Celer need food?" Seren asked.

"No," Ben said. "Celer runs completely on magic. He needs rest, though." Ben and Seren each took another strip from the bag, finishing it off.

Soon, the sun had set below the horizon. The chill of an autumn night on Andaros quickly set in. Ben and Seren zipped their jackets up to their chins and tried to curl up into balls to conserve precious heat. All the while, Ben's teeth chattered, and he cursed his inability to produce even a spark of magic.

Seren was working on something in the dark. She crept out of the lean-to and felt around the immediate vicinity for something; exactly what, Ben couldn't tell. She brought a small bundle of dry wood back to the shelter and began arranging it in the dark. She threw leaves into the center, then started working with some small object that was obscured by the dark. A moment later Ben saw the birth of an ember and a wispy tendril of smoke in the middle of the woodpile.

"Go get more wood," Seren said.

Ben obliged, running around the forest, buoyed by the prospect of warmth and light. He provided Seren with a pile of sticks that fed a respectable fire. It was no roaring blaze, but the comfort of warmth brought a smile to Ben's face as he held his hands close to the flames.

"How did you get the spark?" Celer asked Seren as they settled into the shelter again.

"I salvaged parts from my translator earpiece," Seren said. "The most delicate circuitry had been damaged beyond repair by the electromagnetic pulse, but a few larger wires and the power cell were not damaged. I created a short circuit near the fuel."

"Genius," Ben said. "Thanks. Now, we should get some sleep. We had a big day."

"Understood," Seren said before rolling over and going to sleep. Celer settled into rest as well, drifting to the ground like a balloon losing helium. Ben lay down on the ground, but could not fall asleep. Too many thoughts were spinning around in his head.

"Feeling okay?" Celer asked softly.

"Just shaken, that's all," Ben whispered back. "Never thought that on my first trip off Earth, I'd end up witnessing a murder, getting chased by an alien mafia, and ending up..." Ben lowered his voice until he was nearly mouthing the words, "…hiking across an alien forest with some girl I don't even know."

Celer flew out over Seren's head and did a quick circle, checking that she was asleep. He said, "Ben, I have to admit she scares me. She looks at us like she's going to dissect one of us as soon as our backs are turned. Gives me the shivers."

"It kind of freaks me out too," Ben said. "Right now, though, we don't have a choice. We can't just leave her here."

"Fine," Celer said. "But, we should be careful. Now, go to sleep."

"Good night, Celer."

"Good night, Ben."

The next morning, Ben awoke to the sun shining through the trees. It was already a hand's breadth above the horizon, but Ben was so tired that it seemed to be much earlier. A memory fought its way through the thick fog that pervaded his mind: something that Dennison had said the day before.

Andaros only has twenty-one hours in its day.

No wonder it seemed so early! The night had been hours shorter than Ben was used to on Earth. Even so, Ben couldn't let himself get behind on valuable daylight. He stood and stretched, before shivering in the cool morning air. Moments later his stomach rumbled. This time, he had no snacks left over from the Festival.

"We need to find food," Ben said to Seren and Celer, who were also just waking up.

"What do you suggest?" Seren said. "We do not know what is fit to eat."

"If we get moving, then we're bound to find wildlife at some point," Celer said.

"Makes sense," Ben said. He looked back at the shelter they had built the night before and said, "We should take this down. If anyone's looking for us, there's no use leaving a trail of breadcrumbs."

"Trail of breadcrumbs?" Seren asked. "Did you bring food that you did not tell us about?"

"I guess Hansel & Gretel haven't made their way to Iyerayñan yet, huh?" Ben asked.

"No," Seren said. "What is that?"

Nevermind," Ben muttered. He broke down the lean-to, and with Seren's help, scattered the remains across the woods. Celer whipped up a miniature whirlwind with his tail, blowing leaves and dirt around to cover the cold patch of scorched ground where the fire had been. Once Ben was sure that no one could discern that his group had ever been at the spot, he turned north and started walking.

The day passed slowly as hunger gnawed at Ben's stomach. No animals had shown themselves, and Ben and Seren were both suspicious of any berry bush they saw. Still, they forced themselves to keep walking. With every step, Ben felt a throbbing in his head, and his tongue felt dry. He cursed himself for not having a way to boil or otherwise sterilize water. They could deal with being hungry for a few days, at least, but without water it wouldn't matter. Dehydration would claim their lives before hunger had a chance to. The sun was creeping lower in the afternoon sky, and Ben still had not seen anything. He was about to announce that it was time to make camp when something unseen rustled in the high branches. Something up in there was sending down flurries of leaves from the canopy. They twittered and chirped like birds, which helped Ben clue into their location. They would not show themselves, though. Ben guessed that the mysterious forest creatures had built the many teardrop shaped baskets that he now saw hanging by strands of webbing from the higher tree branches. Each one was dull gray, about the size of a trashcan. On the ground below the circular entrance to each of the strange constructions was a pile of insect shells. Celer flew up to the entrance of one of the large baskets and peered into the dark recesses within.

A wet, crushed insect shell shot out of the opening. Celer dodged the slimy projectile, and it sailed down into the pile of shells below. He peered in once again, but this time, an obviously irate creature the size of an eagle flew from the hole, chirping and squawking as Celer made his escape away from the nest. The animal looked as if it couldn't quite decide whether it was a reptile or an insect. It had the long, thin body and tail of a lizard, complete with green scales that would allow it to blend seamlessly into the trees. Its back legs were lizard-like, with talons perfect for grasping tree branches. Instead of forelimbs, though, it had two pairs of iridescent green dragonfly wings. Ben and Seren ducked as the creature flew over their heads, chasing Celer. Ben laughed while Celer tried to shake off the birdlike creature. Finally it gave up the chase and returned to the basket, which Ben guessed was the animal's nest. Meanwhile, Seren was examining the broken insect shells that lay scattered on the ground.

"I think these may be edible," she said.

"Why?" Ben asked, approaching the pile of remains that Seren was kneeling by.

"There are no markings that show that the species is poisonous. Usually a dangerous species would display warning colors."

"That works on Earth, sure," Ben said. "But what about Andaros? We don't know that life here is similar at all."

Seren replied, "Species on every planet experience natural selection. Similar patterns can be expected. You saw how that animal followed Celer by sight. Therefore, it would know not to eat a brightly colored poisonous animal."

"Okay," Ben said. "That makes sense. So, how do we find, and then catch, the bugs?"

"We watch the birds," Celer replied, returning his gaze to the treetops. Once he found a creature to follow, he flew high into the branches with it. The animal landed on the trunk of a tree, digging its claws into the bark to anchor itself. Just above the animal, a large, black burl protruded from the tree. The animal coiled its entire body and suddenly sprang upwards, thrusting its beaklike mouth into the burl. It retracted its head, along with a squirming gray beetle. Using a claw on its wing, the animal scraped out the beetle flesh, then discarded the shell.

"Did you see that?" Celer asked as he returned to the ground.

"We did," Ben said, elated that Celer had found something to eat. Ben quickly located another nesting burl that he could just barely touch when he reached above his head. With a running jump, he grabbed it near to where it protruded from the tree. As he fell, gravity wrenched the entire bulb free, leaving him with a sizeable bowl full of wriggling beetles. Ben and Seren gathered firewood while Celer stood watch over the beetles, batting any that tried to escape back down into the wooden bowl. Once Seren had sparked the fire, Ben went about preparing spits to cook the insects on. He reached into his pocket for his knife, but found nothing.

"Oh, great," he muttered to himself. "Couldn't bring the knife through the airport terminal, and now I'm stuck without it! How are we supposed to cook now?"

"We could boil the beetles," Celer said.

"We have no suitable vessel to boil water," Seren said. "The wood will burn."

Ben replied, "Not so fast. Celer, you're on to something. Remember the time on the camping trip when we heated rocks and used those to boil water?"

"Exactly what I was thinking," Celer said. Celer's happiness showed as bands of yellow light coursing like snakes around his neckband. Ben peered into the bulb and surmised that it was clean enough for their purposes. He gathered a pile of rocks, which he placed in the center of the fire. After he had waited for the stones to heat up, he used a forked stick to transfer them into the bowl, which Seren had filled with water from a nearby stream. The rocks dropped into the water with a hiss and a plume of steam. Ben threw the insects into the water as it bubbled and came to a boil. Seren's flat expression broke, letting a smile through for just a second.

"Innovative," she said. "I have not seen that before."

"Thanks," Ben said with a small smile. "I'm starving. Let's eat." He fished the beetles out of the water and piled them on broad leaves that Celer had knocked from the trees. Ben and Seren dug into the first food they had eaten all day, scraping the warm meat out of the shells with their teeth. Ben was sure he had never been so hungry before, and ate as fast as he could.

"Not bad," Ben said through a mouthful of beetle.

Seren remained quiet, staring pensively into the fire as she ate. Finally, she said, "There is a very limited charge left in the remnants of my translator. I may only be able to spark a fire for two or three more uses."

"We should be fairly close to our destination by then," Celer said.

"Close, yes, but we will have two or three more days to travel. We will need another heat source."

"Ben, I don't think it will be safe for you to use magic by then," Celer said.

Ben replied, "If it's absolutely necessary, I may be able to risk a small spark in a few days."

"Good," Seren said. "It would be best for us to sleep now. Hopefully we will soon acclimate to Andaros' short day."

"Hopefully," Ben said. He lay down and looked up at the stars, trying to relax into sleep. Soon, though, he noticed that the night sky was different than at home on Earth. He couldn't recognize any of the constellations what had become so familiar to him while camping on Earth.

Celer said, "They're the same stars, you know. Our vantage point is just different."

"It still feels strange, though," Ben said. To him, the stars were more than a backdrop for nighttime activities. On Andaros, Ben would not be able to navigate at night. The North Star, such a familiar tool in Earth's sky, was just another meaningless pinprick among a trillion other scattered stars. The strangeness above him only reminded him of the complex situation that he was caught in. Ben's hand went to his pocket and pulled out the rectangular data storage device. Who had wanted it so badly that they would kill for it? What secrets did it hold? What could happen if those secrets were revealed to the Iyerani mafia? Who were the proper authorities to give the device to? More questions than Ben could even hope to answer swirled like a dark tempest in his mind. Ben yearned for sleep to come and wash away all the questions, at least for the night. Finally, as the last embers of the fire died, Ben drifted off to sleep.

CHAPTER 3

"**H**elp!"

The cry roused Ben with a start, and his head whipped around in search of its source.

"Celer? Seren? Did you hear that?" he asked. Celer flew in a close defensive orbit around his head. Seren was gone.

"We have to find her," Ben said. "Celer, scout from the air. We might be able to find her that way."

"Got it!" He shot up through the canopy in a flurry of leaves, then returned only moments later. He said, "I can't see anything. The trees are too thick!"

"Seren!" Ben called. There was another scream, and this time, Ben could pinpoint its location. He grabbed a charred stick from the ashes of the previous night's fire. It was about as long as his forearm, and seemed to be a suitable weapon. He took off through the woods, with Celer maintaining the orbit around his head. He pushed through the undergrowth as small trees and overhanging branches whipped at him, stinging his face and arms.

"I'm coming!" he called. He broke into a clearing full of toppled trees scarred with the marks of giant claws. Nesting baskets and bones of the green forest creatures lay scattered on the ground. Seren was pressed against one huge tree that was still standing. Between her and Ben was a bear-shaped reptile that stood a menacing ten feet tall. It had no teeth, but instead sported a razor-sharp, jagged, bone-crushing beak. The animal had a defensive frill covered in crimson markings. It reared up and took a swipe at Seren with a giant clawed hand. Just in time, she ducked. The beast missed her head by mere inches, showering her with wood splinters as it raked the tree.

"Hey, ugly!" Ben called as he threw the club he had brought. It bounced against the beast's frill. Unharmed but distracted, it turned, and looked at Ben for a moment through a predatory yellow eye. It then returned to its intended meal – who had disappeared while it was distracted. It let out a mighty roar and returned its attentions to Ben. The beast reared up and prepared to swipe at him, and Ben hid his face under his arms. He shrank back when the creature roared again.

When Ben looked up, blue blood was spraying from a wound behind the animal's frill. Seren, who had returned to Ben's side, quickly dodged the animal's next enraged swipe. In one hand, she held a long, bloodstained branch with a sharp tip. Ben grabbed another stick from the ground and jammed it into the creature's gaping mouth. Ben's stomach turned at the sound of the animal choking. Seren speared the animal behind the frill once more, while Ben kept ramming the stick further down its throat. It thrashed, splattering the two with blood. Finally, the creature stumbled and fell, succumbing to two gaping wounds in its neck. There was a mighty *thud* and a cracking of sticks as the huge head slammed into the ground. The animal heaved a final breath and went limp. Ben and Seren breathed heavily for a while.

"Ben, are you alright?" Celer asked.

"Fine," Ben replied, wiping blue chips of dried blood from his face. "Seren?"

"I am fine," Seren replied. Celer turned to face her.

"What were you thinking?" he screeched, shrill enough to make Ben wince and cover his ears. "You could have gotten us all killed! In fact, that thing almost managed to knock Ben's head off. Hasn't anyone ever told you not to go running off by yourself in the woods? Especially when we have no idea what's out there—"

Ben shouted, "Celer! It's not her fault!" He turned to Seren and said, "You did give us a big scare just now, though. Please, just don't go running off like that again. Why did you?"

"I am sorry I went off alone without telling you. I wanted to find more food before we began the day's hike. I know I endangered all of us by doing so."

"Don't be so hard on yourself," Ben said. "It was a mistake. Happens to everyone. Don't worry about it anymore."

Ben stood up and retrieved the stave that Seren had used to kill the beast from where she had left it. He spun it in the air, experimenting with its balance. "Nice staff," he said to Seren. "Mind if I keep it?"

"I have no further use for it," Seren said dismissively.

"Let's see if we can use anything from this animal," Celer said. "I'd hate to see it go to waste."

"I agree," Seren said, examining the carcass. "Let us start by removing the claws, as knives."

"And hopefully, we can eat the meat," Ben said.

Seren picked up a rock and bashed it repeatedly on the animal's walnut-sized knuckles. The bones crunched, and the rock became wet with blue blood. Seren twisted two of the largest claws from their positions in the hand. Handing one to Ben, they went to work opening the animal's abdomen. Ben cut and hacked at the carcass until his hands were covered in blue. He fought back nausea. Seren's demeanor was completely unchanged by the task.

Soon, there were piles of meat lying on sheets of hide cut from the animal's underside, plentiful enough that they would never eat all of it before it spoiled. Seren guessed that the meat would be safe to eat fresh. Still, Ben avoided all of the animal's organs just to be careful. Once Seren sparked a fire, Ben used a claw to sharpen a crude, but still functional, spit to roast the meat on. As the meat cooked, Seren burned the remaining flesh off of the two claw knives, then fashioned handles out of wood and secured them to the claw blades with plant fibers she had found. Once she was finished, she handed one of the knives to Ben. He took a moment to admire Seren's work.

"This is great! Thanks!" he said. "This makes up for having left my knife at home. Now if I could only say the same for my boots..." Ben looked down at his feet. He had left his sturdy hiking boots at home in favor of sneakers. The casual shoes had soft, unsupportive soles, and Ben's feet ached terribly. The boots would have made a wilderness trek a lot easier. He sighed.

"Don't worry," Celer said. "It's not like we're spending forever out here. We'll be to the city soon enough."

After eating, the group traveled for the rest of the day. Every once in a while, Celer flew high into the sky to check that they were all traveling in the right direction. Ben convinced Celer to retell stories that they had learned at the base during Ben's training. Celer decided on a piece of dramatic pre-Alliance history, the tale of the Wenifrin Occupation of Daalronna. This story told of the turbulent period of prejudice and war that had preceded the founding of the Daalronnan Alliance. Ben could easily imagine himself alongside the Daalronnan resistance when he listened to Celer tell the tale:

"Daron, Chief Messengersmith of Avni, rallied the forces of the resistance for one final charge against the army of Wenifrin soldiers that was about to overtake the city. The desert sands were like an ocean of ash and fire, as technology clashed against magic. The smell of fire and death pervaded the air, along with the thunderous boom of Wenifrin artillery..." Ben could see the entire battlefield laid out in his mind. The booms of the artillery, too, seemed as real as the rocks and trees around him. It took Ben a moment to realize that the sound he heard had not been conjured up by Celer's engaging telling. He looked up and saw a menacing front of steel-gray, roiling storm clouds that threw off violent cracks of lightning. The front and its heavy, driving rain were advancing quickly.

"How long do we have to find shelter?" Ben asked.

"I'll go check," Celer said. He flew up to the level of the clouds and was buffeted by the strong oncoming winds. Here, his tail came into use as a vital tool; as the turbulent winds whipped through the folds of waving fabric, Celer could determine the exact direction and force of the winds. He paused at several different altitudes and locations along the storm front, feeling out the weather system, then returned to Ben and Seren.

"That front's moving fast," Celer said. "A minute, tops, until the rain hits."

"Alright," Ben said. "We'll spit up, but we have to keep track of each other. Celer won't be able to find us from the air if we get separated."

"Understood," Seren said, taking off to the left. Ben took the right, leaving Celer to search straight ahead. Ben darted through the forest, looking frantically around the woods for any spot the water wouldn't be able to touch. Rain wouldn't have frightened him so much if he were well prepared for it, but without the right clothes, Ben feared hypothermia. Being without shelter on a cold, rainy night would surely kill them.

The first cold raindrop landed on Ben's neck, chilling him immediately. He was hit by one, two, then three and four more drops, and then the downpour was upon him, soaking into his clothes and sinking its chill into his bones. He turned around to see if Seren or Celer had found any shelter, and then froze. He had strayed from their sight.

"Seren! Celer!" he called. "Did you find anything?"

"We did!" Seren shouted. "Where are you?"

"I can't tell!" Ben called. He hoped that Celer and Seren had escaped the rain and were dry.

"Stay put where you are!" Celer called. "Let me follow your voice!"

Ben called Celer's name repeatedly until he saw a soaked, cloth form rustling through the branches. Celer wasted no time and shouted, "Follow me!" over the sound of the driving rain. Finally Celer led Ben to a towering tree. It was raised slightly by its thick roots, around which were several tall bushes. A hand reached out from behind the bushes, revealing a natural cavity the size of a small room. Ben ducked his head and squeezed into the natural shelter beside Seren, who sat with her knees pulled close to her body. To Ben's dismay, she had not escaped the downpour, and was wringing water out of her clothes. Ben held the bush aside for Celer as he flew in, then allowed it to snap back into its natural position. The boom of thunder and patter of driving rain continued outside. The lightning flashed bright enough to shine through the bushes. Ben could imagine the unrelenting wall of gray clouds above them, and wondered how long the storm would last. His teeth chattered. Seren stared stoically at the ground. She was shivering as well.

Ben only managed to sleep in short, fitful bursts, in between which he suffered through long battles with the cold and wetness around him. He could no longer tell whether the pounding rain was really getting louder every minute, or if it was just his imagination torturing him. Every few minutes, Ben tried to check his watch to see how long it might be until sunrise. Each time he checked, though, he looked down at a blank digital screen, which had been fried by the electromagnetic pulse. He envied Celer, who had complete tolerance for cold and wetness because he was enchanted, not made of flesh and blood. When he could sleep, he had strange dreams of Iyerani agents, bears, and unending chases. Only as the sky turned pink with sunrise did the storm abate. Ben managed to get an hour of peaceful, restful sleep until a tap on his shoulder woke him up.

"Ben," Seren said quietly. Ben tried to fight his way out of the muddle of sleep. "Ben!" Seren said, more forcefully this time. "We should continue onward."

Ben crawled out from under the tree and stretched in the morning sunlight.

At the same time, Celer flew into the sky to confirm the group's bearings. When he returned, he said, "The river we're coming up on was flooded by the storm."

"How bad is it?" Ben asked. "Is the crossing you found still safe?"

"I couldn't tell from the air," Celer replied.

As they walked, Ben heard the river before he saw it, and what he heard made his stomach do flips from anxiousness. The unseen water ahead roared and thundered. When the river came into sight in the late afternoon, Ben almost refused to cross. Where stones protruded up above the water's surface, they turned the clear, cold water into white froth. Though the waters were only knee deep, they flowed quickly enough that they looked to be able to sweep Ben or Seren off their feet. Upstream and downstream, the water cascaded over tall rocks, making small waterfalls. Ben's knuckles turned white as he gripped his staff tighter.

"Are you ready to cross?" Seren asked. While Ben had been assessing the situation, Seren had found a long branch of her own to use for stability while crossing. She made her own assessment, throwing a stick into the river and watching it whisked away by the rapid current.

"It will be dangerous," Seren said, "but, I think, still possible."

"But are you sure that's the only way? 'Possible but dangerous' is still, you know, dangerous! Can we find another way around?" Ben said.

"I checked the entire length of the river, Ben," Celer replied. "To the east, the river flows all the way to the sea. Way too far. To the west, its source is high in the most rugged part of the mountains. Going around would add three weeks to our trip."

Ben sighed, his worry growing. "We have to cross it, then. Waiting around won't make this any easier. Let's go."

Ben winced as the icy-cold mountain water quickly soaked through his shoes. Luckily, the stones were not slippery with algae or other tiny plants. Once the water reached Ben's knees, he could feel the insistent tug of the current, threatening to pull his feet out from under him. He grimaced when he thought about the current smashing him against the large rocks on the river bottom. The current shot icy needles through Ben's legs as he trudged on, and soon numbed them. Every step was slow, careful, and agonizing. Ben shivered. Every few steps, he looked back at Seren, who was keeping pace just behind him. Celer flew a tight orbit around Ben's head, watching Ben's step. All three were almost to the opposite bank when Ben heard Seren's voice from downriver, far from where he had last seen her.

"Ben!" she called. Her next words were garbled by water. Ben looked downstream to see Seren tangled in the branches of a large tree which hung down into the river. Trapped against the current, she tried to pull her head above water and gasp for breath. She could achieve this for only a moment or two at a time, in between which the current forced her head down. While Ben had been paying attention to his own crossing, she must have fallen and been swept downstream. She was at least twenty feet from him. He started quickly to where Seren was trapped, and in fact he proceeded quicker than was safe. He tripped but caught himself at the last moment with his staff.

"Careful!" Celer yelled.

Seren's head popped up above the water once more and gave a feeble call for help. Ben pushed onward as fast as he could without making the situation worse, and reached the tangle of branches. Reaching into the water, he grabbed Seren's arm and pulled her head and shoulders from the water. Her lips were pale blue. After gasping for breath, Seren allowed Ben to help her stand up, both of them bracing themselves against the tree.

"Out of the water, NOW!" Celer shrieked. Ben agreed with a terse nod, and helped Seren walk to the shore and scramble up. Her shivering was worse than Ben had ever seen. Once Seren was safely on dry land, Ben ordered her to exercise until he had started a fire, so as to keep her body temperature from dropping dangerously. Ben left her to do jumping jacks on the shore while he searched for firewood. There was enough dead wood untouched by the rainstorm that Ben could start a fire. Inside Seren's waterproof coat pocket, the vital, spark-providing circuitry was untouched as well. Ben's shivering was less violent than Seren's, but nonetheless slowed his efforts to provide a spark. His hands wavered as he tried to maneuver the tiny golden wires close to the bundle of tinder. Finally, Ben managed to touch them together close enough to the tinder bundle that it lit. Flames licked around the kindling as Ben piled more wood onto the fire, and he ushered Seren over. Soon the flame was steady enough that Ben risked putting wet wood on the fire, know-ing that it was unlikely to have been soaked to the core by the rain. Luckily, these sticks did catch, and soon Ben and Seren were sitting next to a small campfire, thankful for its warmth and for their very survival. Ben watched Seren carefully as she kept shivering.

"Thank you," she said.

"Hey, I owe you for figuring out the rain shelter and the food. No problem."

They were silent after that. Ben wondered what it was that made her feel so cold and distant. Iyerayñan must have been a harsh place. Still, he was afraid to ask, and wondered whether he would even get an answer. On Earth, he had plenty of his own secrets to keep, about the base and the Alliance. He wouldn't pry into her inner life just yet.

Dawn broke more gently the next morning than it had on any other day of the journey. It was already late after-noon by the time Seren and Ben had their encounter with the river, and Ben thought it was best to not move from a place where they already had a good fire burning. Feeling refreshed, Ben finally realized how hard he, Seren and Celer had been pushing themselves across the Andarite wilder-ness. He knew that fear was at the root of their motivation, fear that was driven by the small but noticeable weight in his pocket. His hand went to his pocket, checking the integrity of the data device.

"Do you think the water damaged this?" Ben asked, holding it up for Seren to see.

"Our enemies would have planned for such a problem," Seren said. "The device is most likely waterproof."

"You give these guys a lot of credit," Ben said skeptically. Seren shot him a more emotional glance than he had ever seen from her. A strange combination of anger and sadness flashed across Seren's face, as if each emotion was fighting for dominance of her expression. As she spoke, her usual controlled tones were gone.

"You are not familiar with the Iyerani race like I am, Ben," she snapped. "Be glad of that."

Ben took a moment to recover from his confusion over Seren's sudden outburst. "Are you alright?" he asked.

"I am sorry," she said, coldness returning. "My emotions have been inappropriate. I apologize."

"It's okay!" Ben said. "If there's something you want to talk about…"

"Perhaps later," Seren said. She started dismantling the shelter of the night before, and Ben joined her. As he worked, his gaze occasionally strayed back to the roaring river.

We have to be more careful in the future… Ben thought. He resolved to take more safety measures for the remaining duration of the trip. He realized, too, that it was not just his body, but his state of mind as well, being hit hard by the trek. When sheer fatigue wasn't weighing down on his mind, the question of the device in his pocket bothered him and kept him from sleep. With all of these concerns, Ben saw the days of the journey ahead stretching endlessly before him.

"Let's get going," he said, tiredness slurring his words.

"Agreed," Seren replied. Ben could hear in her voice that she was tired as well. He warned himself to be careful in assessing her condition by appearance alone. She was so controlled in her words and actions, and Ben knew she could be concealing feelings far more severe inside. He reminded himself that nothing but continuing onward would help them. He revived his spirits for a moment by looking at the tall, majestic mountains around him. He reminded himself of the many hikes he had gone on over Earth's mountain ranges, smiled faintly, then turned north and continued onward.

That day, they came upon a section of forest that was full of the huge, gray nesting baskets of the winged creatures that Ben had taken to calling "Silk-spinners." They hung off every branch for as far as the group could see, weighing them down and making the branches creak under the weight.

"Ssh," he said to Seren and Celer. They paused and looked at Ben quizzically. Ben slowly reached his hand above his head, inviting one of the strange reptiles to land on it. After a few moments of remaining perfectly still, a Silk-spinner juvenile, only a bit larger than a canary, flew down and alighted on Ben's hand. The animal looked up at Ben with wide, curious eyes and squawked. Its talons felt cool and rubbery, and had not yet hardened into the formidable tree-grasping tools of its parents. Celer giggled, sending cascades of yellow magic down his tail.

"It's cute," he said, flying slowly and carefully closer. The baby squawked again and pushed off from Ben's hand with a small gust of wind. Its small wings blurred because of how fast they beat as the tiny creature made its way back into the canopy. Roused from his position by the baby, an adult Silk-spinner took flight, disturbing a few others around it. More followed, and every second the number of airborne Silk-spinner birds grew. The air above them was filled with a living, flowing mosaic of iridescent wings that glittered and sparked when they caught light through the trees. The stunning show of brilliant flying crystal was over in another blink of an eye, as the birds settled back down into new positions among the trees.

"Wow..." was all Ben could manage.

"I wish you could have seen it from up there! It was amazing!" Celer said.

"It was stunning from our vantage point as well," Seren said. "I wonder what draws so many of them here."

"I think I know," Celer said as he drifted through the air. Ben turned to where Celer was looking and saw a glint of sunlight on water through the trees. Ben and Seren followed him as he drifted, trancelike, towards the source. Ben pushed through the bushes and came out at the foot of a tall, rushing cascade. Water poured down from the hills, glistening and gurgling as it flowed over moss-covered rocks. The stones ranged in size from looming monoliths to only as big as Ben's fists. Interspersed between, and sometimes growing on, the stones were a rainbow of flowering plants, and twisting, gnarled trees that entwined with each other and reached out in all directions.

"This is a nice place," Celer said. "Too bad we can't stay for a while."

"Who says we can't?" Ben said. "We could afford to relax for a while, I think."

"That would be inefficient," Seren said. "Remaining here will not speed our arrival at the city."

Ben said, "Pushing ourselves to the farthest limits of what we can handle won't help either. If we take a while to recharge here, we'll continue on better once the morning comes. It's already afternoon anyway. Let's just take the remainder of the day and rest."

"If you insist," Seren said. At the same time, Celer gave a yelp of joy and sped out over the sparkling water, taking in the view. Ben looked for the highest vantage point from which to take in the entire scene laid out before them. The hills from which the water flowed seemed like the best point around.

"Come on," Ben said to Seren. "Let's get a look from up there." They made their way up the piles of mossy rocks, careful not to slip where water had slicked the surfaces. Soon, though, they reached a wall of rock just high enough to make passage impossible. Tangled branches of the trees on either side made a barrier to going around. Seren appraised the rock wall for a moment, as if she was sizing up possible options.

"I will help you up," she said, cupping her hands to give Ben a foothold. She boosted him high enough so that he could pull himself up over the edge of the rock face easily.

Returning the favor, Ben reached down and took Seren's hand, pulling her up onto the ledge as well.

"Thank you," she said. Ben nodded in reply as he stared out over the landscape. From their vantage point above the trees, the landscape was even more beautiful. Ben could see the entire mountain range spreading out around him, covered in the thick canopy of tall trees. Even Seren's eyes widened, and the corners of her mouth crept up a little. Ben wondered again about her reservedness.

Ben had the creeping feeling that he and Seren were similar in how they dealt with emotion. The secret base in Mongolia was his home, and there, he was surrounded by people who may not have been his family by blood, but were by his love for him. None, however, had children of Ben's age. Summers with his parents, away from the base, were also difficult. He had been to a summer camp once, and had tried to meet new people and be honest with those who he wanted to call friends. Still, he spent the school year in a place that he could not discuss without being charged for high treason against the Alliance. He knew that friends were the people you were supposed to be honest with, but how could he? That week at camp, he glazed over his face with a mask of indifference and hoped to go through the motions without getting his hopes up about anyone. Was Seren so different? He looked over at her. She knew about the Alliance. Ben took a deep breath.

"Seren?" he asked. "Look, we've been through a lot together. You can trust me. You said that we might talk later about Iyerayñan, and while we're just sitting around, it might be a good time if you still want to."

Seren nodded. "Yes. You deserve to know. Do you know my grandparents?"

"Yeah. Dennison told me that they left Earth."

"My grandmothers on both sides of my family agreed that Iyerayñan's culture would provide them with more opportunities than Earth's could. However, a cultural revolution seized the planet soon after they moved, and Iyerayñan withdrew from the Alliance. The new government sees emotional control as one of the great virtues of a citizen. My parents and grandparents worked in a low laboring caste, and most people exect that I will, too. My parents hope I will aspire to a higher caste with greater privileges. Socially, I struggle because of the ways in which humans process emotions differently than Iyeranis, and that handicaps me from my parents' desires."

"And you've never had another human your age to lean on?" Ben asked.

"No."

"I'm sorry," Ben said. "I understand what you're going through."

"How could you?" Seren asked. When she looked at Ben, rage blazed in her eyes. "Do not presume."

"Hey, just hear me out," he said. "When Dennison and the others joined up with the Alliance, the Council made the decision that humans were too warlike to be contacted. There's a military edict that makes it so we can't tell anyone.

We wait for the order that lets us introduce Earth to the galaxy, but until then, I'm the only human kid who knows about the Alliance."

"You would never be able to tell your friends important details about your life," Seren said. "You would have to lie to them about where you live."

Ben nodded. "I tried making friends like a normal kid, but then we got into conversations about schools and family work... But I couldn't lie to them like that. Eventually, I just gave up on it."

"I'm sorry I presumed that you would not understand. I think we have more in common than I ever believed was possible."

"I know that when this is all over, we may never see each other again," Ben said, "but I'm willing to hope that we can find a way to change that. You don't have to deal with this alone. I'm your friend."

"And I yours."

Ben extended his hand and Seren shook it. Ben was surprised, almost disbelieving, that his previously emotionless friend was smiling. Seren's smile was the warmest, most genuine one that Ben had ever seen, like a lifetime of unused smiles poured into a single moment. Which, Ben supposed, it actually might have been.

Chapter 4

Ben and Seren spent the next few hours exploring the fantastical landscape. They discovered extensive caves beneath the hills, and explored them by the light of a million blue-green bioluminescent fungi that glowed like stars on the cave ceiling. Aboveground, they smiled at each other's presence until the sun went down. Ben couldn't remember the last time he had doubled over in laughter, but it felt great to be so joyful again. He stared into the embers of the fire as dinner cooked and tried to think of a time when he had been this happy. He couldn't. Still, something lingered in the back of his mind.

"Wait a minute," Ben said. "How are you in a laboring class? You're really smart! You knew about the beetles, immediately figured out the EMP, you speak both Iyerani and English. What's up with that?"

"The Iyeranis are smarter," she said.

Ben's insides clenched. Such intelligence being the norm did not bode well for their chances of evading the mob. Still, he didn't want to ruin the suddenly cheerful mood of the day. He lifted his spit of beetles into the air as if he were about to make a toast. "To new friends," he said.

"Hear, hear," Celer replied. "And to only two more days of travel. We're close to the meadows that border our destination. We'll be at the city very soon."

"Great!" Ben said. Seren nodded her agreement. That evening, Ben and the others were so relaxed that for the first time, they sat back and devoted their full attention to watching the Andarite sunset.

"It looks so similar to Earth's," Ben said as he watched the orange skies.

"There are similar conditions in the star systems of Earth and Andaros," Seren commented. "The planets both orbit around yellow stars. The compositions of both atmospheres are comparable. The factors that make Earth and Andaros capable of supporting life are also factors in how light reflects through the atmosphere and causes the brilliant sunset."

"Aquila once told me about the seven star systems of the Wenifrin Empire," Celer said. "One of the colony planets, Varafri, has a bright green sky, and it orbits a red giant star. Aquila flew there once, carrying a message to a Messengersmith there. He said that sunrise over the cyan grasslands is the most beautiful thing he's ever seen."

"One of the greatest reprieves from daily life on Iyerayñan is snorkeling in the sea-grass forests in the bay of Tara Zarin, near my home. My home overlooks the bay, and so I can explore the underwater forests at my leisure. The mollusks are very intelligent, and on warm days, they are especially playful."

"Sounds beautiful," Ben said. "I wonder what Aquila and Dennison are doing right now."

"They're probably worried out of their minds about us," Celer replied. "Hopefully, they weren't caught by the mob agents."

Ben sat bolt upright. "Do you think they could have been?" he asked.

"I don't know," Celer said, equally worried. "He's a powerful magician, though. All master Messengersmiths are. You managed to take out one Iyerani by yourself, so imagine what Dennison could do."

"Yeah, I managed, but I messed up my ability to use magic pretty badly too."

"Dennison knows better than to use a full-on frontal attack like that. Besides, he might have just played it smart and laid low."

"Seren, who were you travelling with?" Ben asked.

"I travelled alone," Seren said. "My parents will most likely have heard that I am missing by now."

"You're not worried about them at all?" Celer asked.

"Do not mistake my control for lack of concern," Seren said. "It does not make sense to worry about that which we cannot control. Everyone, get some rest. Focus your minds, and control your emotions. No good will come of losing sleep. Good night."

"That might be easy for you to say, but I'm still worried about my great-uncle." Ben lay awake for another hour worrying about Dennison and the alien mob, and whether reaching the city would truly be the end of the journey. Once again, he found himself staring at the blue rectangular device from the crime scene, imagining it would reveal something to him if he looked at it for long enough. Soon, though, his eyelids drooped and he fell asleep, the blue rectangle still held in his hand.

By the time Ben and Celer awoke, Seren had already rekindled the fire from the few embers that remained from the night before. She offered Ben some food: the same beetles they had been eating for days. Ben's stomach turned. He was starting to get *really* sick of having beetles at every meal. At least they would reach the city soon, and he could get something else to eat. Nevertheless, Ben took the cooked beetles and mustered a small smile for Seren's efforts. He ate quickly and saw to it that the fire was extinguished, and they were on their way once more.

That day, the sun shone, lifting everyone's spirits. Celer began to sing. As he darted through the high branches of the trees, he spouted a lilting Voleric tune that carried through the forest. Though Ben couldn't understand the words, the tune was lively and uplifting. Near the end, Ben could make out a repeating chorus as Celer's singing grew softer and softer. In the silent lull after Celer had finished, Ben picked up singing repeat-after-me campfire songs, during which Celer and Seren did the repeating. They filled the forest with joyful song and laughter. Seren tried to teach Ben and Celer a pre-revolution Iyerani song, but Ben mangled the delicate vowels and tripped over foreign consonants. He and Seren both laughed at the attempt. Where Ben had failed, however, Celer carried the tune with crisp enunciation. The songs took everyone's minds off of the rigors of travel, and it seemed to take no time at all before the trees started thinning out. The three emerged from the forest and climbed to the top of a bare hill overlooking the meadows below. Down below, short, scraggly trees dotted the land, but the terraing was otherwise smooth and open.

"All smooth sailing from here," Ben said, and smiled.

When they reached the meadows, Ben was surprised that the water from the rainstorm had not yet evaporated from the land. The ground was squishy and wet, and covered in plants that seemed like some sort of dense, land-dwelling algae. The plants were thick in some places, forming mats that were springy underfoot. Mud covered the ground where the plants were absent. Ben started to doubt whether the rain alone had saturated the meadows. As he and Seren walked, they many times found themselves squishing through ankle-deep mud. It seemed unavoidable, as it was hard to tell where the plants were thick and where they thinned. He became seriously worried when he fell into knee-deep mud. He kicked and struggled for a moment, to no avail.

"Let me help," Seren said, offering her hand. Ben took it gratefully, and together they pulled until he was free. He was covered in mud up to the knees, but otherwise alright.

"Thank you," he said.

"No problem," Seren replied.

"This is getting too dangerous," Ben said. "Next time it could be worse. Just think about what would happen if we were both stuck, with no way out."

"I should have checked this out more," Celer said. "I'm such an idiot! I'm so, so sorry. I thought it was just meadows. This looks like swamp all the way through. We have to find a safer way."

"Do you suggest going around?" Seren said. "It may be more dangerous. Each night that we have been out here has been colder than the last. We cannot afford that risk. The battery of my earpiece may soon be depleted, leaving us without fire."

Ben nodded. "And I don't know when my magic will come back... I'm still worried, though. Last time we decided *not* to go around something dangerous, you almost drowned. I don't want something like that to happen again."

"You don't need to remind me of that, Ben," Seren said. She shuddered. "This time, though, is different. I have been trying to find a pattern in where we find the mud. We have never encountered it near the trees. My guess is some sort of symbiosis between the ground plants and the trees: They aid each other, and so grow thickly close together. As long as we stay near the trees, no harm will come to us. When we must stray farther from the trees, we must maintain distance from each other at all times. If one of us is trapped, the other can come to their aid."

"Alright," Ben said reluctantly. "If you're sure."

"I am."

"Well then, let's go."

They made only slow progress across the swamp that day, traveling in tortuous zigzags to avoid the mud. When they did stray from the areas of sure stability, they walked slowly and carefully. Ben prodded the ground with his wooden stave before each step, thankful for the warning whenever it plunged into the mud. The swampy terrain hindered their travel so much that Ben feared they would spend days more than expected in the swamp. He looked up at the sky every few minutes, checking how far the sun was above the horizon. If he were on Earth, he would have thought he was imagining how fast the sun was moving towards the horizon. However, he was well aware of Andaros' shorter day of 21 hours. If he were on Earth, he also wouldn't have paid much mind to the winged silhouettes in the sky. They appeared at random at first, but then there came six or seven at a time, circling the group from the air. They were calling out with complex sequences of whistles.

"I don't like them," Celer said.

"Mind checking them out for us?" Ben asked. Celer nodded, flew up into the center of the circle of silhouettes, and returned to Ben.

"For lack of a better description, I'd call them dragons," Celer said. "They're small, but well armed. Sharp teeth, claws, and bundles of spines on their tails, kind of like porcupine quills."

"What's going on over there?" Seren called, while maintaining the twenty-foot separation between her and Ben.

"Do you see those animals up there?" Ben called.

"I do. Why?"

"Celer says they're armed to the teeth. Sounds like trouble." A moment later, one of the dragons gave a long, low-pitched whistle. Each of the other six dragons whistled two shrill notes in reply. They landed in a wide circle, surrounding Seren and Ben.

"Pack hunters," Seren called. "They're assessing who is the strongest of the two of us. They will try and single out whomever they deem weaker. Come over here, they'll be more reluctant to attack."

Seren was standing at the base of a tree, the absolute most stable place to be. Without a moment more of hesitation, Ben bolted for her position. The dragons gave chase within a second, taking to the air and closing in quickly. One dragon whistled in a complex pattern, and two closed in on Ben. They stared him down with emotionless black eyes, baring teeth from circular, leech-like mouths. Though only the size of housecats, they had long tails ending in bundles of spines, and large, bat-like wings. The two chasing Ben landed, turned around, and raised their tails at him. Blue skin sacs directly behind the spines inflated like balloons. Ben realized what would happen when the balloons released their air pressure, and ducked as the dart-like spines shot from the dragons' tails and whizzed over his head. He kept running toward Seren, and knocked the dragons aside with his staff.

Their bones snapped audibly, and they hissed. Ben winced at the sound but kept running towards the tree. The creatures were still closing in.

"You saw what they can do with their tails?" Ben asked.

"Yes," Seren replied. "We will have a few seconds' warning when they strike."

The dragons encircled Ben and Seren, pausing for a moment as they waited for a whistle from their leader. Ben swung with his staff, but they beat their wings and flew deftly out of the way. Celer hovered above Ben's head.

The leader whistled. Two dragons turned their tails and the launching sacs filled with air. Both projectiles struck Ben, and within a few heartbeats, his vision blurred. When he moved, his step faltered.

"Careful," he said, slurring the words. "Poison."

Up against the tree, Seren knelt down and held her jacket out in front of her, using it to block the darts. With the command of a complex whistle pattern, the dragons lunged at Ben and Seren, forcing them to step away from the tree. Back to back now, they expected another volley of poison darts. Seren still hid behind her jacket, while Ben tried to shake off the venom.

"Celer?" Seren called. "Ideas?"

"You'd think that if I had and idea, I would have acted by now!" Celer called. "What do you want me to do against *dragons?*"

"Never mind then," she said. After yet another signal, two dragons fired darts at Ben and Seren's feet, forcing them to jump out of the way. At the same time, two more of the pack lunged at their faces, throwing them off balance. Ben and Seren went reeling backwards, and they felt only the unstable mud yielding under their feet. The dragons' coordinated attack had driven Ben and Seren into knee-deep mud with a fierce suction that kept them from moving. As the dragons circled, Ben and Seren struggled to free themselves from the trap, but to no avail. Another dart hit Ben and he fell to his knees, the world a confused, poisoned blur. All of the sounds around were distorted as if by water, and Seren, Celer, and the dragons were indistinct forms moving through the gray haze.

Seren blocked another dart as she struggled to pull together everything she knew about their attackers. They were pack hunters, obviously following a single leader. They had a form of whistled communication based off of calls from the leader and responses from the hunters. How could they convey such coordinated actions so concisely? She nearly lost her train of thought after barely blocking another dart with her jacket.

Focus! She thought. *They key to our escape lies in the whistles.*

"Celer!" she shouted. "Whistle a song!"

"Seren, I hardly think this is the time for—"

"DO IT NOW!"

Celer started whistling the same Voleric tune as earlier, and Seren followed close afterwards with her Iyerani melody. The two songs overlapped, creating a single chaotic song that caught the dragons off guard. One fired a dart, which

Seren caught on her jacket. Another lunged right at her, and she punched it in the chest, cracking the delicate breastbone. It fell to the ground and gasped for breath.

"They're confused!" Celer said. The leader was trying to reassert dominance with his own whistles, but Celer and Seren drowned him out. However, the creatures still circled. Seren looked at Celer, hoping he had another idea. He was staring intently at the dragons, but doing nothing.

"Stop singing!" Celer finally called. Seren fell silent. The chaotic attack stopped abruptly. The frustrated leader of the dragons stopped growling at its subordinates. Celer whistled three notes, and captured the dragons' attention. He whistled the same combination, and they seemed even more attentive. Continuing to whistle, he led them away from Ben and Seren. The leader gave a command, and Celer echoed it.

"What are you waiting for?" Celer asked between calls. "Help me out!"

Seren herself thought she could use some helping out. Grabbing her leg at the knee, she struggled against the mud, taking ponderous steps over to Ben. She grabbed his staff once she was close enough, and slammed it down on the head of one dragon. While Celer sowed discord among the pack, Seren fought, smashing and swiping at the disarrayed creatures. Eventually, the pack leader and Celer were fighting for the attention of only two uninjured creatures. The leader gave a final defiant snarl and flew off, his decimated pack trailing behind.

Seren turned to Ben, who was flopped in a limp heap on the ground. When she struggled over to him through the mud and examined his face, his eyes rolled aimlessly around.

"Se… Sere? Drgguh…"

"The dragons are gone, Ben. We're safe," Celer replied. "Come on. Get him up to dry land."

It took at least an hour for her to struggle back over to the tree, taking each hard-won step through the thick mud while pulling Ben's limp form. When she arrived on dry land, she flopped down and took deep gulps of air.

"What do we do about Ben?" Celer asked. He looked over at Ben, who was taking shallow breaths and responding in slurred gibberish whenever Seren or Celer tried to tell him something.

"Keep him comfortable, I suppose," Seren replied. "We know nothing about the poison. Either he recovers his faculties, or…"

"We're not going on without him."

"We will not. I promise. "

"Do you want to cook up those wolfdragons we killed?" Celer asked.

"Wolfdragons?" Seren asked.

"The things that were attacking us just now!" Celer replied. "They look like little dragons, but they attack in packs, like wolves."

"I do not know the Earth animals with those names, but I trust you," Seren replied. "I agree that we should eat them. It will be a welcome break from beetles."

Seren took the carcasses, and twisted off the tails, with their venomous spines attached. She explained to Celer that she was wary of the meat becoming poisoned. Gathering firewood was a struggle in the marsh, with its few trees, all of which were too small to provide much dry wood for burning. After searching a square mile of swamp, she finally gathered enough dry kindling to start a fire. Luckily, the fire grew hot enough that she could place green wood in the flames, and it would burn. Seren cooked and ate the wolfdragon meat, and for the first time in days, she felt full.

"Seren?"

Ben sat up slowly. Seren rushed over to him, kneeling beside him to look into his eyes to check their focus, take his pulse, examine the pinprick-sized wounds, and ask how he felt according to a few medical diagnostic questions.

"I feel fine," he said. "Thank you for saving me." He looked down at his muddy shoes, and Seren's. "You pulled me out of there all by yourself?"

"Yes. Now, you should eat something. I cooked the creatures we killed."

"Sure beats beetles," Ben said as he dug in hungrily.

"Definitely," Seren replied absently. She was leaning against the tree near which the fire was built. After she had made sure she had done all she could regarding Ben's health, she took to analyzing the wolfdragon spines that she had taken out from the creatures' tails. "Ben, come look at this," she said. Ben came over and sat down, followed closely by Celer, who hovered at Seren's shoulder. She said, "The dart is perfectly adapted for being launched as an offensive projectile. Notice how it is weighted at the front for momentum, and how it flares into four distinct fins at the back."

"Amazing," Celer said. "It's built like an arrow. On Earth, humans designed and perfected something that nature evolved all by itself on Andaros. Where does the poison come out?"

Seren pointed at tiny hairs about half an inch from the sharp tip. She reached out and brushed one, and a small rivulet of clear liquid dribbled from the tip of the arrow. "The mechanism that ejects the poison can probably remain functional for some time after separation. These may be valuable weapons."

"Weapons?" Ben asked. "I thought you said you didn't want to risk eating anything that was poisoned by the darts."

"When we arrive in the city," Seren said, "we may still have to face the people who made us flee from Alarzi. They may have control over more than one city. I hope not, but it is good to be prepared."

"Expect the unexpected," Ben said. "I always take that saying to heart when I'm camping. Extra socks, rain jacket, emergency whistle… I never thought I'd to be prepared to fight alien mobsters. If only we could find out what's on this thing." He took the blue data device out of his pocket.

"Ben, give me that thing," Seren said with a tone of concern.

"Can you get information out of it?" Ben asked.

"No, of course not," Seren replied. "But Ben, you stare at this thing almost every night. I can tell it's weighing on your mind more than it needs to. Remember, we aren't going to change anything so long as we're stuck out here in the swamp. I hate seeing you look so frustrated. Give me the device and get some rest." Ben handed the little blue rectangle over to Seren, who slipped it into her pocket. "Thank you," she said. "Now, go to sleep. You too, Celer."

Ben awoke the next morning and stretched, his mind slowly unfolding from sleep. When he stood, dried mud fell off his jeans in pieces. His and Seren's clothes were still caked with mud from their many brushes with entrapment. They continued cautiously on, following a meandering path through the swamp that kept them as close to trees as possible. Even such a path did not keep them from getting stuck in the mires. Sometimes, there was no truly safe path, and Ben and Seren risked everything by wading through the mud, often times pulling and pushing each other along towards safety. Reaching the city with two days' travel, as Celer had promised, was no longer possible. The three went to sleep exhausted, and woke up without even beetles to fill their stomachs. The insects didn't live in the swamp. Clean water, too, was also almost impossible to come by. In the forest it was easy to boil water with heated stones and the burl of a beetle nest. In the bog, there was no way to purify the muddy, foul-smelling water that sat in stagnant puddles on the ground. Both Ben and Seren contended with pounding headaches from dehydration, while at the same time their stomachs pained them terribly for want of food. Halfway through the fourth day in the bog, Ben stumbled, legs and arms shaking. On the ground, he stared at what looked like fairly clear water. He pursed his lips, drawing close to drink in as much as he could. Just as his lips touched the water, Seren lifted him by his shoulders, dragging him away. He struggled in her grasp, then broke free, only to be pulled back again. Ben looked at her pleadingly as they lay on the ground, both too tired to fight more.

"Seren, the water looks fine! We have to drink."

She shook her head. "Ben, our judgment is impaired by the dehydration. I need you to think this through logically. It is not safe."

"I'm so thirsty… Never been so thirsty like this before…"

"I know. I feel it too," Seren said. "But we need something safe to drink. We can find water if we look hard enough. We cannot find something to save you from an Andarite bacterial infection."

"I don't know if we can go another day."

Seren stood shakily and looked around at the plant shoots that grew up in infrequent stands around the area. Ben and Celer followed as she walked over to the plants, and knelt down next to one. She dug a hand into the mud and pulled out a tangled root ball. Using her claw knife, she cut away the dirty outer layer, revealing a wet, cream-colored center. She cut the bulb in half, squeezing the juices from one into her mouth. She handed the other half to Ben.

"Eat this," she said. Ben took the root unquestioningly and bit into it. Fresh, slightly sweet water flooded over his tongue. Having water again felt amazing, and they wasted no time digging up more roots and eating greedily. The supply ran out quickly, and they were still hungry and thirsty afterwards.

"The root acts as a natural purifier," Seren said. "Though it is not perfect, drinking from this is much safer than taking water straight off the ground."

"If only we had some more food available," Ben said, his stomach still crying angrily out.

"If only," Seren replied. "We do not know what plants or animals are edible in this environment. Even the root was a risk."

Ben and Seren went to sleep without food, both hoping that the ordeal would be over soon. They woke up the next morning and walked for three more days. They drank water from plants where they could find it. On the second day, they were just lucky enough to find a few strange-looking mud shrimp that Seren examined, and guessed were edible. Once they gathered firewood, though, Seren's remnants of circuitry failed to produce a spark. They risked eating the shrimp raw. That second night, they could see a few city lights in the distance, but they were not the blazing beacon of life and urbanity that he had expected. What he had hoped would be a lively place showed only a few dim, flickering points of light at night. He wondered what he and Seren would find once they arrived.

Next morning, Ben and Seren could barely rouse themselves to continue on, and Celer had to shout at them to get moving. When they finally did set out, it was only Celer's constant prodding and encouragement that kept them going. He tried to raise their spirits, but still Ben and Seren could not ignore their biting hunger, parched mouths, and sore muscles. Ben started to wonder what was keeping him from collapsing on the spot and never waking up. Feet dragging, eyes downcast, he kept walking through a landscape inhabited by only him and his agonies. He walked in this isolated, tired state for so long that he thought he hallucinated the tall, chain-link fence in front of him. He reached out and touched the cool metal, running his hands along it like he had never experienced the sensation before. He and Seren looked at each other. Seren smiled broadly, making Ben smile back. They laughed.

"We made it," Ben said. "We're alive."

Chapter 5

The fence that stood before Seren and Ben was still a considerable barrier. Celer could fly over, but that would not solve the issue of how the humans could surmount it. Ben wasn't sure if he could climb over, and there did not seem to be a gate that they could enter through anywhere near them. Off to his left, there was a thick, blanket-like ivy that covered the fence. It started to rustle.

"*Vadzi, lederei!*" a voice from inside called. "*Wavaw rijoreg! Dayalir wiei liru?*"

"What's he saying?" Ben asked.

"He's offering you food!" Celer said.

"Tell him we would gladly take his offer," Seren said. She and Ben walked over to where an Andarite's head poked out of the ivies. He pulled aside the plants, revealing a door-sized hole in the fence, and allowed them into a small hut constructed out of two large, metal crates. There was a mattress of old sheets and matted grasses to one side, and to the other there was a single, small metal box that held a few cans with Andarite lettering on them. The improvised shelter was completed at the front by patched blankets that hung over the open end of the crates. Ben wondered why the Andarite needed the back exit from which he, Seren and Celer had just entered. The occupant of the small shelter had sagging skin around his eyes and his cream-colored horns were brittle-looking, and broken off at the tips in two jagged edges. His back was stooped and he walked with a limp. He wore a scuffed, dirty jacket and trousers that were so patched that they looked more like the cobbled-together remains of a few different jackets and other pieces of clothing. Ben tensed for a moment when the man pulled a knife from his belt, but he was only interested in opening one of the cans from his small supply. His hand shook as he sawed off the lid. He handed the can to Ben, along with a two-pronged fork twisted from scrap wires. He took another can and a similar fork for Seren.

"Irij arei aghakyadh wiei ulga, yadiae didi edel areiro," he said. Celer translated, "I hope you two can share a container, because I have little."

"We're very grateful for your generosity," Ben said, and then Celer translated.

"I'm happy to help," the man said. "I've never seen people of your species before. Where do you come from?"

"Earth," Seren said. She went on to tell the story of how they witnessed the murder at the festival and made their way through the forest and swamp. Ben and Celer added details where necessary, but otherwise left Seren to give her fast, concise summary of events. The old man listened intently the whole while.

"You three are lucky," he said. "Smart, too. Takes a sharp wit to survive out there for long."

"Sometimes I doubted whether we'd survive," Ben said. "I still do doubt, if those mob agents are around in this city."

"Rekyari galovra..." the man muttered.

"Um... It wouldn't really be polite to translate that," Celer said.

The man continued with Celer's translation, "They've brought more harm to this city than almost anywhere else. Latched on to it like a parasite and drained it for all it was worth. Everything you can imagine comes in through here. Drugs, weapons, all of it. The city council's corrupt and the police are too. Welcome to Joraw, kids. The center of the Iyerani problem."

They passed the rest of the meal in silence, except for the scraping of their makeshift forks against the insides of the metal can. Ben and Seren passed the can between them, taking turns forking sweet red fruit into their mouths. They ate quickly, and in their hunger they barely noticed the fruit juice dripping down their chins. When they had finished, their stomachs felt fuller, but not so full as to be satisfied.

"Do you kids have a place to stay tonight?" the man asked. "It'll be a bit cramped, but I think I can spare some space in here."

"We would be very grateful for a shelter for the night," Seren said. Ben nodded his agreement, and within moments all four occupants of the shelter were asleep. Soon, though, calloused, scaly hands shook Ben and Seren awake.

"What?" Ben asked. "Is it morning already?" he still felt far too tired.

The old man stood over him. "No, we've only been asleep two hours. Those Iyeranis are in cahoots with other gangs in the area. Running night patrols. They'll kill you kids if they find you here! Come on! I know a back alley." Seren and Celer followed the man, while Ben stood in the doorway with frustration clawing at him. He stared down the alley-way, waiting.

"Ben, come along!" Seren whispered. "What are you doing?"

"I want to know what's going on."

"You're not seriously planning on confronting them, are you?" Celer asked.

"Why shouldn't I?" Ben asked. "I haven't used magic for the whole trip, so my burns should be healed up by now."

"Ben, do not do this!" Seren demanded.

"Sorry," Ben said. "You three get to safety." Before he ran off, Ben remembered his bag of Andarite coins, from all the way back at the Festival. He pulled it out of his jacket and gave it to the man. "Thank you for your generosity," he said, and then ran off to face his pursuers. He rounded the street corner, and found a single Andarite standing in the street, illuminated by a flickering streetlight. Slowly, almost leisurely, the Andarite raised his arm, upon which a weapon was mounted. On an impulse, Ben gathered up magic and extended his hand. No beam of hot golden energy shot out, but rather, searing pain, even worse than last time, surged through him. He fell over in shock, his mind overcome with agony, and with the realization of his grievous miscalculation: His burns had not properly healed. Two Andarite agents stepped out from the shadows on either side of the street. One stabbed a long needle into the side of Ben's neck, relieving the pain of his magic burns, but also drugging him into a deep sleep.

When Ben awoke, a sharp, sterile smell hung in the air. He lay on his back, what felt like a metal slab, with his head, arms, and legs restrained with wide rubbery straps. The slab was large enough that his limbs were pulled outward in a spread-eagled position. His jacket had been taken, and his left arm was especially cold. That shirtsleeve had been cut off. He wanted to survey his surroundings, but the room was pitch-dark and his head was strapped tightly enough to the slab that movement was near impossible.

His next thoughts were of Celer and Seren. Undoubtedly, Celer would be ready to rush in to save him, even if he had to bludgeon every Iyerani to death with his ping-pong-ball-sized head. Seren might sit back and try to formulate a better plan, but Celer could be awfully convincing when he wanted to be. Ben's greatest fear was that Celer and Seren would be captured, and most likely killed, by Iyerani agents. He cursed his own stupidity. If only he had been a bit more careful, he and his friends wouldn't be in this mess.

He contemplated his own situation. He had never heard of a criminal organization strapping their prisoners to tables before.

Why would they go to all the trouble to do this to a prisoner? Ben wondered. *It's almost like they're going to dissect me.* The sharp smell and the missing shirtsleeve finally made sense. The room had been sterilized, and his kidnappers wanted access to a large vein. Whatever the Iyeranis intended, it involved needles.

Ben imagined they would have some drug to pry information out of him, and his mind immediately went to Seren and Celer. If he told his captors anything, they would surely hunt his friends down. He shouted for help and struggled hard against the bindings. He activated some sort of trigger, and the bonds tightened around his wrists, squeezing down until he dared not struggle anymore.

He heard footsteps in the hallway. He pulled against the restraints again, hoping to escape before he had to undergo whatever they were planning for him. The restraints tightened again, cutting off the flow of blood. In the darkness, Ben couldn't tell how long it took for his hands and feet to start tingling with pins and needles. Thankfully, after another unknown amount of time, the restraints loosened, just enough for blood to start flowing again. Ben forced himself not to wiggle his fingers and toes to get the blood moving, because he didn't know how much stimulus it would take to tighten the restraints again. He lost track of time in the dark room, deprived of any sensation except for the bindings on his wrists and the cold metal against the back of his head. Within the walls of the compound, it seemed as if days had passed, unmarked by any change in the darkness.

Outside, only a few hours had passed, marked by the slow march of the stars and Andaros' reddish-gray moon across the sky. Seren and Celer hid outside a three-story gray block of a building, to where they had followed Ben's captors. The old man who had fed them had followed them for a while out of concern, but had left rather than stick around at the criminal compound.

Celer vibrated nervously. Beside him, Seren took deep, deliberate breaths followed by ragged exhalations.

"Come on!" Celer said. "We have to get in there and save Ben! We're not going to just sit out here!"

"You cannot expect us to engage in combat with trained Iyerani criminals. We need to find the proper authorities to report this to."

"There are no proper authorities report this to!" Celer hissed. "You remember what the homeless guy said! The government and police of this city are corrupt. Going to them is no better than knocking on the front door of that building over there and saying, 'Hey! You know that prisoner you've got in there? He's our friend. Can we have him back, please?'"

Seren nodded. "So we are Ben's only hope for rescue." She withdrew the poisonous wolfdragon spines from her pocket while scanning over the area, eyes darting rapidly from one place of interest to the next.

"Mind telling me what you're planning?" Celer asked.

"We will not be able to get those heavy steel doors open by ourselves. However, if we could draw one or two of the Iyerani guards into somewhere vulnerable, I might be able to disable them and find some sort of access key. The only problem would be evading the four guards occupying turrets on the four corners of the roof." She pointed to the guards, Andarites who stood on the flat roof with guns almost as large as themselves.

"I can distract them for you," Celer said, rising slowly into the air. He made his way through the shadows to the opposite side of the building, then gave out an ear-splitting scream and a nimbus of angry red light.

"*Vadzi, rekyari!*" he shouted, using the potent Andarite insult he had heard earlier. He darted unpredictably around the four turrets, spouting insults in Voleric the whole time. Then he shouted a final bit of Voleric and flew behind another nearby building. The guards' attention had been effectively diverted away from Seren's position as they trained their weapons at the darkness where Celer had gone.

Below, Seren ran to the building and flattened herself against the wall. The turrets couldn't hit her when she was so close. Celer flew down beside her.

"Nice work," he said. "But now there are two agents coming towards this position."

"Can you hinder them in any way?"

"I can try," Celer said. Seren followed him around the building. Celer turned to corner, and when Seren heard his angry shriek, she followed. The two Iyerani agents on their robotic legs were swatting at Celer, who circled their heads too quickly to be caught, screaming into their ears and flashing bright red and orange. Disoriented by the light and sound, neither could find Seren. She analyzed one agent in a split second, then plunged a fistful of venomous spines into the shoulder joint between two plates of armor. The potency of the venom, combined with the alien's small body size, dropped the agent to the ground in seconds. Seren spun and stabbed another handful of spines into the gap in the other agent's shoulder armor. He fell. On the ground, both Iyeranis breathed softly, sedated by the wolfdragon venom. Seren searched the unconscious bodies for a key card of some sort. There were none.

Of course, She thought. *They must use biometrics.* Seren dragged one of the Iyeranis over to the back door to the compound. Sure enough, there were a large eye scanner and a four-fingered fingerprint scanner. She pulled the Iyerani's head and hand into position. A blue light flashed and the door lock clicked. She pushed it open slowly, checking for enemies before opening the door all the way. There was no one in the hall, but still Seren kept up her guard.

The distinct thud of metal feet echoed around the corner, and Seren bolted for the door. Once outside, she looked around. There was no time to get to a safe hideout. She looked at the two Iyeranis lying unconscious on the ground and dove for one, grabbing the handgun out of his limp hand.

"Celer, incoming," she said.

"Got it!" He flew back into the building just as two more Iyeranis rounded the corner of the hallway, and once again screamed and flashed to disorient them. Seren used the outside wall as cover from which to aim at them, but feared hitting Celer. She shrugged it off: statistically, hitting Celer at the speeds at which he was moving would be impossible. She fired erratically, bullets ricocheting off the walls, but managed to hit one Iyerani in the leg. She surged with excitement upon seeing the green blossoming of blood on the cement. She fired again, hitting the other agent once as she emptied the weapon of its bullets. The Iyerani fell to the ground, bleeding out of a deep graze in his side.

Seren ran back away from the wall to grab another clip of ammunition, when a voice sounded in Voleric over a loudspeaker. She couldn't see the source, but it was coming from outside.

"Stand down. Lower your weapon. This extraction is being handled by…" Celer's translation faltered, "…*Sildial*. I don't know that that last word is in English."

Seren looked around. An armored truck rumbled down the dark road, its headlights blinding Seren. As she squinted through the light, four uniformed, armed Andarites disembarked from the still moving vehicle, trailed by their Messengers. They approached her.

"Yiyal veroi valolag?" one asked.

"Are you injured?" Celer translated.

"No," Seren said. "But our friend is inside the compound. Are you equipped to help me get him out?"

"You met a man who lives on the streets. He tipped us off. We can help. You're sure your friend is in there?"

"Yes."

"Good. Stay here."

"No. Let us come in and talk to him. He doesn't speak Voleric."

"Fine. Now let's go."

The team of Andarites entered the building, Seren and Celer trailing close behind.

Inside, a team of Iyeranis started firing from around the corner up ahead. The Sildial team fired back, stopping the Iyeranis' advance. The leader of the team took a spherical object from his pocket and twisted its two hemispheres in opposite directions. Once he threw the device around the corner, the team all covered their ears. Seren followed suit just before a loud explosive blast and a burst of yellow flames. The team kept moving through the halls and exchanging fire with the Iyerani defenders until they reached a room with a door labeled *Interrogation* in the Iyerani language. One Andarite pried off the front plate of the biometric reader, then cut and reconnected a few wires. The machinery hummed for a few moments before the lock bolt slid with a dull thump. They ran inside and clicked on flashlights. In the room was a metal table. Ben was stretched out on it, restrained in such a way that his arms and legs were pulled far from his sides. Seren ran forward to him and started to tug at one of the arm restraints.

"Don't—" Ben started, only to stop as the restraint tightened, constricting on his wrist. He cried out. One of the Andarites came to the table and pulled a blade out of a sheath on his hip. Seren expected to see something about the size of a combat knife, but this was a weapon better described as a short sword. With a succession of precise blows, the Andarite cut the restraints from Ben's limbs. They fell to the floor and twitched reflexively, like the severed limbs of a spider.

"Are you alright?" Seren asked. "Did they hurt you, or inject you with anything, or use psychological torture?" She looked him up and down for any signs of injury. "What happened to your shirt sleeve? How is the blood circulation in your arms?"

"Seren! Don't worry, I'm fine!" Ben said.

Seren sighed. "Good. I am glad."

"Thanks," Ben said, sitting up. "I'm glad you two are alright, too. I didn't think you'd be able to get past the guards. But I guess you found some help, huh? Who are those guys, anyway?"

"We don't know, exactly," Celer said. "They guy who fed us tipped them off that you were in trouble.'"

"Thank them for me," Ben said.

"Weviw arivi!" the leader called. He pointed to Ben, Seren and Celer. *"Arizilvi wavaw wiei."*

"He wants us to come with them," Celer said. Ben nodded agreement and allowed the team of Andarites to lead him, Celer and Seren out of the building. They jogged out of the compound and up the road to where two armored vehicles were parked. Each one had a large gun mounted on top, on a circular track that let it pivot in 360 degrees. An Andarite opened the two-inch-thick armored door and Ben, Seren and Celer piled in, followed by the rescue team. The interior of the vehicle was all gray metal, except for the thin black padding on the seats. An Andarite opened a circular portal in the ceiling and climbed up to his position on the turret.

"Weviw arivi!" the leader shouted again. The vehicle rumbled as it started to move. Across from Ben, an agent of Sildial looked him and Seren over for injuries, and asked a few medical questions. Ben said that he felt fine physically, though quite shaken by the experience.

"That's good," the medic replied. "I'm Edor."

Celer made introductions for the group.

"So how long have you three been in Joraw?" Edor asked.

"Less than a day," Seren replied. "We met in Alarzi, and had an encounter with Iyerani mob agents which forced us to flee across the wilderness." She then narrated the summary of their adventures.

"So you haven't been here long, then. Seen much of the city?"

"Nothing at all," Celer said. "It was dark out, and we were focused on rescuing Ben from the compound."

"I think you should have a look," Edor replied. "You should know what really goes on in Dawta Volaero, outside of Alarzi." He shouted in Voleric up to the Andarite manning the vehicle's gun. The round door in the ceiling swung up and the man at the gun climbed down, allowing Ben to take his place. Celer followed him.

The vehicles rumbled through the mere skeleton of a city. The sun had risen while Ben and the others were in the transport, and the decrepit buildings now cast long shadows over the street. The paint had flaked off most of the buildings, and spiderweb cracks in the brickwork threatened collapse. Fire had reduced many to piles of charcoal and blackened brick. On one building, a sign reading *Going Out Of Business Sale: 50-70% Off Everything in Store* was riddled with bullet holes. The storefront was dark and bare. On the road surface, plants burst up through the cracked pavement. Trash barrels lay empty of anything edible. As the vehicles passed a group of Silk-spinners, the creatures sqwawked with bloody mouths and flew away, revealing the corpse upon which they had been feeding.

"The Iyeranis did all of this to Andaros?" Ben asked.

"The problem was started by the Andarites themselves," Edor called from below. "The economy destabilized because of our own bad judgment. The Iyeranis saw a country with a weak, easily manipulated government. The perfect place to grow a strong base for their organized crime. The group is rooted into Andaros like a malicious parasite."

"What type of crimes?" Ben asked.

"The group runs a massive operation based off of the illegal sale of Iyerani drugs and weapons, and is allied with most of the major crime rings that are native to Dawta Volaero. In cities where the local economy is still alright, Alarzi included, they stay low key, but extort the most profitable businesses. The shopkeeper whose murder you witnessed most likely didn't provide a good or service they ordered from him."

Ben descended from the turret, and gave Seren a chance to see the destruction.

"I never imagined the destruction would be so severe," she said when she returned. "Does this Iyerani group have a name?"

"We call them KTAN," Edor said. "It's an acronym for their full name for themselves: *'Kiei Tañanin Anarnge Ñatange,'* which is Iyerani for—"

"The Master Warriors' League," Seren finished.

"Right," Edor said. "You speak Iyeñavan?"

"It is my native language as much as English is," Seren said. "I have lived my life on Iyerayñan. Does your group have a name?"

"*Sildial Radaejoraro,*" Edor replied. "The Shield of Andaros." At that moment, the crunch of loose pavement stopped as the treads ceased turning. "We're here," Edor said. "Sildial Headquarters."

Chapter 6

The Messengers exited the transport first, eager to be back in the open air. The Andarites filed quickly out of the transport with practiced coordination. Not wanting to disrupt their precision, Ben and Seren waited to exit last. They stood on the edge of an open area about the size of a city block. The lot, which was covered in dull gray concrete, was surrounded by a fifteen-foot-high fence of metal spikes with artfully carved tips. In the dead center of the lot was a black rectangular building, four stories tall. The roof was flat, but had a thick parapet. On each of the building's corners, there were two large, swiveling guns.

"Looks like a fairly well-designed fortress," Celer said. "If KTAN blows by the fence, they have barely any cover while they're running across the lot. You could cut the attack force down significantly before they're in range to fire at you."

"That's the idea," Edor replied. "The founders of Sildial bought this entire lot when all the buildings on it were set to be demolished. They saved the old factory in the dead center, and remodeled it into the headquarters. That was several years ago. Our founder was a retired police officer, Varyal Ralodaro. He recruited a former officer from Dawta Volaero's military, and a business magnate who sold outdoors equipment. They had the money and training to put together a resistance against the Iyeranis."

"So you do not operate with the permission of the government," Seren said.

"We do what we have to in order to stop the spread of the violence."

The leader of the Sildial team waved at a guard who was manning a parapet gun. A Messenger from the team flew up and conferred with the guard, and then the lock to the gate clicked open. Ben watched the headquarters building grow and start to loom over him as he and the others approached it. They stopped in front of a pair of double doors. Above the doorframe, there was an emblem: Two circles were inscribed, one within the other. The central circle was gold, and had the word *Peace* written within. The outer circle was divided into four quadrants, each of a different color. The topmost, the green quadrant, read *Hope*. Clockwise around, there was *Compassion* in red, *Bravery* in blue, and *Diligence* in orange.

Edor pointed and said, "The four qualities around the edge bring us to the center, peace. Varyal created the emblem as a reminder." He said it with a certain reverence that made Ben want to get to know the founder of Sildial.

"Can we meet him?" Ben asked.

"Unfortunately not," Edor said. "Varyal's part of *our* history now. His son took command just a short time ago."

"You sound like you admired him very much," Seren said. "That must have been a great loss for you."

Edor nodded, eyes downcast. "And for the rest of Dawta Volaero as well." He turned to a Messenger and said, "Ridad, Kalar will want to know that we're back." The door clicked open and the team entered. Ridad departed from them and flew down the corridor, which turned left at a right angle. The corridor itself was dull gray metal, but beyond that, Ben recognized the hallmarks of Andarite décor that had also adorned the train. They exited into a grand dining hall illuminated by cozy yellow light. Ben couldn't tell if the hooded fixtures that were set into the ceiling were candles or lightbulbs. The room itself had a surprisingly rustic feel for a building in the middle of the city, almost like walking into a rural cabin. The walls, floor, and ceiling were all made from Andarite wood that had a marbled grain and flowing patterns of light and dark browns. One wall was dominated by a creeping ivy with broad leaves. The hall had six long, wooden tables. At the end of the room that was opposite the door, there was a podium with the Sildial emblem engraved into its front, elevated on a stage so that the entire room had a clear view of the speaker. Ben immediately felt warm and at home in the hall, as the plants and wooden construction reminded him of the outdoors. Edor motioned for him and Seren to sit down at the tables.

"Can we do anything to make you more comfortable?" he asked.

"We have been without enough food for a while. A meal would be appreciated," Seren said. She turned to Ben as Edor left. "You are sure you are alright?"

"Yeah, thanks. So what happened out there? You fought the Iyeranis?"

She told him the story of her fight. Ben looked at her, wide-eyed, as Celer confirmed every detail.

"Thank you," he said. "I'm sorry, I know I made a really stupid decision to try and fight them. I put you in too much danger."

"Try to be more careful," Seren said.

"Pardon me," said a Messenger, flying in from another room. "We have found someone who will be your guide for the duration of the stay. His name is Javrel Darialaro. He is about your age, which you might like."

The Messenger flew away and returned with an Andarite. Ben froze, staring at someone who was wearing the same metal augmentation as the criminals who had kidnapped him. Javrel smiled and waved. Ben took a deep, measured breath.

He sat down next to Ben and Seren. On closer inspection, Ben saw that Javrel had three limbs amputated, their stumps connected by wiring into the controls of the robotic suit. He wore plain clothes with the Silidal emblem printed on the shoulder. A pair of work gloves with rust and oil stains poked out of the pocket of his knee-length, kilt-like garment. One half of his face was concealed by a form-fit metal plate, the eye of which was an immaculately polished lens of dark glass. He was about the same age as Ben and Seren.

"Good morning," he said, and introduced himself.

Ben, Seren and Celer introduced themselves.

"Nice to meet you. I'm sorry about everything you've had to go through. So, Seren, Edor says you're from Iyerayñan?"

She glanced at Ben with nervousness in her eyes. "Yes. Please understand that I did not know about any of the ways Iyeranis had harmed Andaros."

Celer and Javrel conferred for a moment in Voleric.

"I understand," Javrel said. "Do not fear that we will have prejudice. And Ben... He's a Messengersmith?"

"Apprentice," Ben said. "And an apprentice without magic, too. Lost it in Alarzi, with some pretty bad burns to show for it."

"I see. Come now, you should to wash up and get some rest!"

"That would be great, thanks," Ben said. With that, Javrel led Ben, Seren and Celer out of one of the four doors leading out of the hall, and down a corridor lined with doors on one side. Ben and Seren left muddy footprints all the way down the hall.

"A set of clothes will be delivered to your quarters short-ly," Javrel said. He, Ben and Seren came to the very end of the hall, and he opened the second and third doors from the end.

"Luckily we have a few extra rooms in case we get new recruits, or rescued captives. There are towels in the baths, final door in this corridor. You're right next to them. Midday meal will be ready shortly."

"Thank you," Seren said. Ben and Celer thanked Javrel as well, and they departed to their quarters. Seren went to the baths first. While Ben waited for the facilites to become available, he surveyed the quarters he had been given. There were two bunk beds, each of which had a top and bottom bunk, and ample drawer space for a number of possessions. These beds all had blue quilts decorated with multicolored bands of Voleric writing. There were plants in brown clay fixtures set into the wall, and a few hooks for hanging clothes. The room was lit by the same daylight-emulating bulbs that lit the main hall. Ben was sorely tempted to flop down on the nearest bed and fall asleep, but he was still dirtied with swamp mud and didn't want to soil one of the beautifully decorated quilts. He felt the fatigue of two weeks' hard trek through the mountain pass, combined with his capture and the sleepless night, weighing down hard on him. He resolved that once he washed, he would sleep right through until lunchtime. Moments later, Seren knocked on Ben's door, and he let her in. She had washed the dirt streaks from her face and had cleaned the dust out of her hair. She was dressed in the native Andarite style, with thickly folded cloth over the shoulders of her long-sleeved shirt, and a skirt that reached her knees. The whole outfit was black, except for light blue detailing on the cuffs. The Sildial insignia was embroidered on one shoulder. She was barefoot.

"They have not yet found shoes for us," Seren explained. "The baths are ready for you."

"Thanks," Ben said. He entered the large bathroom area, which was made all of gray tiles, and went to one of the stalls. Two basins were set into the back wall, along with a shelf holding a perfectly orb-shaped piece of soap. Ben locked the door, stripped down, and turned on the faucets above the two basins. One dispensed only scaldingly hot water, the other ice-cold. He lathered the soap on thickly, letting the hot water soothe the aches and strains out of his muscles. He let out a deep sigh. The dirt caking his skin fell off and flowed down into the drain into the floor. He finally felt clean, for the first time since the Festival. The cold rinse felt brisk and refreshing. He peered out of the stall to find towels and a Sildial uniform waiting for him outside. He dried and quickly changed into the new clothes, then returned to his room and tucked himself into the nearest bunk. Celer floated down beside him and rested as well.

Ben woke up to someone knocking quickly and insistently on his door. He felt refreshed and fully awake, but still hungry. The knocking on the door continued.

"Coming," he called, and made his way over to the door. He opened it and found Seren waiting for him.

"You slept in," she said. "Lunch has been going on for a while already. I worried about whether you would be awake in time to eat."

"Thanks," Ben said.

They made their way down the corridor, then turned left, going through double doors that led into the spacious dining hall. Whereas the dining hall had been somberly quiet in the morning, it was jovially loud and cacophonous once its five long tables were packed with Andarites, all loudly enjoying each other's company. Messengers hovered above every head. As Seren led Ben in between two tables toward her seat, Ben heard the deep, throaty warbles that passed as laughter on Andaros.

"Do you have any idea how many of them there are?" Ben asked.

"Around three hundred twenty present at this time, judging by the length of the tables and the amount of space each Andarite occupies. As I was coming to get you, I saw a few others going about various duties. I would guess that there are at least an additional thirty agents that I could not account for here." She ushered Ben over to a table with two empty places saved.

Just next to Seren's place, Javrel was talking with an adult Andarite. His uniform was different than the others': the shoulder folds and trim of the shirt were bold crimson. The folds were larger, as well, and draped like a short cape over his shoulders. He had several gold medals with intricate designs pinned to his chest. His horns and the broad scales of his frill were exceptionally well polished, glinting brilliantly from the lights in the room. The horns were also tipped with ornate golden caps. As Ben and Seren sat down, he turned his attention away from Javrel and towards Ben. He smiled. Celer began his translation.

"You must be Ben," he said. "I'm Kalar Ralodaro, leader of this organization. Javrel has told me the bare bones of

the tale of your trek across the mountains. That you survived out there for so long is quite impressive. Now, I believe
that Javrel mentioned a device that you captured from the
Iyeranis in Alarzi?"

"Yeah, I have it right here." Ben reached for it, only to
find the empty pocket of his Sildial uniform. "It must be with
my other clothes." His next realization set his heart pounding. "They could have taken it when they captured me!"

"No, I have it," Seren said. "You gave it to me, remember?" Ben sighed. She handed the blue rectangle to Kalar,
who held it close to his face to examine it.

"Can you tell me more about how you came to find
this?" Kalar asked.

Seren told him the details. "The KTAN agent was be-
rating the shopkeeper because he had failed to deliver the
device to him on the previous day. He dropped it after Ben
attacked him, and we fled."

"Interesting," Kalar said. "And thank you. Any information we can get from this will be valuable. It will take a while
for our computer team to crack it, though. Breaking the en-
cryptions on KTAN devices is like trying to negotiate with
wild wolfdragons."

"I know what you mean," Celer said. He chuckled.

"I'll send this right up to the computer team as soon as
possible. Is there anything I can do to make your stay more
comfortable?"

"Not at this time. Your organization has already been
very accommodating, thank you," Seren said.

"I should take the flight out to Earth to contact Dennison Smith, at the Alliance base," Celer said.

Kalar smiled. "We can work out your journeys back home in the morning. For now, I think it's best you stay here, Celer. There's just a bureaucratic issue about taking refugees in and out of the headquarters, so nothing to worry about. Believe me, if I could forego that paperwork, I most definitely would." Kalar laughed at his own joke. "Javrel will show you three around and tell you more about our work here at Sildial. Now if you'll excuse me, I need to discuss something with my advisors. I'll see you all at dinner, I hope."

"Sounds good," Ben said. "Thank you."

"Of course. If there's anything at all you need, please don't be afraid to speak to someone about it." Kalar departed, leaving Ben to turn to the wide spread of food before him. The assembled Andarites passed bowls and platters up and down the long tables. He didn't waste time trying to discern between what looked good and didn't, and sought only to satiate the hunger that still gnawed furiously in his stomach. He intercepted each bowl as it passed, putting a bit of each food on his plate before passing the bowl on to someone else. He imitated everyone else, eating the many different dished with his fingers. Beside him, Seren was also digging into the food. They only stopped to take gulps of water. At the end of the hastily eaten meal, Ben's stomach ached from the sudden abundance of food, but he felt replenished. He and Seren smiled.

"Your cooks are very good," Ben said.

"I'll tell them you said that," Javrel replied. "Now, if you and Seren are ready to go, I can give you that tour of the headquarters."

"That would be excellent," Seren said. Javrel nodded and led Ben, Seren and Celer out of the dining hall, out the opposite side of the dormitories.

"I'll show you what I can," Javrel said, "But I can't even really talk to much about our more vital systems. Power, water, computers, things like that. I am allowed to show you our library and games center. Places you might like to visit during your stay here."

Javrel led the group into the large, low-ceilinged room that was Sildial's library. Ben, Seren and Javrel entered at casual walking speed, but Celer shot in like a supersonic six-year-old in a candy store. He zipped around the titles in a blur.

"You guys have *everything!* Ben, Seren, you guys have to look at this. There are works from the whole Alliance here! Giral Volaero from ancient Andaros, Tribune Alsariso from Wenifri, Rem-sen Ko-nqa-sit from Daalronna..." He flew around the many bookshelves, surveying titles from every world, many of which were bilingual editions in Voleric and the original text. Meanwhile, Seren focused in on one large shelf stuffed with carefully labeled and numbered papers.

"What are these?" she asked. The others crowded around her.

"Records of the conflict," Javrel said. "They'd probably bore you. I'll find something else.

"No, thank you. If you don't mind, I would like to read these."

Celer read over each of the headlines until Seren told him to stop. "Yes, read that one," she said.

"Tenth in the month of Valzai, year 3416. That would be five years ago in the Andarite calendar, right?"

"Yeah," Javrel said.

"The headline is 'Public Statement from Iyerayñan Foreign Affairs Bureau Chief Fails to Placate Demonstrators.' For the first time since the end of her government's isolation from the Alliance, Maiane Teminnaian Seteyenatan, head of the Ministry's Bureau of Migration, travelled personally to Darjae to speak to the people of Dawta Volaero on the issue of organized crime. The Bureau, she says, "has taken all possible measures to screen prospective travellers for criminal connections. No one with a prior criminal record has been permitted to leave Iyerayñan." Teminnaian went on to personally apologize for the behavior of Iyerani citizens involved with Voleric criminal organizations, and expressed her hope for continued expansion of trade between Andaros, Iyerayñan, and the rest of the Alliance."

"The month of Valzai is the first of the autumn," Javrel said. "Andaros and Iyerayñan signed a trade agreement in the spring of that year. She didn't speak out until we'd dealt with a whole summer of Iyeranis—" he looked at Seren, "Sorry, KTAN members, running guns and drugs through Diwo Rovisiro. Whatever screening measures they used somehow didn't catch those being sent down on Iyerani trading spacecraft. Nobody's caught him yet, but I don't think it's a coincidence that the head of Dawta Volaero's Bureau of Foreign Trade suddenly had enough money to buy a new lake house up on Alza Island."

"When was Sildial founded?"

"Shortly after that announcement. Month of Dalerjo, which is the middle of winter. Varyal and his co-founders moved fifty volunteers into the factory in order to provide hot food and armed protection for the homeless. Things were getting bad here. There was a turf war between KTAN and smaller rival gangs, and KTAN won Joraw. After that, most people either joined up with Sildial, got their families out if they had the money to move, or just hid if they didn't."

"And you?"

"Varyal adopted me and my sister during that winter."

"Sister?" Celer asked. They hadn't met any sister. "Is she..."

"Dead? Oh, no. She's out on a mission with her squad. She's older, so Kalar lets her fight. I fix machines, mostly the transports and some appliances. Thank the gods I can even do that, all because of Varyal."

"You cared for him very much," Seren said.

"I can't think of anyone else kind enough to take in a kid after the kind of accident I was in. He didn't even hesitate to take some confiscated KTAN tech, give it to the medics, and tell them to rebuild me. He couldn't get me back on my own feet, so he made sure I had another pair." Javrel took a deep breath. "But enough of my story. We can move on to the next part of the headquarters, if you want.

"If you don't mind, I'd like to remain here," Celer said. "We don't have much to do until dinner, so this is as good a place as any."

"Of course," Javrel said. "I have duties to attend to. I'll see you three at dinner, then."

Ben looked through the unintelligible Andarite books until he found one that was illuminated with beautiful drawings in the wide margins. He opened to a page depicting two Andarites, each dressed strangely and holding deadly-looking weapons. Both were tall enough that they towered over the seaside town drawn in the bottom margin. One was a woman dressed in living plants, woven and plaited into a dress with the same heavy shoulder-folds as most Andarite clothing. The trees of the forest below reached only to her ankles. Rising over the ocean was another Andarite. He had blue scales that were pale enough to be almost white. His horns, in stark contrast, were pitch-black. Rather than being truly clothed, most of his body was obscured by swirling blizzard clouds. Celer looked up from his reading and came over to Ben.

"What's that?" he asked.

"I was going to ask you," Ben replied.

"Hmm… It's an older dialect. Give me a moment to read it over." When Celer was ready, he began. "The Turning of the Seasons: The Battle of Idrazi and Dalerjo. Before the time of the first writings, the goddess Idrazi presided over a verdant and eternally warm land. The land was large and there were many things to be kept in balance. To help her, she brought forth four children. Three of the four were kind and benevolent, and dutifully helped their mother control the winds, the tides, and the forests. The fourth was an ungrateful and malicious son named Dalerjo. He, having been born later, was jealous of his older siblings, with their prestigious duties to the balance of life. Dalerjo made it his mission to bring their domains under his command, and so he conjured up great, icy storms that lashed viciously against the land. The people suffered under his great winter, and called out to their goddess to help them. Idrazi responded, and challenged Dalerjo to a great battle. The battle lasted five whole months, at the end of which Idrazi finally overcame her son. Still, her love for her son would not permit her to kill him. Instead, she banished him to the north and instructed her other children not to disturb him in his domain. Still, Dalerjo was not satisified. Each year he gathers his strength and returns. When the first frost comes, it is the duty of those who dwell on the land to burn offerings to nourish Idrazi for the coming battle."

"Cool story," Ben said.

"No pun intended?" Celer asked. "Dennison has a few volumes of ancient Andarite myths at the base. I've read a version of this story before. There are quite a few different ones, actually. They differ mostly in how Idrazi and Dalerjo are related. In the one I read, Dalerjo is Idrazi's ex-lover who just doesn't get the message that they're not together anymore."

Ben laughed. "You'd think that after the first few centuries he'd figure it out."

"That hardly makes for a reasonable explanation for the changing of the seasons," Seren said.

"Oh, come on," Celer said. "Can't you just appreciate it for the story? Have some fun with it once in a while?"

Seren thought for a moment. "I will... try. Are you satisfied?"

Celer chuckled. "It's a start. Small start, but still a start." He floated back over to where his other selection of epic poetry was sitting, and started to read aloud. For the sake of his listeners, Celer translated the meaning of the story, rather than try to give a word-for-word translation of the ancient verse. He picked and chose the most exciting parts from the twelve books, much to his listeners' delight.

Celer read on until dinner arrived. Ben had not yet memorized the way back to his quarters, but Seren already had the route firmly imprinted in her memory. She led Ben and Celer back to their quarters. A steady stream of hungry Sildial agents and their Messengers pointed the rest of the way. As the group was entering the dining hall, a Messenger with a deep purple neckband flew towards them.

"Kalar is requesting Seren's presence in his office," Celer explained.

"Alright," Ben said. "We'll save you a seat."

"Much appreciated. I will see you soon." Seren followed the purple-banded Messenger down one edge of the hall. Soon Ben lost sight of her in the crowd. He found Javrel, and sat down with him near the end of a table. They waited for the many bowls and platters to be passed around. Ben filled his plate with the strange leaf-fruits and his favorite tortoise liver strips. Javrel took one of the bowls and dropped a helping of thick, sludgy orange food onto Ben's plate.

"Dagob," Javrel said. "Trust me, you'll like it." Ben took a bite and was greeted by a sweet and sour flavor. Its consistency was thick, smooth, and oily. On Earth, Ben figured it would be served as a dessert, it was so sweet and tasty.

"It's good," Ben said. As Ben continued eating, Celer asked Javrel,

"So what happened that caused you to need the prosthetics?"

"Celer!" Ben scolded. "Don't you think that's a pretty private thing to ask about?"

"No, don't worry. There was…" he was silent for a moment, "…an accident with magic. I was lucky that Vuri, my sister, was there to help me after it happened."

"I wonder what Kalar wanted with Seren?" Ben said. Javrel cast a nervous eye out the door that led to Kalar's office.

"I don't know. Don't worry yourselves, though. Maybe he has questions about her part in the rescue."

"You're probably right. I'm just tense from everything that happened, I guess." Ben cleaned his plate and tried to relax. His time in KTAN's captivity still weighed on his mind.

As dinner was ending, Seren had still not returned from her meeting with Kalar. Ben caught two leaf-fruits as he got up from the table, in case she was hungry. As he went to his room, the same purple-banded Messenger who had summoned Seren intercepted him.

"Commander Kalar requests your immediate presence in his office. Please follow me," Celer translated. Ben followed, wondering why Kalar needed to talk to him, and why he needed him and Seren to be separated for the conversation. The Messenger led Ben up a flight of stairs and into a large office. The walls were decorated with a multitude of awards. There were also pictures of Kalar, smiling and waving from monuments and tall buildings. Ben searched the walls for pictures of Varyal, but found none.

The Commander himself was sitting in a high-backed, cushioned chair upholstered in blue, scaly leather. He stared at a plant on his desk, pulling off bulbous seed pods with his fingers and breaking them with a wet popping noise. There was a look of great unrest on his face. The purple-banded Messenger assumed an obedient position, hovering in place over Kalar's shoulder. Celer translated as Kalar spoke.

"How much do you know about the Iyerani girl?" he asked, looking up from the plant.

"You mean Seren?" Ben asked. "Well, she's very smart, for a human or an Andarite I mean. She wants to move up from her parents' laboring job. She's quick and brave when one of us is in trouble, and she saved me a couple times. Other than that, I don't know too much. She's quiet, you know? Keeps to herself, doesn't make conversation. Why? Is she in trouble?"

"So you don't know about her affiliations?" Kalar asked. Celer sounded uncertain as he translated it.

"What's this about?" Ben asked. He narrowed his eyes at Kalar. "I asked you, is Seren in trouble?"

Kalar gave Ben a sympathetic look, like what adults give to little children at friends' funerals. "I'm sorry to tell you this, Ben. I really am. Tragedies of this kind come far too often to good people in times like this. Ben..." Celer stopped translating. His tone was of disbelief and horror when he replied to Kalar in Voleric.

"Celer, what is it?" Ben asked.

"Ben, just remember, this is his words, not mine, I don't think—"

"Tell me. Now." Ben demanded.

"Kalar told me that Seren is working for KTAN."

CHAPTER 7

"Celer, are you absolutely sure you translated that right?" Ben's stomach clenched in fear of Celer would say.

"Yes," Celer said.

Ben felt a burning tingle on the back of his neck: magic about to well up and slam Seren's accusor into his wall full of trophies.

"Don't try it," Celer said. "You don't want to open those magic burns again, and you don't want to make Kalar any angrier."

Ben pushed the urge back down. Still, it took a substantial effort not to resort to slamming Kalar into the wall with his bare hands, and an even greater effort for him to calm down enough to growl through clenched teeth, "You're wrong."

"Ben, many people here in Sildial have found out loved ones are working for our enemy. It's never easy to believe at first. Count yourself lucky that the traitor wasn't family or a long-time friend. I envy you that you only knew her for a few weeks."

"She saved my life. Repeatedly."

"To put together an admittedly ingenious cover story."

"Prove it."

Kalar spoke to the purple-banded Messenger, who exited the room through a small hole, designed for Messenger transit, in the center of the door. The Messenger returned with a Sildial agent who placed three small, metal objects on Kalar's desk. Kalar gestured for Ben to examine them closer. Each one was an inch-long, quarter-inch wide piece of metal in the shape of a half cylinder. Descending from each were four metal legs. The body had a small camera lens on one end, and a set of small holes on the other, suggesting a microphone on the inside.

"These are KTAN ambulatory audio-visual recorders, designed for autonomous entry into small spaces. All three were found on the KTAN agent's clothes by Sildial laundry staff. Fortunately the devices did not begin transmitting data to KTAN before we disabled them," the agent said.

"Why?" Ben asked. "Seren hates living on Iyerayñan. She told me herself."

Kalar sighed. "Ben, is the girl you've seen capable of hate? Of love? Any emotion that would make her question the cold philosophy of her leaders?"

"Yes. I've seen it."

Kalar slammed his hands on the desk. "Don't you see? She's manipulating your emotions! If we had let this go on longer, she would have convinced you that I'm your enemy. That Sildial is your enemy."

Seren, working for KTAN? Ben thought. It seemed impossible, and yet here was the proof. She had brought listening devices straight into Sildial headquarters.

"What are you going to do with her?" Celer asked.

"That hasn't been determined yet."

Ben sighed in relief. There might still be time to sort everything out and find an answer. "Can I speak with her?"

"One last time," Kalar said. "But, like I said, she had made you care about her. Therefore, she is in a position to influence you. Please be careful. And Ben?"

"Yes?"

"I really am sorry about your loss."

"Yeah, whatever. Let me see my friend."

Kalar spoke to his Messenger, who took up a position in front of Ben, then led him out of Kalar's office, down the stairs, and to an elevator. Kalar's Messenger had to provide multiple access codes at each door before they could reach the cellblock. A thick metal door hissed open. On the other side was a hallway lined with ten cells on each side. Everything was made of bland metal. Each cell was just large enough to accommodate a bed with two sheets, and a toilet, and there was limited space to stand up and walk around.

There was an armed guard stationed at the front of the room. He directed Ben and Celer to the last cell at the right, then unlocked and slid back the reinforced glass door. Inside, Seren sat cross-legged on the bed, eyes closed.

Occasionally her lips moved, forming barely audible fragments of English and the Iyerani language. Between those phrases, Seren breathed slowly and regularly. Ben wondered for a moment whether it would be alright to disrupt her meditation. He sat down next to her and waited. Moments later, she concluded with a rhythmic verse in the Iyerani language, inhaled and exhaled deeply, and opened her eyes.

"What have they told you?" Seren asked.

"That you're working for KTAN. You brought listening devices into the HQ, and you manipulated Celer and me."

"I did not mean to do it," she said. "Ben, Celer, please believe me. I truly care about you. Whatever Kalar says, I would never manipulate you for my own gain."

"I know you didn't." Ben said. "Don't worry. It can't be that hard to convince Kalar that you're innocent, can it? This will all blow over soon, and we can go home."

"Can we really?" Seren asked. "I envy you if you can simply forget all the suffering we have seen here. Besides, Iyerayñan is not truly a home for me."

"Well then, I'm sure Dennison would love to have you on Earth," Celer said. "But first, we should focus on clearing your name. Ben, come on. We should get started."

"Rest first," Seren said. "It is late. Go back to your quarters and sleep."

"Alright. See you tomorrow." Ben got up and left the cell, with Celer close behind. As he was about to turn the corner, he remembered the leaf-fruits he was still carrying.

"Oh! I almost forgot. Here, I brought these from the dining hall for you." Ben handed them to Seren, and she smiled.

"Thank you," she said. "Now go. Sleep, then worry about solving this tomorrow." Ben nodded and started out of the cellblock once again. Kalar's Messenger spoke what Ben guessed was a signing-out to the guard, who opened the door from a keypad. They took the elevator and walked back to Ben's quarters. Here, Kalar's Messenger took off to return Kalar. To Ben's surprise, Javrel was standing outside of Ben's room, waiting for them.

"You were in the Commander's office for quite a while," he said. "Where's Seren?"

"Kalar charged her with spying on Sildial," Celer said. "They found tracking devices on her clothes."

"Planted by KTAN agents, I assume," Javrel said.

Ben raised an eyebrow. "You don't sound surprised about that."

"I had hoped this wouldn't happen, but I knew to expect it. Faced with something like this, Kalar becomes a fanatic. In his mind, any Iyerani is automatically part of KTAN. He will seize on this opportunity to make an example of an enemy."

Ben's heart skipped. "What is he going to do to her?"

"That will depend on how, or if, he is swayed by his advisors. His brother Sarad and friend Thoral Gosali advise him on most important matters. Sarad is a fanatic too, but isn't particularly creative. He usually only supports Kalar's ideas. If they weren't brothers, I doubt Sarad would even be an advisor. Thoral is… Well, Sildial only functions because Thoral keeps it going. He's quiet, but convincing when the need comes. Hopefully he can convince Kalar to give Seren a fair trial."

"How likely is that?" Celer asked. "And don't you dare sugarcoat it."

"Not likely," Javrel said.

Celer sighed. "So, our friend's fate is being held in the hands of nepotism and bigotry. Great."

"Celer, you and Ben must know a master Messengersmith," Javrel said. "He may have the influence to negotiate for Seren."

"I can't go," Celer said, while pulsing in despondent blue. "If I leave, Kalar will only become suspicious of us. Also, things are changing fast around here. As your translator, looks like I'm the closest thing Ben and Seren have to a legal advocate. Besides, I've never made a stellar jump like that before. It would be dangerous."

"Well, it was worth the suggestion," Javrel said. "Seren will have my prayers tonight. I believe Valzai and Doria favor us." With that, Javrel departed. Celer explained about the gods of strength and love whom Javrel had referenced.

Ben went to his quarters and flopped down on the bed. His bed, that he suddenly thought, wasn't in a small, metal-walled cell, and wasn't behind a reinforced door locked from the outside. He didn't like thinking about Seren being locked up in Sildial's detention level. He wondered if she was worried, or scared, or hopeful. Emotions, Ben realized, that Seren knew weren't productive at a time like this. Ben took that and tried to repeat it over in his head.

Worrying isn't doing anything for you right now, He thought. *Get some sleep.* He focused on that to the exclusion of anything else until he drifted off.

Celer circled above the bed, pulsing red and orange. What scared him the most was his ignorance of how Sildial worked. What was the presumption in a trial: innocence or guilt? Were trials fair, or just shows to preserve an image of fairness? Was the head Commander of Sildial bound by checks and balances? Were there protocols for his impeachment? Would precedents set by Kalar's reputedly heroic predecessor be upheld? Celer decided to take a short flight to clear his head, and then hopefully catch some rest. Moving out into the hall, he started a slow, meandering flight without any real destination in mind. He simply kept moving, letting his mind wander as much as his body. Being a Messenger, he could feel how magic flowed through the compound, permeating solid surfaces, only bent or redirected by the presence of a magic user's mind. Celer himself caused a substantial disturbance as he kept himself aloft, alive, and thinking. Every once in a while, he felt the tug of another Messenger, strong or weak depending on the distance. The pulls didn't distract him until he felt a particularly turbulent group of pulls coming from somewhere to his left, and one floor up. From so far away it was hard to get details, but it felt like three Messengers.

Normally the pull would have been unremarkable, but in the darkened, nighttime hallways when most Messengers and magic users were sleeping, the pulls should have been weaker. If Celer's memory served him right, then the pull was coming from Kalar's office. Celer didn't find it particularly polite to eavesdrop, but he decided to make an exception for the fanatical Andarite who had given the order for Seren to be imprisoned. Celer darted quickly up to Kalar's office and made his final approach in complete silence. Three rapid, loud voices were discussing something. Celer listened, focusing on every word of Voleric.

"You can't do this just on a whim and a few scraps of evidence," one voice said.

"A few scraps of evidence?" another voice retorted. Kalar's voice, growling. "We discovered three autonomous trackers on the body of an Iyerani who came sneaking into Joraw and so conveniently avoided the KTAN patrols. What more do you want, Thoral?"

The first voice, which must have been Thoral, responded, "Anything that can prove that she *knowingly* brought those devices into Sildial with the intent of harming our cause. They could have been planted on her."

"Does that matter?" a third voice asked. Presumably, it was Sarad, the other advisor Javrel had spoken about. "We have an Iyerani in custody. We have the three devices that were found on her clothes. We have a city that hasn't seen hope for a long time. The people of Joraw need a sign that

Sildial is still strong and ready to strike again. Kalar, we've got to kill the Iyerani."

A red flash of angry light surged across Celer's body. He hoped it hadn't been seen.

"You cannot do that!" Thoral said. "The poor child languishing in our prison cell has a right to a trial, regardless of what your racist excuse for a shriveled conscience has to say. I am not going to let you kill an innocent to satiate your bloodlust."

"Varyal set precedent on a similar matter, when an Iyerani captured by Sildial agents was summarily executed without trial," Sarad said.

"That was different! The agent shot seven of our own and was witnessed by five more, including Varyal himself!"

Kalar took on a sympathetic tone. "Thoral, you've lost loved ones to this conflict, haven't you? We all have. People have been sacrificed, sometimes unwillingly, for our cause. Might I remind you, Thoral, we aren't just fighting for Joraw. We aren't just fighting for Dawta Volaero. We are fighting for Andaros. *Five and a half billion Andarites.* If one more piece of Iyerani scum has to be killed to show our enemies we mean business, so be it. Sarad, send Messengers out to the city. I want the people to see me doing justice. The firing line demonstration will be in Diwo Square at noon tomorrow."

"I will kill you before you do that," Thoral said.

Celer felt a great influx of magic into the office, like someone unstoppering a bathtub drain and letting a torrent of water out. Celer felt Kalar concentrating energy between his hands.

"No, you won't," Kalar said, and he let it go. There was a flash of light that Celer could see in the crevice between the door and its frame, and then there were moans and a thump as a body hit the floor.

"Call someone up here to bring him to the cell block," Kalar said. "He can stay with the Iyerani."

Celer realized a Messenger was about to exit the room. Magic swirled invisibly around Celer as he took off, flying down the corridors at incredible speed. In an instant too fast for a human or Andarite to perceive, Celer returned to Ben's quarters. He had traveled so fast that he had made a stream of air behind him perceptibly warmer.

"Wake up! Wake Javrel! Now!" Celer screeched. Ben awoke with a start, holding his ears and flinching from the verbal assault.

"Celer? What the—"

"Kalar is going to kill Seren at noon tomorrow." Celer said. Any hope of sleep departed from Ben as he jumped from the bed as if it was his own life in immediate danger.

"He can't do that!" Ben said disbelievingly. "There has to be some rule that makes sure he doesn't."

"Kalar is in absolute command, as far as I can tell," Celer said. "He's accountable to no one."

Ben found Javrel in his quarters and roused him, and Celer explained the situation.

"Please tell me I'm wrong," Celer said.

"I can't, sorry," Javrel said. "He'll follow through. He can't back down now that he attacked one of his own advisors. Was Sarad encouraging him?"

"He went so far as to cite a precedent from Varyal that convinced Kalar that he was right. Thoral tried to stop Kalar, but he got magic-blasted as soon as he spoke up. Javrel, how did this happen? Why did Sildial let Kalar lead like this for so long?"

Javrel thought for a moment. "He was charismatic. That, and KTAN's people and their allies almost always fight to the death. Sildial has only had to put enemy combatants on trial once or twice, and there was always overwhelming evidence for their guilt. Kalar made most people here feel like he was best thing that ever happened to Andaros."

Celer said, "So, all we have to do is show Sildial who the real evil one is by noon tomorrow. How easy do you think that will be?"

"Kalar's good at making things seem like they fit into his views. We need some really good evidence if we can even hope to save her."

"The trackers," Ben said. "If we know more about them, we can figure out when Seren would have picked them up, and how. We might have to break in."

"No, I have the passcode for the tech department. I can get you in."

Javrel led the party to the second floor, where they came to a large metal door secured by a keypad on one side.

"Let me go in first," Javrel said.

"Your territory," Ben said. Javrel keyed in the code and walked confidently into a forest of technology, populated by treetrunks of huge computer processors, wires hanging like vines all over the room, and power cables like roots in tangles on the floor. Javrel, with his mechanical limbs, seemed to fit perfectly into the space. There was a single Andarite in the back of the room, surrounded by a multitude of monitors, and the flashing lights from piles of small devices. She hunched over a monitor with sullen eyes, but snapped upright upon seeing Javrel.

"Javrel? What are you doing here so late? And who are these?" she asked, pointing an accusatory finger at Ben and Celer.

"We're here to look at the three listening devices that were found on an alleged KTAN agent," Celer translated as Javrel spoke.

"And why should I let anyone barge in on a whim and look at evidence that needs to be left uncorrupted until trial?" she asked. "They don't have clearance."

"Because there's not going to be a trial," Javrel said. "Kalar's going to put on a big public execution tomorrow in Diwo Square. He doesn't care if she's guilty. He just wants everybody to know that Sildial still knows how to kill Iyeranis."

"Thoral wouldn't allow that."

Celer retorted, "Kalar shot Thoral with magic, then shoved him in the detention wing."

"He's gone insane," the technician said.

"He went insane a long time ago," Javrel replied. "You're just seeing it now."

"You're trying to give her a defense, then?"

"Yes. We need to see those devices. There might be some evidence we can use. If we can show something substantial to all of Sildial, no one would consent to this execution."

The technician opened a drawer and pulled out a clear-topped box containing the three devices. Ben took it from her and opened the top.

"May I?" he asked.

"Of course. Anything you need." Ben examined the device closer than he had been able to in Kalar's office. Its front tapered to a rounded point, with the small camera at the very tip. *Almost like a bullet,* Ben thought. He played with the limp legs for a moment. Each one had small hooks on the feet.

"Hey, guys. Look at this."

There were gray fibers caught in the barbs from where the devices had been removed from Seren's jacket. By pushing the joints in just the right way, he could slide them into the abdomen, completing the bullet shape.

"Do you have any captured Iyerani guns?" Ben asked. The technician walked to a locked cabinet and returned with a long-barreled weapon. Ben took it and slid the bullet-shaped listening device down the barrel. It was a perfect fit.

"The Iyerani agents who shot at us in Alarzi," Celer said. "They shot these. I bet they use their legs for drag, so they slowed down enough that you two didn't notice their landing."

"But then I should have been bugged, too," Ben said. "Nothing was found on my clothes."

"The Iyeranis took your jacket when you were in the compound, remember? Whatever they wanted to do to you, they didn't think you would escape," Celer said.

"That proves it, then!" Ben said. "Seren's innocent! We can tell everyone tomorrow at breakfast. That way, everyone will be assembled, and it will be before noon."

"Thank you for your help," Javrel said to the technician.

"Of course. Just doing what's right," she said.

With that, Ben, Celer and Javrel departed.

Ben lay awake in bed, imagining everything that could go wrong. He could not fail Seren, not after everything she had done for him in the wilderness. Still, despite his worries, his body dragged him off to sleep for a few hours before sunrise. He managed just enough rest to wake feeling ready for the battle of wills pitting Kalar against him, Javrel and Celer, with Seren's life hanging in the balance.

"So what's the plan?" Ben asked. "When do we make our move?"

"Kalar's an egomaniac who loves to hear himself talk. If he's going to the effort to go public with this bloodletting, he'll try to get Sildial fired up about it beforehand."

"So we wait for him to make an announcement about it, then make our case," Celer said.

"Exactly. That will be at the beginning of breakfast."

They sat down to a table at the very corner of the dining area, near to the front, where Kalar would make his announcement. Already, the Commander was standing at his podium, smiling, dressed in his unique red Sildial uniform. His scales and horns were freshly polished and glinting in the light of the dining hall. On his horns were the same golden bands he had worn when Ben had met him, also freshly polished.

"He sure does like to put on a show, doesn't he?" Ben said.

"Quiet. He's starting," Celer said.

Kalar's purple-banded Messenger gave out a high-pitched, warbling coo that lasted until every last person had settled and was ready to listen. Once he saw that he had captured the crowd's attention, Kalar raised a crescent-shaped magical item to his chin so it framed his mouth, and began speaking. The device amplified his voice until it filled the room.

"Gathered friends," he started, "let us take a moment to remember our fallen comrades. The Iyerani *rekyari* have taken many of our friends and family, combatants and civilians alike. Let us remember Darva and Aeizi Zolaro, who perished while bravely escorting homeless children of Joraw northward to Albir. Reydh Galelijo, a civilian who died, but took with him five of KTAN's criminal lackeys by triggering one of their own mines. Many more have died, valiantly in combat or minding their own business, just trying to get by. They are not lost, however. The honored dead are cheering for our efforts from the halls of the gods!" The crowd shouted and cheered.

"They are watching us, and as we remember them, we are encouraged to continue onward. We are doing just that. I am here to tell you that we are succeeding. I say that because recently Sildial has captured an Iyerani agent trying to gain access to our secure facility. The woman from Iyeraynan who entered this compound with the young Messengersmith, Ben Taylor, was in league with our enemy." A wave of disapproving murmurs made its way through the crowd, and Andarites all over the room gave Ben suspicious glances. "However," Kalar continued, "our friend Ben is not to blame. His kind, caring sensibilites were cruelly manipulated by an Iyerani who only needed him as a tool to help her cross the wilderness, setting up her devious cover identity as a poor, starving victim in need of our help. She manipulated us into allowing her to enter this compound, carrying with her three listening devices meant to relay our plans back to her soulless leaders. For this infraction I have cited Varyal's precedent regarding similar situations, and I have authorized the execution of this Iyerani agent." Several Sildial agents whooped and hollered.

"We are succeeding in defeating our enemies! All of Andaros will know that fact at noon today! The public execution will be in Diwo Square! KTAN will see that we mean to rear our collective head and strike back! With this stroke we will begin anew and tear down the oppressive virus that is the Iyerani *rekyari!*"

Andarites and Messengers all over the room roared in approval, joined soon by more and more, until the entire space was filled with the cheers and shrill calls of the entire bloodthirsty militia, ready to see red human blood soaking into the ground of the square. Ben's stomach turned as he looked out over the sea of raised fists. He paled.

"We can't do this," he said. "Kalar has them all convinced."

"Mob mentality, Ben. We just have to make them think. Don't give up on her," Celer said. He gave a high-pitched call similar to that which Kalar's Messenger had given. As the crowd quieted, they turned to look at Celer.

"Go ahead," Celer whispered. "I'll translate."

Javrel handed Ben a glass of water, from which he took a grateful sip before starting his speech.

"Hold up," Ben said. "Before you decide to do this, at least listen to all of the evidence. Yes, Seren is Iyerani. But, she's also my friend." Ben got a barrage of derisive hisses and shouts from the crowd. Celer withheld the translations of their remarks.

"Just keep going. You're doing fine," he said.

Ben continued, "Kalar didn't mention how Seren, my friend, got the listening devices."

Javrel stood. "If you believe in real justice, you'll all listen to Adoro from the tech department. Please."

The technician Ben had met last night stood on her bench. "The three devices discovered on the alleged agent's jacket were small, four legged robots, each equipped with a microphone and a camera. The interesting part is the shape of the devices. When the legs are folded in, each one matches the shape profile of a small-caliber Iyerani-made bullet."

Now the crowd was completely silent.

"Thank you," Ben said. "I met Seren in Alarzi, at the Literature Festival. After we were attacked by an Iyerani agent, we were shot at in an open area by Iyerani members of KTAN, but neither of us thought we were hit. Those devices were planted on us."

"Commander Kalar, do you accept that the evidence does not conclusively prove Seren's guilt?" Celer asked.

Kalar laughed. "Of course not. What do you know of our wily enemy? The Iyerani planned this all along. She will die at noon."

Javrel took a deep breath. "In that case, I believe that Kalar has moved outside the bounds of moral leadership. We can't continue like this. I call for everyone in Sildial to declare that Kalar is no longer fit to lead, and should be removed from command." There was murmuring and hushed discussion all over the room. Still, no one was getting up to throw the Commander off his lofty podium. Kalar himself was looking at Ben with mild, condescending amusement.

"My friends, are you going to trust this newcomer instead of your beloved leader?" he asked. "The Iyerani has played Ben's emotions, and he has become an unwitting accomplice to her plan. If we show her leaders that we are not afraid to kill, and that we can see through their devious ploys, *they will fear us.*"

"Everyone knows that Iyeranis don't think like we do," Javrel called. "They don't feel fear in the same way. All you will do is make our own civilians mistrust our justice system."

"The people love me, Javrel. They respect my will. They will tell their children the story of our victory over the Iyeranis. Hatchlings will be named after us! We will strike down this enemy and be remembered as heroes of Andaros!"

One of Sildial's agents stood up amid the crowd. Ben immediately recognized Edor, the medic from his rescue. "I hope that I can tell stories of victory to my children when Andaros is free," he said, "but I cannot, in good conscience, call the people of Sildial heroes if they are willing to go along with this crime. I agree with the human boy. Down with Kalar Ralodaro."

Murmured assent spread through the crowd. "You would turn on your leader, who treats you all as brothers and sisters in arms?" Kalar asked. "Who would you have replace me?"

"Thoral Gosali!" Javrel shouted. "Your advisor, who attends to the feeding of your brothers and sisters in arms and the upkeep of this building. Doing what needs to be done, while you're off waging your supposedly glorious holy war against every Iyerani you see!" There were numerous shouts from the crowd, both in support and derision. Individual arguments broke out out among seatmates all around the room.

"Who says it isn't glorious?" another Andarite called from the crowd. "All you who are siding with the Iyerani are short-sighted traitors! Kalar's my leader to the end!"

Kalar smiled. "That's the spirit! You should all strive to be more like this righteous man, who defends our goals to the last. This comrade of mine is loyal to me, as you all should be."

"We're not loyal to you, you selfish *bulgadh!*" Edor called. Celer had no translation for the expletive. "We're loyal to Andaros and Sildial. We're loyal to the ideals we had, before we started trying to justify the murder of civilians. We were loyal to Varyal, our *real* visionary leader!" There were cacophonous cheers from all over the room. Andarites surrounded Edor and urged him up to standing on a table. "Thoral for Commander!" he shouted.

"Thoral for Commander!" the crowd echoed back. Ben looked away from the cheering crowd for just a moment, to watch the satisfyingly dumbfounded look on Kalar's face. Ben looked back at the cheering throng, and echoed the Voleric chant as best as he could.

"*Yavil Thoral Dalvalijo!*" Ben called. Still, though, there were derisive, riotous shouts from those who supported Kalar.

Cloaked in anonymity among the hundreds of other shouting Andarites, a supporter of Kalar called forth a great bolt of magic, the light from which blinded everyone for a split second. When the flash passed, Edor had fallen, a smoking hole bored straight through his chest. The crowd broke into a full-out riot and chaos reigned. For a moment, Ben was jostled about among the sea of brawling Andarites. They fought not with fists, but with their horns. They charged forward from range, or swung their heads low, catching opponents in the chest and drawing blue blood. Ben dodged the attack of one of Kalar's supporters, but fell to the ground in his haste. Another Andarite stood over him, ready to stomp his face in with a booted foot. Not a moment too soon, Javrel drove his robotic elbow into the attacker's abdomen with the sickening crunch of metal breaking bone. He gave Ben a hand up to his feet.

"Thanks," Ben said. Another attacker rushed at him, blue-stained horns aimed at his chest. He ducked and punched the Andarite in the gut, winding him.

"Now would be a good time for some magic!" Javrel called. Ben's body grew warm, but there was the sensation of hot needles pricking his flesh.

"Magic burns!" Ben replied. Around them, other magic users were using their own abilities, and both sides fired golden bursts. The room was in total chaos. "How do we know who's on what side?" Ben asked.

"We don't," Javrel said. "But people will recognize the only cyborg and the only human. Just defend yourself." An enemy Andarite ran at Javrel, screaming and wielding a table leg. He made a wild attack at Javrel's head, only to have his wrist seized and broken in Javrel's mechanical grip. Javrel threw the table leg to Ben, who caught it just in time to strike an assailant across the side of the head, sending him reeling. Javrel was just fine without a weapon; he was using some kind of Andarite martial art composed of elbow and knee strikes, combined with grappling and the use of his formidable horns. He dealt devastation to each enemy with a single blow, power amplified by his robotic limbs. He sidestepped a charging Andarite and grabbed the sides of his frill, using the attacker's own weight to slam him into another brawler. One's horns met the other's flesh. Meanwhile, Ben held his own by dodging and making use of his splintered table leg. Above the fray, Messengers milled about ineffectually, unable to affect the physical struggle below. Celer descended from their midst.

"Behind you!" he called. Ben spun and struck an Andarite squarely in the face with his table leg. It sent the Andarite reeling, but the weapon itself also broke into two useless halves. Javrel defended Ben while he scrambled for another weapon, searching for a fractured bottle or another fragment of furniture.

Celer kept watch for any more aggressors. "I can't see Kalar!" he called, returning to the ground. "His supporters are demoralized! Some are even fighting for us now!"

"Where did he go?" Ben asked. Celer flew up again and saw a number of injured combatants fleeing the dining hall through the double doors.

"I think he left the headquarters!"

"Filthy coward," Javrel growled. He kneed one of Kalar's last supporters in the gut, smashing bones with his mechanical limb. The Andarite crumpled in a heap. Javrel and Ben could now see what Celer had reported. Kalar's supporters, discouraged by the sudden flight of their fearless leader, were in retreat. They didn't bother to help their injured allies, who were left bleeding and broken on the floor of the hall.

The adrenaline drained out of Ben, and his arms ached from the exertion of dealing out so many blows to his attackers. Out of range to strike physically, Javrel lashed out at the retreating loyalists with a string of obscenities that Celer refused to translate. Once the last of Kalar's followers had left the building, the remaining agents of Sildial were left to survey the carnage of the dining hall. Breakfast lay toppled on the floor, and anything that was once edible was trampled or soaked in Andarite blood. The walls were pockmarked with the charring of magical blasts. Some rebel had gone so far as to destroy Kalar's podium with magic, leaving its remains scattered around the hall. The dead and injured lying on the ground were numerous, and it was impossible to tell which side they had fought for. Of those who were still standing in the hall, barely half of the assembled crowd was still present. Ben thought that in this moment he should be relieved; Seren was no longer going to be executed by an unjust dictator. Instead, though, he was held by fear and regret in reaction to the death around him. Had he just traded Seren's life for the survival of Sildial? For the freedom of Andaros? He surveyed the wreckage and realized he had made a grave mistake. Javrel was pacing aimlessly around the room, eyes downcast.

"I'm sorry," was all Ben could think of.

"Don't say that," Javrel said. "Thank you. Thank you more than I can describe. You have freed Sildial."

"But I destroyed half of it!" Ben said. "How does that work?"

"When there's a fungus on half of your food crop, you must destroy it to save the rest," Javrel said. "We will rebuild, and Thoral will lead us."

"Speaking of Thoral," Celer said, "I think he spent the night as Seren's neighbor. We should probably take care of that."

Accompanied by their Messengers and a throng of expectant Andarites, Ben and Javrel made their way to the elevator. They took the highest-raking Andarite they could find with them so he could intercede with the prison guard. The three of them and their Messengers took the elevator down to the detention level. Once there, the Sildial agent explained everything to the guard, who then opened the only two cells in use. Seren and Thoral looked up from their respective places, then exited their cells. As Thoral exited, Ben could see burns in wide swaths across his face and body. Many of his scales had sloughed off after Kalar's attack, revealing blistered blue flesh below. Javrel faced Thoral almost reverently, then bowed his head deeply and made a high-pitched hum from deep in his throat.

"Thoralol jevalvor," he said.

"Hail Thoral," Celer whispered the translation reverently into Ben's ear.

The two other Andarites and their Messengers followed Javrel's lead. Thoral looked greatly confused, and started conversing in rapid Voleric with Javrel. Meanwhile, Seren was coming over to Ben. She smiled.

"Thank you," she said. "I had no doubt that you would convince Kalar to release me. I am grateful for your intervention on my behalf."

"You're welcome," Celer said. "We didn't really convince Kalar of anything, though."

"Things got messy," Ben continued. "Somebody got shot with magic, and there was rioting, and now about half of Sildial is still here."

"Were there fatalities?" Seren asked. "You should not have risked the operating capacity of Sildial just to save me. That was inefficient."

"Kalar's supporters were breaking Sildial down from the inside," Celer said. "You did these people a service."

"If you insist," Seren said.

"Anybody else hungry?" Ben asked. There was resounding agreement from Seren, Javrel and Thoral.

Back in the dining hall, Sildial had already begun the massive cleanup necessary after the riot. The dead and injured had been taken away, and now crews were cleaning up the destroyed furniture, ruined food and spilled blood covering the floor. Thoral was visibly dismayed at the destruction. Still, when he arrived in the hall, every Andarite paused from their work and looked up.

"*Thoralol jevalvor,*" one said, raising his fist. The rest of the crowd joined, chanting the words loudly and triumphantly.

After a moment, the crowd's cheering faded into expectant silence.

"*Zilri sildialaro,*" he started. Celer began translating. "People of Sildial, Javrel has given me your list of grievances against Kalar, and has told me about the riot and his retreat from the headquarters. As his advisor, I know all too well where Sildial would have gone if his rule had continued. I am grateful that you intervened, for the sake of Andaros and for the sake of the humans and Messenger caught in the middle of our conflict. Thank you. I am reluctant to take the public stand as official leader of Sildial, but nevertheless, I accept." The cheers restarted, reaching a deafening height.

Thoral blinked and took a shaky step back from the wave of noise. "Unless anyone has further concerns, I will be going to the office of the Commander to begin sorting out the paperwork involved with this transition. Thank you." The crowd parted in respectful silence. Thoral was joined by an entourage of Sildial agents armed with brooms and mops, removing the scattered waste from in from the path of their new leader.

"They love him already," Ben remarked.

"And why shouldn't we?" Javrel asked. "He did all of Kalar's dirty work and kept him from completely destroying us. Remember, he also defended Seren from Kalar, even if it didn't work out as well as it could have. You should respect him too. Now come on, help us clean up." He called for two more mops to be given to Ben and Seren, and they helped the cleanup crews until the sickly odor of blood and destroyed food was replaced by the sharp tang of cleaning fluid. Many of the tables and benches were sent to Sildial's carpenter for repair, and one small crew was working on rebuilding the podium, levitating the fractured pieces back into place with magic. Andarites came out from the kitchen with steaming bowls of rich, brown porridge mixed with white seeds and small insects. Ben's stomach flipped at the idea of eating more bugs after his stint in the wilderness. He was hungry, though, after a morning of fighting and cleaning, and sat down to breakfast anyway. He, Seren and Javrel sat down in a circle on the floor, with Celer hovering above them.

"I hope your first impression of Sildial hasn't been completely ruined," Javrel said.

"Because of Kalar?" Ben asked. "Of course not. If Sildial kicked him out, you guys can't be that bad. Sounds like you're doing some good work here."

"You represent your organization well, Javrel," Seren added. "If the rest of Sildial is like you, then you are part of a very honorable group."

"You flatter me," Javrel replied. "There are a lot of good people here. Fewer people like Kalar, since this morning. Fewer cowards. Now if you'd excuse me, I have duties to attend to. If you need me, I'll be working in the transport garage."

"Understood. Javrel, thank you for your efforts," Seren responded. "If they approve, then Ben, Celer and I will be in the library."

"I'd love to," Ben said. "See you later, Javrel."

In the library, Ben and Seren found a couch between the fiction and history sections, while Celer perused the titles for something everyone would be interested in.

"Thank you for visiting me last night," Seren said. "Knowing someone was advocating for me was comforting."

"Hey, I wasn't going to leave you alone down there without making sure you were okay. Plus, you missed dinner, so I had to bring you something."

"Also, I had to make sure Ben didn't kill Kalar immediately after he accused you of being a traitor," Celer said.

Seren smiled. "I had a feeling you would have to do that."

Ben laughed. "A feeling?"

"A reasonable assumption based on your previous actions."

"Ah, okay," Ben replied. "Too bad you weren't in the mess hall to see Javrel. He was awesome during the fight. Although, I still cringe every time I remember the sound of him driving his metal knee into some poor Andarite's bone."

"That robotic suit is quite the enhancement, I see," Seren said. "He said it was made from recovered KTAN technology?"

"Yeah. Doesn't make me want to take those soldiers head-on again."

"Agreed. What about you? Have your burns healed yet?"

"I didn't want to risk testing that during the fight," Ben said. "I spent the whole time defending myself with a chair leg. Surprisingly effective, actually."

"Hey you two!" Celer called. "I found a book that looks good. I'll bring it over and—" He was stopped by the lightning-fast approach of a gray-banded Messenger, who shouted a message at Celer.

"This is Dalivei, Thoral's Messenger. He says that there's going to be a Takathist attack on Sildial tonight," he translated. "Apparently KTAN has an alliance with them, too."

"Takathist?" Seren asked.

"Anti-magical sect of the Voleric religion," Ben said. "Extremists. I thought they were dormant since Andaros formally joined the Alliance, but I guess not."

"All that remains of Sildial is preparing for the attack," Celer said. "Sounds big."

"Can half of Sildial defend well?" Ben asked.

"I don't know," Dalivei said. "They obviously chose this day to attack because they saw our weakness."

"How can we help?" Ben asked.

"You will remain in your quarters for the duration," Dalivei replied. "Thoral doesn't want you three putting yourselves in danger. You're still not technically Sildial agents, and we don't think you should be acting like them now."

"Come on!" Ben protested. "I can fight! I don't care about the magic burns, I can find another weapon for—"

"Understood," Seren cut in, shooting Ben a cautionary glance.

"Thank you, Seren," Dalivei said. "Now all of you, get moving. We have a battle to prepare for."

Chapter 8

For the rest of the day, the mood in Sildial was drawn tight like a bowstring waiting to be released. There was little chatter except for clipped phrases, orders being given and acknowledged. At one end of the base, Javrel was busy readying the armored transports for battle: Ammunition was loaded, turrets lubricated, all the gauges checked. Seren and Ben helped distribute a small midday meal, grainy bars of high nutrition and low flavor.

Meanwhile, Celer attached himself to one of the Messenger teams that roamed the streets, warning tenement dwellers and vagrants of the impending battle. Most knew where to find empty, sturdy buildings, where they could ride out the attack. Celer saw all manner of people who couldn't fight for themselves, among them a single parent of three recent hatchlings, and an old, frail man living off rainwater, a small fruit tree, and a colony of edible insects. He checked the home of the old man who had welcomed him and the humans to Joraw, but found it empty. Every able-bodied Andarite in Joraw was fighting, for Sildial or simply for the survival of their loved ones. Anyone else who had inhabited the city and had the means to get out had long since departed. Still, being out in the streets was a reminder to Celer of why exactly Sildial existed. By the time in mid-afternoon when he and his team returned, Celer found all of the preparations complete. Now, everyone in Sildial sat at their assigned posts, tense and with nothing to do except wait for the battle. The sliding of metal against metal, the dull clicks of guns being cocked, filled the halls. Messengers flew through the battle stations, giving the latest on KTAN's troop movements. Celer returned to Ben's quarters. Ben and Seren sat together just outside their rooms. Ben looked anxiously up and down the halls, as if expecting KTAN agents to storm the hallway at any moment. Seren kept her normal, inscrutable blankness.

"The report is in," Celer said. "The attack force is made of three hundred Takathists, and a number of elite KTAN agents. They have three huge artillery pieces."

"The Takathists will have to deal with huge losses before they can even breach the entrance," Ben said. "There will be a lot who get killed by the roof guns and the grenades Sildial can launch from the parapet."

"Still, I don't like our odds," Celer said.

"We could be up there, helping," Ben grumbled.

The first crackling of gunfire began with the last light of the sun. It was dull, muffled, and far away. If Ben closed his eyes and focused on the sounds, he could almost imagine himself on the parapet, watching the advancing force below and breathing in the tangy scent of the accelerant in the guns. He wondered where Javrel was among the soldiers. He longed to know anything that would tell him how the battle was going.

Now, he could not only hear, but also feel, the huge, pounding booms of KTAN artillery fire. Feeling the resonant boom, coming at regular intervals, was like being inside a monumental clock. The artillery was the giant hands of the clock moving from one moment to the next, the gunfire the soft clicking of gears and springs. Perfectly, mechanically, and with calculated Iyerani precision, the bombardment continued. Ben began counting the blasts and the seconds between them. One blast, then seven seconds. The next blast, and another seven. Eight blasts, and just over a minute had passed. It had felt like an eternity. At fifteen, Ben wondered who was suffering under the clockwork assault. Twenty, and Ben noticed that Seren had closed herself off, eyes shut, deep in meditation. Thirty, and a Messenger flew into Ben's field of view.

"The artillery has broken through the front wall!" Celer translated. "Thoral is ordering us to hide in the library. Let's go!" Seren stood up and immediately began sprinting towards their new hiding place. Ben, though, was unsure. Here was his chance to fight, while the enemy was on Sildial's home field. He ran towards the sounds of the battle.

"No! We're going to the library!" Seren called. Ben paid her no heed as he kept going.

"Ben, this is a clear violation of our orders," Seren reprimanded him.

"Sildial is about to be overrun! We have to help somehow! Celer, come on. You know we have to do something."

"Hmm…" Celer said. "I may have translated that order wrong… You know, it's an easy mistake to get all those infixes confused… Let's go."

"Celer, don't support him on this, please," she said. "We could be killed. We're not even armed."

"Sorry," Celer said.

"Fine, then. You give me no choice," Seren said. "I will not allow you to go alone, but let it be noted that I still highly object to this course of action."

"Duly noted," Celer said. With that, he whizzed off, leading the way. They reached the dining hall to find a huge part of the front wall blown away by artillery, leaving brick, mortar and huge wood spliners all over the dining hall floor. Sildial had built a semicircular defense around the door, crouching behind small, portable metal walls. Only a fraction of the Takathist force could awkwardly scramble over the pile of jagged rubble where the wall once was, but the entirety of the Sildial force could fire at them while they were climbing. Still, the extremists put up a fight to their final breaths, firing wildly into the Sildial's line before falling and yielding the attack to their fellows. Medics worked tirelessly, carrying the wounded and dying to a makeshift infirmary in the kitchen. One medic paused to look at Ben and Seren.

"I thought Thoral ordered you to... Never mind. There are too many of those Takathist *bulgadhi* out there for us to pass up two fighters. Guns are over there."

He motioned to boxes at the back of the room, where there were a few extra guns, and boxes upon boxes of ammunition. Ben and Seren ran to them, finding weapons of a thoroughly alien configuration. Seren figured it out first: Holding the padded, loop-shaped handle so that the holder's palm faced the ground made it so the barrel lay across the top of the forearm. The trigger was set at the correct angle to be pulled by the thumb. She helped Ben get the weapon into position.

"Thanks," he said. He saw the glint of polished metal among the Sildial soldiers. "Javrel's down there!" he called. "Come on!"

They ran off across the dining hall towards the line of their allies. Ben felt the wind from a barrage of bullets pass by, missing him by just inches. They ran all the faster towards cover, hoping not to have another such close call. As Ben ran, he nearly crashed into two medics carrying a badly injured Andarite on a stretcher. A blossoming stain of blue blood was quickly overtaking the white bandages wrapped around his torso. Ben's stomach turned, and he tried not to think about the wound cloaked beneath. Finally, they reached the metal perimeter and ducked down behind it, startling Javrel.

"What are you doing here?" Javrel shouted over the roar of gunfire. "I thought Thoral ordered you to stay in your room!"

"He did," Ben replied tersely. "But we couldn't just sit around and do nothing."

"Somebody gave you guns?"

"Yeah."

"I don't know what Thoral will do to you when he hears about this, but it won't be good for you…" Javrel muttered. "You defied a direct order." Javrel stood up, taking quick, mechanical aim and firing three times, before kneeling back down below the barricade. Ben followed his lead, firing a few times before sliding back into cover. He didn't take the time to check where his shots had gone; he had never practiced with any weapon, let alone this alien one. With the multitude of Takathists on the battlefield, though, he was bound to hit something. Ben continued firing for a few more intervals of shooting and hiding. His breath became ragged from the rapid repetitions of standing up and ducking down. Beside him, Seren was also winded, though she seemed to recover more quickly. Ben paused to catch his breath, closing his eyes and breathing deeply. As he did so, he was surprised that the gunfire had suddenly subsided, leaving him alone with the ringing in his ears. The silence was disturbing rather than calming. He opened his eyes and peered over the barricade at a battlefield empty of approaching soldiers. Sildial peered outward over the metal barricades, searching for a trick.

A rocket shot towards Sildial from the Takathist line.

The next few seconds were a loud and violent blur. There were short bursts of Voleric shouting, cut off by a great force, heat and light that propelled Ben back and tumbled him along the floor like a doll. The world spun for a few moments, filled with the tumultuous roar of close-quarters battle. Ben was too disoriented to move. There was a heavy, blunt throbbing in his head as he opened his eyes. It took him a moment to recognize the flames that seized the wood paneling of the hall, the Takathist and Sildial lines dissolving against each other at close quarters, and the soldier standing over him, raising a knife and shouting an invocation. The blade plunged toward Ben.

Not a moment too soon, he swung his leg up and kicked his enemy in the knee. The blade cut the air as its owner faltered and stumbled to the ground. The soldier made a sound between a yelp of surprise and a feral snarl of anger. Recovering quickly, he fixed his eyes on Ben and growled with zealous rage. Ben raised his wrist-mounted gun and squeezed the thumb trigger. The weapon clicked ineffectually.

The Takathist laughed and swung the knife with light-ining speed. Ben recoiled fast enough to escape a killing blow, but still, cold steel sliced across his forehead, opening a line of biting pain that dripped with a warm, wet trickle of blood. Ben backpedaled away from a second wild swing. The Takathist took yet another wide, predictable attack. Ben ducked and lunged for his attacker's midsection, sending both crashing to the ground. The Takathist's blade clattered on the wood floor as it dropped. Seizing the opportunity, Ben tried to sprint away. The Takathist reached out with one hand, catching Ben's ankle and pulling him to the ground. With his other hand, the soldier reached for his blade. Ben lunged for it too, breaking the grip around his ankle and reaching the weapon with an infintessimally small lead. He closed his hand around the leather grip, raised the weapon, and swung it downward. It sank diagonally into the junction of the enemy's shoulder and neck. Vital arteries sprayed blood on Ben as his enemy died. In his last breath, the extremist muttered something in a venomous tone before slumping to the floor. Ben's breath was fast, and his heart pounded in his ears. As blood from his forehead started dripping into his eyes, he realized that he had sorely over-estimated his ability to help in the chaos of battle. He was untrained and had neglected to bring enough ammunition to defend himself. He stared blankly at the knife, soaked in blue, that he had used to end the life of an enemy. His fervor for battle died, overrun by fear and confusion. It was then he felt a hand on his shoulder. Terrified for a split second, he spun around and nearly slashed Javrel open with the weapon still in his hand. After wiping away the blood that was still dripping into his eyes, Ben saw him, his face contorted with worry. Celer floated around his head, streaked with soot and blue blood.

"Where's Seren?" Ben asked. He had lost track of her after the explosion.

"She's safe. Come on, I'm getting you out of this battle." Javrel closed a metal hand forcefully around Ben's upper arm and brought him to a medical station in the hallway. He placed him in front of a medic and said, "Check him for injuries, then keep him here. He was *supposed* to be under Thoral's orders to stay out of the battle."

The medic nodded and gave Ben a sharp look. "You are now under dual orders from Thoral, as commander, and me, as your attending medic, to remain in this ward for the duration of the battle. Do I make myself clear?"

"Yeah, got it. Now where's Seren? Is she okay?"

"Sit still, let me treat this wound," the medic said, wiping the blood of Ben's face.

"Now!"

The medic slapped on a piece of stinging, disinfectant-soaked gauze and a short piece of medical tape, then led Ben to another section of the tent. Seren, with a bandaged head wound of her own, glared at him. Ben beamed back.

"You're okay!" he said, rushing towards her. "After the explosion, I—"

"Ben, never do that again. I warned you what would happen."

"I know. I'm sorry."

"Good. I am glad you are safe."

After that, Seren was silent. Ben tried to stop thinking about the chaos of battle, but the gunfire was still too close to allow him any reprieve. Instead, he was trapped amidst the images of death and destruction imprinted on his mind. He listened to the gunfire and felt the fresh burn of memory even as the real battle faded. Visions of fire and the spraying of blood flashed before his eyes, with the shouts and screams echoing in his ears. He was jerked awake when he realized there was barely any gunfire outside. Now, there were only the sporadic shots of an enemy covering its retreat.

Javrel came into the medical area, all rage drained out of his face. He was absently rubbing an oiled rag into one of his metallic arm joints. He had pulled back his uniform sleeve, and Ben saw that he had no biological arm whatsoever, all the way up to the shoulder.

"Do you feel able to help the cleanup crews?" Javrel asked.

"Sure," Ben mumbled. Anything to occupy his mind was welcome now. He stood up and walked along with Seren, back to the now empty dining hall-turned-battlefield. The able-bodied survivors, a group that seemed pitiful and small compared to just one day before, were shoveling rubble, moving bodies, and trying to brace parts of the walls that threatened to collapse. The gaping hole gave a broad view of the destitute town surrounding Sildial's headquarters. So exposed, the dining hall was definitely not ready to be used again any time soon.

The bitter tang of burning chemicals and smoke filled Ben's nose. Outside, there were two giant fires, hissing, crackling orange suns blazing against the pitch-dark night sky. At one fire, Sildial agents wrapped dead Takathists in fuel-soaked paper and heaved the bodies onto the flame. At the other, they did the same thing to Sildial's dead, except with greater care. Silhouetted against the pyre, a man with a notebook took the names of each of the fallen, rescued their possessions, then sent them to the flame. Each body was heaved onto onto the mass pyre without any apparent ceremonial rites or reverence.

"Do you guys not have funerals or something?" Ben asked Javrel. "You just throw your dead in a big heap?"

"Perhaps your people attach a lot of importance to the body," Javrel said, "but for us, it's just another vessel for our essence. Sometimes we call death the 'second hatching.' We leave the body for something greater, just like we left the egg at our first hatching. Discarded eggshell, discarded body, same thing."

"That makes sense," Ben said. "But still, humans don't lay eggs."

"They don't?" Javrel asked. "Well then how do you— never mind. Let's go help with the cleanup."

Ben nodded, and Javrel called for two shovels for Ben and Seren. As they toiled to clean up the mounds of pulverized rubble, Ben let his mind sink into the monotony. Everything about the battle disappeared, and his thoughts and feelings simplified into the beating of his heart, the dull ache in his arms, and the repetivite motion of scooping up rubble, then depositing it in a nearby wheelbarrow. The simple, yet attention-consuming task helped him forget, though just for a few minutes, the carnage and death. However, the bloody sight and scorched scent of a stretcher being carried past reminded him of the battle. The body lying there had distinctive injuries that Ben had always hoped he would never see up close. It was covered in long, tortuous trails of burns, which charred the flesh black and melted straight through the synthetic uniform fabric. It was so covered in the gruesome, burnt patterning that barely any skin was left untouched.

"What are those?" Seren asked.

"Extreme magic burns," Ben said. He shivered at the sight. "That's what happens when a magic user gets completely burned out." He shuddered and rubbed his arms, remembering his own burns. And to think he had pushed his luck with magic *twice!* He resolved to be more careful in the future.

"He probably burned out trying to shield everyone from that explosion," Celer said. "I saw a couple others who went the same way he did."

"Then these men will have a special place in our celebration of the second-hatched," Javrel said. "They will be remembered well." He muttered a private Voleric prayer under his breath and went back to work. Ben was still impressed at how Javrel never showed effort, not even heavy breathing, as he shoveled more and more refuse into wheelbarrows to be carted away. The only sound that came from him as he worked was the occasional whine of motors under strain. Ben supposed that Javrel didn't deal with the same fatigue that was now overcoming him. Still, Ben liked watching the progress of his own work, and the work of those around him. He took comfort in watching mountains of rubble turn to hills, then scattered gravel and dust, and then disappear entirely. By late afternoon, the rubble was gone, leaving only the hole in the wall, irreparable charring, and a multitude of bullet entry holes in the walls. No magic had been used in the cleanup; all of the magic users had already reached or surpassed their safe limits during the battle. The rest of the day sat in a mournful, disoriented fog. A man who Javrel identified as Sildial's chaplain stood on the remnants of the stage and read the names of the dead, giving the belongings found on their bodies to friends, siblings, and spouses who came to claim them. Each claimant received a blessing and then moved off in stoic silence. After the reading, Ben watched from the sidelines as soldiers told stories and jokes about their departed friends. There was a thin mask of humor draped over the building. Because of the destruction of the front wall, someone had defaced the sign reading "Main Dining Hall," and replaced it with "Sildial Courtyard." Someone had played along with the joke and placed a few potted plants beneath the new sign. Ben didn't hold much hope that they would survive for long. Harsh, frosty air filled the space, heralding the bitter winter. As soon as the cleanup of rubble and bodies was complete, everyone retreated back into the heated parts of the building.

The sun was rising. Ben was tired, but accepted the small breakfast distributed among the fighters with gratitude. He, Seren and Javrel ate their dried fruit, smoked meat, and dry, chewy bread in silence.

"You three should get some sleep," Javrel said. "Thoral will deal with your disobedience when you wake, though."

"We understand," Seren said with finality. Satisfied, Javrel left. Once he was gone, Ben, Seren and Celer went to their rooms and all fell asleep within moments of lying down. Ben slept deeply and dreamlessly until about an hour after noon. He awoke then to find a note atop a stack of books, placed on his beside table, right next to his pillow. His first reaction was a twinge of fear at the idea that someone had entered his quarters unnoticed. He reached for the note, and Celer translated it:

Celer and Ben,

Thoral has put you two and Seren under <u>strict orders to remain in the dorm sector!</u> Thoral wants to speak with you when he is able, but you will only leave this area when escorted by his gray-banded Messenger, Dalivei. I left you some books, paper, and ink for if you become bored.

-From Javrel

Ben looked at the thick tomes, all with titles unreadable to him. Disinterested, he was relieved when he heard the knock on the door.

"Come in," Ben said. Seren entered quietly and sat down next to him on the edge of the bed.

"How are you feeling?" she asked.

"I'm still trying to sort everything out in my head," he said. "All of the death... I killed someone. I know he was trying to kill me too, but I can't help but wonder if he had a family. What are they doing now?"

"You will most likely never know," Seren said, "But ask that in regard to yourself. You are alive because of your actions, and your family did not have to lose you. And... I didn't, either. I care about you."

"I care about you, too," Ben said. "Not that I'm doing a good job acting like it. I know I was being an idiot when I went to the fight, and now we're probably going to be punished by Thoral. I'm sorry I put you in this position."

"Ben, I know you wanted answers before you were kidnapped, and I understand the need to help the people who helped us, but you must not do so recklessly."

"Yeah, seriously," Celer said. "You can't use answers that you got killed for. Be careful."

"I will, I promise," Ben said. He rubbed his arms, while seeing the haunting image of the soldier killed by his magic burns. He wanted badly to get that image out of his head.

Soon, Thoral's Messenger came floating down the corridor.

"Commander Thoral will see you now," he said. "Please, follow me." Ben, Celer and Seren followed the gray-banded Messenger up the familiar stairs to the Commander's office. They went inside and found that Kalar's pictures and awards had been removed, leaving only the blank, wood-paneled walls. Thoral sat behind the large desk, which was now clean, and empty except for a lamp, a small plant, and a single folder of files. Ben and Seren stood nervously before him, while Celer maintained a disciplined, stationary position floating over Ben's shoulder.

"Before I start," Celer translated from Thoral, "You should know I would hold you to much higher standards, and I would be well within my responsibilities to punish you, if you worked for Sildial. That being said, your conduct was extremely foolish. What in Idrazi's name possessed you to run onto that battlefield?"

"I thought I would be able to help," Ben said. "Seren told me not to go. She was being a good friend to help me, even though I didn't listen to her in the first place. I am sorry."

"Ben, no, I will share fault with you in this matter—"

"Celer, don't translate that," Ben said. "Seren, I'm grateful for what you did, even though it was against the rules. Just take this as a thank you, okay? Besides…" Ben searched for something that would convince her. "…arguing about this would be inefficient, because I'm not backing down." Seren nodded.

Thoral cleared his throat and pronounced his decree: "Ben, you will be required to help with all repair work and other upkeep of this building, until such time as you leave under the protection of a parent or other legal guardian. Between meals and work, you will not be allowed to leave your quarters. By the power given to me by the office of Commander of Sildial Radaejoraro, this decree is effective immediately." Ben nodded and waited to be dismissed to his new duties.

A Messenger flew into the office. It was different than others Ben had seen recently: It was not made with the blue cloth and thin yarn associated with Andarite Messengerwork.

Rather, it was made of heavy, brown cloth with a thick, seemingly woolen ribbon tied around the neck. Ben recognized it as the robust construction of a Messenger from the planet Daalronna.

"It seems," Thoral said, "that our resident enchanter would like to have a word with you. Dalivei will escort you."

"Okay…" Ben said. He turned to Seren. "I guess I'll see you at dinner?"

"Of course."

Ben, Seren, Celer and Dalivei left Thoral's office, walking together until Seren turned off towards her room. Ben and Celer continued following Dalivei until they reached a wooden door, indistinguishable from any other door in the building, except for the writing. Any other door in the area was marked with a vertical band of Voleric script on one side. This door, however, had horizontal writing inscribed on a bronze plaque set in the center. Ben immediately recognized the system: Traditional Daalronnan pictographs. Each glyph was a picture of an object, simplified into a collection of straight lines and small circles. He scrutinized the writing for a moment, trying to remember its meaning. The very first Messengers were made on Daalronna, and it was those first Daalronnan Messengersmiths who spread the craft to Wenifri, Andaros, Naris, and finally, Earth. They brought their language with them, making it the official language of Messengerwork, and so Dennison had required that Ben learn to speak and write Daalronnan. Most modern writers, however, often replaced the pictographs with the easier-to-use Wenifrin alphabet. He could speak and read fluently in the modern system, but he had to dig through his brain to find the meanings of the old symbols. After a moment, finally pieced together the meaning of the sign:

Daal-Na Kon-Ren An-Tun
Messengersmith

"Dennison never told me that An-Tun came here," Celer whispered.

Ben was equally surprised. Dennison's friend, Master Messengersmith and Representative of Daalronna on the Alliance Council Kon-Ren An-Tun, was working for Sildial? Dennison had also not told them that An-Tun had achieved the prestigious title of *Daal-Na* in service of Daalronnan culture. Ben could count the number of living recipients of the award on his fingers. He knocked on the door.

"Come in," a voice said in the Daalronnan language. Ben obliged, opening the door and stepping into the room. It was a large space, well lit by orbs of frosted glass emitting a homely yellow light. The walls and wide, stone-topped desk were densely packed with tools and materials, yet they displayed a clear and regimented organization. One entire wall was given over to small cubbyholes lined in many colors of silky cushions – Messenger resting places. At least a dozen Messengers of Daalronnan make were drifting about the room, but they all came over to Ben, forming a floating cloud of curiosity. At the desk, Kon-Ren An-Tun was pounding a pungent herb with a pestle and mortar. At seven feet tall, an average Daalronnan was an imposing presence compared to a human. An-Tun, like most Daalronnans, had sandy colored scales, small eyes with wrinkly eyelids, and the orifices of three breathing vents on each side of the oval head. He had four arms: a long, muscular upper pair for heavy work, and a short, dexterous lower pair for aiding in detailed tasks. An-Tun, however, was obviously not the picture of health. His scales were graying and pale, and his eyes were more deeply wrinkled and squinting than most. The glistening marks that crisscrossed his arms spoke of decades upon decades of complex magic usage. Most prominently, he sat on a cushioned, black wheelchair with a small Sildial insignia on the back. By now, An-Tun must have been over two hundred seventy five years old. He turned to look up from his mortar.

"Apprentice Ben! Celer! It's nice to finally meet you. I know I haven't been in communication with the Earth base for quite some time. Is Dennison well?"

"Um…"

"I suppose not, since he doesn't know whether or not his grandnephew is alive. The better question is, are you well?"

"I'm getting better, since the battle," Ben said in Daalronnan.

"Good," Celer said.

"That's good. However, Ben, I should tend to your magic burns."

Ben motioned to the herbs that An-Tun had been grinding. "Is that for the burns?"

"Anetan, yes. A traditional Daalronnan healing herb that will keep you from feeling the pain of the operation. It needs to be applied to all of the skin around the burn area, so I must ask you to remove your shirt." Ben complied, and An-Tun started the procedure, taking a sponge from a basin of hot water, and squeezing water over Ben's arms and back. He then took a wide brush and swirled it in the paste of Anetan. Up close, it was a sickly yellow-green color and smelled like badly soured milk. Ben's nose wrinkled up, and An-Tun chuckled. "I know people can find Daalronnan traditional medicine repulsive, but I think that is part of its effectiveness. I don't think you'll want to go burn your nerves again after this procedure." He continued laying the anesthetic thickly onto Ben's skin, surrounding Ben with a pungent aura. Already, numbness crept across the region where the Anetan had been applied. An-Tun said, "We will wait a few moments while the herb finishes sinking in."

Ben felt an uncomfortable question itching at his throat. "So, I know you were a Messengersmith..." he began.

"Yes, why?"

"During the attack, I didn't see anyone using the amount of magic a Messengersmith would be able to deal out. I know this is blunt, but... There were a lot of agents who died. Could you have helped?"

"I wish that I could have helped, but I have a nerve cancer found only in my species. It is why I am paralyzed from the waist down, as that is where the cancer is worst. Elsewhere, it interferes the steadiness of my hands, and with all but the smallest magical tasks. I can maintain Messengers when they are cut, torn, burned, and many other injuries of battle. I can do the smaller, finer enchantments, but unfortunately I have to send badly damaged Messengers to the Ziggurats in Darjae or Albir. My ailment, and *Thoral's orders,* kept me here during the battle."

"I'm sorry I asked," Ben said. "That was thoughtless of me."

"You have great capacity for caring, Ben, even for these freedom fighters you have only known for a few days," An-Tun said. "You should not apologize to anyone for standing up for those you care about. Now, I think that anesthetic has been sitting for long enough." An-Tun brought over a cup of familiar-looking needles soaking in a viscous blue fluid.

"Are those wolfdragon spines?" Ben asked.

"Debarbed, they work even better than the glass needles used on Daalronna for this procedure. Now, give me your burnt arm." Taking three of the needles, he grabbed Ben's arm firmly, and swiftly jabbed them in. Ben winced unnecessarily, as the medicated needles went into his numb flesh with only a small, itchy tingle. The process went on, each needle used only once, then discarded. "I have heard rumors from Messengers," An-Tun said, "but I would like to hear the story of how you got such *extensive* magic burns!" He listened intently as Ben related the Iyerani attack that forced him and Seren together, summarized their time in the wilderness, and told of their arrival in Joraw. At the end An-Tun said, "You and Seren know more about our plight than many

Andarites of your age. Now that you are no longer trying to evade KTAN, I can help you find Dennison. He and your parents must be terribly worried. Surely when your parents let you go to the Festival, they weren't expecting you to be chased by criminal aliens."

Ben felt a sharp pang of worry for his parents. In the chaos and violence of his adventure, he had barely thought about how much he missed them. What he wouldn't give to see them now, he thought. The recent events were more than he had bargained for when he stepped through the worm-hole into Alarzi. "I miss them a lot," he said. "I don't even know where Dennison is, though. How will you find him?"

"Once Neralja finally managed to force my exit from government service, I lost my security clearance, so I can't send Messengers directly to the Earth base. My Messengers haven't been able to find Dennison here on Andaros. However, Celer has the proper military clearance, if I remember the charter correctly. Has he ever made a stellar jump?"

"No, I haven't," Celer said.

"That's fine. You can piggyback on Qan's energy field." An-Tun motioned to a large Messenger of brown cloth. "As long as she stays near the Sun, there should be no problem with Celer crossing to Earth alone and alerting the base staff about Ben's whereabouts."

A borad smile overtook Ben's face even before An-Tun had finished speaking. "I can't wait!" he said. "Thank you, thank you so much." Suddenly the cluttered room, the pungent smell of Anetan, and even the needles plunging periodically into his arm, seemed distant, like Ben had begun waking from a long, unpleasant dream. He could stop running, and fighting, and wondering who could be trusted and who couldn't. Just a few hours, An-Tun had said, and then he would be reunited with Dennison, and they could return home to where things were certain, stable, and peaceful.

"I am finished with the procedure." An-Tun said after wrapping Ben's arm in clean cloth bandages. "You can go now, but for the gods' sakes, don't use magic for a few days! Let those burns heal. Now, go down to the dining hall. Even if it is only for a few hours, I understand that you have some orders from Thoral to fulfill."

"Oh! I almost forgot!" Ben said, still joyful. "Thank you again, Daal-Na."

"I'll go with you," Celer said. "I should say bye to Seren before I lead Dennison here."

Ben nodded, then went to the door and down the hall, almost forgetting to wait for Dalivei, his escort. He nearly bounded as he went down to the front wall. There, he found a job carrying stones to the repair workers. The numbness of the anesthetic was replaced with the numbness of excitement, and no pain of exertion touched his mind. He was going home, to familiar plants and animals, twenty-four hour days, his family, and his destiny to be a Messengersmith.

"What did the enchanter have to say?" Seren asked, surprising Ben as she walked over, carrying a bag of mortar powder to one of the bricklayers.

"He fixed up my magic burns," Ben said, "and he said he was helping find my uncle Dennison. I'll be able to go home by tonight!"

"That's wonderful, Ben!" Seren said, with a smile that seemed to die just as soon as it had blossomed on her lips.

"Don't worry," Ben said, "Dennison's a Messengersmith, and that means he has a lot of connections in the Alliance. We'll find your parents and you can go home, too."

"Thank you very much for your concern," she said. "I am happy that you will be going back home, where you belong. I wish you a long, prosperous life. I will be remaining here to work with Sildial."

"What?" Ben asked. "What about your home? You have family on Iyerayñan, don't you?"

"My parents sent me here unaccompanied. They work long hours at a food processing plant, barely seeing me except for short, infrequent vacation periods. At home, everything feels cold and dead. Efficiency and productivity have strangled the love and beauty from our lives. Here there is still life, and love, and so much more beauty than on Iyerayñan, but this life is threatened. Ben, you deserve to go home to your family and enjoy all the beauty Earth has to offer you. I have to stay here and do what I can to help."

Ben's hopes crumbled and died. Returning to Earth would mean abandoning his friend to the suffering of Andaros. The prospect sickened him. He said, "I want to be someone who deserves all those things, but I won't be if

I leave you here alone. If you're staying, we are too. Right, Celer?"

"Of course."

"No, Ben, you must not. I cannot be responsible if you die here."

"And how do you think I've feel if you died, and I did nothing?" Ben asked.

"Celer," Seren said, "You must know how dangerous this is."

"Yeah, and I know it's only going to get more dangerous if you have no translator. I'm the only one who can go back to Earth, because I'm the only Messenger here with security clearance for the base. Ben and I won't leave until I say so."

"There is nothing that can convince you to leave me?" Ben smiled. "Nope."

Seren shook her head. "I won't argue any further, but I hope you reconsider."

"Sorry," Ben said.

"We need to tell An-Tun," Celer said.

When Ben and Celer arrived back in An-Tun's office, Ben explained, "Seren is staying here. We're her friends. We can't leave."

"She will be working with the entirety of Sildial," An-Tun said. "She won't be alone."

"Who's going to translate Voleric for her?" Celer asked. "You're busy enough doing Messenger maintenance."

"You've seen the death and suffering here," An-Tun said. "You could not seriously wish to remain here when you could be comfortable at home."

Ben felt a wave of nausea at the idea of going back into combat, but he pushed it back. "It's not about what I want anymore. I know I have to be here for her."

"She can do this on her own, Ben," An-Tun said. "She is strong enough."

Ben slammed his fist on the desk. "I know that! She's stronger than me! More disciplined! But I can't just sit around on Earth studying classic literature and memorizing the thread counts of good Messenger cloth while my friend is out here being shot at!"

"Please, Ben, calm down," An-Tun said. "You're making this decision so hastily." He placed a placating hand on Ben's shoulder, but Ben pushed it away.

"How could you even think that?" Ben shouted. "Whether or not I should help my friend, who is in mortal danger, isn't up for debate! I don't have to contemplate that. It's wrong for me to sit around when I could be helping her."

"I have the greatest respect for you, Daal-Na, but honestly, you can't force me to make that stellar jump," Celer said.

An-Tun was silent for a while. Finally, he said, "You fully understand the risks involved, up to and including permanent disability and death?"

"Yes," Ben and Celer said simultaneously.

"And are you willing to obey the orders you are given?"

"Yes."

An-Tun nodded, then reached for a paper and pen from his desk. "Very well, then. Sildial needs as many people of loyal character as we can get. I will have your service recommendations to Thoral by tonight."

CHAPTER 9

It took several more days for the work crews to rebuild Sildial's headquarters, rebuilding the front wall, mending the outer fence, and getting several damaged armored vehicles back in working order. Ben went to bed aching every night, awoke with stiff muscles, and went back to work. He awoke one morning and saw a pile of items on his bedside table. There was a uniform, a stack of books, and a short sword. Along with these items was a terse note in unfamiliar handwriting:

> *Commander Thoral has changed your orders. Be in the*
> *main training room next to the firing range, in squad uniform,*
> *2 baoguvi after breakfast.*
> *-Vuri Darialaro*

"Baoguvi?" Ben asked.

"Time measurement," Celer replied. "We have about half an hour until we have to be there."

Ben nodded, and began looking over what Javrel's sister had sent. He started his examination of the delivery at the books. Celer translated the titles. "*Voleric Grammar Reference*, and Deidhoi Veraro's *Mythic History of Dawta Volaero.*"

"They want me to learn Voleric now?" Ben said with a sigh. "Well, I guess we can't avoid it if we want to help out around here."

Ben picked up the sword. The crossguard was small, offering protection barely to the edges of Ben's hand. He slid off the scabbard of black, scaly leather, revealing a bright, reflective steel blade that tapered to a sharp point. The weapon was simple, yet elegant in a manner of stream-lined practicality; unadorned by any decoration, the sword was a refined, effective tool for close combat. Ben sheathed it slowly and carefully in admiration of its craftsmanship. Next, he looked at the neatly folded uniform that had been left for him. Unlike the one he had been given on his arrival, this one had a design embroidered in deep green thread on the left shoulder. Encircled in calligraphy was an animal Ben recognized all too well. The huge reptile Ben, Seren and Celer had encountered in the forest, of ursine shape and covered in armorlike scales, was posed in a terrifying posture of aggression on the sleeve. Mouth open and lined in deep blood-blue, the creature leaned forward towards an unseen enemy.

"Fierce insignia," Celer said.

"No kidding," Ben replied. "I think we've earned it, though!"

Celer laughed. "I'd say so. Now go on, wash up and change so we're not late. If we have extra time you can start learning the Voleric alphabet."

"You sound just like Mom..." Ben said, chuckling. "'Don't be late for your first day of boot camp, Ben! Make sure you do your homework!'" Celer sighed and gave off light waves of yellow amusement and orange annoyance. Still, Ben obliged, going to the stalls and washing himself with the soap, cloth, and basins of scalding hot and freezing cold water. The temperatures invigorated him. Once finished, he changed into the squad uniform and admired the new look in the reflective surface of the Andarite sword. Not in the mood to begin wrestling with an alien alphabet, Ben decided to leave his quarters early and see if Javrel was down at the training area already. He was, along someone Ben guessed was Vuri, Javrel's sister, who had been on a mission since before Ben had arrived. She had pale blue horns that matched with faint swirls on her frill. She was slightly taller than Javrel, and had none of his robotic prosthetics. Twisting, gnarled magic burn scars covered her arms. They were years old, but were far more severe than anything Ben had ever incurred. The scars were prominent as Vuri shadowboxed in the corner, thoroughly destroying an imaginary opponent with a martial art composed of kicks, knees, elbow strikes, and the occasional dive forward, horns aimed for a goring blow. The entire display, Ben imagined, would be brutal when brought down on a real opponent. Vuri paused as she heard Ben and Celer enter.

"*Vadzi*," she said.

"Greetings," Celer translated, as Vuri continued, "Thoral wants you to get used to speaking Voleric," Vuri continued. "I'm your squad leader, Vuri Darialaro. Javrel's sister. Arwi, where are you?"

A Messenger with a green neckband and wide, round eyes flew to Vuri from another part of the room. "Here! Are these the trainees? Hi, I'm Arwi. Nice to meet you."

The recruits smiled and made introductions.

"Are we the only recruits?" Celer asked.

"The only ones for quite a while," Vuri replied. "And of course, the only Earth-spawn to ever join us. Welcome, all three of you." Ben turned around to see Seren walking in, looking battle-ready in her new uniform, and wearing a focused, hard expression. She had cut her hair since it had grown out during the trek, returning it to the short style she had worn when Ben and Celer had met her. Ben smiled at her in silent greeting, and she returned the gesture. Moments later, Javrel came in, wearing a matching squad uniform. Upon entering, he saluted Vuri, placing one hand flat on his chest, thumb pointing upward so its tip touched the base of his throat. Vuri returned the salute.

"Welcome to Daolor Squad," Vuri said. She tapped the embroidery on her shoulder, which displayed the same beast as was on Ben's uniform. "I heard from Javrel that you three have already met our namesake animal. Before we begin, I would like to make a few things clear. Until now, you were guests and were to be treated like it. Now, you are members of this organization, and you will be treated like it." Her voice took on a sudden, surprising harshness. "I am here to give you the necessary strength and skill to throw alien invaders off of this planet! *Rovidzi jevalval!* Trainees, salute!"

Javrel snapped back to attention and performed the salute. Ben and Seren imitated him. Once she was satisfied with their form, Vuri saluted back.

"In our faith, Audir placed the soul in the throat. To point to your throat in this salute is to place your life and your soul in the hands of the people fighting alongside you. Do not forget that this is what it means to be a part of a Sildial squad.

That's enough talk for now. Form up, we're headed outside!" Javrel and Vuri broke into a jog, heading for the door out of the training room. Ben and Seren followed, falling in line just behind them. They took the elevator up to the ground floor, then jogged out through the repaired dining hall. The air hit them like a wash of cold water, and as the four ran, they chased the white clouds of their own condensing breath. Around them, the already desolate city of Joraw seemed even deader in the biting cold. Broken windows were infected with creeping, white frost, which did not glisten under the thickly cloudy sky.

Arwi was laughing and flying in an erratic, loopy pattern around Vuri's head.

"What's so funny?" Celer asked.

"The land-walkers are stuck down here in this weather, but we get to do flight exercises! Come on, Earthie! Let's go!"

The final 'o' carried joyfully into the air as Arwi flew up into the cloudy sky. Celer followed, rocketing headfirst into the clouds within seconds of launching himself from near the ground.

Catching up with Arwi, Celer accelerated up through the thinning atmosphere until they reached orbital velocity. The Messengers sensed the great flow of magic around them, propelling them up and up into the free, starry blackness. Once the Messengers of Daolor Squad felt the loss of gravity, and the accompanying freedom from the concepts of up and down, they paused. Celer glanced around, taking in the view. Below him, he could see the entirety of Andaros. The small continents, narrow straits and seas, and swirls of white clouds appeared to have been painted onto the surface, for they were so deceptively tranquil from such an altitude. Farther out, the Andarites' yellow home star was a lantern on the nighttime sea, casting bright, comforting light that was inevitably swallowed by the black void beyond. The void was populated by stars, thrown like handfuls of glittering sand onto black silk, not twinkling as they did when seen through an atmosphere. In the calm and silence of a weightless orbit, the sight was grand to behold.

"Wow, I haven't been in orbit for a while," Celer said.

"It never gets old, does it?" Arwi said, giggling. The Messengers' speech was now transmitted by waves of magic. Sound would have been useless in the void, for it depended on an atmosphere to carry vibrations.

"Makes me feel bad for the land-walkers every time," Celer said. "They have to hide in their air suits and launch cans."

Arwi laughed again. "Launch cans, ha! Good one."

"Have you ever seen the Wenifrins build a fast space-ship?" Celer asked.

"No... *But neither have they!*" They both cackled madly and tossed off a few more scathing quips. To Messengers, the concept of technological spaceflight was absurd. The craft themselves were noisy, cumbersome and could barely navigate compared to small, agile Messengers. Besides, spacecraft could barely accelerate to a tenth of light speed with days of thrust, let alone half or more in a few minutes.

"You're early," said a voice coming from below. Celer and Arwi looked down towards Andaros to see a blue-banded Messenger approaching them.

"I am Yadho," he said. "Thoral assigned me to train Celer and to sharpen Arwi's skills. We should begin our first circuit of the star." Without waiting for an answer, he sped off, and the Messengers felt the waves of magic throwing him through the starry depths. Celer and Arwi followed close behind, rapidly accelerating through the flow of magic until they were pushing the upper limits of their speed, over half the speed of light. Huge cones of magic stabbed out in front of them, pushing aside micrometeors, motes of gas, and other tiny, invisible particles that could impart deadly force if impacted at such high speeds. They dodged any larger particles with their immensely fast reflexes.

Up ahead, the star around which Andaros orbited threw immense magical energy into deep space. The Messengers drew closer, reaching the closest safe distance in just under half an hour of the fastest flight possible. Back on Andaros, magic had washed over Celer like a morning mist, damp and cool, yet calm and unobtrusive. Here, Celer had just stuck his head under the full force of ten Niagara Falls. The feeling of being this close to the source of a star system's magic, the very life force of all the Messengers, was euphoric past the limits of human understanding. It had taken many small excursions to the Sun in years past for Celer to master the feeling, and not let himself plunge thoughtlessly into the deadly ball of plasma. Yadho barely paused before taking a sharp turn towards the star's northern pole, then doubling back along his original course and shooting back towards Andaros. Soon the three passed the little green planet by, hurtling off towards a gas giant that grew slowly in their fields of view. The orb of bright purple and deep red gas was surrounded by glittering rings, like ripples on the deep black sea. Close up, the tranquil ripples were actually belts made of huge chunks of rock, iron and water ice. Floating inside the ring and dodging the occasional ice boulder, Celer stared at the planet's sporadic flashes of lighting as electrical storms prowled around the thick atmosphere.

"Can we go in?" Celer asked, mesmerized by the colorful, flashing display.

"Not in that weather," Yadho replied.

"The view from inside is all dark and cloudy," Arwi said. "It's much prettier up here.

"We're wasting time," Yadho said tersely. "Follow me. We're doing agility exercises today."

"Wait, how do you define 'today' in a context where there's no rotating planet to define day and ni—Hey! Wait up!" Celer called, as Yadho and Arwi were already far ahead, darting around boulders and dust clouds like fish in a dense reef. Celer followed, trying to match the experienced Messengers' speed. As they accelerated, he had to follow faster and faster. The time of straight flight between dodging meteors became shorter and shorter as he sped up, until he was at the very upper limit of his reflexes and focusing intently on not running into things. He no longer had breaks between dodges; he dove and weaved, bobbing continuously between ice chunks and rocks. For a moment, he looked far ahead to regain his sight on Yadho and Arwi. Distracted, he impacted with a small ice shard. He felt a sharp, overwhelming burn, like his head had been torn open and it was being filled with molten metal. Shocked by the immensity of it, he ricocheted off into empty space without the awareness to realize what was happening and stop himself. Space spun madly around him, stars drawing long, blurred lines, occasionally interrupted by the fleeting purple blotch of the ringed planet. Finally, he regained enough focus to steady himself in space. His vision was blurry and imprecise, but he could see the other two Messengers flying out to meet him.

"What happened?" Arwi asked. "Are you alright? I told Vuri you probably weren't ready for the asteroid field! I'm sorry, if we——"

"I'm okay," Celer said, though he listed to one side. "I think I burned out a shielding enchantment, though."

"It was unwise to bring you out this early," Yadho said. "We will go directly to the Ziggurat at Darjae and have the spent threads replaced. You will share our protective cones for the return trip." Arwi and Yadho stayed just inches away from Celer as the three flew away from the gas giant, letting it shrink into a tiny light in the distance behind them. Re-entry was a careful, controlled descent, spiraling wide so as not to burn up in the atmosphere. Joraw, the mountains, and the marshes were far off on the horizon as the three Messengers descended to a city set among wide, rolling hills of windy grassland. The air was warmer; winter did not have the courage to spread frost so far south. Across the fields far below, unidentifiable beasts roamed in single-minded herds. From such a height it was impossible to pick out their individual forms.

Soon, the Messengers arrived at the proud, sprawling city of Darjae, growing out of the ground like a forest of metal, brick and stone. The roughly circular city surrounded a hill, atop which stood a grand Ziggurat. These Ziggurats were the centerpieces of the greatest cities all around the Alliance. Rising hundreds of feet into the air, the many-terraced structure dominated the skyline and reflected the light of the sun off every one of its polished surfaces. It was constructed of tan stone, so precisely cut and finely polished that it was impossible to tell where each building block ended and the next began. On its many levels, the building held aloft gardens and courtyards, intermingled with walkways of the same tan stone. Inside the building, Celer knew that Messengersmiths, city government leaders, and foreign dignitaries would be housed on the upper levels. Below them were many secretaries and recordkeepers, and in the deepest bowels of the building would be the craftsmen who made glass, cloth, and yarn to be made into Messengers by the Messengersmiths. A powerhouse of politics, craftsmanship, and magic, the Ziggurat was the nexus of power dominating the entire city.

As the three flew in, the city welcomed them with an open atmosphere: The buildings were spaced well apart and decorated with flowerbeds and trees. Streets with wide sidewalks bustled with foot traffic and a number of different varieties of man-powered vehicles. There were no motorized vehicles or anything similar to cars or motorcycles. As they flew closer to the Ziggurat, Celer saw another grand building, five stories tall and occupying the equivalent of an entire city block. Made entirely of white stone and wide windows, the building's exterior was decorated with bright, calligraphic tapestries.

"Is… Is that… what I think it is?" Celer said, pausing to look back at the building.

"Yes," Yadho said. "Behold the Grand Library of Darjae."

"Is it true that the library contains every piece of litera-ture ever created on Andaros?" Celer asked.

"No, but really close," Arwi said. "The library has bet-ter security than the house of the Legislative Assembly, or the palaces of the nobility. There are sitting rooms with re-ally comfy couches because you can't remove books from the building. They all have to be read inside. It's Dawta Volaero's greatest cultural treasure."

"Can we go in?" Celer asked.

"We are already late in returning to Joraw," Yadho said. "Another day, when Thoral grants you a day of leave. I will return to Joraw now so that Vuri knows what happened. Arwi, go with Celer to the Ziggurat."

"Fine," Arwi said, flicking her tail dismissively at Yadho as she flew away. Celer took a glance back at the magnifi-cent library as he followed, still longing to go inside. He and Arwi flew to the Ziggurat and ascended to its higher tiers, then entered through a small, round, magical door above one of the land-walkers' doors, which opened auto-matically once it detected the Messengers in close range. Inside, Arwi navigated the halls, marked clearly with signs to Messengersmiths' workshops, clerical offices, and stair-ways to the lower floors. She led Celer to an office about the size of a shoebox, set neatly into the wall and manned by a Messenger clerk.

"Do you have an appointment?" the clerk asked.

"No. I was wondering if you could fit in a procedure today. My friend here has a burn to his anterior shock protection enchantment. Rammed right into a boulder in the rings of Telliar."

"Oh, my. I'll see if there's a Messengersmith who can take him." The Messenger clerk took off down the hall and returned a few moments later. "Messengersmith Veildir can see you now." Celer followed the clerk down the hall and into a Messengersmith's workshop. He entered, lying down on a table covered in silky white fabric.

"Name?" asked an Andarite man, staring over a clipboard, pen in hand.

"Celer."

"Burn to the anterior shock protector?" he asked.

"That's right."

"Got it. This won't take too long. I'm going to disable your tactile enchantments so you won't feel a thing." The Messengersmith picked up a polished wooden talisman in the shape of a teardrop, then tapped the tapered end at several places around Celer's head. Celer didn't feel anything as the Messengersmith drew a razor blade across his head, breaking his cloth skin in a clean line. Out of the corner of his eye, Celer saw the Messengersmith drawing a long strand of black, crumbly ribbon out of his head and dropping it into a small metal bucket. The Messengersmith found a wooden box and took out another ribbon, unburned and intact, and started feeding it delicately into Celer's head. The ribbon, made of blue cloth and marked with golden lines, held the same enchantment that Celer had burned out.

"So, where are you from?" the Messengersmith asked.

"Joraw," Celer replied. "With Sildial."

"Do you… work for them?" the Messengersmith asked reluctantly, almost disbelievingly.

"Just started. The Iyeranis attacked my friends and me in Alarzi, and then…" Celer related the most important details of his adventures to the Messengersmith.

"Quite a tale," the Messengersmith said, nearly whispering.

"You don't believe me?" Celer snapped.

"I believe every word, Celer," he said, "but these Iyeranis are little more than organized criminals. Maybe strong in places like Joraw, but they are well controlled here, and in any city where police forces are organized and strong."

"But I've seen them!" Celer shouted, his shrill call piercing the walls of the workshop. "They've kidnapped my friends and used Takathist fighters in their forces! They're more dangerous than you know!"

"Celer, try to stay calm while the procedure is going on. You sound like that vagrant who's been wandering from city to city, spouting end-of-times nonsense like a false prophet."

"Who's that?" Celer asked.

"I can't recall his name exactly. If I didn't know he was a fellow Andarite, however, I would have thought you were him. His name is similar to yours, Kilyur or Koler or something like that. He has a little gang of homeless people who run around with him, shouting about how the Iyeranis are about to destroy the world, and brandishing guns at whoever derides him. He's made some very wild accusations. People say that he's charismatic, but it's a bit hard to give credit to someone who does nothing but wander the streets and shout about how Andaros is doomed if they don't do as he says."

"He sounds like a maniac," Celer said. The Messengersmith's face betrayed smugness, like he believed that he had convinced Celer to give up his fight. Celer wanted to knock that look off of his face. "But, he has a point! The Iyeranis *are* stronger and more numerous than you know. Homeless or not, that guy knows his facts."

The Messengersmith scowled. "You're young, and I'm sure this experience has been stressful for you. I have been on Andaros for my whole life. I admit we have some economic troubles and crime is higher than anyone would like. However, KTAN is not an invasion force, and they are well contained inside a few hopeless cities. You and your friends should leave Joraw, take the opportunity to visit our fine library, and go home."

"I—" Celer stopped. Aggravated, he hissed and allowed himself to bathe in his own aura of red light, darting angrily around his body. The rest of the procedure passed in bitter silence, interrupted only by the dull, feathery rustle of ribbon passing through the Messengersmith's fingers. Finally, the Messengersmith drew another talisman from his table full of tools, drawing it slowly across the gaping wound in Celer's head. Where it touched, the fabric drew itself together and closed seamlessly, as if the incision had never been made. A moment later, Celer's sense of touch returned. He lifted himself off the silky tabletop and turned to face the

Messengersmith. He forced a nimbus of happy yellow light around his body.

"Thank you, Messengersmith Veildir," he said, bowing his head slightly.

"Any time," Veildir said. "Have a good day, and good travels homeward."

"Yeah," Celer said dryly. "Have fun... um... not worrying about stuff. Thanks. Bye."

Without another thought, Celer shot out the door, finding his way back to the small Messenger door and flying out into the cool air. Red-orange sparks jumped from his form as he met Arwi high above the Ziggurat.

"Are you alright?" she asked.

"Yeah," he replied. "Just an annoying Messengersmith. Nothing to get angry about. How do I look, by the way?" Celer turned down so the top of his head faced Arwi.

"Like it never even happened," Arwi observed. "Wait a minute, why didn't we just go see Ben to get that fixed?"

"It's not like he carries the right talismans around with him all the time. Dennison hasn't even given him his own set yet. Now come on, let's go back."

While the Messengers were away, Vuri led the squad through a punishing routine of physical training: Running, crawling, jumping, arm and core exercises, all outside in the snow. Ben's lungs felt parched as he breathed in the dry winter air. He and Seren were sweating in their uniforms. The moisture chilled them to the bone in the whipping wind, but Vuri didn't seem to care about their chattering teeth as she pushed her recruits through her routine. Not much could be done without Celer's translation, but Vuri could shout and pantomime simple actions well enough to keep them moving through the workout.

"Halt," Vuri called in Voleric. They had heard the command enough times to recognize it. Bent over, hands on knees, the recruits shivered and gasped for breath. Vuri was watching the Messengers come back down through the clouds.

"We're moving on," she said once Celer was back to translate. "But go into the dining hall first and warm up. I'm not going to kill you two. Yet." She cackled and sprinted off back into the headquarters building. Ben and Seren followed at a slow jog, then sat down for warm drinks in the dining hall. Snow on their uniforms melted and puddled at their feet. Ben gulped down the last of his steaming mug when Vuri called, "Move out."

"How much do you keep below ground?" Seren asked as they took an elevator down.

"Anything dangerous or anything that needs really good defense. We're going to the firing range, which is on the level closest to the surface." The elevator doors slid open with a soft hiss and a definitive *clunk*. Vuri led the way down a hall, to a thick metal door with bright orange Voleric lettering going down both sides of the frame. Javrel handed out safety goggles and ear protection. Ben struggled for a moment to figure out how to put the goggles on correctly. It didn't help that the straps had been fitted to accommodate the wide head frill of an Andarite. Javrel spotted him having a hard time, and took the glasses. Going around to Ben's back, Javrel pulled deftly on the many straps until they were fitted snugly on Ben's head.

Once the protective equipment was secure, the group entered the firing range. The long room had accommodations for an impressive twenty shooters at a time. It was all gray stone and dull metal, except for the targets, which were paper silhouettes on metal clips. Standing out from the black silhouette was a series of red markings on the head and chest: the locations of lethal shots.

Vuri unlocked a cabinet and pulled out guns for each of them. "Javrel tells me that you're already familiar with these," she said. Ben laughed sheepishly.

Vuri popped the magazine out of the gun, showing Ben that it was made of two metal cylinders fused along their length. "Liquid propellant goes in this side," she said, indicating the right cylinder, "and solid shot goes in this one," indicating the left cylinder. "Now, let me see you shoot."

"Sure." Ben slipped the weapon onto his arm, then secured the straps so the weapon fit snugly around it. Vuri demonstrated that rotating the chamber at the rear cocked the weapon. She showed Ben how to sight down his arm. When Ben affirmed he was ready, Vuri gave him permission to place his thumb on the trigger and fire. There was a flash of light, a harsh recoil, and a bitter, sour smell in the air after he fired. Ben looked at the target, an Iyerani shape about ten feet away. The shot had just grazed the silhouette's arm. Ben fired again, and this time saw the spark of the projectile as it hit the sloped back of the firing range, missing the target entirely.

"You thought you could fight off extremists with that aim?" Vuri said. "I wouldn't expect a Messengersmith to use a tech-weapon anyway. No recoil on a magical fighting staff, right?"

Ben laughed and unstrapped the weapon from his arm, then handed it to Seren. She didn't perform much better than he did. However, when Vuri said she wouldn't mind her taking a third shot, she managed to place the round in the target Iyerani's right chest.

"Nice shot," Ben said.

"Not a fatal injury," Seren said.

"What do you mean? You hit him right in the heart!"

"Iyeranis' circulatory systems are very different from humans'. They do not really have hearts as you understand them."

"How do you kill them, then?" Ben asked.

"Shot in the head or lungs," Javrel said. He took a gun from the cabinet, then walked over to the firing line and aimed. He fired three shots, piercing the target twice through the chest and once perfectly through the center of the head.

"How long did it take you to practice that?" Ben asked, amazed. Javrel laughed and waved his metal arms in the air.

"Barely any. Just mechanical accuracy. Being part-robot does have its perks, you know."

"People must hate playing darts with you!" Celer said.

"Yeah, no kidding. Keep practicing."

They practiced at the range for a while. Seren's bullet holes were quite scattered across the head and chest of the Iyerani-shaped target, but her spreads were still smaller than Ben's. At least Seren had managed to place all of her shots on the target.

"Have you practiced with one of these before?" Ben asked Seren, after he had barely nicked the corner of the paper.

"Never, except my attempt to rescue you, and during the attack," she replied. "I think, however, I am taking more time to observe my mistakes."

"Thanks," Ben said. As soon as his burns had fully healed, he resolved to start training with magic, rather than keep dealing with this. He kept firing until his target was perforated all over, and looked enviously at Seren's smaller, cleaner placement of shots.

"That's enough target practice for today," Vuri said. She led them to another part of the training area; a room empty except for a few punching bags, its floor made of a dense foam that yielded only slightly underfoot. Javrel withdrew four swords from a small rack on the wall, all identical to Ben's except for the thick rubber edges on the blades. He handed one each to Ben, Seren, and Vuri, and then he and Vuri moved to the center of a circle marked in white on the floor. Taking up positions opposite to each other, they saluted by raising the swords above their heads, then dove into an unrestrained flurry of combat. The action was fast, blades flashing back and forth without hesitation. The siblings matched each other strike for strike while maintaining carefully measured stances. Ben tried to focus on the movement of blades until he was overwhelmed and the line between attacks, parries, ripostes and more parries blurred into a single, fluid yet chaotic display. Giving up on trying to follow, Ben noticed how dulled the sound of rubber-edged swords clashing was. The absence of a satisfying, dramatic clash of metal on metal made the spectacle oddly surreal. The sparring stopped with a suddenness Ben hadn't expected. Vuri, eyes slitted with focus and determination, stood with her arm outstretched, sword hovering just below Javrel's chin.

"Just because my brother's a robotic hotshot on the firing range doesn't mean he's the best fighter here. That's me. Well, if the records from the intramural sparring club have anything to say about it. Let's see how you newbies do!" She and Javrel retreated from the ring, leaving Seren and Ben to take the center.

Seren asked, "Shouldn't we receive some formal instruction before being asked to—"

"Just fight. I'll correct you when you need it, as I'm sure you will."

Seren complied, a scowl crossing her face for a single moment. Then her face froze over and she fixed Ben with that signature look that made him feel like he was about to be dissected. Ben felt creeping dread grasp at his insides, knowing that the most intelligent, calculating mind he had ever met was about to face him in combat. He became doubly glad that the rubberized swords were only meant for training. Seren raised the sword above her head as she had seen Javrel and Vuri do, and Ben followed suit. Ben and Seren stared at each other, each tempting the other to strike.

She knows you're reckless, Ben thought, not daring to take the first strike. A few seconds stretched painfully on as neither combatant acted. Ben's fingers tightened almost imperceptibly around the handle of the sword as he prepared to attack. *Almost* imperceptibly. Seren seized the moment and swung hard and fast at Ben's side. He moved to block, but Seren's blade dropped slightly, missing the parry and continuing on to his chest. She missed by centimeters as Ben made a swift, last minute block and stabbed towards Seren's chest. She parried and retreated, back foot touching the edge of the ring. She lunged forward and delivered a wide, arcing strike over her head, and it came down upon Ben's blade, raised in a parry. She overwhelmed him with three more rapid strikes, and Ben felt like there was no technique, only reflexes, saving him from the blade. Seren paused and retreated, cold eyes fixed unwaveringly on Ben. He rushed at her, swinging wide. Seren dodged then slid a foot into Ben's trajectory. He tripped and fell, his head and shoulders landing outside the white circle. His forehead smacked the foam floor, which was soft enough to save his skull, but dense enough to remind him not to fall on the ground again.

A moment later, he felt the point of Seren's sword pressing into his neck.

"Spinal cord severed, opponent killed," she summarized.

"That… was not fair," Ben said, pushing himself up from the ground.

"We're not playing this for sport, Ben," Vuri said. "Life or death. Seren gets that, and fights like an Iyerani to boot. She observes *everything*. Besides, you swing that weapon like you're drunk. We could all see you preparing your attacks a mile off. And Seren, don't get cocky. You're just as sloppy as him, just a bit more clever."

Seren nodded. Vuri put her and Ben through a few more bouts, interspersed with repetitive drills and a few shouted, profane admonishments. When their arms already burned from repetition and exertion, Vuri demanded that they both spar against her before stopping bladework for the day. She was merciless, and left both Ben and Seren feeling like incompetent civilians in under thirty seconds each. Then she ordered Daolor Squad to take two laps around the compound. Both humans lagged behind and finished with cheeks bright red, both from the cold air and the exertion. They gulped water as it was provided to them in the dining hall, then Vuri ordered them down to the library.

"Celer, you can take over from here?" she asked.

"Yep."

"Don't even think about going easy on them."

"Oh, I won't. Ben, Seren, grab your books. Language time."

From training until dinner, Celer lectured and drilled the Voleric language into Ben and Seren's heads, starting with a few basic phrases and the writing system, and then lunging ahead into a monstrous table of noun suffixes that governed most objects in the language. Voleric nouns, Ben learned, could end in 22 different suffixes depending on their role in the sentence, some of which only differed by a single accent mark. Celer wanted them to know the first ten by the end of the session: The singular and plural forms of the genitive, dative, benefactive, malefactive, and allative cases. Ben struggled to get past Dative, while Seren had the suffixes and their usage summaries memorized with time to spare. At the end of the session, Celer dictated the first list of vocabulary, which Ben and Seren wrote down to be memorized later. Most of them were benign, household terms, but Celer ended the list with *gun, sword, attack, retreat, enemy.*

"Vuri says you won't go into battle until she can trust you without a translator. We should go to dinner, and then you two had better study until you go to bed."

Ben felt queasy. He didn't know how long it would take for him to even trust himself with the language. He closed his vocabulary list into the appropriate page in the book and set off to dinner.

Ben and Seren ate their lightly seasoned meat, steamed vegetables, and unidentifiable bitter mush, while sitting on wooden benches that still smelled like freshly cut lumber and tacky chemical sealant.

"I dislike Vuri," Seren said between bites.

"Why, because she's hard on us?" Ben asked.

"She comports herself like an unrefined barbarian," Seren said. "That, and her choice of vocabulary is offensively imprecise."

"Come on," Celer said. "You probably would have said those things about Ben when we first met."

"Hey!" Ben protested.

"Vuri is worse," Seren replied. Ben felt hurt that Seren didn't deny that he was an unrefined barbarian. "I believe she dislikes me as well."

"I think we'll just have to get used to her," Ben said.

"And until we're not recruits anymore, she ranks above us," Celer added.

Ben finished off his meal and stared loathingly at his pile of Voleric books. "We have homework to do, don't we?" he asked.

"I believe so," Seren replied. She sounded tired, but otherwise indifferent. The humans and Celer went to the library, where they could at least enjoy the larger space and comfortable chairs. Sitting at a large, round table, they opened their books and set paintbrushes and sheets of vertically ruled paper beside them. Seren and Celer helped Ben through the memorization of the noun case endings, and they quizzed each other on the vocabulary until they had them thoroughly memorized.

"At this rate, I'm never going to learn enough to fight on a team," Ben groaned.

"No, no, you're doing fine!" Celer said. "In fact, I think we have time tonight to start on verbs!"

Ben groaned louder.

"Verbs are simple as long as you're using the indicative mood, because you just put the right particle on the front depending on what tense you want to use. The present doesn't take a prefix. Now, when you get to the passive voice…"

Ben, and even Seren, had to stop Celer as he passed over things he thought would be obvious. After a while, Ben's eyelids struggled to stay open, and his head was propped lifelessly on his arm.

"…except for nominal and optative infixes, which replace the vowel when the preceding consonant is not an alveolar, the dental *edh,* or an approximant, so—Ben? Ben, are you awake?"

"Wha? Um, yeah. Infixes and different merb voods and all that. I'm kind of drifting off, though."

"Verb moods, Ben. I think we should stop for tonight."

"Agreed," Seren said. "No doubt Vuri will drive us to our limits again tomorrow."

"And I want to get you two through the ablative, locative and comitative cases tomorrow, at least," Celer said.

"Alright," Ben said. "Let's go before it gets any later." He closed his books and shoved the papers inside of them, not caring that they wrinkled and creased. Upstairs in his room, he half walked, half stumbled in the dark towards his bed. Nothing would feel better than sleep.

Ben woke up the next morning with every part of his body moaning that he should go back to sleep. His blankets, so warm and comforting, took a great mental effort to remove. Celer chattered about how Ben had already slept in too late, and how he needed to get down to breakfast or else he wouldn't have anything to eat at all. Ben looked down at himself, noticing that he had slept in his uniform. He ran his hands along the front of his shirt and pants in a futile attempt to get the erratic creases out, then went out to the dining hall. Seren waved him over to a table where she had saved him a spot at the end, and had prepared an extra bowl of vegetable stew and smoked meat.

"Late," Vuri growled. She and Javrel were sitting with Seren.

"Sorry, sir..." Ben replied. He ate the now-cold breakfast and tried to arrange his hair in the reflection of a spoon. He needed a haircut badly.

"Celer, is something bothering you?" Seren asked. He was hovering, but staring off into space and drifting absently with the slight air currents in the room.

"I'm thinking about the Messengersmith I talked to in Darjae," he said. "That guy was so apathetic when it came to KTAN, and us, and everything that's going on. He treated me like a little scared kid. It hurt. That, and he was talking about this drunk homeless guy who knows that KTAN really is a threat. It was really weird, because he said the guy had a name that sounded like mine."

"Kalar," Seren said.

"The guy who tried to get Seren killed?" Ben exclaimed.

"Whoa," Vuri said. "Who would have thought our 'grand and fearless leader' would turn into some street bum? Oh, wait. Everybody. Probably had some kinda mental breakdown after we kicked him out. Guy's a total waste."

"Still, that's pretty extreme," Ben said. "Even for him."

"The dude was *always* extreme," Vuri replied.

Celer spoke up again, saying, "The Messengersmith said Kalar had a bunch of gun-toting disciples. Probably the remnants of the guys he fled with."

"Hopefully he's not getting violent against other Andarites!" Arwi squealed. "We might have released, like, another angry problem when we kicked him out!"

Vuri said, "Hopefully he hasn't gone *that* crazy. But if he wants to go kill some more Iyeranis, I say go ahead. Hey, maybe he'll even croak in the process." Ben suddenly wondered how excitable, flighty Arwi and snarky, nonchalant Vuri had ever been paired as Messenger and Keeper.

"What if he really does become a problem for us, though?" Ben asked.

Vuri snorted. "How? You heard Celer. Kalar and his buddies are all drunk and homeless, wandering around Darjae."

"Darjae is far away and Kalar's followers are few," Javrel said. "Sildial is limping already. We don't have the resources to go deal with him. Now come on, we're going for our run."

Ben shoved a final mouthful of stew and meat into his mouth, chewing even as he left the table and went out the door. He was still hungry. Daolor Squad went outside and was hit by the biting cold of the winter air. Snow was falling lightly. Ben was glad for the heat of exertion while running, even as he became tired from the laps that Vuri demanded of him and Seren. Once again, the Messengers flew up through the clouds and went to do flight exercises.

"Be careful today!" Ben called, hoping that Yadho wouldn't get Celer injured again.

"I have modified our practice regimen," Yadho replied before shooting off. Satisfied, Ben continued his run. He and Seren settled into a comfortable pace, keeping stride with each other.

"You were really good yesterday, with the swordfighting and Voleric and all that," he said.

"Thank you," she said, breathing hard. "You sparred well. I had one superior move, that is all."

"Less chatter," Vuri said tersely. "You're both lucky, training is shortened today. Everyone participating in the procession of remembrance has finished their preparations. We'll be honoring the fallen this afternoon."

"Alright," Ben said. "Thanks" felt wrong for a funeral, even though he was pleased about shortened training. He was also curious to see how the Voleric people honored their dead.

The day's run once again left both Ben and Seren gasping for breath by the time they were done. Still, Vuri wasted no time bringing her squad down to the firing range. Seren was still learning fast, and Ben was catching on. He missed the target less than he had the day before. By the end of sword training, Vuri had corrected the humans' technique more times than they cared to count, but both could see it helping. Ben rather enjoyed Vuri's teaching style, heavy on practice combat and light on repetition or drills. Out of ten bouts, Ben had won four. Training adjourned and Daolor Squad went directly to lunch, which they ate quickly and in silence. The mood of the funeral had already settled over Sildial, and somber brown and black tapestries had been hung around the room. The tables were cleared and stowed away without a word.

Soon, Sildial was gathered in the hall, everyone standing for the ceremony. Some agents, who reverently clutched elegant scrolls to their chests, stood in a crowd at the center of the room. The rest of the organization hung close to the walls. At the front of the room, just in front of the podium, a pitch-black rug embroidered with golden calligraphy was laid out on the ground. The lights were turned down until the forms in the crowd cast long, wavering shadows in the flickering light. The ceremony started in silence, and then, from somewhere unseen, a single flute played a languorous and haunting melody. Ben shivered. The ethereal flute sounded exactly like wolfdragon calls set to music. The music mounted to a higher pitch and its speed increased, and from the crowd around the edges of the space there came singing. All the mournful singers shared the same melody, but it seemed no words had been agreed upon. Each mourner joined his or her own personal lament to the collective song, which swelled into a cacophonous yet strangely unified call. The music increased again in speed and volume, and the singing became frenzied, degenerating into the mournful screams and moans of friends and loved ones. Struck by the sheer volume of emotion, thoughts of Ben's parents, and uncle Dennison, and all of his family at home suddenly flooded into Ben's mind. He blinked rapidly, feeling long-restrained tears gather and drip from his eyes. Immediately as he felt their wet trails down his face, Ben joined the great cathartic release, throwing his full voice into the air and letting it mingle with those of the mourning Andarites. He let rage and longing and fear flow momentarily through every fiber of his being until he lost the distinction between shouting and crying, between his voice and those around him. The Wolfdragon flute was the feeble cry of a child next to the overwhelming roar of shouts and moans. The cry died down naturally and slowly, until each had released the full measure of their own pain. Those who had finished stared stoically outward, allowing the still-crying mourners to finish their lamentations without shame. At the end, Ben felt lighter, having thrown off the unexpressed weight of his emotions. He understood why this had become a part of the Voleric funeral tradition. He didn't notice until the end of the ritual, however, that Seren had moved over next to him and delicately twined her fingers into his. Her presence was wordlessly comforting. Ben squeezed her hand gently, and she squeezed back. They stood close enough together that Celer could keep his voice to a respectful whisper as he translated the opening remarks of a chaplain dressed in pale teal robes. The Andarite took to the podium, eyes closed in respect and solemnity as the longest wails of the congregation faded into peaceful silence.

"Thank you for the fire of your voices," he said. "Those who have taken to their second hatching remain here, with those who remember them. We have shed our grief here, and now we may bear witness to the great and honorable deeds of our loved ones. Now we lay their lives down to the examination of their patron gods. Now, we grant them passage into their eternity." With that cue, the Andarites in the crowd at the center of the room took their scrolls and opened them, laying them on the rug. Fully unrolled, each scroll was at least twice as long as Ben was tall.

"The scroll-bearer is a close friend or relative who the dead person chose while they were still alive," Javrel said, coming up beside Ben. "That person's job is to write a scroll that tells everything about the dead person's life, good and bad. The patron god of each dead soldier will read their life and decide if that person's good enough for their chosen afterlife."

Ben didn't think it would be polite to ask what happened if they weren't good enough.

The whispering was attracting disdainful glances from people around them. He whipped his head around and focused on the ceremony. The Scroll-bearers were still carrying their written memorials and placing them upon the sacred rug.

"The scrolls go to our mausoleum in the back of the library, so anyone can read them," Javrel said.

The scroll-bearers finished their procession and formed an orderly line near the podium.

"Now it is our turn to remember and cherish those who we have lost recently. Though it may now be impossible to tell who fought for what side when Kalar deserted us, we will remember them all as those who fought fiercely for what they believed in. The first eulogy today will be given by Viraj Deloro, Scroll-Bearer for Djera Deloro."

The first eulogy was followed by many more for the other 'second-hatched,' and while emotion hung thick in the air around him, Ben felt conspicuously alienated. He had fought alongside these people and felt sorrow at their loss, but the stories about the lives of the dead reminded Ben that he was still largely an outsider to the affairs of this organization. He stood straight and silent out of respect, even as his legs grew restless. When the eulogies were finally over, the congregation sung a soft, hopeful tune that left Ben with a deep-seated sense of calm. After the chaplain gave closing remarks, Thoral took the stage.

"Thank you, Chaplain Relaro," he said, while motioning for the lights to be raised. "Now, I'd like to announce some changes in our organization. First, congratulations to the newly organized squads; Vyurzo, Aqwero, Zolidae, and Daolor." Ben waved along with the rest of his squad and the members of the other new squads, all sporting patches with fearsome animal mascots. "Our new recruits from Earth are in Daolor, under their new squad leader, Vuri Darialaro. I'm sure she will lead this young squad well. I have also come to a decision on who will take positions as my advisors. For these positions, I have chosen Valerija Dyalaro and Daal-Na Kon-Ren An-Tun." A tall Andarite woman with grass-green scales and sandy colored horns took the stage, along the Daalronnan Messengersmith. An-Tun made eye contact with Ben and Celer as he waved at the crowd. He mouthed something that Ben couldn't hear.

"Did you hear that?" Celer asked.

"No," Ben said.

"I did. He just asked you and me to meet him in his office after the ceremony. It sounded like he was right in front of me. I think he used a spell."

"Whoa," Ben breathed. "That's some complicated magic. He might not have all his raw power, but he still has the skill."

Satisfied that he had covered all of his points, Thoral dismissed the crowd. Ben followed An-Tun, catching up with him quickly and walking alongside him as he pushed his wheelchair down the halls.

"That was a really cool spell," Ben said.

An-Tun smiled. "I'm glad you liked it. It's not that hard, actually. I can teach it to you if you like. After you're fully healed, of course."

"That would be great!" Ben replied as he reached the stairs. For a moment he worried if An-Tun's wheelchair would be able to make the climb, before it raised itself up and confidently levitated ahead. An-Tun set the wheelchair down on the second floor and led Ben into his office.

"I don't think I've ever had a young Messengersmith come through here, so determined to stay. I like your reasons, too. I know many people who come here only to kill, but not you. That's why I have something here that I think you deserve to use." An-Tun wheeled to the back of his office and withdrew a long object wrapped in purple cloth from a neat pile of other possessions. He handed it to Ben, who pulled back the purple veil to reveal a three-foot long staff of polished wood, in a deep, rich brown color like soil in the deep woods. It was naturally twisted and gnarled, yet still polished and comfortable to hold. The tip looked like a fist-sized, irregular and wavy ball of red-orange glass, like sunset dissolved in water and frozen.

"A staff for amplifying magic?" Ben asked. "Daal-Na, it's beautiful. Thank you."

"Built and enchanted for combat, as well," the Messengersmith said. "That tip is amber from the deepest mine on Daalronna. The wood, from the core of the Eldest Trees of the northernmost forests. I built this when Kalar was younger, hoping to give it to him when he became a great leader like his father. I couldn't bring myself to do it, though, as I saw how he was acting as he got older. I give this to you with the understanding that you will fight bravely and never lose sight of why you do so. Agreed?"

Ben stared at the weapon in his hands, feeling the physical weight, but also the heavy expectations attached to it. An-Tun had made this staff, anticipating greatness from its wielder. Ben swelled with pride at the fact that a *Daal-Na* had conferred that honor to him. He looked up from the staff with teary eyes and met An-Tun's gaze. He said, "Agreed."

CHAPTER 10

An-Tun sent Ben away with the staff, carefully wrapped in its purple cloth, and a baseball sized, polished stone. The stone was unremarkable in any magical sense, and was intended only as an exercise tool. Ben was to lift and drop the stone with magic, for a prescribed number of repetitions after each meal, until An-Tun judged that Ben was allowed to practice with the weapon. After dinner, Ben went to the library with Seren and Celer to practice Voleric. While Celer lectured, Ben took the stone and tried levitating it, as instructed. The magic sparked in his chest, seeping with faint warmth, and with a slight tingling sensation, down his arm, as it had before he had burned himself. It slid out of his fingers, making the faintest ripples of light in the air. Like an extension of his body, Ben's own incorporeal fingers wrapped around the sphere. The sphere wobbled uncertainly on the table for a moment, as Ben hoped that the magic wouldn't let him down. Slowly, and then more confidently, Ben lifted the sphere from the table.

"And so the Ablative can be used with quite a few preopositions, all of whi— Ben! Your magic's back!" Celer said, diverting himself from Voleric nouns.

"Congratulations!" Seren said, her rare smile released in full, spreading to Ben and making him feel that much happier.

Ben told them about his meeting with An-Tun, describing the weapon with as much detail and reverence as he could. "It's weird," he said in closing, "but I feel more at ease now. I've spent my whole life around magic. I feel like this is the weapon I'm supposed to have."

"As if you were fated to have it? Do you really believe such a superstitious concept?" Seren asked.

"Haven't thought about it much, really. I guess you don't?"

"I was not raised to believe in any supernatural entity or deity. It leads me to believe that we can control our own destinies."

Ben nodded, considering what she had said. Her words seemed particularly relevant now, when everything seemed so much in flux. He wanted as much control as he could get.

Fourteen days later, Ben, Seren and Celer had been pushed harder and faster through training than any previous squad. The new Daolors were tired, mentally and physically drained, and all leaning on each other to share the few bits of remaining morale. Javrel and Vuri had maintained emotional distance from them, a pair of drill instructors passing the high expectations of the organization onto their new recruits. Once again, the squad took its morning run. They had been given new coats and warmer clothes, and were glad for them in the fearsome, demonic blizzard that had swallowed Joraw. Ben looked outward into an unforgiving vortex of pure white, snarling and howling as the winds blew and rattled old windows and whipped through alleys. Celer had fallen back into his habit of staring off into the distance, saying nothing. This time, though, the thick snow conglomerating around his windward side was almost comical.

"Come on!" Ben said, jogging in place to keep up much-needed body heat.

"There are people out there," Celer muttered. "In this weather."

"Well, there'll be a few less if you hurry on up!" Vuri shouted. Celer followed, spinning to throw off the snow.

Ben, though beaten down by training, could tell that he was faster and had more endurance than when he had started. Running back into the compound, he turned to go down to the firing range, where Vuri still required him to train with an Andarite gun, even after he had begun training with the staff. He stopped, noticing that Javrel and Vuri were speaking with a Messenger whom Ben did not know.

"Apparently," Vuri said, "Advisor Dyalaro wants Daolor Squad up in her office immediately. Her Messenger said it takes precedence over all of our current orders."

"That sounds ominous," Ben said. "Let's not keep her waiting, then."

"Pardon the mess," Ms. Dyalaro said as Daolor Squad entered. Her office, with the same layout as Thoral's, was occupied by several well-organized stacks of boxes with white labels. Pictured were already hung on the walls, all featuring Ms. Dyalaro and another Andarite. In one picture, they held two bluish, speckled eggs as proud parents. The other pictures were of the couple and their children at various milestones. "I'm still moving into my new position," she elaborated, while retrieving a teapot and five large cups from the back of the office. Into the cups she poured a generous measure of steaming, red-violet drink.

"Is this Ko-Imensi?" Ben asked.

Ms. Dyalaro smiled. "Yes, it is. Daal-Na An-Tun was kind enough to give me the tea and spices as a gift for becoming an advisor, and I thought I'd share it with you after your run out in the cold."

"Thank you very much," he replied, taking the warm mug in his hands and taking a drink of the beverage, which Dennison had sometimes served at the base when he could get it. Ko-Imensi tasted sour and spicy, but warm and familiar. Seren, Javrel and Vuri also took their mugs, then sat down on the chairs that were set out around Ms. Dyalaro's desk.

"Now to our business," she said. "Javrel and Vuri, you will remember how devoted Varyal was to not only fighting KTAN, but also to evacuating the people of this city, people who have no means of their own to get out. Thoral has charged me with restarting that initiative."

"No offense, sir, but I'd like more time to train my recruits," Vuri said.

"Our magic-users are spread thin, Vuri. Many are recovering from severe burns from the last attack, many more have been killed or have deserted. There are few left. I need you and Ben on this mission."

Vuri looked down at her feet and scowled. "Understood," she said. "But sir, if I may speak freely?"

"Go on."

"I don't think the recruits are ready."

Ben, Seren and Celer looked at Vuri, feeling betrayed.

Ms. Dyalaro said, "Your recruits spent more than ten days, with no supplies or training, in the wilderness. They survived multiple animal attacks, and crossed the Barali mountains, the Irizu river *after a rainstorm,* and the Awizila marshes. Aside from how to shoot a gun and swing a sword, I don't think there's much you *can* teach them. Am I understood?"

"But what about the language?" Vuri asked. "They're not fluent."

"Celer?" Mrs. Dyalaro asked.

Celer said, "Vuri, they've memorized all of the vocabulary you've given them, and all the basic grammar. We can get by."

Mrs. Dyalaro stared Vuri down, daring her to defy her. She didn't.

"Yes, sir," Vuri said. "Daolor Squad will be ready as soon as you need us."

Ms. Dyalaro smiled. "Thank you, Vuri. I'll be briefing you in the transport garage tomorrow, immediately after breakfast. Get some rest, that's an order. First mission is a big day for anyone. Oh, and you can drop by anytime to return those mugs. Dismissed."

Everyone left, Vuri still with an annoyed look on her face. "I'll be in my quarters," she growled, then stalked away.

"I said you're good enough for the mission tomorrow, but we should keep practicing Voleric," Celer said. "Javrel, mind coming along to help with speech exercises?"

"Sure."

As they headed to the library, Ben felt the need to ask Javrel about what he had overheard earlier.

"Hey, so about Vuri... I've never seen her use magic. Why hasn't she told us more about that?"

"It... just slipped her mind, probably," Javrel said tersely, then sped up, leaving the humans and Messenger behind. Ben didn't think he was being completely honest. Still, it wasn't something he wanted to pry about if they didn't want to discuss it.

Though Advisor Dyalaro had given the squad the day off from physical work, Celer and Javrel still drilled Ben and Seren on the Voleric language. Javrel smiled and nodded approvingly at their mastery. However, once the books were

closed and everyone dispursed after dinner, an air of nervousness settled over Daolor Squad.

That night, Vuri still fumed at Advisor Dyalaro. When she
and Javrel were alone in their shared quarters, she said, "I'm
still worried about the recruits."

"They'll come through," Javrel said. "Besides, we have
our orders. We have to go out there tomorrow, and apparently Ms. Dyalaro thinks they'll do just fine. Otherwise,
she wouldn't have put us on this. I'm more worried about
you."

"What, because you think I don't trust them?" Vuri
asked.

"No, it's not that. Advisor Dyalaro doesn't know us that
well. I know it's *technically* true, but she maybe shouldn't have
counted you as another magic user."

"You don't have to remind me, Javrel," Vuri said.

"I know," Javrel said. "I'm sorry. But you're still one of
the best fighters I know, even with… that."

"Yeah, sure. Night, bro."

"Good night, sis."

Outside, Celer floated around the halls. Arwi floated up beside him. "You're worried about tomorrow," she said gently.

"I think we all are," he replied.

"First mission is always scary, I know," Arwi said. "Well,
they all are. But this one is even more than all the other ones.
You're going to be fine, though. You're a good flier."

"Any Messenger worth his own cloth can dodge bullets," Celer muttered. "I'm worried about my friends."

"Ben has that staff from An-Tun, and he's been getting really good with it. Seren is, like, genius smart, and she can shoot pretty well. I get it, you're scared for them. But they need you tomorrow, too. Get some sleep."

Inside his quarters, Ben was also trying unsuccessfully to get to sleep. A few days of training was doing nothing to ease his mind, and terror was churned up whenever he thought back to the last battle. Images of the violence were burned into his mind with the same fury as his over-used magic. The explosions and shouts echoed in his mind, and above all he remembered the aftermath, watching an unidentified soldier being carried from the scene, so consumed by magic burns that they had charred the entirety of his flesh. Such images disturbed his sleep as he tried to get some rest before the morning.

Breakfast was tense, though Arwi tried to lighten the mood with her indomitable cheeriness. Once plates were cleared, Daolor made its way up to the office of Advisor Dyalaro. She had no tea this morning, and looked just as solemn as everyone felt.

"Meet the Fyetalí family," she said, placing a few portrait sketches on her desk. There were a mother and father, with three young children. "The mother has been of frail health since the beginning of the season, and has been trying to support her husband, who has one leg, and their three hatchlings.

You will be escorting this family from their home, back to headquarters. After that, a caravan can take them to the secure supply road that we maintain in and out of Joraw. Other squads will be taking other families by other routes. These families live deep inside territory controlled by KTAN, ignored because of their relative neutrality in our conflict. They know KTAN's de facto curfew and they respect the defensive perimeter around each of their buildings. Once they are in our care, however, KTAN will not discriminate between combatants and civilians. There are five other squads with all the magic users I could muster, taking other families. I hope that by forcing the KTAN patrols to respond to multiple incursions at once, you and the others can keep them scattered for long enough to make successful escapes. Messenger scouts will inform all of the squad leaders of the most recent KTAN positions as soon as you get to the transport garage. Be fast, be brave, and may the god Balgar favor us this day." Advisor Dyalaro saluted in the Andarite fashion, and Daolor squad returned the salute. They turned to walk out the door.

"Oh! I almost forgot! Come back!" Advisor Dyalaro called. Daolor returned to her. "You need your identification tags."

Advisor Dyalaro handed Ben and Seren metal tags with their names, squad name, and the words *Not Specified* punched into the metal. The tags were on black necklace strings.

"I suppose it doesn't seem like a very good omen, giving you these right before the first mission, but if we were ever to need to identify your bodies, these are necessary."

Ben's stomach flipped. "What's 'not specified?'"

"I had to get these printed quickly and I didn't have a chance to ask for your religious identities, in the event that we would need a burial. Again, I'm sorry to make you think about all of this right before I send you off on your first mission. I hope you'll never need them. Dismissed."

The squad then headed to the transport garage, Ben feeling thoroughly disturbed.

"You look worried," Ben observed of Seren. It seemed to be about more than just the tags.

"We should be lying low until we recover from the attacks," Seren said. "I worry that we will not be able to handle a punitive strike."

"You're right," Ben muttered, disturbed by Seren's realization. "But I don't think Thoral or his advisor are going to take 'no' for an answer. Let's just focus on staying alive and completing the mission, alright?"

"Agreed."

The Andarites and Seren went to the armory, while Ben retrieved his staff from his quarters. They all arrived in the transport garage, and Ben was immediately appalled at the state of his squad's transport. The thing must, at one point, have been one of the imposing and heavily armored vehicles that had been Ben's introduction to Sildial. Now, its armor was blackened, twisted, and amateurishly welded into a mere semblance of its former protectiveness. Many of the plates were altogether missing, leaving protection around the cockpit, and a twisted birds' nest around the gunner's postion, but scant shielding anywhere else. None of the other squads seemed to have any better accomodations.

"We did what we could, and there are a few enchantments on it," a worker said, "but this is the best we can give you, after what those *golibra* Iyeranis did to our fleet. Good luck to you."

"Thank you for all your hard work," Javrel said. "Audir would be proud." He turned to the squad. "Vuri, you drive. Ben, take the turret with me. Seren, it looks like there's a hole in the rear armor you can fire from. Arwi and Celer, you scout our perimeter. But first, everyone gather around." He bowed his head reverently, and the others followed, forming a small circle. "*Valzai, Balgar, Degadh, ziyeudeb wi arizi velorij arizari.*"

Celer translated, with explanations, "Valzai, god of strength, Balgar, of war, Degath, of justice, protect us on our journey."

The prayer finished, Daolor Squad mounted their transport. The machine gave a lively roar as the engine started, and the squad rode out into the snow-covered city.

As soon as the other squad vehicles peeled off to their own courses, Ben felt exponentially tenser. He knew no landmarks, and the Messengers had not yet returned with reports of the KTAN troop positions. The desolate buildings, with their many dark corners, glassless open windows, and piled rubble, provided possible hiding places for the enemy everywhere. Fear and cold kept Ben's bare hands tightly grasped on his staff. He tensed even more when he saw the nearly imperceptible movement of pale blue Messengers flying towards him over the white, snowy landscape.

"Andarite mob agents just ahead," Celer reported. "Five, maybe ten if they're hiding." Sure enough, Ben saw the darkened forms of Andarites situated in the open windows, barely visible in their unlit positions. They raised the weapons. Automatic gunfire pounded through the air, and Ben and Javrel ducked into the relative safety of the twisted armor. Javrel was first to reappear, firing with calm confidence and mechanical accuracy, sighting and ending his targets with brutal efficiency. Ben popped up and sighted an enemy who poked out from behind a window. Letting magic cascade through his body and into the staff, he loosed a miniature sun of golden light that met its target like a small grenade. The dispatched target never reappeared from where it had slumped. Whirling around, Ben dealt a swift, cauterizing death the next enemy that aimed at him.

He was taking aim at another criminal when the vehicle jolted, tilting suddenly downward and coming to an abrupt halt. Before he could figure out what had happened, he looked up to see more Andarites than he and Javrel could kill before they fired. Ben threw up a bubble of magic, invisible except where the bullets ricocheted off a few feet from the vehicle. The impacts set off bright yellow ripples, as if in a pond of molten gold.

"Can I fire through this?" Javrel yelled, nearly breaking Ben's concentration. He had to keep his mind both on the Voleric and the shield.

"No!" Ben called. He looked up to see a mob agent with a menacingly large weapon aimed out of a rooftop installation. It fired a grenade trailing a line of white smoke, which crossed the distance in the blink of an eye and detonated against the bubble shield. Momentarily blinding, a flower of bright yellow and fiery orange bloomed across the shield, spreading and nearly engulfing it. An acutely painful tingling spread through Ben's nerves; one of few warnings he was going to get that his magic was being taxed. "I can't block another one of those!" he called. "Vuri, what's going on?"

"Pit trap under the snow!" she called. "We can't move!"

"Everyone out of the vehicle!" Javrel called. "I see cover! Ben, can you shield us?"

"Just against the guns," Ben replied, jumping from the transport. Seren and Vuri followed, and Javrel led the team into an unoccupied alleyway. Javrel had situated them in an area where only two of the positions could fire upon them. One, however, was the grenade launcher, reloading quickly yet safely from behind the parapet of its roof.

"What are we supposed to do from here?" Vuri asked her brother. Ben asked for Celer's translation. Under the stress of the battle, the Voleric words just weren't coming. "There's no way out of this alley!" Vuri said. Indeed, the other side was closed off by half of a collapsed building. The most pressing problem was the grenade position, already reloading for a shot that would put an end to Ben's defenses and burn him out again. Ben poked a hole in his shield for a split second, long enough to fire another bolt of energy near the grenade launcher. It exploded with an impressive flash, collapsing the edge of the roof. A still-flailing Andarite fell with its grenade launcher among the rubble, landing amid the crash of debris below.

"Nice one!" Vuri said. Javrel fired at the other shooter, rendering the entire area silent except for the wind.

"Move out," Javrel ordered.

"Wait," Seren said quickly. "There are multiple placements that can shoot us when we leave cover." Her Voleric was crisp and unaffected by stress.

"And they're already converging on us," Celer said, flying into the alley from where he had been scouting with the other Messengers. Sure enough, the mob agents had come down from their positions and were moving in a wide circle, closing in on Daolor Squad.

"Give us a way to fire though," Seren said.

"Everyone get down," Ben commanded in Voleric. At least he had the basics. The squad obeyed. A plan formed tentatively in his head. Dropping the shield for just a moment, Ben touched his staff to the ground, effecting a quick enchantment on the ground and raising a shoulder-high wall of asphalt and rubble. His arms burned as he formed the barrier. Now, he could focus his remaining magic on the attack. The squad fired confidently at their attackers, who were forced to dance between the meager spots of cover on the road. One of those was the squad's own trapped vehicle, half-buried in the snow.

"We cannot stay here until we run out of ammunition and magic," Seren said between shots.

"I can get our ride out of the trap if you cover me!" Ben shouted.

"Go for it!" Javrel called. Without hesitation, Ben threw as much magic as he safely could at the wall, turning its many particles into hot, fast-moving projectiles that bombarded the enemy cover. The squad ran at full speed towards the transport, forming a tight circle around Ben and firing at enemy stragglers. Once at the transport, Ben jammed his staff beneath the chassis.

"Everyone in!" he shouted. "Vuri, drive!" Vuri revved the engine and the tires spun in the deep snow, finding no traction until Ben poured magic into the space below, pushing the trapped vehicle up on a vibrating plate of light. It slid forward and the tires grabbed the road. The vehicle took off as soon as it gained a grip. Seren shot out her hand, helping Ben pull himself into the fleeing vehicle. They left the enemy positions far behind.

"Ben, how's the magic?" Vuri called over the engine roar.

"I won't be able to do shields for the squad, and my ability to shoot is close to dead. One or two more shots before I can't do anything. How close are we to the family?"

"Funny you should ask," Vuri said as she stopped the car outside a decrepit tenement building. The door opened, and a family of five made their way out. All were wrapped in strange, patchwork cloaks that looked to be the remnants of many dishtowels, pieces of old clothing, and any other cloth that could be patched, sewn or tied together. The three small children ran out through the snowbanks, followed by the mother and father. Leaning on the woman, the Andarite man hobbled out on his one leg, the stub of the other wrapped in dirty, blue and brown bandages.

As the family got into the transport, Ben and Javrel kept nervous watch on the city. Inside the vehicle, one of the small children reached up and grabbed Seren's hair with a curious hand.

"*Zer yil veroi radaelo,*" the child said simply, while twirling strands of Seren's hair around her fingers.

"No, I am not an Andarite," Seren replied, putting her Voleric to use. Annoyed, she brushed the child's hand insistently away.

"Where are you from?" another of the children asked.

"Earth. Now be quiet, the agents of the mob are still near."

"But mommy said that if we didn't go near them, they leave us alone!"

"That is not true anymore. Let me focus or they will hurt us all." Cowed, the little child hushed and squeezed closer on the seat to its siblings and parents.

"Gods, Seren... You're terrible with children," Vuri said. She started the vehicle in motion once again, taking a separate route from the one they had travelled before.

"I am sorry, I did not know I was here to be the squad's public relations officer," she replied, while pushing strands of hair behind her ear.

"I'm just saying it wouldn't kill you to lighten up, miss Iyerani logic queen," Vuri shot back. "Come on, the kids have to deal with enough already, with the poverty and the—the mob!"

"There is no need to shout, I understand your point!"

"No, I mean they're here!" Vuri called. A second later, the sounds of gunfire broke out. The children screamed and clutched tight to their parents. Bullets struck the haphazard armor of the vehicle with rapid clunking sounds. The engine roared louder as Vuri pushed the craft to the upper limits of its speed. Above, Javrel fired at every opportunity, while trying to stay protected within the metal nest. Ben had taken an extra gun and was firing with mixed results. He used up ammunition more quickly than Javrel, firing several times at each position in hopes of getting one hit.

Vuri wove the vehicle between alleyways, sliding recklessly on ice and making it hard for Ben or Javrel to get a steady shot. Then, the vehicle took a curve and lost traction entirely, sliding and ramming hard into the side of a building. Vuri shouted something long and profane in Voleric as she got out of the vehicle, followed by Seren and the family. Ben and Javrel had been slammed painfully up against the side of the nest. Javrel was bloodied, and one arm was bent backward at an unnatural angle.

"Are you alright?" Ben asked. "That arm looks bad."

Javrel gave a crooked, joking smile that ran up his face to the blue-bleeding wound on his cheek. The arm twisted around, unharmed. "Robot, remember?" he reminded Ben. "Just fine. Now, shield me."

"I can't."

"Not at all?" Javrel demanded.

"No!"

"Fine." Javrel jumped out of the craft unprotected, sliding down its side to where the rest of the party was taking cover in a dead-end alleyway. Ben followed. Behind the craft, the entire squad was looking around furiously for an exit.

"Vuri," Javrel said. "If you can, we'd really appreciate it." Ben, Seren and Celer looked at each other in confusion.

"I can't," she muttered.

"I believe in you," Arwi said, circling close to her keeper. Vuri clenched her fists, shook them and screamed into the air.

"Work, you stupid magic!" she shouted furiously. Still, not a single spark. Vuri stole a glance out at the approaching Iyeranis. She looked at her brother, eyes wide, breath shaky. "It's not coming. Javrel, I'm sorry…"

"It's alright," Javrel said, though he sounded unconvinced of his own reassurance. "We'll find another way out."

Seren, though, was already well on the way to finding out how to escape. She scrutinized a heavy padlock on the door of one of the buildings that walled in the alley, then wedged her sword into the ring and tried to break it off.

"Javrel, help me with this," she grunted. With their combined strength, they broke the lock. The door swung open into a dark, long unused apartment lobby.

"Shelter, great," Ben said. "But now we're just trapped in another building."

Not dissuaded, Seren climbed the stairs until she reached an apartment, where she and Javrel once again broke the lock. Wasting no time, Seren searched for and found a myriad of cleaning supplies in the pantry, and demanded Celer read their labels. She chose a few different bottles, returned to the lobby, and showed the chemicals to the group.

"I need a larger supply of these," she said. "And also, find glass jars and any construction hardware you see. Bring them down here." The squad and the children nodded and ran off, leaving Seren to begin mixing the cleaners, solvents and other pungent household chemicals. Ben and the kids returned with some glass jars, a handful of nails, and a bottle of sanitizing alcohol. The others brought more chemicals, some small batteries, and a bunch of rubber tubing that Javrel guessed could be helpful.

"Chemistry's real interesting and all, but could you tell me what you're doing?" Vuri asked. Seren didn't respond. She placed two chemicals in a bucket, added a third, and the mixture began to bubble and froth. She placed a few more buckets of chemical cocktails around the mixture, which was reacting and pouring out a sinister fog that covered the floor.

"Find a first floor window on the farthest extreme of the building," she said as she continued working. "You will know when to make your escape. I will cover it from the second floor and follow as soon as I can."

"Be careful," Ben said.

"Of course," she replied. "See you soon. Now go, before this entire room floods with gas."

Everyone exited, leaving the chemical reaction to its own devices. Seren mounted the stairs while the rest followed her instructions to the other end of the building. Ben looked back to check on her one more time, but she had already disappeared.

The squad and their civilian charges crouched in the shadows, waiting for something.

"We should go now," Vuri said.

"No," Javrel grabbed her arm before she tried to move. "Seren said that we would know. We don't have a cue yet."

From the other side of the building, a deafening boom resounded from the lobby and shook the whole building.

"I bet that's the cue!" Ben said.

Vuri and Javrel broke the window and cleared away the broken glass, then helped the civilians through. In the time it took for everyone to get through the window, smoke was already spreading rapidly through the building and pouring out from the windows. The noxious chemicals stung Ben's eyes and itched like terrible poison ivy in his throat. His eyes watered. They all moved silently, the parents' hands clamped over the teary-eyed childrens' mouths. No one gave into the urge to cough as they slipped into yet another back alley. The enemy was probably preoccupied with the fire, but no one wanted to take the chance that they weren't.

"Headquarters is barely a half-mile off now," Javrel said. "We're in the clear as soon as Seren catches up."

Ben looked back at the building. Behind them, flames started by the explosion licked out from the first story windows, moving about the broken glass like tongues around sharp teeth. Seren had not yet come out. "Stay here," Ben said.

"Oh, no you don't!" Vuri said. "I am not going to be happy we lose two recruits on this squad's first mission."

"Let me shield you," Ben said.

"No. You could seriously hurt yourself."

Vuri ran off back towards the building. Javrel surveyed the last three magazines of ammunition, and slammed one into the gun. Stepping out of the alley, he and Ben watched the street for any enemy approach. They glanced back at the apartment complex every few seconds. The fire blazed on both the first and second floors now. The part of the building closest to the center of the explosion collapsed, sending up a column of sparks. Ben clenched his fists and growled, hating the knowledge that there was nothing he could do, and starting to believe that his friends were gone.

It was with surprise, therefore, that he looked up to see two soot-covered forms running back across the opening between the buildings. Vuri and Seren collapsed, panting and coughing, on the ground. Both girls sat up, relatively unharmed save for a few minor burns. Ben literally jumped at Seren, wrapping her in a tight hug.

"I'm so glad you're okay," he said.

"Ben…" she whispered, "I cannot breathe."

Ben released Seren, letting her catch her breath. Blood seeped through her uniform sleeve, glistening against the black surface. "Were you shot?" he asked.

"Broken glass," she said. "It will heal quickly."

"Glad you're okay, both of you," Javrel said quickly, "but let's get going. Sildial's close." He led the group at a slow jog through twisting alleys and passages between buildings, taking a meandering route through shelters and destroyed buildings. Everyone cheered when the headquarters building loomed in front of the squad. They entered in through the front, greeted by medics who started an immediate examination of the civilian family. Advisor Dyalaro was there as well, clipboard in hand, Messenger hovering at her shoulder.

"You're back, good," she said. "How was the workmanship of the vehicle?"

"Yeah, about that…" Vuri started, and then she related a summary of the tale to the advisor, including the abandonment of the transport. She concluded, "You'll have my official report by tonight."

"Good. What matters is the family is safe."

"How are the other squads?" Arwi asked. "Did they get back okay?"

"All of the other squads have returned," the Advisor said. "All safe and alive, no critical injuries. All of the families are going to be moved to safe houses outside of Joraw. And Daolor Squad, congratulations on a successful first mission. Have some food and drink, relax. We'll worry about your transport issues later."

Daolor Squad filled plates of hot food and gathered around a table together to eat. "Good work, everyone," Vuri said.

"Thanks," Ben said. "And Vuri, thanks for going back for Seren."

"Yes, thank you," Seren concurred.

"No problem," she replied. "What was that stunt, anyway?"

"Mixing basic household chemicals can yield a number of poisonous or explosive gases when they react," Seren explained. "I left my gun with a mop in the shadows, and the shape of a head was convincing enough that the enemy fired, providing the spark. I... I did not account for how fast the fire would spread through the building."

"Either way, we're glad you're alright," Celer said.

"I would like to know what stopped Vuri from using magic today," Seren said bluntly. Arwi and Javrel looked at Vuri nervously.

"You don't have to go into it if you don't want," Arwi said softly. "I know it's hard."

"No," Vuri said, strong but obviously pained. "This squad has to be able to trust itself. I'll tell you why I'm a crappy magician. Javrel and I are Takathists."

"What? How does that work?" Ben asked. "Takathists are supposed to hate magic and have a military devoted to killing Messengersmiths. Besides, I heard you praying to other gods."

"Henotheism. We worship all of the Voleric gods, but revere Takath, god of justice and order, above the others. And will you try to keep the stereotypes to a minimum, please?"

Ben bowed his head shamefully. "Sorry."

"Don't worry, we get it a lot. Now, did you ever use magic by accident?"

"A couple times when I was younger, yeah…" Ben wondered what she was getting at.

"Well, Javrel and I were born in the same Takathist cloister that is allied with KTAN today. I don't even remember the first time it happened, but somehow, I accidentally used magic. My parents beat me for it, and I thought that it was over once the magic subsided. The problem is, hardline Takathists believe that magic users always choose to use their powers, rather than having accidents like mine. The community treated me like…" Celer struggled to translate an idiom, and came up with, "like a leper, but worse, and that doesn't even convey the full scope of it. Very, very bad." Vuri continued, "They tried some religious therapies to make sure it would never happen again, but there was another accident. The council of respected laypeople and the High Priest decided that I should be expelled from the compound."

Ben's mouth hung open. "Your parents went along with that?"

"My parents suggested it." She smiled at Javrel. "Javrel came along because he didn't want me to be alone."

"Where did you go?" Seren asked.

"Diwo Takathar, the cloister city, is west of Joraw. We were rescued by a moderate Takathist sect here that had a support program for people who had been expelled. The shelter they ran was firebombed as soon as the extremists allied with KTAN. Javrel was with me in a part of the building that didn't burn, but as I saw the destruction…"

"The magic came again," Ben said. Anger could bring magic forth very easily.

"Yeah. I exploded. We woke up in Sildial and when I saw what I had done to Javrel, An-Tun had to sedate me before I started to burn again. After I calmed down and tried to train with magic, I could never call it on my own. An-Tun said something about a psychological something or other."

Psychosomatic magical blockage, Ben thought. That was how Dennison had translated Daalronnan papers on the subject of trauma and magical failure.

"So there. Me, Javrel, magic, all of it. That's the story," Vuri said.

"Thank you," Ben said solemnly. "I always heard that Takathists were just people who had a religion that told them to hate magic-users. It's… definitely more complicated than that."

"I am sorry," Seren said. "It was insensitive of me to ask that personal information from you."

"What?" Vuri asked. "No! It's about time somebody stopped treating me like a hatchling about it. Everybody tiptoes around it, all the time. Facing up to it… it felt good. Thanks."

"You're sure you're feeling alright?" Arwi asked.

"Yeah," Vuri said confidently. "Oh, forgot to mention we got Arwi at that shelter. Before that, she was orphaned."

"It's a funny-shaped family, but we wouldn't like it any other way," Arwi said.

"Definitely," Javrel replied. "Good job on the mission today, everyone. Now eat up, and go get some rest. You've all earned it."

"If Celer doesn't mind," Seren said, "I need a translator. I would like to speak with your computer staff about the device we found at the Festival."

Ben's eyes widened in shock. "I totally forgot about that."

"You handed that thing to Kalar, didn't you?" Celer said. "How do we know it's still here?"

Javrel jumped up from his chair. "We have to go check the computer center, immediately."

Upstairs, the computer technician, Adoro, rooted around several drawers before finding the little blue box that Ben, Celer and Seren had brought from Alarzi. "Lucky you remembered this," she said, while searching for the correct input port among a mess of cords and adapters. "I think we all got caught up in the chaos after you had your little scuffle with Kalar. Ah, here it is…" She pushed the device into a port, where it clicked into place and started glowing blue. One of the many screens in the room came alive with a cascade of sharp, blocky Iyerani lettering. "I'm going to start running the decryption programs," she said, "Which takes forever because the Iyerani encryptors are so darn clever. Feel free to take a seat while it works." She motioned to the chairs at several other desks. After a wait of what Ben guessed was half an hour or more, Adoro reported that the file had finally been decrypted. What resulted was an intimidating block of text indecipherable to most of the occupants of the room. "Now, we'll call a translator up here to tell us what this all is, and—"

"Shipping records," Seren said.

"Oh yeah, you're Iyerani," she said. "So? What does it say?"

"These are shipping records for a variety of supplies, mainly wiring and conduit. All of them have what seem to be very high safety certifications in regard to how much energy they can direct. Can you show me more of the list?"

"Sure."

"Refined antimatter. We have to tell Thoral immediately. Handled incorrectly, or *correctly* by someone trying to build a weapon, antimatter will wreak massive damage upon contact with an atmosphere."

"Hey, hold up," Adoro said. "Translate those other components again before you go running off."

She did so.

"Wait a minute," Adoro said. "You said the VN-790 Flow Regulator?"

"Yes," Seren said.

"A company called Venosha Nalo makes parts for wormhole generators. KTAN isn't a terrorist organization. They don't want a bomb. They want a way to ship whatever they want on and off of this planet."

"Seren, does it say where?" Ben asked.

"Several locations. Seaports of Albir, Koldaro, and Everoi, for multiple dates."

"Can you find any connection between those ports?" Vuri asked the technician.

"Running it through the database now," she replied. "Here we are: Dhilnara Enterprises, a company from the planet Wenifri, regularly docks ships at each of those ports."

"Dhilnara..." Ben muttered. "I know that name from somewhere."

"Alarzi," Celer said. "We saw one of their billboards at the Festival. Secure transport and delivery."

"They must be working with KTAN somehow," Seren said. "If anything needs secure transport, it is definitely volatile antimatter."

"Daolor Squad?" Javrel said, "I think we have a new mission."

Chapter 11

"**Absolutely not!**" **Advisor** Dyalaro decreed, once the squad had gathered in her office. "I have read the Dhilnara enterprises charter. Their ships have special contracts that allow them to operate under Wenifrin imperial jurisdiction. We operate solely within Dawta Volaero. Operating on a Wenifrin-owned transport ship would not only be outside our charter, it would be a breach of *interplanetary law.* So no, I cannot authorize an investigation into Dhilnara Enterprises."

"We don't need to actually go *on* the ship," Celer said. "We can watch from the shore. Once a ship lands in the nearest port, we can spy while the ship is docked."

"You're that interested in this lead?" Advisor Dyalaro said.

"Ms. Dyalaro, Dhilnara is a powerful company. We need to know how they are interacting with our enemies. The resources available to the Wenifrin corporations could be enough to cause a decisive shift in this war," Javrel replied.

Ms. Dyalaro sighed. "Fine. When is the next time a Dhilnara ship will be in a nearby port?"

"Three days from now, at the port of Albir," Seren said.

"Be there," Ms. Dyalaro ordered. "And you keep dirt and concrete under your feet at all times, understand? Yes, the docks are still under Voleric rule, but I do not want you tempted. Under no circumstances are you to get aboard that ship, understand?"

"Understood," Vuri said. "We won't let you down."

"Glad to hear that, Ms. Darialaro. Dismissed."

The squad turned and left. "Celer, please come with me," Seren said. "If I can, I would like to learn more about the Iyerani computer language, in case we encounter it."

"I'm going to see if An-Tun can coach me through a few new spells," Ben said.

Vuri replied, "Alright. Three days. Train, stay rested, be ready."

Three days later, Daolor Squad had gone through all the magical and technological preparation they could in such a short window. Javrel had procured civilian clothes for the mission; "So we attract less attention," he explained. The cold weather made it easy to conceal both the humans and Javrel's mechanical limbs. All four wore hoods and gloves and kept their heads down. A Sildial transport worker had even managed to find a non-military vehicle; an old, boxy, abused thing that had been refurbished by Sildial mechanics. At the very least, it would attract less attention than an armored vehicle with a prominent gun turret. Daolor Squad piled in.

The transport rattled and bounced along the snowy, unmaintained road out of Joraw, setting everyone's teeth on edge, until the road merged with the well-maintained highway between Joraw and Albir. Everything was quiet; the air was full of anticipation, and Ben still felt far too inexperienced to be going on missions. Celer's speculations weren't helping.

"I was thinking," he said, "that maybe KTAN won't just ship supplies through that wormhole. They could move an army through there, too. And the fact that Dhilnara Enterprises is shipping wormhole components to a private group is scary, too. Wormholes require such good supervision that the Alliance government requires everyone who deals with them to have really good certifications."

"What are you getting at?" Javrel asked.

"Either Dhilnara is knowingly doing something *very* illegal, or someone in the Alliance government signed off on the transfer of goods to KTAN."

"Great," Vuri said. "I don't know which is worse. Makes me *really* confident about this mission, Celer. Thanks." The squad returned to an even more uncomfortable silence as they completed their journey to Albir. Finally, the vehicle ground to a stop outside a huge shipping yard. The smell of seawater and oil permeated the air. Cranes towered over the skyline, some stationary, some maneuvering huge shipping containers onto barges and freighters. All this was far off in the distance, where a crane could fit in Ben's palm if he held his arm out straight. In the immediate vicinity, freight trucks passed occasionally and pedestrian traffic meandered through Albir, unaware of the alien threat operating at the port. The port itself was surrounded by a high wire fence, guarded at its entrances by men with wooden staffs, no doubt enchanted for many of the same feats as Ben's. Even so, Vuri walked up to the nearest guard, not flinching as she faced up to the burly Andarite. Their Messengers took to tensely staring each other down, feet above their keepers' heads. Celer narrated the conversation between them.

"Bureau of Commerce, Department of Marine Trade Regulation," she said. As she did so, she raised a small metallic circle for a split second, not long enough for it to be recognized. "You have a shipment going out to Dhilnara Enterprises today. Mind if we take a look?"

"You seem a bit to young to be an inspector, ma'am," the guard said, choking up his grip on his staff. Vuri only smiled.

"Why, thank you!" she said. "I think I'll take that as a compliment today, instead of an attack on my credentials. Now can I see that shipment? I'm running late as it is, and if I miss this shipment then my boss gets involved with yours, and the bureaucrats start asking *so* many questions..." She sighed for dramatic effect. "You get what I mean."

"Got it. Go on in, please. Sorry about that," the guard said, sliding the gate open for Vuri.

"My associates will be coming in as well," Vuri said. She went back to the car to retrieve them. "We're in. Javrel, stay with the car. I can't think up an excuse for your robo-face right now." Ben, Seren and Celer entered, only to be asked by the guard to pull down their hoods.

"Your associates are… I don't recognize your species," he said, raising an eyebrow.

"Quite frankly, sir, I am insulted by your insensitivity and prejudicial species-bias," Seren retorted accusingly, through Celer's translation. With that, she and the others walked confidently away into the shipyard.

"Nice bluff," Ben commented. "What was that thing you showed him?"

Vuri threw a metal disc back to him, which was adorned with crudely carved decorations and a few lines of calligraphy. "Flash this fast enough and people believe anything. Sometimes it doesn't work, and that's when you have to break things."

"I am uncomfortable with the fact that we just impersonated federal officials," Seren muttered, "but in comparison with the possibility of a growing KTAN army, I suppose it is a small risk."

"Remind me why we had to ditch Javrel?" Celer said.

"It was hard enough to pass myself off as an adult," Vuri said. "He's the little brother, and half of his body is made of hijacked Iyerani tech. *Really* hard to explain to people. No one here has seen a human before, so nobody knows how old you should be compared to how you look. Anybody who asks, Seren can take care of. Nice call with the racist thing, by the way."

Seren nodded appreciatively. "A bit of a warning next time would be welcomed."

"Sure," Vuri said. "Celer, Arwi, go scout above. See if you can get a better perspective."

The Messengers flew off. Vuri stayed cool and confident as she bluffed through asking directions to the place where the Dhilnara Enterprises freight ship was docked. She negotiated with another official, who allowed her to start opening crates and inspecting the contents.

"What are we looking for?" Ben asked through his teeth.

"Anything that looks like it could be linked to KTAN, I guess," Vuri said. "Maybe Seren can identify Iyerani stuff getting shipped in?" She looked at Seren expectantly.

"I have seen nothing suspicious," she said.

Celer and Arwi flew down into the yard. "There are Wenifrin dock workers carrying some very large boxes with hazard labels on them out of the ship."

"Sounds like a good lead," Vuri said. "Let's go."

The squad ran out of the port before the slow, carefully moving guard detail around the antimatter containers could make it down the docking ramp from the ship. They got back into the car with Javrel and told him what had happened.

"We should follow them," Vuri said.

"No," Seren said. "Our orders were to observe. You already overstepped them by impersonating a government official. We can do no more."

"The only limit Advisor Dyalaro placed on us was that we don't go on the docks," Vuri said. "The thing we want, conveniently, has not only left the docks, it is leaving the entire freaking port! We can follow it!"

"Yeah, and get spotted," Celer said. "Shady Wenifrins with mob connections probably know how to tell when someone is following them. They…"

"Celer? What?" Ben asked.

"Everybody shut up," he hissed. "Vuri, open the door a bit."

A large trailer truck had pulled up outside the port, and the Wenifrins were moving the boxes out of the port gates. The driver and the dockworkers were talking rapidly.

"What are they saying?" Ben asked.

"It's a dialect that I don't know, but I recognize the phonology. Plosives and post-nasal fricatives."

"Which means?" Javrel asked.

"Rim dialect," Celer replied.

"As in the Wenifrin Rim Planets?" Vuri asked.

"Yeah."

"Someone tell me about the Alliance politics of which I am apparently ignorant!" Seren snapped.

Vuri closed the door now that Celer was done listening. "In the last year, there have been protests and violent revolts all over the outer planets of the Wenifrin empire."

"The protesters could want help fighting the empire," Javrel said. "Maybe they and KTAN are trading favors. Dhilnara probably operates out of the colonies."

The Wenifrins finished loading the huge, warning-labeled boxes into the truck, then the truck pulled away from the port. It gained speed slowly under the weight of the box.

"Now or never," Vuri said. "What do we do?"

"I'll follow them from the air," Celer said. "Arwi can relay where I am back to you, so you can follow at a safe distance. Let me out of the car."

Vuri opened the door, and Celer shot out, Arwi in close pursuit.

Daolor Squad's vehicle followed the truck onto the highway, keeping a safe distance, far enough away so as not to be spotted. Celer and Arwi kept track of the truck, relaying its movements back to Vuri. They were travelling through familiar mountains.

"Wait a minute," Ben said. "Isn't this the highway back to Joraw?"

"Yeah," she said. She revved the engine even higher and started closing in on the vehicle.

"Vuri, what are you doing?" Javrel asked. "If we get any closer, we'll be spotted!"

"We have to cut them off before they start setting up in Joraw," she said. "Celer was right before. They could start moving troops into our city as soon as they get that gate completed."

"We are unprepared and we have no backup," Seren said. "This was a survey mission, nothing more."

"We have to make sure this thing doesn't get there," Ben said. "We don't have time to get approval."

When Arwi came down the next time she was to report the vehicle's location, Javrel sent her off to warn Advisor Dyalaro of the possibility of attack. She flew back to Sildial headquarters as fast as possible.

When Arwi arrived back at Sildial, she made a supersonic rush straight for the Advisor's office.

"It's as we feared," Advisor Dyalaro said. "Messenger patrols already showed that KTAN was gathering more Takathist troops in the city to overwhelm Sildial. They're probably a temporary safeguard until the Iyeranis have wormhole contact, but still too much for us. We barely fought off the last attack. Trying to pull that off with our current numbers would be suicide."

"So what are we doing?" Arwi asked.

"We will be evacuating this building as soon as possible. We've been making preparations ever since we saw the Takathist buildup in the city. Thoral managed to call in a favor and rent a warehouse in Albir where we will be basing our operations from now on."

Arwi moaned. To her, the building seemed just as much a part of Sildial as any living member. This was where she and the siblings had been taken in by Varyal. This was where they had trained to save Andaros. After the attack, this was where everyone had labored together to rebuild. The place resonated with memories. "Understood," she croaked awkwardly.

"I'm sorry," Advisor Dyalaro said. "I know how much this place is a home to you. If there were an alternative…"

"I know," she said.

"Go back to your squad," Advisor Dyalaro said. "If they believe they have the ability to stall that truck's arrival, let them do it. It might give us valuable time."

When Arwi returned to the transport, Vuri and Javrel cursed at the news.

"Alright," Javrel said, "Let's get on with this. Vuri, bring us up alongside that truck. I'll stop it."

The engine roared, and the vehicle surged forward. Ben looked nervously out the window at the icy road surface.

"Careful of the cargo," Seren warned.

"Yep," Javrel said.

The car came up swiftly behind the truck, then moved out of its travel lane to drive alongside. The Wenifrin driver looked over at the car just in time to see Javrel lean out the window and shoot the tires. Even as the air hissed out of them, the driver would not stop. Javrel raised his arm to fire at the driver, but the Wenifrin opened the truck door and began firing back with a pistol.

"Duck!" Javrel called. Everyone hid their heads inside the unarmored civilian car, hoping the cheap metal would keep away bullets. Javrel peered up again and fired back, a single shot from his unerring robotic arm. The driver clutched at the chest wound and fell out of the open door, hitting the pavement. The truck drove on under its own momentum.

"Vuri, U-turn, now!" Ben called. "The antimatter is about to crash off the road!" He pointed ahead at a bend in the road, off which the vehicle was about to hurtle into a large drainage ditch. Vuri slammed the brakes, jerking everyone forward in their seats, then turned turned the vehicle back around, racing away from the truck. The truck ran of the road and crashed into the ditch with the groan and screech of metal on metal, but there was no explosion.

"The cargo must be intact," Seren said. "We should try to recover it."

"What if it breaks open in the engine fire?" Ben asked, motioning back to the truck. There were flames pouring from the ruptured gas tank.

"Then the blast will be larger than that of an atomic bomb and it will not matter how quickly we drive away," Seren said.

"Oh. Yeah, let's go try and get it, then."

Vuri made yet another jarring U-turn and drove back to the site, only to be met by a firing line of six Iyerani guards. They were bloodied and their robotic enhancements were soot-stained, but they stood with their weapons, resolutely staring down the squad.

"Shield?" Ben asked.

"Yep," Vuri replied.

Ben punched his staff through the windshield, throwing out a conical field of magical energy. Vuri drove straight for the guards and they scattered, moving into a circle around the car. Ben shifted his shield into a dome around the whole vehicle.

Without warning, the vehicle screeched to a halt and Ben's shield died. Bullets ricocheted off of the vehicle as Ben tried to get a spark of magic back. Everyone cowered inside. They were surrounded.

"Magic burns?" Javrel asked.

"No! I feel fine!"

"Then what?" Vuri demanded.

Ben felt magic flow back into his fingers, but in the same instant the squad car was thrown through the air. Ben felt the ripples of someone else's magic all around him. The car landed upside down, suspending everyone inside the vehicle by their seatbelts. They struggled out of the restraints, crawling over broken glass to get out of the car. They hid behind its useless metal mass to stay away from the gunfire, now coming from only one side.

Ben scrambled to his feet and peered over the car. Down the road, there was a Wenifrin in oil-stained work clothes, wielding a staff of ivory and amber. Ben fired a blast of magic, which the Wenifrin blocked easily off a personal shield. He tried another, which was blocked just as easily. The Wenifrin smiled and pointed at his arms mockingly. Ben got the picture.

"That Wenifrin shielded the Iyeranis from the crash, threw the car, deflected both of my attacks, and he still isn't straining his magic."

"We're outnumbered by the Iyeranis," Seren said. "We cannot take them on in the open like this, not if Ben thinks he cannot handle the magician." She glanced over her shoulder. "We have to run for the woods. Ben, shield us as best you can. Hopefully they will give up searching when they realize we've been defeated."

Vuri nodded. "Three, two, one, go!"

Ben threw up a shield, under which the squad ran for the side of the road. The Wenifrin lashed out with a blast of heat and light that destroyed Ben's shield and sent pain rocketing up through the back of his neck. The squad made it to the woods, losing sight of the Wenifrin. Before slowing down, they came to a steep, rocky, downward slope. Running down, Ben tripped and fell over the ice-encrusted rocks, rolling and flopping over them before finally slamming into a tree. The others fell similarly, unable to gain traction on the icy slope. They stumbled to their feet at the bottom and kept running, going into the woods as far and as fast as they could. When the burning in their lungs and legs demanded that they run no further, the squad huddled silently in the snow, listening for sounds of pursuit.

Ben said after a while of listening, "I think they might have given up."

"What now?" Arwi asked. "KTAN will get another truck to come along and pick up the antimatter, and Sildial is already in full retreat."

"I have no idea," Vuri muttered. "We're all out of options."

Celer said, "Arwi, you and I should watch from the air to see them move out with the antimatter, then we can call someone to pick up the rest of the squad."

The Messengers flew up over the truck. They watched another KTAN team come, recover the durable antimatter containers from the ruined truck, transfer them into another truck, and drive off towards Joraw. There, they met an armed

Takathist guard division that brought the supplies to the same compound where Ben had been kept by KTAN. Now, it was far more heavily guarded, with a high perimeter fence and a guard every few feet. The Messengers returned to Sildial to make the report of the failure to Advisor Dyalaro. She sent out an inconspicuous civilian vehicle to pick up the squad.

Back in the woods, Daolor Squad had nothing to do but sit by the roadside, shiver in the cold, and think about the fact that they would not be returning to the headquarters for long.

"Are you okay?" Ben asked Javrel, who was staring forlornly out at the mountains.

He took a deep breath. The exhalation billowed out as a cloud of steam in the chill air. "I hoped that we would never have to leave that place. It was home for us. I never thought that things would get so bad that we would have to leave."

"Things are going to get better," Ben said.

"How do you know that? We just gave up the last base of resistance we had! We didn't stop the antimatter from getting to Joraw, either."

"I know. We can't give up, though. Not on Andaros, not on each other. I won't."

Javrel smiled. "Thanks," he said. "The gods were good to us when they sent you three to us."

"Thank you."

They waited hours for Sildial's vehicle to arrive to pick them up. Without vehicles or much ammunition, they were defenseless and could not risk a fire, so they shivered in place until a vehicle rolled up to take them back to headquarters for one last night. Daolor Squad drank warm, bitter tea and joined the other agents in a low, mournful hymn during dinner. In the morning, everyone rose before the sun to make the final preparations for evacuation.

The sun was rising by the time everyone had finished loading the essentials and anything else they could into Sildial's few remaining undamaged vehicles. A few agents cast bitter eyes at Daolor when they found out that they had abandoned a vehicle. Someone was going to have to leave some belongings behind to make up for the loss of space. The owner of the warehouse had sent a small truck that would carry some more of their supplies, but not much more. Soon, the caravan was rumbling away on the broken streets.

From their seat in a transport, Javrel, Arwi, and Vuri looked back one last time at their old home, now empty of any life or signs of it. One team had remained behind, just outside of the soon-to-be blast radius. The building itself was too valuable to leave for the Iyeranis to take. Somewhere, someone pressed a detonator. There was a yellow flash, brilliant in the dim light of the overcast morning, and then smoke and dust clouded up around the bottom of the building as it collapsed in on itself. Javrel and Vuri kept their eyes on the dust settling over the dead rubble until the vehicle turned, obscuring it from their sight. For the rest of the drive, they prayed. Ben, Seren and Celer listened, and soon it seemed the siblings had prayed for every individual soul on Andaros.

Still, as the vehicle came to a stop in Sildial's new home, it didn't seem that there could ever be enough time to pray for all the troubles of the planet.

As everyone got out, they were confronted by a tall, plain, warehouse wall. Sildial was silent as they marched into this cold, unfamiliar place with the knowledge that they would never return to the base that had been their symbol of rebellion and hope.

Ben looked around, concerned for his friends as they abandoned their home. His second concern was the obvious lack of any tactical considerations in the construction of this civilian warehouse. Something told him the owner wouldn't take kindly to the organization building a parapet on the slanted metal roof. Nevertheless, he and the others heaved the first of many boxes out of the transport and started carrying them into the empty space of concrete and metal. The inside was dim, as at least half of the light bulbs were dead in their ceiling fixtures. The rest of them shed weak white light that faded and died before it illuminated the back and corners of the huge room. Ben kept hauling boxes while others around him set up cots, and arranged boxes, and the few sheets that could be spared, so everyone could have a bit of privacy. He looked out at the rest of the organization, with its meager pile of supplies that was dwarfed by the empty concrete grimness of the warehouse. *So now we're the refugees,* he thought.

After the unloading of supplies, a task that did not take very long, the crowd began to settle. They eyed Daolor

Squad and muttered in hushed tones around them. Ben heard Voleric words like *enemy* and *danger,* but still didn't have the fluency to tell what exactly was being said.

"Rumors are spreading quickly in these close quarters," Javrel said. "The people want to know what happened out there, and Thoral's been very secretive."

"And with good reason," Celer said. "They could panic."

"Not to mention the fact that we failed the mission," Seren muttered.

"How do you think Thoral's going to take it?" Ben asked.

"Who knows?" Javrel said. "He's new to command. But let's find some beds first." Javrel talked to another agent, who led them to three very basic cots, essentially canvas stretched taut over a thin, wobbly wooden frame. The squad retrieved their personal belongings and stowed them under the beds.

Dalivei, Thoral's Messenger, zipped out of the air and hovered in front of Vuri. "Ms. Darialaro, Commander Thoral would like to speak with your squad."

Chapter 12

Thoral's new "office" doubled as his quarters, and was made of a ring of curtains hung around his bed, a few old boxes for seats, and a small desk made of more old boxes. Thoral, Daal-Na An-Tun, Advisor Dyalaro, and Daolor Squad somehow all managed to squeeze into the space, with their Messengers hovering close to their heads. Everyone sat on boxes except for Thoral, seated on the bed, and An-Tun, in his wheelchair. The three leaders were clearly worried.

"I was briefed on this matter by Ms. Dyalaro, via Arwi," Thoral said. "But I would like to hear your official report."

Vuri retold the adventure to Thoral, while Celer translated the Voleric discussion into English to keep Ben and Seren updated. At the end, Thoral muttered to his Messenger, who flew off to another part of the warehouse.

"I'm having Adoro, the tech expert who I believe you've met, look up more details on Dhilnara Enterprises. Once we're firmly planted at this new base, we're going to focus all of our attentions on taking control of these wormhole stations."

The squad nodded.

"Dismissed," Thoral said. "Now go make yourselves useful."

After the squad walked out, Thoral whispered to his advisors, "What do you think?"

"We need to watch the revolutions developing on the Wenifrin Rim," An-Tun said. "We don't know how deeply their alliance with KTAN runs."

"Are you saying they'll fight for KTAN?" Thoral asked.

"We can't discount the possibility," An-Tun replied.

"For now, I think we should focus on gathering more information on the wormhole ports themselves, and on this Dhilnara Enterprises business," Advisor Dyalaro said.

"Agreed," Thoral said. "I'll read their charter and interplanetary laws that matter to this situation. An-Tun, coordinate Messenger surveillance on any locations that Adoro finds important. Valerija, see to it that our people are comfortable and morale is at least afloat."

There was a resounding "yes, sir," from walker and Messenger alike.

Outside Thoral's improvised office, on the warehouse floor, Javrel brought breakfast for the rest of his squad. Without a dining hall in the new establishment, they ate on their bunks.

For days, they all trained apart in their chosen fields. Between the hours of menial work around the warehouse, Ben trained with An-Tun, who taught him new spells and enchantments, including the powerful magic innate in the staff. Seren, already familiar with the fundamentals of Iyerani computing, learned KTAN's unique computer language at a speed that astounded her teacher. Celer practiced with formations of Messengers from other squads, becoming even more agile. He learned the arts of moving unnoticed through any space, wide open or enclosed. He watched enviously each day as Messenger recon parties were sent out, reporting on the goings-on aboard the Wenifrin-KTAN positions.

The mood was grim around the warehouse. Sildial radiated a general feeling of distrust to Daolor Squad, for letting the antimatter into Joraw. Fighters and Messengers avoided eye contact with them.

One day at lunch, Ben felt an ominous disposition settling over the crowd. People spoke in hushed tones. Ben's Voleric was still quite bad, but what he heard involved words like *attack* and *bad fortune*. Javrel snatched a newspaper from a passing fighter. Shock and uncertainty were painted across his face by the time his eye and lens reached the bottom of the page. He read for Ben and Seren:

"JORAW POPULATION DEAD AFTER MYSTERIOUS PURGE: The corpses of approximately 1500 homeless, often disabled residents of Joraw were found piled along the roads in and out of the city. Autopsies show

that all of these victims suffered violent deaths by gunshot or be-heading. Authorities do not currently have suspects, but Zdai Olaro, district police supervisor of the greater Albir area, has denied that it has anything to do with the large freight truck crash that interrupted commutes several days ago."

"Everyone in Sildial knows Zdai's corrupt," Javrel said. Now, listen to this part."

"Kalar Ralodaro, known in Darjae for the past weeks as the 'Prophet of Iyerayñan,' was seen parading with a small group of followers holding what witnesses claimed was the sev-ered head of an Iyerani. He and several others of his group have attributed the attack to the Iyerani organized crime organiza-tion known as KTAN, or 'The Master Warriors' Alliance.' They have stated that the head belonged to one of the escaping perpetrators of the massacre, who he and his armed followers caught trying to return from the attack. He also produced a written threat, allegedly from KTAN themselves, stating that if any of their assets were threatened, there would be another massacre. Authorities have yet to confirm either allegation."

"That was just this morning?" Ben asked, appalled.

"It happened overnight," Javrel said. "They want to keep us away from that wormhole port."

"Kalar's going to use this thing like a podium to shout his message from," Celer said. "People will freak out, and they'll want answers."

"And they'll take them from whoever shouts the loudest and fastest," Vuri added. "Great. Kalar's going to recruit another resistance movement under him."

"Divided resistance against a united enemy," Seren said.

"Exactly," Javrel said.

Ben was glad that there were, at least, some new recruits to Sildial. Citizens of all skill levels from Albir and the surrounding cities followed the threads of rumor, hunting down the new headquarters of Sildial. Thoral took them in indiscriminately. They were more than Sildial could handle in its facilities, but the people were determined fight KTAN. It was better, Thoral had said, to take them here than let them go to Kalar's army. By the end of the day, Sildial had no more recruits to take in. The rumor mill of the Messengers, however, carried the name *Ralodaro's Righteous Swords* from Darjae, along with tales of an impressive militia growing there. Sildial scrambled for a reply from Thoral, who needed his advisors to fend of questions as he stayed in deep deliberation in his office.

"Maybe we don't need to worry about him just yet," Dalivei suggested, while slowly circling around Thoral's head. "Darjae is a long way away."

"No. Kalar is reckless, and innocent people will be killed if he keeps whipping them into a frenzy. If we wait and he gets out of hand, it really will be our fault."

"It's not like we can force him to stop," Dalivei said. "He won't listen, not after we took sides with the humans over him. However, if we could convince his followers not to work for him, then we might have a chance."

"I think I might know how to do that," Thoral said. He didn't smile. The plan would be risky, and that was putting it lightly. "Valeri!" he called, to his advisor. "Do you know if we have a copy of the Ceremony Statutes around, latest edition? I need to check if my plan is still legal."

By that night, the frenzy of rumor was even greater, as Messengers were seen dispersing to the far reaches of the city, on the strange mission to bring back news reporters. No one in Sildial had ever known Thoral to be an attention seeker, and Ben wondered what was so important about this press release that no one in the organization could be told beforehand. By sunset, there was a crowd of Andarites in front of a podium, which Thoral had put up in the front of the warehouse.

"No camera people?" Ben observed.

"What?" Vuri asked.

"News reporters. I thought that's why Thoral sent all those Messengers out. Who are these people?"

"They *are* reporters, Ben. *Writers*," Javrel said. "We are a very traditional people. The written word can be carried and shared. Now quiet, Thoral is beginning his speech."

"*Zilri dawtaro volaero,*" Thoral started. "People of Dawta Volaero," Celer translated, "By now everyone in this nation and beyond has heard of the horrific mass murder of the remaining citizens of Joraw. Former Commander of this organization Kalar Ralodaro, now head of his own

'Righteous Swords,' has already made his intent against the Iyerani group KTAN clear. However, we know Kalar is dangerous, and unstable. It was for this reason and others that we had him removed from our own ranks. That is why I say this: Kalar of the line of Ralod, *rol arey avardo vroil: Djelab Verathari. Dalval ravelari eili riri eidjedzol, dai zejerald ravelaghe izurezol."*

The crowd and reporters erupted into shouting.

"Thoral zeir!" Vuri shouted angrily.

"What's going on?" Ben asked. "Celer, translate the end!"

Celer asked Vuri in Voleric, "Did I hear that right?"

"If you heard what I heard... I really hope not."

"What was said?" Seren asked insistently.

Vuri replied, "Thoral just challenged Kalar to single combat for control of the two factions."

"That is obscenely barbaric," Seren said.

"Which is why the Ceremony Statutes on Djelab Verathari haven't been used in over seventy-five years," Javrel replied. "I don't think the rituals were ever actually taken out of the lawbooks, so the challenge is still valid."

"When is this going to happen?" Ben asked.

"As soon as Kalar accepts the challenge, which I'm sure he will, and a venue is arranged," Javrel explained.

"What is Thoral *thinking?*" Vuri said. "I mean, he's been a great leader, but, well..." She made a vague gesture in Thoral's direction. It was easy to see what she meant: Ben remembered Kalar being a fit, muscled man with imposing posture that only amplified his charisma. Thoral was short and thin-limbed, a good leader, but likely not a fighter to match Kalar.

"What are the rules of the Djelab?" Celer asked.

Javrel explained, "Wrestle the opponent out of the arena circle, or keep him on the ground for more than a count of eight. Using magic, or striking with the horns or teeth is an immediate loss, and an *extreme* dishonor. Other than that, no rules."

"I don't know if either of them are really trained in Djelab combat, but Kalar obviously has the advantage," Vuri replied.

"And we have a few days, at most, before a venue for the challenge is arranged," Javrel added. "It's not as if he can train for this."

"What do we do until then?" Ben asked. "Is there anything we can do?"

"Pray," Vuri said simply, before stalking off in frustration.

Ben had to admit, even though Kalar wasn't a good commander, he still knew how to put on a spectacular show. By that evening, Kalar and his new lackeys had already managed to send an acceptance letter to the challenge, secure a venue for the fight, and send invitations and an army of reporters to Sildial. The arena was far away, in Darjae. Still, Kalar's militia was very accommodating. They offered to pay for the trip via bullet train. Kalar, Ben thought, was trying to make his chance to bask in the applause of an arena crowd go as smoothly as possible. All Daolor Squad could see as a result, however, would be an even more dramatic fall for Sildial in the arena. They were even more surprised when Thoral called them to his office after dinner.

"The train leaves tonight," he said, "and there are limited seats. I can't take all of Sildial. Only Daolor and Aqwero Squads will be coming with me."

"May I ask why?" Javrel said.

"No."

"But why challenge him?" Vuri demanded. "There has to be a better way than a *Djelab!* Do you seriously think you can take him on in physical combat?"

"What would you have me do?" Thoral snapped. "I never expected that Kalar could rebound this quickly, but he's used this massacre to throw the people into a frenzy. His organization is bigger than ours, ten men to one, after a single day. Trust your Commander, and be ready first thing in the morning when I call for you. Dress uniforms. Go."

"Yes sir," Vuri said through gritted teeth. She turned and left, leading the others. As ordered, they were ready the next morning, directly after breakfast, wearing full dress uniforms with long sleeves embroidered with calligraphy. The train ride was just over an hour long, pulling into the station in Darjae at noon. There, a welcoming party stood outside the terminal, wearing smug smiles. Thoral stood tall and straight, met their eyes, and smiled back. This, the appearance of two humans, and a scarred Andarite in an Iyerani robotic suit, obviously confused the welcomers. Unsettled, they opened the doors of two limousine-like transports upholstered in fine polished leather with gold trim. Thoral, his advisors, and the chosen two squads piled in. The ride was blurred; Ben fidgeted nervously in his seat as the limos passed though the streets of Darjae, a large, pedestrian-heavy city with short towers and business complexes, decorated with slightly underwatered trees and the occasional small fountain. The huge Ziggurat and Library rose above the rest of the city like mountains. The limousine route was lined with Andarite civilians, wearing hard expressions as they analyzed the prey passing through the gates of their den. The limos arrived at what appeared to be a converted college campus at the edge of the city. Idyllic cobbled walkways lined with flowering plants linked several tall, stone buildings. There were many windows, half of which were covered with posters and banners, all depicting the same gory scene: An Iyerani in cartoonishly over-stylized armor, mouth agape as a green sword pierced its chest. The calligraphy at the side: *Andaros Is Safe Under Ralodaro's Righteous Swords.*

"They've descended from fighting KTAN into outright speciesism," Celer muttered.

"And this is who Thoral's about to give our oaths to," Vuri grumbled. The Sildial representatives got out of the car and marched to where Kalar's followers had made an arena out of a large plot of open land in the back of the campus. In what must have been record time, enough bleachers for at least half of the 'Righteous Swords' fighters had been erected around a perfectly circular wooden platform of about twenty foot diameter. The platform area was edged in bright red paint. Step off, Ben remembered, and game over. Eight seconds on the ground, pinned or unconscious, game over. No using teeth, horns, or magic. No other rules. The bleachers were already filled with a raucous crowd of Kalar's favorite people; the battle-hungry masses that were high on their leader's charisma and the approaching scent of enemy blood. Even more of these folk crowded the area around the bleachers, packed like fans at a rock concert, craning to get a look at the arena. Messengers hovered at the arena edge, ready to pass commentary along to those who packed in behind the over-filled bleachers, too far away to see. Close to the arena, there were two covered areas similar to dugouts at a baseball field, set into the ground at exact opposite sides from each other. These were completely veiled by heavy curtains, so each team had no view of the other.

"Those are for the fighters and their ceremonial guard of two representatives," Javrel said, indicating the dugouts. "The rest of us will have to sit in the bleachers."

"Who's the guard?" Ben asked.

"Javrel and Dalivei, Seren and Celer," Thoral replied. He had changed out of his uniform and into a ceremonial fighting outfit; a small, dark blue kilt, and tightly fitted sleeveless shirt of the same color.

"Commander," Seren protested, "Surely I am not qualified to attend such a ritual. I know none of your traditions."

"Just look confident and imitate Javrel," Thoral said absently. His nervous gaze was averted from her, towards the arena. Seren looked at Javrel and Vuri quizzically.

"Beats me why he chose you," Vuri said. "But you'll do fine." Just then, a long, high-pitched flute note sounded, holding until the entire arena and surrounding area quieted. Ben was reminded of the flute played at the funeral. Thoral departed with his guard to the dugout, while the rest of the squad went to the bleachers. Inside the dugout was dark, with all light blocked by the billowy curtains. Celer translated the words of the announcer, who stood at a podium to the side of the arena.

"Fighters of Andaros, we are proud to play host to the first *Djelab Verathari* in over seventy years, and even prouder that this battle will once and for all settle who is to be the leader of our resistance from the evil Iyerani corruption. Without further ado, per the Ceremony Statutes proceedings, I would like to introduce the leader of Sildial Radaejoraro, the challenger and our guest, Thoral Gosali!"

Taking his cue, Thoral exited the dugout, calmly pushing aside the curtains and walking, flanked by Seren and the other ceremonial guards, to the center of the wooden arena floor. The crowd in the bleachers gave him weak, polite applause. Every eye was upon him, sizing up the challenger with disdain.

"And his opposition, the challenged, our leader and hero of the resistance, Kalar Ralodaro!"

Kalar burst forth from his dugout, throwing the curtains dramatically aside and being met with wave after wave of thunderous applause. He raised his arms and reveled in the love of his friends, smiling and waving at everyone. For a man who had just recently pulled himself off the streets, he looked good. His followers' funds had gone to a slick black fighter's outfit similar to Thoral's, along with a good bath. His scales and horns had polished and waxed to a reflective glimmer in the afternoon light. Kalar and his ceremonial guard, two tall, bulky Andarites with the same polished scales, walked with a confident, crowd-pleasing swagger to the center of the arena, where they stood almost nose to nose with the Sildial team. Seren detected a distinct aroma of liquor wafting from Kalar.

"Keeping up with old habits, I sense," Thoral observed dryly. For a moment, rage flashed behind Kalar's eyes, and he glowered cruelly at Seren.

"Still harboring *rekyari,* I see," he retorted. He made eye contact with Seren. "Not for long. In half an hour you will be dead, little *rekyar.* My organization will not harbor enemies of the cause."

Thoral's gaze remained locked on Kalar. "Nor will mine." He smirked and gave Kalar a pointed look. Kalar clenched his fists for a moment, before returning to waving appreciatively at the crowd.

"Let's get this over with," Kalar said. "And may the best patriot win."

"Agreed." Thoral said.

The ceremonial guards turned and walked back to the dugout. Seren and Javrel went over to the bleachers, where they sat down next to Ben and Vuri. Thoral and Kalar dropped into low fighting stances and waited for the announcer to call. He counted down, along with the chant of the crowd.

"*Va... Ro... Gal... Ďo... Er...*" The crowd was gaining fervor. "*Jeb... Ya... Ao... Wavaw!*" At the call of *go,* Kalar jumped forward to grapple Thoral, but met empty air as Thoral jumped out of the way. Kalar spun, reacting quickly to the evasion, and ran at Thoral again. Thoral rasied his knee and jabbed it into Kalar's stomach, then followed up by elbowing him hard in the face. Kalar reeled for a moment, before growling savagely and grabbing Thoral's shoulders. He threw Thoral to the ground, but Thoral rolled away and jumped to his feet before Kalar could keep him down. The crowd jeered and cheered according to their allegiances. Thoral moved around the edges of the arena, tempting Kalar to attack him, then jumping out of the way.

"He can't keep this evasion game up forever," Vuri muttered. "Kalar has better stamina."

"There must be some plan," Seren said. Still, Thoral didn't seem to be doing anything effective. In fact, he wasn't even making an attempt to get Kalar out of the ring. The strategy, though, was getting Kalar angrier and angrier. After so many dodges and jumps, Thoral's chest heaved from the exertion, and Kalar seethed with frustration. The evasion game kept up until Thoral was unsteady on his feet, and Kalar bellowed with rage every time he tried to catch Thoral.

"You're winning, Kalar," Thoral shouted, "but you know that I'm the better leader."

"Everyone who truly loves Andaros loves me!"

"That is a lie. We tolerated you for a while, and only because we loved your father. Never you."

Kalar roared, and charged Thoral again. He lowered his head, aiming his polished horns at Thoral's stomach. Kalar's attack struck, horns sinking deep into Thoral's flesh. Thoral gasped in pain and fell to the ground, clutching at the wounds. Blood gushed through his fingers as he tried to stop the bleeding with shaking hands. Kalar stood up, shouting and shaking his fist in the air, a savage grin on his face.

"I have won!" Kalar shouted. "Bow, Sildial, to your new leader! Kalar! Champion of…" His smile faded and his words trailed off. The crowd was silent. Occasionally there were murmurs, as the crowd tried to put together the pieces of what had happened. Finally, someone shouted from the Righteous Swords crowd.

"*Kalar Zedarialaro!*"

Others shouted their assent. "*Kalar Zedarialaro! Arizijage wavaw!*"

"What does *zedarial* mean?" Seren asked.

"Dishonor," Celer said. "Kalar the dishonorable."

Javrel said, "He struck with his horns in the arena. The crowd is calling for his removal."

"That was his plan," Seren realized. "Thoral knew he couldn't remove Kalar in a conventional way, but he knew how to get Kalar to remove himself. And it worked."

Kalar was also working out what he had fallen for, as emergency medical technicians tended to Thoral in his pool of blue. "This man sympathises with the enemy!" he said, pointing at Thoral. He then pointed to Seren. "And he houses that heartless scum in his headquarters!" Still, his popularity was dissolving around him. Defaming the man who lay beaten and bloodied on the ground did not help him gain back favor with his people. The crowd shouted and ridiculed Kalar, and on the arena floor, below all those voices, it seemed his former glory could never be farther away.

"The gods favor me!" he shouted. "Valzai respects my determination! Audir's will guides me! Listen to me! I am the instrument of their will! You are using ancient rituals to usher evil into our midst!"

The crowd still jeered, and the determination drained from Kalar's face. He ran to the arena exit and disappeared from sight. All eyes turned to the cluster of medical technicians around Thoral. They were loading him onto a stretcher. Thoral raised his head just enough to close to one of them and whisper something weakly.

"Hail Valerija Dyalaro," the technician relayed to the crowd. The crowd took up the call like a sacred chant, slowly and solemnly. Their fervor grew by the second, until they screamed Advisor Dyalaro's name for the world to hear.

"Accept the position, Valeri," An-Tun said to her. "Go down there and meet them."

Valerija Dyalaro shook, eyes locked on the crew taking Thoral away. Still, she stood and walked to the arena center. She looked around the arena and raised her hands in acceptance. The crowd cheered. One of the grunts from Kalar's ceremonial guard walked forward to meet her.

"I am Vodir Balaro, second in command to the dishonored," he said. "You have the facilities and the loyalty of everyone here." Then, he grabbed Ms. Dyalaro's wrist and held her hand up like she was a wrestling champion. "We are Sildial!" he shouted.

"We are Sildial!" echoed the crowd.

Balaro called to the crowd, "I will escort our great leader and her advisor to the office of the dishonored. The rest of you, see to it that the friends she has brought with her are cared for." A group of finely dressed men and women, former followers of Kalar, escorted Daolor and Aqwero squads into the compound, where they went to a lounge set with all kinds of food.

"Please make yourselves comfortable here," one of the escorts said. "Eat anything you like. And... we are sorry for your loss." Everyone nodded solemnly and thanked the escort. No one ate.

"I didn't see where exactly Thoral was hit," Arwi said. "Are they sure he's dead?"

"I do not believe so," Seren said. "However, he may likely die in the hospital."

"So that's why he wanted you and Javrel as his guard," Celer said. "Thoral knew Kalar would freak after what you did to him the first time."

"So do we get these digs now that Valeri's in charge of everybody?" Vuri asked, with a wide, sweeping gesture around the well-appointed room laden with rich food and lavish decorations.

"That's seriously what you're worried about right now?" Arwi asked.

"Come on, I'm not the only one who's wondering. It's way better than the warehouse, right?" She snatched a crisp fruit from the table and bit into it loudly.

In another part of the compound, Valerija and Vodir walked down the halls to Kalar's former office, with Daal-Na An-Tun wheeling along next to them. They came to a door, upon which hung a flag reading, *Kalar Ralodaro, Supreme Commander of the Righteous Swords*. Below it was the same impaled, charicatured Iyerani on the flags outside. Valeri hissed with displeasure.

"Have this thing taken down," she said.

Vodir nodded understandingly. The three leaders entered a spacious, second story corner office with windows overlooking a courtyard garden. Silky tapestries hung on the walls, surrounding an obviously expensive desk of dark, polished wood, and a chair upholstered with soft cushions covered in black leather. Valerija opened the desk drawers, finding them full drafts of inflammatory speeches, labeled in Kalar's uneven scrawl. There were a few very thin files of unorganized paperwork. Valeri picked them up and showed them to Vodir.

"Are there not more?" she asked.

"Kalar delegated most of his paperwork to me and other advisors," Vodir replied.

"Classic Kalar," she said, sighed. She turned to her Messenger. "Go back to the delegation, tell them they don't have to wait for me."

Vodir nodded to his own Messenger, a larger-than aver-age one with small eyes, blue neckband, and stoic compo-sure. "You may show them to new quarters."

"What's the prognosis?" Javrel asked when Mrs. Dyalaro's Messenger returned.

"Thoral was flown to the hospital just after we left the arena," she replied. "Not much was said…" she flared with melancholy blue light. "…but they don't expect him to last the night. Kalar's followers signed over control of the orga-nization directly to Valeri."

"And what happens to Kalar now?" Seren asked.

"He will live on alms," she replied. "Anyone may provide him with food, water, and soap without sharing his dishonor. He will survive, but he will not truly live after what he has done."

"He won't be sent to jail, or have a trial?" Ben asked.

"What happens in that arena belongs only to the gods," the Messenger said. "Secular law will have no further part in it. As for the rest of the exchange between Ceremonial and secluar law, the interface is complicated."

"So are we staying here?" Vuri asked.

"Yes. Surprisingly, there are still remaining quarters here. We'll be staying one squad to a room, except officers' quarters."

"You may move in now," Vodir's Messenger said. "Follow me." He flew in unerringly straight lines and took corners at precise, military-style angles, leading Daolor and

Aqwero Squads out of the building and into another nearby one. This building was a dormitory house of the former college. The first few rooms they passed had the signs of recent use, including varying degrees of neatness and belongings shoved under beds or strewn around the room. Most of the building's two stories, however, were still unoccupied.

"You have first pick," Vodir's Messenger said. The squads' Messengers looked at each other for a moment, and all simultaneously called for the second floor, so they could be as close to the sky as possible. The walkers acquiesced and followed their floating friends to the second floor rooms. Daolor picked two rooms with two beds each, Javrel and Vuri taking one, Ben and Seren the other.

"Are the rest of Sildial coming soon?" Javrel asked.

"Supreme Commander Dyalaro is organizing their move," the Messenger replied. "Vodir is directing the Righteous—ah, rest of Sildial to be ready to help the transition."

"Thank you," Javrel replied.

"Also, dinner is in an hour," the Messenger said. "The mess hall should be easy to find. Just follow the crowds." He then sped away, back to Vodir.

"I'm going to nap until then," Ben said to the squad. "I slept terribly on those warehouse cots."

"Definitely," Vuri said. "These are super comfortable compared to those things. Sleep tight!"

Javrel woke them all as the rivers of people poured from their quarters and posts, heading to the impressive, three-building complex of dining halls that served the organization. Entire squads were delegated to waiting the multitude of tables underneath the cathedral ceilings of the mess hall. Smooth stone pillars were spaced around the room. Vodir Balaro made sure the members from Albir were well cared for, promising as much food as they wanted. They sat down and were brought fried food on steaming platters, prepared in huge batches inside industrial-size kitchens. They ate their fill of spicy vegetables and savory, salty meats, washed down with cold tea and water. The hall was quiet aside from tense murmurs from the other tables. Seren looked particularly uncomfortable.

"Hey, are you okay?" Vuri asked, looking concernedly at her.

"Fine," she said.

"It's the people, isn't it?" Javrel said, casting his camera and eye around the room. The former *Swords* seemed to mind their own business for the most part, but they stopped once in a while to stare suspiciously at Seren. Kalar was gone, but he had planted in his followers a mistrust that wouldn't leave so easily.

"Don't worry," Ben said. He smiled reassuringly at her.

"We're looking out for you," Arwi added.

Seren smiled and went back to eating.

Moments later, a shrill Messenger whistle pierced the murmured conversations. An-Tun and Advisor Dyalaro stood at the front of the room, awaiting quiet.

"Thank you for your attention," Mrs. Dyalaro said once the room was quiet. "And thank you to the cook staff, for the excellent meal. Now, most of you do not know me, nor I you. I am Valerija, line of Dyal, Commander of Sildial. Not Supreme, not Righteous, just Commander. This is my friend and advisor, Alliance Ambassador Emeritus and Messengersmith Daal-Na Kon-Ren An-Tun." She waited for the applause to die away, then continued, "A lot of you probably came here to kill Iyeranis. Many others hopefully came here to save this homeland of ours. To the latter, I say, I look forward to working alongside you. To the former, I need only say this: Learn your real mission or show yourselves the door. Vodir is coordinating the duty schedule for this afternoon. That is all." She and An-Tun exited the room promptly.

"Admirably concise," Seren commented. The entire organization picked up their plates, trays and utensils, and moved in an orderly fashion to send them back to the kitchens. Vodir's Messenger flew to the Albir group with news.

"Supr—ah, *just* Commander Dyalaro and Vodir hope you will all take the day off today. We know this is a trauma for all of you. Thoral is in our prayers. Feel free to explore the campus."

Daolor Squad left to take in their surroundings, exploring the new headquarters site. The campus itself could easily house twice its current capacity in its extensive dorms. The air here was warm compared to Joraw, and no snow covered the ground. The Library and Ziggurat loomed in the distance, and farther out were the flat, grassy plains of the continent's southern reaches.

"This was an old college campus before the bigger university across town started attracting all of the new students, or so the other Messengers told me," Celer said. "Whoever owned it gave it to Kalar free of charge."

"Lucky us..." Vuri mused. "I wonder what kind of training facilities they have here."

"I wonder if these new fighters ever really got training," Javrel replied. "Something tells me Kalar didn't pay that much attention to things like that."

Sure enough, they walked around the campus and found a few empty gymnasia, but nothing that could be called a training facility; no swords, no guns, no firing range. Ben wondered how many new magic users were here, and whether they knew anything about combat. He was worried about meeting someone who wasn't careful with magic. When they passed members of the former *Swords,* they attracted suspicious looks. Seren in particular was getting venomous glances from the passing recruits. When they muttered to one another, Ben heard familiar Voleric insults.

"How much did Kalar tell them about you?" Arwi wondered to Seren.

"Lies and exaggerations, just like last time," Javrel said. "He might be gone, but it's a lot harder to get rid of their prejudices."

"Don't start any fights for my sake," Seren muttered.

"I don't think we'll have to *start* anything," Vuri said. "Maybe finish it, though." Ben didn't like the sound of that, and balked at the idea of having to repeat the dining hall incident.

"How's everyone settling in?" Mrs. Dyalaro said when she stopped in at Daolor's dorm that evening. Celer related the day's troubling events in detail. Mrs. Dyalaro replied, "Tell me if you ever feel in immediate danger, and *of course* if someone attacks you. Try to stay calm, however. The rest of Sildial know who you really are, and they'll arrive soon."

"This is a good thing," her Messenger said. "We have the resources to face off against KTAN and the Takathists on equal terms now. We're taking our fight back northward as soon as possible."

Just then, another Messenger flew up to Mrs. Dyalaro. His neckband was gray, and Ben recognized him immediately: Dalivei, Thoral's Messenger.

"Dalivei!" Mrs. Dyalaro said. "What news is there?"

"He's recovering!" the Messenger exclaimed.

"That's excellent!" Mrs. Dyalaro said. "And he's coming back soon?"

"Tomorrow morning," Dalivei said. "And he said if you wouldn't mind, he'll take the Commander position back."

Mrs. Dyalaro laughed. "Of course. I don't know how he does it, really. Tell him he's welcome to it, and that all of his advisors are waiting for him to come back." Dalivei nodded and sped back out into the twilight sky. Everyone in Daolor Squad beamed.

"I'll make the announcement tomorrow morning," Mrs. Dyalaro said.

Later that night, a van rolled into the campus under pounding rain. Thoral stepped out, shielded from the downpour by a dome of magic from a nurse of the Darjae hospital. The raindrops made golden ripples across its surface. He made his way to his office by the quietest corridors and least-used routes, hoping to avoid attention until tomorrow. Occasionally, people saw him and saluted as he passed. He only smiled and bade them to continue about their business. Along the way, he met up with Advisor Dyalaro.

"Thoral?" she asked. "I didn't think you were coming back until morning."

He smiled. "I wanted to be back as soon as possible. The nurses wanted me to stay longer, but I insisted. How are Kalar's old friends doing?"

"Ready to follow, and ready to fight. And about fighting, Thoral... What are we going to do about these wormhole gates?"

"I've been thinking about that ever since Daolor Squad told us about them. Part of me is still amazed that KTAN has managed to keep them secret for so long. I'm afraid to act too quickly, though. Did you confirm that news report?"

"Yes. Come with me."

One of the files in the Commander's office was the written threat that Kalar received from KTAN. In the crude, slangy Voleric dialect that was the signature of the larger criminal groups, there was a warning that if a wormhole gate was attacked, there would be another massacre, as in Joraw. Advisor Dyalaro showed it to Thoral.

"KTAN knows they have us paralyzed," she said. "Just yesterday, they moved Takathist troops into Alarzi for the first time. If we fight back, the Iyeranis will kill innocents. But if we do nothing, there's nothing to stop KTAN from taking Dawta Volaero entirely."

"You think I don't know that?" Thoral snapped. "Any move we make could doom thousands of people."

"So could our inaction," Valeri replied. "As it is now, KTAN is free to choose any target they want, no matter how zealously we would otherwise defend it. They could gain an irreparable tactical advantage in just a few days. Adoro from the Tech department also sent me this." She handed Thoral another paper.

PRIORITY EXTREME

ANALYSIS BRIEF: KTAN Data Storage Device (Recovery location: Alarzi)

TECHNICIAN ON DUTY: Adoro Galiro

> *Analysis of the decrypted data shows the details of a KTAN plan to construct several wormhole gates in key cities around Dawta Volaero. Components and fuel transport to the Joraw location appear to have been expedited due to the contested nature of the city between KTAN and Sildial. The other locations listed will receive wormhole gate components between Doria 11 and 14, with antimatter to follow on Doria 15-17. Research into wormhole gate construction shows 4-5 days for safe and proper completion.*

Thoral checked the calendar on Advisor Dyalaro's desk. Doria 18.

Thoral thought this over for a long time, and Valeri waited for any word from him. Finally, he said, "We will take all of the listed locations tomorrow. Seize control of all of them at once."

"You can coordinate that in a day?" Valeri asked, stunned.

"I must," Thoral replied. "Do you think KTAN will really take the time for safe and proper construction? They could be moving in soldiers if we take time to deliberate. I will give my plans to An-Tun, and his Messengers can coordinate resources across the continent. We will not let another day fall into the hands of the enemy."

CHAPTER 13

Yuri roused the squad early in the morning to ensure that they wouldn't miss Thoral's announcement at breakfast.

After everyone had eaten, Mrs. Dyalaro took to the stage in the dining hall and quieted the anxious crowd. Thoral stood beside her, looking in good spirits for someone who had just recovered from the hospital. Ben saw familiar faces in the now enlarged gathering; the rest of Sildial had moved to the new facilities between last night and early this morning. Ben was happy to see that both factions seemed to be integrating well, sitting at the same tables, laughing and conversing without prejudice.

"Good morning," Thoral began, "and welcome to all of you who made the night trip from Albir! I can't express how important it is that we are now unified. We now have the resources and the manpower to take our mission for Andaros on the offensive. Of course, we cannot hope to win if KTAN manages to ship weapons and soldiers through even one wormhole gate. This is made worse by the threats KTAN has made since the Joraw massacre. They have promised a similar killing if we threaten their wormhole operation again. Therefore, I am regarding this as a hostage situation. What we need to take this threat out is a coordinated, covert assault. Attack every port simultaneously, giving them no chance to respond. We have ascertained the locations of each illegal port, and my advisors and I have worked out insertion points into each city. We anticipate highly defended perimeters around all of these stations. The coordination and skill necessary for this attack make it what may be our most difficult undertaking yet. However, Adoro Galiro, who analyzed all of the data I used to make this decision, has some words of hope for us. KTAN has invested greatly in buying and keeping secret the components of these wormhole gates. Thus, they have taken a great risk. If we succeed today, it is possible that they will not be able to recover from this loss. We will have taken Andaros back."

Everyone cheered and pounded the tables, with more volume and fervor than they ever had for Kalar. Thoral raised his hands above his head, and lowered them for silence. Everyone obeyed.

Thoral said, "Immediately after breakfast, the original Sildial will report to Valeri, or An-Tun, according to your usual assignments. The assimilated *Swords* received assignments this morning, to either Valeri, An-Tun, or Vodir. They have your individual mission details. Dismissed."

Daolor Squad filed out of the hall along with the rest of the organization. They lined up with a number of other squads, where Mrs. Dyalaro was handing out packets and giving orders. Vuri eventually arrived at the front of the line.

"Darialaro, Vuri… Squad leader of Daolor…" she said, while thumbing through the thin paper packets. She handed one to Vuri. "Here are your orders. Report to Lot 3 South, next to the Jederai Center."

Daolor and several other squads followed the campus signs and filed into Lot 3 South. Ben was relieved to see that he wouldn't have to trust any of Kalar's recruits with his life; this entire group was made up of pre-unification Sildial fighters. Thoral had assigned command of the division to Adar Tikari, a man with gray scales and sharp features, who was shouting the roll call as everyone came in.

"Daolor Squad!" he called.

"All accounted for!" Vuri called.

"Tavrai Squad!"

"All accounted for!" shouted another squad leader.

"Igodra Squad!"

"All accounted for!"

Adar checked his roster. "Very good! That's everyone. Now, we have been assigned the Rozala wormhole station. Messenger scouts have pinpointed the location of the wormhole gate at the east end of the city, right in the fishing district near the coast. The city is far enough north that we will have to take a bullet train to get there in time. This means we won't have armored transports for our assault, and we'll have to take the portal on foot. Luckily, we have a few magic users: Ben, Yidara, and myself. Final reminder before we move out: KTAN has promised a civilian massacre if any of these wormholes are attacked. We liberate one, troops go out from another and kill everyone in sight. Thoral hopes that if we all attack simultaneously, we might be able to reduce the casualties. By simultaneously, he means down to the *second*. I have a watch synchronized to Thoral's, as does every division leader. No one shoots before I give the order from *this*, understand?" Adar held up a pocket watch, and the affirmation of the order rumbled through the group. "Good," he said. "Our train is leaving soon, let's go."

The train in question was a Wenifrin-built maglev, which streaked across the plains around Darjae at three hundred miles an hour. Ben was dealing with pre-battle jitters that had now become familiar to him. Seren sat next to him, still appearing unimpeachably calm. Javrel was rubbing lubricant from a squeeze tube into his metal finger joints.

"Something on your mind?" Vuri asked Javrel.

"Yeah. How do we know we're attacking the right place? They could have moved the gate parts to another building, right?"

"I don't think so," Ben said. "Have you ever been through a wormhole?"

"No."

"The whole room rumbles before it opens. They must have to build really solid foundations for the gate."

"That makes sense," Seren said. "But that also means that they have been preparing for this day for quite a long time."

"Great..." Vuri muttered.

The train came to a stop in a rusty terminal that smelled like cheap fried food and salt water. The division went on foot from there, through the mediocre downtown of the coastal city of Rozala, into even less well-off neighborhoods, where the houses were crammed together and the streets were littered with refuse. Messengers led the way through the tightly packed buildings, searching ahead for the enemy lest they be setting up a bottleneck ambush in the dangerously narrow streets. Finding no such trap, the Messengers led onward.

The division walked through the streets, passing by weary-eyed parents glancing out of the windows of tenement houses. They stepped carefully around the dirty children who played with rocks and discarded bottles and strings in the streets. After passing out of the residential district, they came to the canneries, fish markets and docks that spread along the shore, which smelled like the rot of low tide, old blood, and the pungent exhaust of fishing boats and canning machines. One large warehouse stood apart from the others. Daolor Squad hung in the middle of the group of fighters as they kept to the shadows. Arwi flew up to Adar, who led the group, and came back to Vuri, relaying orders.

"We are to hold position in these alleys until Adar gives the signal to begin the attack. When that happens, we take the west side of the building," she said, indicating the side of the warehouse farthest from the shore.

They waited, crammed into the alleyways, being dripped on by snow melting off the roofs. In the bright sun, which was approaching noon, the drips were fast and large.

"Everybody get ready," Arwi relayed from Adar. "Assault starts in a few minutes."

The nearest cannery exploded. The shockwave rushed outward, reaching the Sildial division in their alleyway and knocking them into the snow. When they could stand again, they saw the remnants of the cannery, a blackened, flaming pile of wreckage.

"What was that?" Vuri demanded.

"Who knows?" Adar called. "But I don't think it's a co-incidence. It's no use waiting now. We have to take that port! Go!"

Andarite mob agents, one of them holding a huge grenade launcher, streamed out of the KTAN warehouse. Sildial charged outward to meet them.

"Yidara, shield with me! Ben, take out the grenade launcher!" Adar called. The two Andarite magicians erect-ed a double-walled shield in front of the advancing Sildial force, which the mobsters could not penetrate. The grenade launcher fired, and Adar and Yidara strained under the magi-cal effort needed to keep up the shield. Ben wreathed him-self in a personal shield, skirted Sildial's line, and ran for the grenade launcher. A grenade hit his shield, which absorbed the impact. When Ben opened his eyes after the blinding blast, he stood in a crater, the reach of his shield forming a little untouched pedestal of pavement and snow beneath his feet. He reached out his staff and his personal shield changed shape, firing a bolt of magic at the grenade launcher. Under the weight of the heavy weapon, the holder could not flee fast enough, and was struck. The magic ignited the other grenades, engulfing not only the grenade launcher, but also his allies in the vicinity, in a fiery explosion. Daolor Squad cheered Ben's shot, and the whole division advanced on the building, protected from the guards on the roof by the magical shields. A three-part magical blast broke the metal door off its hinges and threw it down the hallway, where it slammed into a waiting guard. The piece of twisted metal and the broken mobster beneath it landed at the feet of an old Andarite with a mob insignia on his jacket. He had torn the sleeves off of his jacket, revealing snaking magic burns all over his wrinkling, flaking skin. He stood between Sildial and a huge, empty circle of metal, which was secured to the ground with metal beams as wide and strong as bridge supports. The Iyerani engineers attending the wormhole gate fixed their huge bug eyes on Sildial for a second, and then fled. They were replaced by more mobsters, who trained their guns on Sildial.

"Yidara, shield. Ben, offense with me," Adar said.

Adar and Ben, personal shields swirling with magical light, stepped up to meet the primary mob magician. Behind him, the mob had their own shielder, rendering everyone's guns ineffectual until the magical battle was decided.

The mob magician opened the contest, firing a bolt from each of his hands that sent Adar and Ben reeling back, shields straining under the attack. Adar fired back with an energy lance that flew sideways, then hooked inwards. The direction of the attack confused the mob magician, who received a nasty burn across his chest that immediately blistered and bubbled. Taking the opportunity, Ben blasted him, and the mob magician cowered as his skin split open in gaping, bloody lines. He let out a roar and fired back at Ben, who, in his moment of triumph, lost concentration on his shield. He ducked at the last moment, but the hot air thrown from the magical blast scalded his back. Ben screamed. As he tried to get up, he fell on his back, causing the pain of the burns to flare again. Adar diverted the mob magician's attention away from Ben, hitting him with a single sustained blast of heat and light. The image of the two Andarites battling seemed distant as Ben struggled with the pain of his own magical strain and the burns inflicted upon him. He looked around as he tried to stand. Behind Yidara's shield, Daolor had gotten to the front line to see Ben. Five distraught, fearful faces watched him. He had not fought this far to let his friends down.

The mob magician disregarded Ben in his agony. He and Adar fought, standing motionless as tongues of light licked between them. Each of them was in a meditative state that focused each completely on the other; Ben could recognize the blank, intense stares from when Dennison had focused on Messengerwork like this. Ben interrupted the mob magician's concentration with a focused blast. It worked, and Adar clinched victory with a single stroke to the distracted magician's throat. He crumpled to the ground, lifeless.

Ben, Adar and Yidara next focused on the enemy shielder, and the mob gunmen scattered as they sensed their magician's downfall. The shielder, rather than die in vain, used up all of his magic in a single blast at Yidara's heart. Both fell, appearing magic-burned beyond repair.

Without shielders and without much cover in the warehouse, everything erupted into bloody chaos. Neither Adar nor Ben had the magic remaining to shield the whole division, so they ran to their squads and shielded them as best they could. Others on both sides of the conflict ran for the sparse boxes around the warehouse. Blood ran as everyone without cover fell in a swift hail of bullets. All around the warehouse, Andarites and the occasional Iyerani lay dead.

Daolor, Adar's squad, and two other Andarites hiding behind a box faced down a larger group of survivors behind a larger group of boxes. Ben took the two behind the box into his shield, and joined his shield with Adar's. They advanced over the bodies, keeping the shield at shoulder level so the others could fire over or duck behind. Javrel was hit in the shoulder, but the bullet glanced off his robotic limb. Javrel killed several more as they tried to rise from behind their cover, his lens eye and unfailing arm taking each one within a second or two. The final few gave up the fight, and fled from the building.

Adar surveyed the warehouse, looking from the ten living fighters and their Messengers, back to the entrance, where the bodies of mobsters and Sildial fighters mingled on the ground. One or two of the deceased had been hit in the magical blast that had taken out the shield, and their Messengers lay shredded on the ground. Others, too small and too fast to be killed by bullets, hovered despondently over their keepers' bodies, or lay on their chests, quietly whimpering.

Ben saw a weak movement on the ground out of the corner of his eye. One charred Messenger flopped weakly in the pool of his keeper's blood. Ben approached and picked the Messenger up. He recognized the damage done by a long burn: The ribbon upon which the ventral flight enchantment was inscribed had been completely burned off by the burst of magic.

"You're a Messengersmith, aren't you?" Adar asked.

"Yeah. I can give this a temporary fix, but someone in Darjae will have to see to it for it to be permanent," Ben said. He worked with what he had on hand; he used his sword to cut strips of fabric, used the last dregs of his magic on the replacement enchantment, then tied up the temporary bundle of enchanted fabric. The Messenger muttered, "thank you," then went to hover above his dead keeper.

"Where will they go?" Seren asked. "Now that they have no keepers."

"I don't know what Andarite tradition says," Ben replied. He sat on a box and looked at the Messenger whom he repaired, who now mourned so deeply. He next looked over at

Celer, and felt the sudden, empathetic terror that intertwined his mortality with Celer's wellbeing. "Seren?" he asked.

"Yes?"

"If I die, will you take care of Celer after I'm gone?" he asked.

"I will," she said.

"Ben, don't talk like that," Celer said. "I'm not going to lose you."

"I hope not," Ben said.

"Help me destroy this blasted thing," Adar said, his voice choked with grief. He stood for a moment, seething in front of the wormhole gate, before blasting every remaining joule of his magical energy into it, breaking apart every component he could. Seren and Celer attended to the fuel cells, calling in some bystanders from the cannery explosion to help move them out. Ben and Vuri broke apart what they could, while Javrel found a huge wrench and used his robotic strength to take out all of the bolts that secured the gate to its massive foundational supports. He heaved them out of the building in boxes, dragged them to the shore, and dumped them in the sea to sink to the muddy bottom.

Civilians came in to help dismantle the gate. When asked, they had no more knowledge about the cannery explosion than did the Sildial team. A manager who had been out for a lunch break estimated the employees who were inside to be around 1500. Around twenty survivors had been pulled from the wreckage, and several of them did not even survive the trip to the hospital.

Soon, Sildial and their civilian helpers had reduced the nearly operational wormhole gate to a pile of wreckage, destroyed by a myriad of fuel fires, hacksaws, hammer blows, and magic. After emergency services had cleared out, a city councilor in crisp business attire came in to survey the scene, attended by secretaries and newspaper reporters. She listened to Adar tell the story of what had happened.

"By all the gods…" she said as he finished the story. "Those Iyerani gangsters, operating in Rozala for so long… I'll be having someone put the Commerce Board to a criminal inquiry immediately. Is there anything we can do to help you?"

"Transport vehicles for the antimatter so we can deliver it to proper disposal," Adar said. "Also, disposal of the casualties. Rite of Possessions has already been made."

The councilor nodded. "You will have everything you need. I will arrange for your transport back home, if you need it."

"We'll be picked up by our own people shortly."

Back at the new headquarters in Darjae, Thoral was furious. He sat with his advisors and reviewed the reports of the missions.

"How could this have happened?" he demanded. "Everyone was to attack the gates at the same, *before* KTAN had a chance to respond and kill civilians."

"I have the report from the lead Messenger of Toliro Squad," Daal-Na An-Tun replied. "Apparently, the division got anxious and decided that a few minutes early was 'close enough.' Toliro succeeded in getting their gate without civilian casualties, but at the expense of the other civilians."

"Toliro," Thoral said. "Is that one of ours?"

"It was Kalar's up until the Djelab," Valeri replied.

"That would explain it," Thoral muttered. "Casualty report?"

"All divisions are reporting heavy civilian casualties," An-Tun said. "Mostly from pre-planted explosives."

Thoral buried his head in his hands. "What could we have done differently, if we had waited? Fewer people would have died."

"Maybe," An-Tun replied. "Maybe more people would have died. You did what you could."

"I hate this job," Thoral muttered.

"Good," An-Tun said. "You won't make us kill any more people than we have to."

Just then, a Messenger came up, relaying a message to An-Tun in swift, choppy Daalronnan.

"Thoral, Adar Tikari's division just reported in," said An-Tun. "They managed to get their gate, but at the expense of an occupied cannery and most of their fighters. Several members of the mob escaped."

"Thank you for the report," Thoral replied. He made a note on the paper on his desk, then sighed in relief. "So even with the causalties, all the teams that have reported back have captured and destroyed their gates. Joraw's team is the only one that hasn't sent a Messenger back yet."

"What do you think KTAN is going to do now?" Advisor Dyalaro asked.

"Panic," An-Tun replied. "The humans' arrival, the Djelab, the speed with which Thoral took action against the gates... I do not think they ever expected that. We just took their biggest protection away from them."

"Commander Thoral!" screamed a Messenger who came hurtling into the office. "The division attacking Joraw just reported back. They were repulsed by an army of Wenifrin rebels. The wormhole gate there is open."

Chapter 14

Ben and the others stumbled out of bed the next morning amid complete chaos. The rest of their dorm was full with the clipped, urgent babble of preparation. Javrel moved out into the hallway and snatched a passing Messenger out of the air with a lightning-fast mechanical swipe. The confused, annoyed creature looked up at him with scorn.

"Must you *really* do that to get someone's attention? What do you want?"

"Are we under attack?" Javrel asked.

"No," the Messenger squawked. "Thoral is ordering the entire organization to move to the front. We have to aid the militias."

"Front?" Javrel asked.

"*By the gods,* robot-boy! Your squad sleeps like a pile of rocks! The new battlefront. The division attacking Joraw didn't secure KTAN's wormhole port. Wenifrin rebels called the *Jethnara Blade* are going to march on Golaube today, along with a Takathist force. Now go on, get packed! Your squad advisor will have your deployment assignment in the dining hall."

Javrel nodded and relayed the message to the squad. They hurriedly packed what little thay had and headed to the dining hall, falling into Advisor Dyalaro's line with the other squads assigned to her. Meanwhile, fast Andarites ran up and down the lines, distributing breakfast-on-the-go in small bags. Everyone picked nervously at chunks of dried meat, fruit and dense crackers. At the front of the line, Mrs. Dyalaro handed Vuri a folder with their orders. The squad sat down at a table out of the way of the line to read up on the mission.

"We're on the northernmost section of the front," Vuri said. "Our job is to reinforce the militia in Golaube, which is currently under attack by the Takathists from the West, and the Jethnara from the East. From there, we and the other squads assigned with us move northwest, straight towards..." She trailed off.

"What is it?" Seren asked.

"Diwo Takathar. The commune where Javrel and I were born. Anyway, Once we get there, our job is to lay siege to the commune, which will hopefully put the Takathist forces in other cities on retreat." She held up a handwritten note on the bottom of the printed sheet. "Mrs. Dyalaro adds that Ben will be one of very few magic users on this attack force. Most magical squads are being put to use to battle the Jethnara Blade."

"The Wenifrin rebels, unlike the Takathists, will have magicians of their own," Javrel explained.

"But remember, there's going to be a Jethnara force in Golaube," Arwi said. "Ben should be ready."

Ben nodded thoughtfully. "When do we leave? I think I'm overdue with An-Tun for another lesson."

Javrel checked the orders. "About an hour. You have time, but make it quick."

"Good. Thanks. See you all later!"

An-Tun received Ben into his study with a somber smile, of the kind usually reserved for the bereaved at funerals. There was already a pot of tea steaming on a magical heating element, and two clay cups were set out on the desk.

"Are you expecting someone?" Ben asked, hoping he wasn't intruding on An-Tun's business with someone else.

"Just you," An-Tun said. "Come, sit down. You look tired." He waved his hand and sent the teapot levitating across the desk, then tipped it and sent a steaming purple stream into Ben's cup.

"Thanks," Ben said, taking the cup in both hands and letting the warmth relax his fingers. "How did you know I was coming?"

"You have orders to head to Golaube," An-Tun said. "There, you will face magicians in battle. I took the guess that you would want guidance on how to meet your enemy."

"You knew Daolor is going to Golaube?" Celer asked.

An-Tun laughed. "You help your friends, I help mine. One of whom happens to be a certain uncle, who would appreciate the fact that I keep track of you, if he knew you were here."

Ben felt a knife of homesickness through his stomach at the mere mention of his family. "Do you ever talk with Dennison?"

"No. He and I haven't been very good about keeping in contact for the past few years. I do miss him, though. Now, we don't have all day for conversation. You need some lessons. Put up a shield around your hand. Go easy on me, now. Remember, my magic isn't what it was. This is about concepts, not power."

Ben put up a weak shield around his hand. An-Tun dipped his long, scaly fingers into his teacup, then held his hand over the shield and allowed the purple drops to fall down. The rolled off the small orb, making golden ripples as they went. Next, An-Tun wreathed his hand in golden light, and reached right through the shield, unimpeded.

"What? How did you—"

"I changed the flow of magic through the space of the shield. It's a common trick if the shielder isn't properly focused. Also, your shield is a wall, which works perfectly fine on bullets and other physical objects. Try making your shield flow, like this." An-Tun summoned a whirling mass of energy around his hand, that shimmered like water under bright morning sunlight. Ben put his hand on the vibrating surface, which felt strangely like both a solid and a liquid at the same time. He opened his mind to feel the way the magic was manipulating the forces around it, then withdrew his hand and replicated the swirling shield. An-Tun once again tried to pass his hand through it, but his fingers bent against the swirling surface, unable to pass through.

"I was in battle against two other magicians before," Ben said. "They never did tricks like that."

"Who were they? The truck driver and a pair of mobsters? Probably common criminals without training. I know a Messengersmith on Wenifri who has seen the colonial dissent. From what he tells me, I do not doubt the army of Jethnara is better prepared."

"What else can you teach me?" Ben asked.

"Maintaining concentration on your shield will be important against the Jethnara," An-Tun said. "But also, you'll need better attacks. I would guess you've just been blasting your enemies with light and heat?"

"Yes, mostly."

"Other magicians will adapt to that far too quickly for you to keep up. Think about the other forces available to you, and the resources you have at hand. Remember this as well: know what your enemy is shielding against, and find a way around it." An-Tun checked a Daalronnan timepiece on his wall. He said, "You must go. Your squad will be leaving soon."

Ben stood up and drank the last of his tea. "Thank you. See you soon. Hopefully."

"See you soon," An-Tun said. "I have faith in your abilities."

An hour later, a caravan of transports rolled up to the Darjae train station, which was otherwise devoid of life on the outside. Daolor Squad and the other squads accompanying them marched in orderly lines up into the terminal. They passed the large double doors into the facility, above which hung a sign, reading: *Commercial transport suspended to provide immediate, free transport to the Sildial fighters. Balgar and Audir be with them.* The ticketing gates were unattended, and swung freely, letting the Sildial fighters move without payment. Attendants, stewards and maintenance workers cheered and waved as Sildial passed. The train that pulled up was covered in beautiful graffiti that would put any of Earth's street artists to shame. However, the calligraphic words themselves were biting, cruelly poetic slurs against the Wenifrins. Ben remembered that Wenifrins built and installed the train systems for Andaros; now some talented civilians had tried to take misguided revenge on the rebels working with KTAN. The fighting force entered the defaced train with somber determination, splitting into two streams that filled the seats from the front of the train to the back. Daolor Squad found a row of seats where they could sit together, and sat silently as the maglev tracks accelerated the train to three hundred miles per hour, speeding northward and turning the cityscape to a gray blur, which soon yielded to the green vastness of the plains around Darjae.

"What did An-Tun teach you?" Seren asked.

Ben let out a shaky sigh. "Fighting magicians is going to be a lot more complicated. An-Tun showed me some concepts, but I don't know much. Hopefully I can handle it."

Seren smiled reassuringly at him. "I believe you can."

They rode in silence for a while before Vuri spoke up.

"I can't believe KTAN did it," Vuri said.

"Did what?" Arwi asked.

"Got the Takathists and Jethnara magicians to work on the same side," Javrel put in. "I was thinking the same thing. The Takathists would never have worked with magicians in the past. They must be desperate if they agreed to that."

"Or there's some agreement between them that we don't know the details of," Celer added. "Either way, we're fighting a powerful combined enemy."

Over an hour later, the train slowed, granting clarity to the speedy blur outside. Everyone on the train craned their necks to look out the window to the north. Smoke rose from the northern horizon, and several Wenifrin helicopters circled like carrion birds. Even from this distance, Ben instinctively tightened his grip on his staff. The train came to a halt at Golaube South Station, where everyone exited into the city.

Ben had forgotten about the chill of winter in the relatively balmy climate of the south, around Darjae. Here, snow and ice clung tenaciously to the roofs of buildings. The streets of southern Golaube were empty, the civilians having already evacuated away from the fighting in the north. Luckily, it had not snowed since the evacuation; the streets were plowed clear. Sildial marched in tense lines through streets that were silent except for the far-off rattle and drum of gunfire and crumbling buildings. The sounds of battle grew steadily louder. Sildial put out a vanguard of Messengers, who searched around corners and over rooftops for hidden enemies. Ben could feel the currents of magic twisting and pulsing invisibly through the air, manipulated by the magicians of both sides.

Daolor Squad and the rest of the contingent that would be moving on to Diwo Takathar took a wide street leading to the west. They turned a corner and saw the chaos of the battlefield. Ragged, dust-smeared Golaubean civilians cowered in desperate positions against half-broken walls, bullet-marked cars, and improvised turrets in windows. Armed with only small handguns and a motley of magical artifacts, they held a tenuous defensive line against a well-armed, uniformed force of Wenifrin rebels bearing the black and silver insignia of the Jethnara Blade, the Wenifrin colonial rebellion. Andarites and Wenifrins exchanged percussive shots of gunfire and thunderous, flashing blasts of magic across a no-man's-land of fragmented road and debris. A few of the embattled civilians turned to see the approaching Sildial reinforcements, and cheered. The cry of "*Javalvor Sildial!*" rang out among them. Hearing the cry, the Jethnara Blade faltered for a moment, but kept coming forward.

"Magicians to the front!" called the Sildial Mesengers, carrying the message through the ranks. "Shields up! Reinforce the militia positions!"

"See you soon," Ben said to his friends.

"Go get 'em," Vuri said. She gave him a playful salute.

Ben returned the gesture with a smile, took a more aggressive grip on his staff, and charged into the fold with his fellow magicians. Celer orbited close to his head, watching his back and translating occasionally. Ben's Voleric lessons had mostly paid off, and he could now take and receive orders with the other soldiers. He and two other Andarites coordinated a single shield of three swirling layers, under which they ran out to a battered car. Shielded by the hunk of immobile metal, they dropped their magical protection and fired into the approaching force. Their bursts of magic detonated against an invisible wall a safe distance from the Wenifrins. Ben reached his mind out into the swirling flow of magic that was the shield. He felt a way in. If he could ride the flow of the magic just right... Got it! A tentacle of magic hooked in through a break in the shielder's focus, and the Wenifrin panicked as Ben grabbed his skull with fingers of invisible force. The invisible wall dropped as the shielder scrambled to oppose Ben's mental attack.

"*Zei arei dyal wodaro...*" Ben muttered under the strain of the fight with the Wenifrin. "*Wavaw wiei.*" – *I have his shield... go.*

The front lines of the Jethnara Blade force crumpled under a barrage of creative magical attacks to the mind and body. Meanwhile, Ben had found his opponent on the visible plane. He and the Wenifrin stared each other down, invisibly matching wits and power over the distance between Ben's position and a well-fortified position at the top of a building behind enemy lines. This opponent was skilled, with a mind of oil and smoke that slipped out of Ben's magical grasp every time he thought he had seized the upper hand.

Suddenly, he felt the magical landscape. A second Wenifrin mind knifed into Ben's consciousness, and he felt a line of sharp, burning pain slash across his head. He cradled his head in his hands. A hot stream of blood spread through his hair and down his forehead, brought out by no physical blade. He curled into a defensive ball, both physically and magically, fighting to keep out the combined assault of two magicians. Ben felt the welcome magical presence of other Sildial magicians, striking out along the tense cords of magic that connected Ben and the attackers. The attack on his mind abated like a weight being lifted off of his chest. Up on the foritified building where the Wenifrin magicians were positioned, there was a flash of light. The flow of magic around the area became smoother, like a knot being untangled from a rope. One of the magicians was dead, or incapacitated. The other still lived, but soon caved to a combined assault by Ben and the other Sildial magicians. Another knot of magic was untied from the ambient flow. With the Jethnaras' shielders terminated, the rest of the force faltered. Sensing the opportunity, the Sildial front line raised a defiant battle cry and charged. Jethnara's remaining magicians tried to take up a new shield line, only to be thwarted by Sildial's.

Ben ran from his cover behind the car to a more advanced position between two buildings. He felt a Jethnara magician near him try to raise a shield, but caught him before he finished. The panicked Wenifrin fell when Ben's magic twisted his neck with violent speed, precision, and a sickening *crack*. Around him, the other Sildial and Jethnara magicians were locked in their own mental struggles. They were tightly matched; for every Wenifrin who fell, an Andarite did as well. Occasionally, explosions with no apparent cause threw shrapnel across the battlefield, the byproduct of a magical attack thrown off course by a clever shielder. The hot metal and stone thrown by these events struck surrounding soldiers, inflicting wounds without regard for allegiance. Ben lashed out quickly and forcefully against another magician, only to have his attack directed into the ground. The fragments of pavement hit surrounding Wenifrins and Andarites like crude bullets.

The magical landscape of the battle was shifting in Sildial's favor. The Jethnara Blade, it seemed, had not allotted enough force to defend this street. As the Jethnar line broke and Sildial charged up the street, Ben had the sinking feeling that the best magicians were only being reserved for later.

The force turned a corner and was met by a blast of heat and light that detonated like a bomb, leaving a charred crater in the road and a mess of unrecognizable bodies where the center vanguard of the Sildial force had been. Another blast went off, this time creating a gaping hole in the foundations of a nearby building. Most of Sildial's fighters managed to escape the blast and the collapse of rubble onto the street. So great was the change in magical flow after each attack, it was impossible for any magician not to pinpoint the shooter's location by instinct. A lanky Wenifrin with pallid, sagging skin was perched atop a pile of cars and twisted metal, waving a staff of pitch-black wood and shooting magic with reckless abandon. His comrades were hunkered behind all manner of cover, buildings, cars, snowbanks, and more, firing during the lulls in his magical assault.

"What the—" one of the magicians near Ben started. Recognition flared in his eyes. "*Ngalver Eriva.*"

"What?" Ben asked.

"Ngalver Eriva's a modified pain drug that KTAN's been piping onto the Andarite black market to addict people and cripple the population," he replied. "That Weni's on it, big time."

"He can't feel his magic burns," Celer said. Ben realized it too, and formulated a plan.

"Celer, get all the magicians we have. Tell them to distract that guy." He indicated the drug-addled Wenifrin. "Also, tell them to stay fast and light. He won't know when to stop fighting."

Celer flew to the magicians, relaying Ben's idea. They took to forming a wide circle around the magician, while keeping small, personal shields against Wenifrin bullets. The magician looked at them with mad curiosity, pausing his attack for a moment. Ben levitated a fist-sized rock and hurled it at the magician. It deflected off a shield close to his skin, but it got his attention. The ambient magic bent toward the magician like a great inhale of hot air. Ben tensed, magic coursing into every cell of his musculature in preparation for something he *really* hoped would work. The magic came at him as a blast scorching energy, and Ben reacted with adrenaline-hyped reflexes. He pushed off from the ground and, aided by magic, jumped above the blast. The enemy's magic detonated below him, and the outer edge of the blast scorched and warped the rubber soles of his boots. A vortex of magic slowed Ben's fall, and he landed on the flat pavement just outside the last explosion. His feet stuck in place by bonds of melted rubber that cooled immediately in contact with the cold ground. Ben felt the Jethnara magician preparing another blast of magic while he knelt, trying to untie his boots as quickly as possible. One foot in and one foot out of them, he realized he didn't have enough time. The next blast of magic came and Ben threw up a desperate shield that bent all heat and light around him and Celer, leaving them alone in a cold, dark dome. The nerves that carried the magic burned like hot iron through his arms, up and down his spinal cord from his abdomen to his brain stem. He regained his senses when the burning sensation faded to a throbbing that was painful, but not excruciating. Ben lowered the shield, unable to maintain it without feeling dizzy. The light reflecting off of the snow blinded him. Ben struggled out of his boot, then ran, stumbling, into the space between two buildings.

The other magicians rallied to continue the attack. Ben watched from his darkened alleyway as they continued on. Some escaped the blasts, but others weren't quick enough and were lost in the flames of the explosions. The magician was being worn down, and the drug kept him from realizing it.

If only we didn't have to put ourselves in the direct line of fire... Ben realized that maybe he didn't. It would take the last of his magic, but it would be worth it. He wreathed himself in a showy, yet entirely harmless display of twisting, arcing light, like a cloak taken from the surface of the sun. In this form, all features obscured except for his general silhouette, Ben stepped out from the alleyway, and was greeted by confused stares. The Wenifrins hiding behind their walls seemed uncertain as to what was going on, which was good. Ben didn't know how many bullets he would be able to take while keeping this disguise up. The Wenifrins looked to their magician to finish Ben off.

"I... thought... I destroyed... you," the magician growled in slurred, unpracticed Voleric.

"Nope," Ben said, trying to sound casual in a nonnative language. "Try again!" He ducked behind a car, and at the same time caused the indistinct light to dart of to another part of the rubble on the street. He hoped the deception had been fast enough. The enemy magician took the bait, turning and firing another blast of magic at the darting illusion. The form was fairly easy to maintain; a shifting light in roughly human form, without any distinct features. The problem was maintaining it while dealing with magic burns. Ben bit back the pain of fire ants crawling across his arms and kept on controlling the image, darting it back and forth. The Wenifrin grew increasingly irate and disjointed, firing rapidly, callous to the lives of other Wenifrins. Ben ran the illusion around near the enemy positions, and Jethnar agents ran from their own magician, often unsuccessfully. The magician's arms were covered in blistering burns, but he paid them no attention. Ben had a feeling that this might be the last straw. He was curious, and forgot to shift the illusion in front of the blast. The magician fired one more time, and the image was lost to the great ball of energy. The manic Jethnara magician's nerves erupted in smoke and sparks and he slumped. The body slid off the tower of cars and flopped down onto the street below, limp and smoking. Ben stood up from his hiding place behind the car. Sildial roared with approval.

Once again, the Messengers raced ahead to scout the next segment of the urban battlefield. Celer and Arwi were with the group heading straight towards the north wall, where they expected the combined Jethnara and Takathist forces to be pushing into the city. Instead, they found a half-sized force of Jethnara fighters taking up defensive positions around several buildings to the north. There were no Takathists to be seen.

"The Takathists split off," Arwi said. "Vuri was right. They would never work with the Wenifrins."

"Do you think we could negotiate a surrender?" Celer asked. "The Wenifrin rebels must know they're going to lose."

And surrender they did. Not immediately, but as the Sildial force, combined with the armed citizens of Golaube, marched closer and closer to the temporary Jethnara base, the Jethnara Blade surrendered its hold on the city. They began the retreat march back to Joraw. Celer flew back to Ben, finding him amidst the rubble, helping Sildial burn the corpses of the last fighters to die before the ceasefire.

"Why don't you have any shoes on?" Celer asked.

Ben looked down at his feet, which wore only socks. "Long story," he replied. "Where's the rest of the squad? We got separated when the magicians were called forward."

"Right this way," Celer said. He floated above the rest of the crowd, leading Ben back to the squad. "Look who I found!" he called.

The squad turned and stared at Ben in disbelief.

"Ben?" Seren asked. "I saw—we thought you—you're alive! How?"

"Of course I'm alive," he said. "What made you think I wasn't... Oh. The illusion?"

"So that's what it was," Seren said. "That was very convincing magic."

"Ha, I guess so. Thanks. I used up all of my magic for today, though. So what do we do now?"

"We're clearing out rubble," Javrel said, "and helping the Golaubeans with the most important repairs to buildings. Then we're taking our next orders from Advisor Dyalaro."

By the time most of the wreckage had been cleared, it was late afternoon. Advisor Dyalaro gathered the fighting force of Sildial to outline the next steps of the campaign. She stood on the tower of cars that had been built by the drugged magician, which made for a convenient and imposing speaking platform.

"By now, you've all heard that the Takathists abandoned their duties to the KTAN movement into Golaube. I have sent Messengers to other cities, and they returned with similar reports. The Takathist extremist movement is taking up defensive positions around Diwo Takathar, their walled commune. From what we know about the Takathists, they are withdrawing from their alliance with KTAN because of their religious conflict with Wenifrin rebels' use of magic. They are no longer an aggressive threat to our efforts."

The crowd cheered.

"The bad news is, the Takathists are still holding onto several small villages that are near their territory. I will be sending in several squads to liberate the civilians who are unwillingly under theocratic rule. They will be led by Mr. Vodir Balaro, while the rest of us move to Joraw. The squads going to the periphery of Diwo Takathar will be Awera, Zolidae, Divawddir, Daolor, and Kaliyo. At the same time, the rest of Sildial will march to retake Joraw." The Sildial crowd cheered again, but Advisor Dyalaro waved down their enthusiasm. "We do not know much about these Wenifrin colonial rebels, the Jethnara Blade, except that they oppose the Wenifrin Imperial government, and are in league with KTAN. We have no idea how many more Jethnara rebels will be coming through that wormhole gate. Until now, we have been blessed that the KTAN war has been restricted in the number of cities it ravages. A Wenifrin force could consume our entire country. Everything we have done since Varyal founded Sildial has led up to this day. Everyone prepare for the next march."

Chapter 15

The force heading to Diwo Takathar left that day, after a swift resupply with a Sildial quartermaster. They took two transports laden with weapons, supplies and food to last them for the whole of the trek: a journey of a day and a half to the nearest Takathist-held village, and then two days to each further village. All 5 squads wouldn't fit on their two allotted transports, so they rolled along slowly, matching the pace of the walking force. Thoral's general policy had been that Sildial would not accept gifts of gratitude from the recovering citizens of Golaube, but he had allowed Ben to receive a pair of boots of scaly leather to replace his melted ones. They were too tight, and squeezed his toes so they ached on each step. Ben lamented his original pair, which couldn't be recovered from the pavement without cutting the soles off completely. He grimaced as he hiked.

Daolor Squad marched silently in comparison with the other squads; the other, older Andarites bantered and ribbed each other comfortably during the march, but avoided Daolor.

"Uh, guys?" Arwi whispered. "I don't mean to freak you out, but some of the other squads are looking at us weird."

"Yeah, me and Javrel," Vuri hissed. "We're going back to Diwo Takathar, what did you expect? People have their minds on us. The Takathists."

"We know who you truly are, and I believe that is what matters," Seren said. "We will fight alongside our own people. Perhaps you will lead us with your knowledge."

"We were young when we left," Javrel said. "How much do you expect us to remember?"

Seren sighed. "Pardon me for trying to cheer you up, then."

"Oh, just stop, all of you!" Celer said. "Yes, we're a bunch of Iyeranis, Takathists, Earthlings, humans. We're going to do our best to be friends with the people around us. And if they still won't have us? Fine! We still won't be alone."

Everyone nodded assent.

"Thank you!" Celer huffed.

The division trekked hard across the forest for the day. After sleeping bags and rations had been distributed in the evening, everyone settled in for the night. Each squad stoked a fire, building them up until they were confident that the piles of crackling, glowing coals would stay warm far into the night. Everyone pulled their sleeping bags in close the fires to ward off the winter chill. The light of the coals shifted and danced in the light breeze. Ben thought about what had been necessary to survive the day. During the day, he had noticed that his friends had avoided his gaze.

Seren lay next to him, also staring ruminatively into the small flames. Vuri snored fitfully. Whether Javrel was silently sleeping or still drifting off, Ben couldn't tell.

"Seren?" he asked. She turned away from the fire to look at him. Shadow and orange light chased each other across her face and glinted in her eyes.

"Yes?"

"Are we alright? I mean, I think you've been avoiding me today."

Seren thought about this for a moment, then said, "I'm sorry, Ben. You took the right course of action today, against that drugged Wenifrin. The matter is... No. You did well. I need to control this on my own."

"You scared us with that stunt today, Ben," Javrel said. He pulled his head out of his sleeping bag. The firelight shone in his black lens eye. "We thought you were dead. Vuri, Seren and I saw the explosion, and your little light trick caught up in it. We mourned for you. After the fighting died down, Vuri asked Seren if she wanted to write your funerary scroll."

Ben's heart seized up in his chest as he imagined what it would have been like to see one of his friends in the center of that magician's explosion. He remembered how his mirage had stood dead in the middle. They were as convinced that it was him as the Wenifrin was. Seren would have known the statistical likelihood of survival at that epicenter, and would have told the others so.

"I'm sorry," Ben said. It felt weak and inadequate. "I won't do it again. I promise."

"But at the same time," Javrel said, "Your strategy took him out. If anyone here thinks they won't survive a winning move…" He stared into the fire for a long time, as if searching for the right words in the coals. "We all have to do our duty to this planet."

Ben nodded and began to drift off to sleep, then was jerked awake by the sound of engines screaming overhead.

"Enemy aircraft!" a Messenger called. "Find cover!"

"Extinguish the fires," Vuri said. "Split up, find cover."

With the fires out, everyone scrambled blindly in the dark. The cover of trees was thick, but hardly sufficient to defend against any sort of explosive. Ben's heart pounded as the engine noise grew louder by the second. The Sildial division wouldn't have long before the craft began firing. Ben ran blindly out into the forest. He stepped into into empty air, slid down a steep, icy embankment, and tumbled over rocks and broken branches that dug into his sides. He grunted upon hitting the ground hard, with one leg bent under him at a painful, unnatural angle. Blood welled up from the abrasions on his hands – he had left his gloves in camp.

Luckily, Celer had managed to follow him in the dark. "Are you alright?" he asked nervously, while hovering above Ben.

"I hope so. Since when did KTAN have an air force?" Ben whispered.

"Since they opened that new wormhole port in Joraw. Wenifrin ships, probably."

There was the crunching, scratching sound of someone sliding down the embankment next to Ben. He conjured a ball of light in his hands, ready to fight off a Wenifrin. Only Javrel stood over him.

"Three Wenifrin bombers with the Jethnara insignia. Headed right towards us in less than five minutes," he said.

"How do you know?" Ben asked.

"It's not perfect, but I have some night vision in my camera eye," Javrel replied. "Now come on, this embankment won't save us from the bombs. We have to find Seren and Vuri."

Ben tried to stand up, but he screamed at a sudden jolt of pain as he straightened his leg. Putting his weight on it was out of the question. "Find them, bring them back here," he said. "I might be able to shield us. Go!"

Javrel ran off, but Ben feared it was futile. The roar of engines was directly overhead. He erected a bubble of magic around himself, stretching nerves that had already been pummeled at Golaube. Between his leg and the magic burns, the pain was almost unbearable as he waited for the Jethnara firestorm.

The attack never came. Ben was so preoccupied with the screaming of his own nerves that he took a while to register the deathly silence in the air. The roar of engines had faded into the distance. He lowered his shield and waited for the far-off voices of his friends to draw closer. He could make out their forms as they clustered around him in the dark.

"I'm going to examine your leg," Seren said. "It will be painful."

Ben laughed. "At least you're honest," he said. She probed her fingers at his joints and he hissed in pain.

Far above the scattered Sildial squads, Arwi chased the craft as they sped away. Breaking the sound barrier, she closed in behind their dark forms. All three craft shot towards a small, firelit city built near the bend of a frozen river. Against the background of stars, a tall, domed building dominated the landscape. Arwi had never seen the building in person, but it matched Vuri's descriptions. With a sinking feeling, Arwi recognized the great granite temple dedicated to Takath, the center of the Diwo Takathar community.

Seeing what was about to happen, Arwi didn't care whose side the Takathists had been on. She just wanted to warn a city of civilians facing imminent destruction. Magic flared around her as she sped faster and faster, outpacing the Jethnara planes by several factors of the speed of sound. Descending towards the city, she screamed at watchtowers manned by guards day and night.

"Evacuate everyone into the forest! The Iyeranis have sent bombers to destroy you!"

"Begone, devil bird!" the guards called. They waved guns and blessed pendants into the air to scare Arwi away.

She screamed in frustration and dove towards the walled-in neighborhoods, screaming into as many windows as possible. People emptied into the streets, but grew enraged upon finding that the warning came from a Messenger. She was called a devil bird, deceiver, spawn of sin and much worse as the civilians threw ice chunks and food refuse at her.

"Please listen! The danger is up there!" She flicked her tail at the sky.

Arwi screamed in anguish as she saw it was too late: The three bombers appeared as triangles of darkness, black against the black night, only visible where they blocked out the light of the stars. They fired two missiles each. The temple was consumed in a blaze that illuminated the midnight countryside like high noon. A shockwave ran out through the city that knocked people to the ground and drove Arwi into a snowbank. She pulled out, shaking off the snow, and decided it was too late. She flew into the sky, followed by the hot wave of air from yet another missile.

She could only watch, transfixed, as the Jethnara pilots did their work. People screamed in the streets, rushing around to find loved ones or to run for the city gates. They looked to the sky and appealed to Takath to be spared. The planes fired another volley of missiles, and after another great explosion, the city had been silenced except for a few disparate, pitiful wails. The bombers hovered in place and dropped another payload: Silvery lines dropped from the planes, and dark forms slid quickly to the ground along them, landing on the ground amid the wreckage. Jethnara footsoldiers combed the rubble of the streets for survivors, and with short bursts of crackling gunfire, Takath's disciples were systematically silenced.

Arwi cried for the civilians all the way back to the camp. As she found Vuri, she was shrouded in a nimbus of sorrowful blue. She related what she had seen in brief gasps between blubbering cries of horror. Vuri and Javrel sat stoically in the snow, processing the event.

"Why did they have to do that? Especially to civilians?" Javrel asked.

"The Takathists withdrew from their alliance with KTAN as soon as the Jethnara soldiers came. That much we know from Mrs. Dyalaro," Seren said. "It would make sense, according to Iyerani ideas, that KTAN would want to punish them. This also gave them the opportunity to demonstrate their new air power."

Javrel said, "Do you think anyone... Mom and Dad... everyone's gone?"

Arwi only nodded. "I think we can only hope that it was quick for them."

Javrel and Vuri leaned against each other, hugging. Ben sat in silence, wanting but not knowing how to help them.

"If there's anything you need me to help with, I will," Ben whispered.

"Thanks, bro," Vuri said, "but you take it easy. You have your own healing to do."

"What happened to you?" Arwi asked of Ben.

"Seren says I sprained my leg pretty bad, falling down that ridge. I can probably walk in a couple of days. But seriously, guys, if you need help with anything, ask me. I can only imagine, but I bet what you're going through hurts a lot more than what I am."

As Ben was unable to move back to the campfire himself, his friends came to circle around him, carrying him back to his sleeping bag, which he painfully wriggled into. Ben felt small against their desire to help him with his injury, especially after the Darialaro siblings' loss. They all drifted off, hoping to sleep through the night without another roar of bomber engines.

The day greeted them late, as bright morning sunlight was reflecting off of the snow. No one was too eager to be off to confront any remaining Takathists, who now had nothing to lose. Ben's leg ached as he awoke. He feared to move it. Javrel and Seren helped him out of the sleeping bag, and leaning on them, he limped to a large cookfire where everyone had gathered to eat together. People shot a mix of glances in Daolor Squad's direction, ranging from pity, to suspicion, to fear. No one spoke audibly; only in Voleric whispers that the humans couldn't make out. However, Vuri and Javrel could hear them, and judging from their faces, it wasn't good. An anxious soldier passed out bowls of hot gruel to the squad, and Daolor sat on the ground, eating sullenly. People still whispered, and Vuri had had enough.

"Let's just get on with the mission, alright?" she snapped at no one in particular. "There are surviving extremists holding down those outlying towns."

"Unless they're going to check out their bombed-out city," one of the Andarites grunted. "*galovra rekyari* had it coming."

Vuri growled and started to stand up. Seren put a cautionary hand on her shoulder.

"You know that more violence will not help us," Seren whispered. "Be strong in *here*." She tapped the side of her head.

"Can Ben still wield magic from a transport turret?" another soldier asked.

"I really think Ben needs to rest for a while, after yesterday," Celer said.

The soldier nodded. "Fine. Daolor Squad can ride one of the transports today. Javrel will man the turret."

"I'll drive," Vuri said.

"I can take the second gun," Seren added.

"Sounds good," the soldier agreed.

The camp was packed up, fired buried, food put away, all without Ben's help. He sat, watching people do things around him and wanting to help. But no, Seren insisted. He had to stay off that leg for now.

Riding in this transport was a lot better than the last one. This one was made with thick, professionally built armor and had a solid turret. It wasn't hacked together from spare sheet metal, with garish, scar-like weld marks all over its surface, as the last one had been. Ben felt safe. The transport rolled on throughout the day, and at night everyone made camp once again. This time, however, the first of the Takathist-held villages lay just over a tree-lined ridge. People slept uneasily, even under the diligent guard rotation.

Seren, sitting with her back against a tree and a cocked gun in her lap, took the last watch before morning. The rest of the squad slept nearby. She shivered from head to toe, and her toes stung from the cold, even under her socks and boots. Arwi hovered around her head.

"You didn't know Vuri's parents, did you?" Seren asked.

"No. We met in Joraw, after she and Javrel ran away. My previous keeper... He..."

"You don't have to talk about it if you don't want to," Seren said.

Arwi sighed. "Thanks. I'm worried about Vuri, though."

"She is stronger than she believes. Perhaps her anger will help us if she learns to control it. Now come, it is time to wake the others."

"It's still dark."

"The extremists will not see us coming."

The village was small; less than a thousand people by the Messengers' estimates, living in small homes heated almost exclusively with fire. Sildial agents stood on the ridge, eyeing the Takathist camp just outside the village. They said that ten tents sat crowded around a large fire, each one guarded by an armed Takathist. Daolor Squad listened enviously to the reports flying back and forth through the camp, as they were forced to stay behind. At least one person would have to stay with Ben, and sending half a squad into battle didn't make much sense by Vodir's reckoning. Vuri had protested, but Vodir stood firm.

"He hasn't been a member of Sildial for even two weeks, and suddenly we take orders from him," she fumed.

"Thoral apparently trusts him," Javrel said.

Ben secretly let go of a little bit of fear. None of his friends would be in harm's way, at least for this battle.

The sound of gunfire and shouting was distant as Daolor Squad waited for the rest of the division to return. Occasionally, someone got up to stoke the fire with more wood, but there was not much to be found without digging through the snow. Ben didn't disturb the silence as Seren stared meditatively into the coals, and Javrel and Vuri sat, glancing at each other and whispering occasional fragments of prayer. The dialect they used was stilted and formal, with an arcane accent that alienated it from the mainstream Voleric that Ben had been taught. Ben looked around the woods at empty silk-spinner nests that were laden down with snow and ice, trying to occupy his mind with something other than the situation at hand.

Eventually, the gunfire died down. The squad awaited the return of the rest of the division for a time that seemed far too long.

Vuri stood up. "Seren, stay with Ben. Javrel, come with me to investigate."

"Be careful," Ben said.

"We're only going as far as the ridge. We should be safe."

After a while, there was the crunch of footsteps returning through the icy crust on the snow, accompanied by low moans. Seren ran for a medical kit in the transport, opening it up near the fire as Javrel dragged a wounded Sildial fighter through the snow. Vuri was pressing her hand against the fighter's chest, trying to put pressure on a wound. Blood glistened on his uniform fabric.

"Lay him down here," Seren said, indicating the packed snow around the firepit. As soon as the patient was on the ground, Seren slashed open his uniform with the shears in the kit, in order to get a look at the wound. There was a bullet wound in his left chest. She took a wide cloth bandage and pressed it over the bleeding opening. As she tried to staunch the bleeding, the patient coughed convulsively, spraying blood across Seren's face.

"The bullet most likely punctured his lung," she said. "He is bleeding internally into it. Without a hospital, I do not know how he can be saved."

"No... survivors... in the village," the fighter said between coughs that brought up increasingly more blood. "Do not... try rescue."

Seren kept at work, doing whatever she could for the wound on the outside, but unable to help the internal bleeding that was killing him. Celer pressed against his throat, monitoring his pulse and reporting it to Seren as she continued to hold pressure on the wound.

"Can we take him to Golaube?" Vuri asked.

"Too far," Seren said.

Celer was still listening to the pulse. "It's getting weaker," he said.

Seren worked for a while longer before her patient breathed his last, with the sickly gurgling sound of blood filling his lungs.

"Pulse?" she asked.

Celer rose from his position on the fighter's neck. "Nothing."

"Can we tell if his family would want any particular rites upon his death?"

Javrel approached and reached down the fighter's uniform collar, pulling out a nametag and a small jade statue strung onto a black necklace cord. The statue was a tiny representation of an Andarite in simple monastic robes, holding a torch and a walking stick. Javrel explained that it was Birel, Voleric god of discovery and innovation. His devotees had no specific practices for mourning besides the general rites performed by the worshippers of any of the Voleric pantheon. He showed it to the others, who read the nametag:

Galo "Ki" Bivoli
Kaliyo
Birel

Javrel searched the body for any personal property that would be given to his family for the performance of the religious "Rite of Possessions." He collected the nametag and statuette, along with a bag of game chips, a short knife, and a small ring, and folded them all into a cloth cut from the unbloodied parts of Galo's unform.

"We can't help the dead down in the village, but it's the least we can do for this one guy." Javrel put the funerary parcel into one of the transports. He and Vuri prayed according to the general traditions of all Voleric worshippers. When they had finished, everyone sat in respectful silence.

Celer broke that silence. "So what do we do now?"

"Meet up with the force invading Joraw," Vuri replied. "We can't expect to take the rest of the extremists on our own, but we can help the team trying to take the wormhole station."

"We have two options," Seren said. "Take the transport, risking an encounter with extremists on the road, but proceeding faster, or cross the forest on foot, slower but with less chance of an unfortunate encounter. Thoughts?"

"Ben can't walk. We'll take the transport," Vuri said.

Ben and Seren sat inside the cramped, armored machine while Vuri drove and Javrel watched for movement in the trees. Ben asked, "How are you feeling?"

"Rationally, I know that I could not have saved the patient without getting him to a doctor. Still, I cannot shake the feeling that I failed him."

"You did better than I would have," Ben said.

She smiled. "Thank you."

"What do you think is going to happen in Joraw?" Arwi asked.

"We can't judge what will happen without knowing what resources the Wenifrins have on the other side of the wormhole," Vuri said. "Somehow I doubt that three bombers is all they have."

"A Master Messengersmith like Dennison would be able to do serious damage," Celer said. "I hope none have allied with the rebels, otherwise I don't know how we would stop them."

Javrel had insisted that he should drive for the second half of the long night journey, to let Vuri sleep. Seren helped Ben bind up his leg, and they found a bit of Annalalh ointment in the trauma kit. In a few hours, Ben's magic healed somewhat. The transport arrived at the north highway entrance of Joraw only shortly after the red tint of dawn had faded from the sky. Once they rolled into earshot of gunfire and the ethereal ripping sound of magical combat, Dalivei, Thoral's Messenger, flew down to meet them.

"What are you doing here? What happened to the villages? The rest of the division?" he asked.

"They were all killed in the attack on the first village," Vuri replied. "What's going on here?"

"Thoral and Valeri insisted on leading two prongs of the strike themselves. Valeri managed to get her squads to a safe location, but they're pinned down. Thoral... Jethnara had a powerful magician, maybe even a Messengersmith... We haven't gotten the casualty report back yet."

Vuri nodded. "Arwi, go see if you can find Thoral and his group. Check for survivors. Dalivei, lead us to Valeri."

"Follow me," Dalivei said. He raced down an alleyway, with Celer and the walkers in pursuit. "I'm taking you by the least guarded route. Still, there are several sentries. Quiet now, we're getting close."

Daolor Squad crept behind a building of gray brick, crumbling mortar, and small, glassless windows. Ben bit back the pain in his leg with each step.

"Tell Valeri to find a way to distract them," Vuri whispered to Dalivei. "Seren, Javrel, direct fire at that nearest sentinel." She indicated a Wenifrin on a roof, whose eyes were trained on the cornered Sildial fighters. "Ben, take care of the shields. They're bound to have some. I'll take the next sentinel down. Ready?"

The squad waited until they heard the sound of gunfire in the next street, as Advisor Dyalaro's group seized the distraction and renewed their resistance. Seren, Javrel and Vuri fired at the near sentinel, and inevitably, the bullets ricocheted of ripples of magic. Ben reached out his mind to grapple with the rooftop magician, slipping in through the back door of a stray thought. Both Daolor's and Jethnara's shields were nullified, letting Vuri fire at the Wenifrin shielder. Ben felt the opposing presence of magic writhe and die in his mental grasp. Javrel began to run to take down the next sentinel.

"Wait!" Ben called. "We'll take this position. Cover me." Ben limped to the building where the Wenifrin sentinel had stood, and placed his hands against the brick. A bit of magic cracked strategic points up the side of the building, and several bricks fell to the ground. Ben led the way, climbing up the handholds and footholds he had made. He wreathed himself in a shield, jumped through the window, and confronted the second magician in the room. The short Wenifrin, wielding a black scepter, threw loose stones at Ben in tiny vortexes of magic. Ben focused on one and pushed it back, slamming it into the Wenifrin's skull. Milky white blood gushed from a wide gash in its forehead. The others began firing at other Wenifrin sentinels from the window.

Below, the trapped squads rallied, and pushed forward from their hiding place in an alley. They cheered and bellowed ferociously, while firing magic and bullets at the Wenifrins. The Wenifrin rebels were disorganized, not knowing whether to fire upon Daolor or Advisor Dyalaro's troops.

A force like an earthquake shook the building where Daolor Squad stood. Moldy plaster chunks and dust rained from the old ceiling.

"Someone's collapsing the building," Ben said. He reached out his mind's influence, feeling a presence of magic nearby. He recoiled instinctually from the great power. "Everyone huddle around me! Hold on to someone."

Everyone group-hugged as tight as possible. The floorboards groaned and snapped below them. Ben threw up his shield in a panic as the building collapsed around them.

He felt a moment of weightlessness as the floor gave way, and then only the mental shock of the building falling onto his shield. There was another great, fiery magical jolt as the shield absorbed the shock of landing on the ground. Rubble and splintered wood fell around them. Ben's shield snapped as his mind could no longer handle the amount of pain being thrown through his magic-burned nerves. His vision swam and his ears rang. Above him, the wavering, blurry ghosts of his teammates tried to speak to him. It could have been English, Voleric, anything; he was too disoriented to tell what they were saying. He saw a flash of metallic gray and a flash of red move to each of his sides, and felt hands clamp down on his arms. He screamed, his hypersensitive nerves reading Javrel's and Seren's touch as if hot coals were being pressed into his skin. His ears rang upon hearing the tiniest sound, and at the scene of a fallen building with casualties beneath its rubble, there was an orchestra of wails.

Ben drifted in and out of consciousness and lost all track of time. When he awoke with burning muscles, he, the rest of Daolor, along with a few fighters and the soot-covered Advisor Valerija Dyalaro, were in an alleyway. Presumably, this was the same place from which Daolor had intended to rescue their comrades. When he managed to slur out that suspicion, Seren confirmed it.

"Eerywon okay?" Ben said, as coherently as he could.

"Daolor Squad is alive," Seren said. "Several other fighters died in the building collapse. There are wounded that we cannot reach without being fired upon."

"Wenifrin magician?" Ben asked, focusing on his lips and tongue, forcing out the words one sound at a time.

"He hasn't attacked with magic since that demolition attack," Advisor Dyalaro said. "His burns may be too severe."

"*Tiñatso ngantaxe!*" a voice called from outside.

"What was that?" Ben asked.

"The Iyerani language. One of the rebels has demanded that we surrender," Seren relayed.

"I don't think anyone is seriously considering that, right?" Vuri demanded. "There has to be something we can do."

"Make it quick," Advisor Dyalaro said. "The south flank of the attack isn't going any better than this one. Someone has to get to that wormhole station and stop Jethnara from sending more aid."

Celer was trying to peek out from the alleyway without being shot at. He dove back to cover, then returned to peeking, once, twice, three times, and finally a fourth.

"What are you looking at?" Seren asked.

"I think there's an armored Wenifrin vehicle farther up the road."

"Yes, we disabled one before we had to retreat to this position," Advisor Dyalaro said. "It was carrying a large-caliber gun on the roof turret."

"Is it operable?" Seren asked.

"I think a magician destroyed the wheels. Besides, how would we get over there? We have no shielding, do we?"

"No," Ben groaned.

"How much of a shield could you produce?" Javrel asked.

"I can't!" Ben said.

Javrel took a robotic fist and slammed it into the alleyway wall. Fragments of brick and mortar broke of with the force. "Don't tell me that you *can't!* This is the key battle of this war. We don't need a shield for a whole person." He waved his alloy hand in front of everyone's faces. "Tell me you can shield a torso. A little bit of magic for my head. That'll do it. I can get to the transport."

"I—"

"If it is possible, you must try," Seren said.

"He could die!" Celer shouted. "That much magic usage could kill him. You saw how bad he was after the building fell. I'm not about to let my best friend do this."

"You think I don't realize that?" Seren snapped. "You and Ben are my first and best friends. I saw the deaths from magic burns. I don't want him to do this. But what we *want* does not matter here. A planet hangs in the balance. The needs of the many—"

"Please," Celer pleaded. "Don't make him do this."

"I will," Ben said. He took a few deep, shaky breaths to prepare himself. "Javrel, get ready. I'll shield you as well as I can."

Celer said, "Don't, Ben…"

Ben gave Celer a small smile, then fluffed his tail fondly. "Go back to Earth and tell Dennison it was for a good cause." He gave Seren a tight hug. "Keep yourself safe."

"I'm sorry," she whispered. "Truly, I am..."

"Don't be," Ben replied. "Just catch me when I fall." He steeled himself and breathed in the bitingly cold air of the Andarite winter. The spell formed in his mind. He touched Javrel's jacket, and screamed as magic rushed through his nerves. The burning feeling only faded when he lost feeling in his limbs. His vision faded, and he slumped into oblivion.

Celer hovered over Ben's limp form as Seren lowered it to the ground. He looked over at Javrel, who was shielded along the places where metal didn't cover his body. Golden light flickered faintly in the wind. "Use that shield well," Celer said.

"I will," Javrel said. The Wenifrins fired upon him as soon as he stepped into the street. Bullets ricocheted harmlessly off both magic and metal as he sprinted down the road to the destroyed vehicle. He climbed up to the turret, where a cold Wenifrin body lay. The weapon was still loaded. Javrel worked quickly on the locks that kept it attached to the vehicle. The entire automatic weapon assembly, once freed, was bulky, heavy and unwieldy. Javrel's motors whined against the strain of carrying it off the turret. He raided the cockpit for its safety belts, and lashed them onto the gun to make a rough carrying harness. He carried it back to the squad's position, then began firing upon the sentinels. His steady robotic hand fired true, and under the hail of automatic bullets, the Wenifrins cowered.

Yet, one brave enemy stood up from his position: a Wenifrin magician. Javrel looked at him for a split second, and in that moment the short, pale-skinned being gave him a crooked smile, and raised a staff. Javrel's mechanical knee joints failed, and he fell to the ground, his head slamming into the icy pavement. His camera eye exploded. His metal fingers froze. Javrel looked at the magician through his one biological eye before the magician slid back into the shadows.

Chapter 16

Back in the alleyway, Vuri watched in horror. The Wenifrins were taking careful shots at Ben's last shield, weakening it bit by bit. Seren clutched Vuri's arm, restraining her from going to help Javrel.

"Seren! Help Vuri," Javrel called. "You need each other. Vuri, I'll see you later. Love you."

The next bullet, aimed at Javrel's flesh eye, met no resistance from magic. A ring of deep blue spread through the snow around his head.

Vuri screamed. Then, she looked over at Seren. "You have to get away from me. Or I'll kill you."

"Vuri, you can't go out there and try to take them on by yourself. It's not—"

"No, I mean *you*," she said, panic rising. "My magic is coming."

"I won't leave," Seren said. "You can control this. You can control your emotions, and your magic."

"I can't! Get away!"

The air around Vuri started to warm. Light flicked around her scarred fingers. Seren grabbed Vuri by the shoulders and glared at her, straight in the eye.

"Vuri Darialaro, sister of Javrel, disciple of Takath," she said, "I will not pretend to know how terribly you are suffering now. I also will not pretend that you are some out-of-control, powerless hatchling. You are not. I know you."

The snow melted at Vuri's feet, and she grimaced. "I've never been able to! I can't, Seren. Run while you can."

"I don't care!" Seren shouted. "I did not subject Ben to the injury of his own magic to be lied to! Javrel did not die so you could lie to yourself and maul the rest of us!"

Heat like a bonfire radiated from Vuri. She growled and gritted her teeth, trying to restrain her power. Seren remained, looking into Vuri's eyes.

"Control it, Vuri," Celer said. "Just a little. No artful spellwork. No fancy lights. Just think. Determine the shape of the magic in your mind and it will be."

"You've grown since I met you as a little child, Vuri," Advisor Dyalaro said. "We believe in you. Javrel believed in you."

Vuri nodded, and the heat faded. Cold winter air rushed back into the alley. "Stand back," Vuri said.

Everyone stepped away. Seren smiled at Vuri and said, "You can do it."

Vuri shouted a war cry and ran out of the alley. The Wenifrins fired, but all of their bullets bent in their paths, deflected into the ground. The snow melted under her feet. Standing over Javrel's body, Vuri literally burned with rage, focusing it into sharp beams of magic that slashed open the Wenifrins' positions behind the walls and windows. They screamed and flailed under the one-warrior magical assault. She looked back at her squad.

"Stay close," she growled. The fighters fell in behind her, and they ran down the street under the protection of Vuri's shield. Advisor Dyalaro carried Ben over one shoulder, but there weren't enough hands to fire at the enemy and carry the body of Javrel.

"Vuri!" A Messenger streaked across the sky, settling in front of the enraged Andarite. It was Arwi. "The other branch of the attack is rallying forward again! Follow me! We'll meet up with them! Where's Javrel?"

"He sacrificed himself for us," Seren said.

Turning a corner, Daolor Squad met up with the bedraggled remnants of Sildial, who were storming the same gray building where Ben had once been a prisoner. Vuri caught one Jethnara magician off guard by diving at him. Enwreathing her sword with magic, she bisected him with fire and steel, head to toe. His shield dropped, and Sildial gunned down those he was protecting.

"You're controlling your magic!" Arwi exclaimed.

"Thank Seren," Vuri growled.

"You need to stop soon," Arwi shouted over the sound of the battle. "I feel the amount of magic flowing through you. You'll burn out soon. Help Seren bring Ben to the medics."

Entering the medical tent on a secure street away from the battle, Vuri and Seren found Daal-Na An-Tun himself helping those who had been magic-burned. He was applying his traditional salve to a conscious patient when he noticed Daolor Squad enter. Celer circled around Ben's nose, monitoring his weak breathing.

An-Tun's eyes widened. He set down his salve and pushed the patient away. "Go sit on that bench, I'll finish you up later," he said.

The patient glared. "But you're already almost done—"

"Now! Your life isn't in danger, this patient's is! Vuri, Seren, put Ben up on this cot." An-Tun placed a scaly hand on Ben's throat and closed his eyes. "Yes, I can feel it by my magic... The damage has reached almost up his brain stem."

"Will he wake up?" Seren asked.

An-Tun paused and looked at her for a moment. He sighed. "I will do what I can for him."

A Messenger burst through the door flaps of the medical tent. "Where is Daolor Squad? Commander Dyalaro has ordered them to the frontal assault of the wormhole station!"

"Half of our squad is incapacitated or dead," Vuri said. "And why *Commander* Dyalaro—Oh no. Thoral?"

"Died on the battlefield," the Messenger replied. "Is the girl from Iyerayñan still alive?"

"Here," Seren said.

The Messenger sighed. "Good gods, thank you. We had two official translators of the Iyerani language. They're dead."

"Are we negotiating a surrender?"

"No. The wormhole is open, to planet Nalofri. They left the airlock open."

"But Nalofri is a dwarf planet with no atmosphere! They would suck all of the air out of their building!" An-Tun exclaimed.

"Exactly. We think preparing to move troops through in pressurized transports. The winds from the atmosphere suction are making it difficult for us to fight in there. We haven't broken though into the port room yet, but everything in that building is labeled in the Iyerani language."

"I'm not a wormhole technician," Seren said.

"You're a native speaker of the language, and that's the best we have," the Messenger replied. "Now come on, before the reinforcements gain a foothold."

"Coming," Seren said.

"Right behind you," Vuri said.

Seren and Vuri readied their weapons and ran through the streets, trailed by the Messengers. Sildial had broken a path through the city, and the surmounted KTAN and Jethnara positions were marked by bullet holes and the charring of magic. Seren and Vuri arrived at the wormhole port building, where KTAN and Sildial were exchanging rapid fire in the twising hallways. Casualties on both sides lay on the ground, slicking the floor with blood. Vuri took the lead, pushing through to the front lines and releasing a savage aurora of magic. Sildial fighters dove out of the way of the minimally controlled forces that arced around her body like solar flares. Seren remained back, held by the insistent hand of a Sildial escort on her shoulder.

"We need you alive to translate," he said, shouting over the wind that filled the halls. Air from all over the compound was being drawn towards the pressureless expanse of Nalofrin space on the other side of the open wormhole. Seren pointed to a sign written in the Iyerani language.

"This marks the way to the wormhole," she said. Her escort shouted orders to the other fighters, and they pushed on.

The buffeting of the wind grew stronger as the Sildial force approached the room containing the massive wormhole generator. When they arrived in the room, the wind was so strong as to threaten to pull in anyone who didn't cling to the walls. The other side of the wormhole opened into a gray, rocky plain dotted sparsely with pod-like buildings. At the nearest one, Wenifrins in pressure suits were attending to transport vehicles.

There was a terminal with scrolling Iyerani writing on the door frame of the wormhole chamber. The Sildial escort indicated it to Seren.

"Is this the right thing?" he asked.

She scrutinized the screen. "Yes!"

"Good! Close the wormhole!"

Seren stared at it, then opened and closed several tabs in rapid succession. "I told you, I'm not a wormhole technician," she said. "This could take a while."

A blast of magic fired out of the wormhole, catching the escort in the shoulder. He lost his grip on the wall and was pulled by the winds toward the wormhole, where a magician shrouded in shielding walked through, unperturbed by the winds. Sildial agents fired at him, but to no effect; the shield that kept him from the winds also redirected the bullets away from him. Vuri fired a blast of magic, crying out at the pain of the burning energy. The magician faltered, but kept coming.

"Fast would be nice!" Vuri shouted.

"I could destabilize the antimatter equilibrium and widen it! Cover me!"

Seren stared at the controls, and the dense Iyerani script wavered uncertainly in front of her eyes. She hadn't read from her home language in months, let alone about antimatter flow, rift dilation, reference gravites... All things she had never been taught. A blast of magic narrowly missed her head. Another Sildial agent fell towards the gaping wormhole. Seren hoped she understood the controls correctly as she started punching commands into the computer screen.

Cutting the antimatter regulator should collapse the spatial singularity... she thought. "I'm starting the closure! It will take a few minutes to close correctly!" she shouted over the rush of the wind.

"Do it faster!" Vuri ordered.

Seren tried, but was met with a warning light. "The gravity shockwave could kill everyone in the building if I do."

"Could?"

Seren checked the warning again. "Probability above 95%!"

"Good enough odds for me. Shut it!"

Seren slammed the button.

The aperture collapsed and the shockwave knocked the air from Seren's lungs. She was thrown across the room. She couldn't tell which surface she was hurtling towards, there was a flash of light, and then everything went black.

Chapter 17

Seren awoke in a warm bed, covered in thick quilts that smelled like wood smoke and tea. The room was small and somewhat cluttered with clothes and shoes. There was a magical lamp on the bedside table, emulating flame in a wooden dish but giving off very little heat. By the dim light, an Andarite child was reading. She looked up at Seren.

"*Vadzi*," she whispered tremulously.

"*Vadzi, oguvi*," Seren replied, returning the greeting. Still in Voleric, she asked, "Do I know you?"

"Joraw," she replied, then ran from the room.

That's right... Seren thought. *We rescued this family. But why am I here?*

The Andarite girl returned with Daal-Na An-Tun, who smiled at Seren. "I'm glad to see you're awake," he said.

"Where are we?"

"Tareila, a small town fairly close to Joraw. The family you rescued was more than happy to quarter Daolor."

"I thought I was the only one left," Seren said.

"Oh, no. It was Vuri who shielded you from the blast! Neither of you would have made it out otherwise. She and Ben are both conscious, and have been for a day or so. Ben is well enough to be out of bed."

"How long since the battle?"

"Five days. We believe that KTAN's operations have been put down on this planet, now that they have lost the support of the Takathists, and have no way to get Jethnara reinforcements."

"What about the corrupt police? The organized crime?"

"Everyone made quite a big scene, between the bombings and our attack on Joraw. The public is calling for thorough investigations into the executives responsible. I expect there will be impeachments. Would you like to see Ben now?"

"Yes!" Seren cheered. "Please, send him in. Oh, but Daal-Na? I have one question."

"Anything."

"Vuri was as powerful today—I mean, at the battle, as Ben, in the way of magic. But she hasn't practiced."

An-Tun considered this. "I didn't see her firsthand, but magic burns do tend to have that effect on a body. If they heal at all, they heal stronger than ever before. I understand she had quite a few. And, if you will pardon the philosophical clichés of a tired old man, I think people heal in much the same way. I'll let you see Ben now."

When Ben came in, he rolled slowly in on a tarnished metal wheelchair. He wore warm robes of deep blue fabric, with a big hood that piled and spilled over the shouders. Celer hovered around his head.

"Is it permanent?" Seren asked.

"The wheelchair? No, just until I feel steady on my feet again. An-Tun has me on Daalronnan cures that will help my nerves heal. I'm just glad you're okay. I heard about what you did at the wormhole port. Remember Adoro, the lady from the tech department? She says the shockwave blew out all of the wormhole technology, so KTAN won't be able to call their allies back anytime soon. And I heard you could have died. That was brave."

"It was necessary." Seren wiped tears from her eyes.

"We're glad you're okay," Celer added.

Ben rolled the wheelchair close to the bed and awkwardly hoisted himself up with his arms so he could sit next to her on top of the quilt. They hugged each other tightly.

"Do you want to talk about it?" Ben asked.

"I hated putting you in that position. I thought I had killed you."

"It was necessary," Ben said.

"That did not make it easier."

"What about you?" Celer asked. "Are you feeling alright after what happened with the wormhole?"

"Yes. I owe Vuri. An-Tun said that once Ben heals, he'll be a stronger magician."

"He told us, too," Ben said. "I think I'll need it."

"I know. I understand that being a Messengersmith is magically strenuous work."

"Not that," Ben said. "I have a feeling this isn't over."

"But the Wenifrins were repulsed, and An-Tun said the organized crime rings are being dismantled as we speak, the corrupt politicians being investigated. Andaros is safe."

Ben smiled at Seren. "I know what's happening. It was just a feeling, like I said. Now, we'll go. You should rest."

"If you don't mind, I would like to walk around for a while."

"Okay. We'll come with you."

The rest of the house smelled like baking and wood smoke. Ben took a deep breath of the scent that reminded him of Earth, and not of the acrid oil smoke of burning vehicles, nor of gunpowder smoke or of the stinging fumes from when Seren had set a building alight with herself in it. The father of the house looked at the two humans as they came out of Seren's room. He smiled at them and pointed to a clean prosthetic leg where there had once been only bloodied, dirty rags.

"Thank you for everything," he said. "We cannot repay this. We pray that the gods bless you with all you could ever want."

"We only performed our duty," Seren said. "But thank you."

"Please, at least take these." He pushed warm breads into Ben and Seren's hands.

Celer flew in from another room to greet his friends, Vuri and Arwi following close behind. Vuri could walk on her own, albeit shakily. Arwi monitored her closely.

"Hey," Vuri said, waving at Seren.

"Vuri, I'm sorry," Ben said. "I should have done better for Javrel."

She avoided his eye. "Commander Dyalaro has a special message for us. Daolor is the only squad she wants to talk to."

"About what?" Ben asked. "Why us?"

"Why would I know?" she snapped. "Go figure it out yourself."

"Vuri, I said I'm sorry about—"

"Just leave me alone. Now." Vuri looked into the distance, away from Ben.

Ben hung his head and wheeled his chair away, leaving Vuri and Seren alone.

"He did everything he could," Seren said.

"I don't want to talk about it right now," Vuri replied.

"Okay. That's fine. Is there anything else you need?"

"I want you to say Javrel's eulogy at the funeral," Vuri said.

"Me?" Seren asked. "I'm honored, but Vuri! I don't know anything about your culture, your traditions... How would I do it?"

"Better than me," Vuri replied. "I hate public speaking on a normal day. I'll handle writing his funerary scroll and performing his Rite of Possessions. I just need you to think of something nice to say. There's a mass funeral soon, for Sildial. They'll be honoring him."

"I will honor his memory to the best of my ability," Seren said.

Vuri smiled, just a tiny upturn that crept across her mouth for a second and then vanished. "I know you will."

Commander Dyalaro gave Daolor the remainder of the day to rest, then summoned them to her home. Vuri stepped up and gave three solid knocks on the door. Momentarily, an Andarite man wearing reading glasses opened it, trailed by two small children. Their horns were but ungrown nubs set above bright eyes. They toddled up to Ben and Seren, eyeing them curiously.

"Human?" one asked.

Seren knelt in front of the child and let him put his curious fingers in her hair. "Yes," she replied in Voleric. "You must be Commander Dyalaro's children. Your mommy is very brave. Ow! Please, you mustn't pull my hair like that."

"Sorry," the child said.

Seren stood and faced the father. "I understand it must have been hard to be safe while your wife was in danger. Thank you."

He shrugged and smiled, scooping up the children in his arms. "Someone had to take care of Iri and Balke. Now come in. I understand you're still on Sildial business?"

"Yes. Do you know why? I thought Sildial would be disbanding now that the threat has passed."

"I don't know. At least come in out of the cold and have something to drink."

Mr. Dyalaro led the squad inside, to where the other selected squads were already packed into the family's living room. He poured them tea. Ben surveyed the room, and noticed that Daal-Na An-Tun was situated in his wheelchair right next to the Commander. He waved and smiled at Ben, but his normally warm eyes were hiding something. Commander Dyalaro cleared her throat conspicuously. All heads turned towards their leader.

"Thank you for being here. You are the squad whose skills are most necessary for this next mission. Because of the delicate nature of the next stage of our mission, I can only afford to have a few people along. We're going to Iyerayñan itself. An-Tun will explain."

An-Tun adjusted his reading glasses and focused on the thin, delicate paper in his hand, the type of stationery that was meant for sending letters by Messenger. "This is a letter from a friend living on Iyerayñan," he said.

Dearest An-Tun,

Apologies that I could not be writing to you under better circumstances, and condolences to you, and to everyone else in your resistance movement, who have lost loved ones in this conflict. I write to you to report disturbing activity in the higher levels of the government of Iyerayñan. A political faction that has long lay in obscurity is gaining popularity among the people. I am concerned with their current stance in regards to the Alliance. Because of my experience with the tactics of Iyerani politics, I find that it would be neglectful of me to dismiss out of hand the possibility that this faction and KTAN are connected. I would like to humbly request of your superior officer that he send his own personnel to advise on KTAN-Andaros activity and aid my staff with research and investigation on Iyerayñan.

Yours truly,
    Kiyernin Alaranaian Pelairan

"Kiyernin is a Messengersmith, living at the embassy of the Alliance on Iyerayñan. I trust her word, and I brought this letter before Commander Thoral as soon as I received it."

Commander Dyalaro said, "You have the next ten days to rest here. After that, we will take a wormhole to Kiei Zarin, Iyerayñan. I need Sildial to have its own Messengersmith and an interpreter, two if possible. Celer, how long will it take you to pick up the basics of Iyeñavan?"

"The Iyerani language?" Celer asked. "I'll learn the essentials by the time we leave."

"Are you coming with us, An-Tun?" Ben asked.

"I'm afraid not. My health has been taking a turn for the worse... I think the nerve cancer might be trying to spread to my lungs faster than expected. Iyerani air is too low in oxygen for a healthy Daalronnan, let alone an old-timer like me. I'll be here until you leave for Iyerayñan, to help you brush up on your Messengerwork. Then, I'm off towards home on Daalronna. If you need anything, send Celer to the Kavnos Ziggurat. I just bought a small cottage on the foothills of the Skygate Mountains. The Kavnos Messengersmiths will know to forward the message to there."

"Ben, I know that Daalronnan is the language known to all Messengersmiths, so between you, Celer and Seren, I hope you'll be able to translate for me and the others," Commander Dyalaro said.

"Of course."

"Hey," Vuri interjected. "What am I supposed to do? Last I checked, I speak Voleric and that's about it."

"I wouldn't want to be the one to order the breakup of any squad," she replied. "Unless you had other plans, you may come to Iyerayñan."

"Yeah, as the useless tagalong," Vuri muttered.

Celer rested comfortingly on Vuri's shoulder. "We wouldn't have left Andaros without you anyway. Daolor sticks together."

"Definitely," Ben and Seren said.

"Would anyone like some more tea?" Mr. Dyalaro asked, poking his bespectacled head out of the kitchen. "There's plenty on the stove."

"Oh, yes please," An-Tun said. "Where do you buy this blend? It's excellent."

"I think we should head out," Celer said. "Seren, I don't want to waste any time. You should start teaching me Iyeñavan once we get back to the house."

"If he doesn't mind, I'd like to keep teaching Ben now," An-Tun said. "I have a few more tricks for him before he heads off to Iyerayñan. Is there a place where we can work?"

"My home office is a bit cluttered, but will it work for you?" Mr. Dyalaro said.

"Perfectly, thank you."

Seren's face was downcast as she walked with Vuri and Celer out of the house. She seemed to be scrutinizing the forms of the snowflakes on the ground in front of her boots. When they arrived back at the house, Vuri went back to her room. At the kitchen table, Seren fumbled with the papers and pen as she prepared to teach Celer his new language.

"Something on your mind?" Celer asked.

Seren sat down and let her head fall to the table. When she looked up, there was a line of tears streaming down her face. "I'm afraid to go back," she choked out. "I haven't told you everything about that place. You would be horrified that I complied with that government. I saw the members of Vetokan who couldn't make caste qualifications..."

"What?"

"Profiles of denizens who fail to reach the qualifications of certain castes are reviewed by the Board of Genetic Advancement. They are terminated, bodies recycled for organic resources."

"A eugenics program," Celer whispered. "That's the kind of government we're investigating."

"I can't go back there, Celer. Can't watch another shipment of outcastes on its way to a processing plant. And there's much more. I can't tell it all."

"It will be hard," Celer said. "But we need you. Be brave for us."

Seren hugged the little Messenger, and a teardrop hit his head and soaked into his cloth. "I will try," Seren said. "I will try."

"I know you will. That's all we can ask for."

Acknowledgements

There are a great many people without whom the first draft of this story never would have gotten finished, let alone the second draft, the editing, or the publishing. I am immensely grateful to everyone who helped in this process, and each deserves a very special thank-you.

First and foremost, Mom and Dad, for everything. I could spend another 100,000 words describing how they go above and beyond for me every day. Because of them, I had the tools to put this book together, from the computer that stores my files, to the classes that shaped my writing ability, to the many, many books that fueled my desire to write. Also, they were very helpful in giving me publishing deadlines to shoot for, without which I may have procrastinated for much longer.

Anna Haber's help as an editor was invaluable to the project. Without her, this book would still be a mess of POV-hopping, grievous ellipsis overuse, and a myriad of other crimes against the prescriptive law of Standard Written English. I especially appreciate Anna's thoroughness in the midst of what must have been an extremely busy schedule. Through all of it, she kept emailing with updates, keeping my spirits up with positive comments, and keeping me grounded with many, many, necessary criticisms. It has been a great honor to have you wield the editor's blade on my work, and to be the conlanger for yours.

Brooke Solomon has been an immense inspiration to me for the last four years, and it was amazing to be able to collaborate with her and share each other's rough drafts for so long. Her emotional support has kept me moving on a great many slow spots, and knowing that someone has already claimed the role of Vuri in the hypothetical movie adaptation of *Winter's Corruption* was heartening. Brooke was the first person to make me really believe in my characters, by way of her praise of their antics in the rough draft.

A great many teachers also helped me along the way. Every one of the English teachers I had during the writing process of course influenced my style, but there are several, English and in other subjects, who deserve special credit. In rough chronological order: Mr. Curry, for recognizing that 7th-grade Brennan needed to write his ideas down rather than just let them ferment inside his cranium, Magistra Goulson, for the encouraging interest in my conlang (*gratias tibi ago*, and sorry the *Aeneid* reference couldn't make the final draft!), Dr. Christerson, for looking at the rough outlines of the

Andarite biosphere, and Mrs. Lahar, for encouraging me to share my ideas, even during a very frustrating time.

Also, a big thank-you to all of the neighbors and friends who asked about my progress on the book, gave encouragement, read chapters, and promised to buy the finished product. The sum of all of this emotional support gave me the perseverance to move forward through many slow spots.

Also, to the reader: Thank you for your support. Thank you for buying this story, believing in my invented world, and taking this ride along with my characters. I hope you enjoyed.

Sincerely,
Brennan Danaher Knowles Corrigan

ABOUT THE AUTHOR

Brennan Corrigan is an independent author and linguistics enthusiast. Aside from writing and designing languages like Voleric, he enjoys reading, chess, acting, fencing, and collecting notebooks with nice covers. He lives in New Hampshire. *Winter's Corruption* is his first novel.

Find more information about *Winter's Corruption*, Andaros, and future books at brennandkcorrigan.tumblr.com.

49062201R00222

Made in the USA
Lexington, KY
24 January 2016